# STUDENT PROTEST
## AND THE LAW

# STUDENT PROTEST AND THE LAW

Edited by

## Grace W. Holmes

The Institute of Continuing Legal Education

Hutchins Hall  •  Ann Arbor, Michigan

Library of Congress
Catalog Card Number
78-627818

Printed in the United States of America by
R. W. Patterson Printing Company, Benton Harbor, Mich.

# FOREWORD

Society's current concerns with war, race, and poverty are nowhere more vigorously debated than in academic communities—universities, colleges and, increasingly, secondary schools. These debates are not new; millions in the over-thirty generations argued similar questions during their own school days. What differs, and markedly, on today's campuses is the mode of the debate. Now, positions are expressed by actions as well as words, and even the words tend to be employed as missiles rather than missives. Indeed, "confrontation" is now a more accurate characterization than "debate."

As campus tensions are exacerbated by incivility and attitudes are polarized by insensitivity, relationships deteriorate into conflict, sometimes armed. A search for ameliorative measures leads naturally to the law, which Western civilization considers a mandatory alternative to violent self-help. Although universities and colleges wisely seek to govern themselves without intervention of the civil authorities, they have found their procedures increasingly inadequate and have come nearer and nearer the brink of disaster. The law's devices thus appear more attractive.

To help educators and lawyers—and all others interested in our educational system—understand the law's role in matters of student protest, The Institute of Continuing Legal Education presents this book. It consists of an edited transcript of a national conference on Law and Student Protest held in Ann Arbor in May, 1969, and of useful supporting documents, such as pleadings, injunctive orders, judicial guidelines, and student codes. The speakers, who here become authors, are distinguished lawyers and educators, most of whom recently have been on the campus firing line (a phrase that all too readily comes to mind). The legal papers they employed to cool off campus crises are here set forth. Counsel for student groups and for universities here give their divergent views. Preventive as well as curative measures are described.

This timely and extraordinarily practical volume is possible because of the generous assistance of the experienced lawyers and educators who participated in the conference and who made available sample documents from their files. We are in their debt.

John W. Reed
Director

Ann Arbor, Michigan
August, 1969

# THE INSTITUTE OF CONTINUING LEGAL EDUCATION

The University of Michigan
Law School

Wayne State University
Law School

State Bar of Michigan
Executive Committee

*Francis A. Allen*, Dean, The University of Michigan Law School

*Milton E. Bachmann*, Executive Director, State Bar of Michigan

*Benjamin Carlin*, Professor of Law, Wayne State University Law School

*Robert E. Childs*, Professor of Law, Wayne State University Law School

*Gilbert H. Davis*, President, State Bar of Michigan

*Charles W. Joiner*, Dean, Wayne State University Law School

*Joseph R. Julin*, Associate Dean, The University of Michigan Law School

*Douglas A. Kahn*, Professor of Law, The University of Michigan Law School

*William J. Pierce*, Professor of Law and Director of the Legislative Research Center, The University of Michigan Law School

*Boaz Siegel*, Professor of Law, Wayne State University Law School

*Hamilton Stillwell*, Dean, Division of Urban Extension, Wayne State University

# CONTRIBUTORS

*William M. Beaney*, Professor of Law, The University of Denver College of Law, Denver, Colorado

*Paul D. Carrington*, Professor of Law, The University of Michigan Law School, Ann Arbor, Michigan

*Richard L. Cates*, Esq., Lawton & Cates, Madison, Wisconsin

*Tom J. Farer*, Associate Professor of Law, Columbia University School of Law, New York, New York

*Robben W. Fleming*, President and Professor of Law, The University of Michigan, Ann Arbor, Michigan

*John P. Holloway*, Esq., Resident Legal Counsel, The University of Colorado, Boulder, Colorado

*Edward C. Kalaidjian*, Esq., Thacher, Proffitt, Prizer, Crawley & Wood, New York, New York

*Robert L. Knauss*, Professor of Law, The University of Michigan Law School, Ann Arbor, Michigan

*Richard A. Lippe*, Esq., Lippe & Ruskin, Mineola, New York

*Marvin Niehuss*, Professor of Law, The University of Michigan Law School, Ann Arbor, Michigan

*William W. Van Alstyne*, Professor of Law, Duke University School of Law, Durham, North Carolina

# Table of Contents

# PART II

## COMMUNITY
## STUDENT — UNIVERSITY

## PART III
### CONSTITUTIONAL CONSIDERATIONS

# Introductory Remarks

## Robben W. Fleming*

The whole area of the law and the university is terribly important today. While the tactical maneuvering that is now going on is very interesting in itself, and will doubtless be the subject of many theses by legal historians, we need to study these controversies for reasons which are far more basic than the determination of the legal tactics that can be employed by either side.

Those of us who are devoted to the law must be able to persuade people that the law is an effective and a fair instrument for dealing with the problems of student protest. Part of our difficulty today, it seems to me, is that many of our young people do not believe that the law is a fair instrument for dealing with the consequences of dissent and protest.

I am gravely concerned with the question of how one uses the law effectively and at the same time persuades the various constituencies that such a use is fair. That is extremely difficult to do in this controversial area of the law and the university student.

The overall problems—at least the problems that have been of concern to me—appear to fall into three general categories: student rights, questions of violence and coercion and the civil liberties aspects of both.

As we study the question of student rights, it is clear that we must not only reexamine the student's internal rights, *i.e.*, his rights within the university, but the rights of the student as a citizen. The latter is, in a sense, a whole new area. It is exemplified by the kind of dispute which we had at The University of

---

* President, The University of Michigan, Ann Arbor, Michigan.

3

Michigan in the fall of 1968. Some 200 of our students were arrested because they participated in a local controversy between ADC mothers and Washtenaw County officials with respect to the proper clothing allowances for those mothers and their families. This was an off-campus affair in which our students were arrested for the peaceful occupation of a public building after closing hours. They were, of course, tried for violation of the civil law and were ultimately convicted and fined.

There was a day, as we all know, when a university student who engaged in activity which violated such a law could expect to be disciplined or to have some action taken against him by the university. Today it is quite clear that students are claiming their rights as citizens—rights separate from and unaffected by the fact that they happen to be students. This claim has some tendency to exacerbate local community relations. Many of the older generation, particularly, think that the university should do something in a situation such as our ADC incident. The students, of course, hold a wholly different view. They feel that where they are in conflict with a civil law, at least when it does not affect university premises, they should be treated just like any other citizen.

This new area of the student as a citizen clearly relates to the university. Such activity may have any of several permutations—factors which bring it closer to or further from the university's orbit. Our case was relatively clear-cut; it had no immediate university impact.

The student's rights within the university—what I call his internal rights—merit our most serious consideration. As we look at our disciplinary procedures, for example, it becomes quite clear that we have not really followed the dictates of the due process concept. Most of us would answer, "Well, yes; but on the other hand, neither have we been arbitrary and discriminatory." The validity of that defense stands somewhat in the eyes of the beholder. It is quite clear now that we must and should accord a student his appropriate rights under due process. The accomplishment of this gives rise to difficulties, because within the university framework we are not really prepared to conduct long trials and adversary procedures as it is done in our courts. So we are struggling today with the question of how we ensure a student the rights of due process without so involving and bogging down the whole procedure that nothing is accomplished. Because we are not really experienced, we have not done it very well. This difficulty is emerging all over the country.

The second category of problems involves the question of violence and coercion. How do we deal with those problems? I think we have to be careful not to lose our perspective. After all, violence and coercion in our society are not novel. They are, it is true, quite new on a campus, in the sense that we are now having to deal with them. But in our society we have always had to try to learn how to handle numbers of people who are bent on violence. Any of us who are familiar with the labor field know the problems of strikes and of violence in that connection. Those who have been interested in farm movements have seen this over the years in terms of farmer boycott problems. Some of us remember the days of the Depression, when homes were being foreclosed and people were resisting with arms. The whole civil rights movement in the last few years has involved the doctrine of civil disobedience; and any time we are dealing with civil disobedience we are riding a very fine line—can we keep it within an acceptable kind of conduct, or will it slip over into violence? Since we are dealing with people whose emotions are heavily involved, it is very difficult to keep it from slipping over. But the point I would make is that violence and coercion, though very difficult for us to deal with on the campus, are not new in this country.

In a democratic society we do not deal well with numbers of people who are resisting whatever it is we are doing. On our campus, where we have more than 30,000 students in Ann Arbor, one percent of our students resisting something means that 300 people are involved. That many persons are difficult to handle with any kind of process, particularly if they are determined to resist. Moreover, we have the terribly delicate problem of how to keep the great mass of nonparticipants from joining the others out of sympathy, even though they do not agree with the tactics of the activists.

In part, our difficulties are multipled because the resistance is what one might describe as a political question; that is, it is coming because of differences over political objectives or national priorities.

The problem is aggravated at this point in time by the fact that both in Congress and in the state legislatures a tremendous number of bills is being introduced for all kinds of controls on campuses. Many of these bills are very badly thought out. On the other hand, those of us who are opposed to such legislative action and are saying before Congress and elsewhere that the universities ought to be allowed to handle this problem must not be blind to the fact that representatives, both at the state level and in the Congress, do truly represent their constituencies. Something must be done; there is no doubt about it. I have never seen the public so hostile to student activities as they are today. Privately, Congressmen and legislators, although they understand that much of the proposed legislation will be either totally ineffective or harmful, emphasize that their constituents demand that they do something. I think the people are wrong, but they do demand it; and the legislation is going to be very difficult to deal with.

The third question which must be considered involves the problem of civil liberties in this entire area. There are the first amendment aspects. To what extent may one, under the guarantees of the first amendment, express his views in the underground newspapers that appear on campus? To what extent are such publications entitled to the protections of the first amendment?

One of the reasons we have so much trouble dealing with these problems, either on a relatively small campus or one as large as

The University of Michigan, is that we cannot readily identify students just by looking at them. From the civil rights movement, students have learned that if they decline to identify themselves we may be able to identify them only by arresting them, which creates another syndrome of problems. Alternatively, we can try to take pictures to accomplish identification. We must address ourselves to what are the legitimate means of identification which do not violate a person's civil liberties—means which we would all regard as satisfactory and acceptable.

Finally, of course, there is the problem of what I call repressive legislation. We are faced with this difficulty right now. We receive communications from the Secretary of Health, Education and Welfare and other officials saying, in effect, that we should make certain that all of our students understand the provisions which may withdraw federal financial benefits from them in the event they are convicted of engaging in certain kinds of activities, or if they are disciplined on campus. To act upon this directive involves us, at the outset, in a civil liberties dilemma. If we say to all students, "Note these provisions and be careful you don't violate them," we may very well be said to have exerted upon them an influence against participation in anything that might be labeled dissent, and thereby infringed upon constitutionally protected rights of dissent. On the other hand, if we say nothing to them, if we do not call this to their attention, we are exposed to the charge afterward that we did not make clear to students the possible repercussions of their activities. I would hope, therefore, that this dilemma might be considered in these discussions, in terms of how one properly informs students of the problems they face without unduly repressing their constitutionally protected right of dissent.

# PART I

# Symposium

# The Challenge to the University

Professor Paul D. Carrington
Richard L. Cates, Esq.
Professor Robert L. Knauss
Professor Marvin Niehuss

# The Lawyer's Role in the Design of a University

## Paul D. Carrington*

### Introduction

The film† you have just witnessed was intended to provide mood music for our program. We are all familiar with the phenomenon of protest, but it seemed worth a few minutes to express the spirit of the problem before proceeding to try to deal with it rationally. Before we begin to express our differences, we should be able to agree that combat between the National Guard and large numbers of talented and spirited young people is what we are all seeking to avoid.

Perhaps we can also agree that it is not wholly within our power to prevent it. There are a number of reasons why this is so. Before stating them, let me assure you that it is not the principal business of this conference to examine the causes of youthful unrest. This is an immense topic in itself; we could easily devote two days to it here while adding very little to the public understanding of the subject. And it has been much treated elsewhere.

We can safely assert, however, that no one has yet exhausted the problem and it seems unlikely that anyone will soon do so. In

---

* Professor of Law, The University of Michigan Law School, Ann Arbor, Michigan.

† Editor's Note: Films of student demonstrations and rioting were shown to the registrants at the Seminar "Student Protest and the Law," conducted by The Institute of Continuing Legal Education on May 16 and 17, 1969, at Ann Arbor, Michigan.

the absence of complete understanding, it is unlikely that we can produce a complete remedy. We can readily see that a subsociety for adolescents has emerged—a subsociety attracted to values and attitudes which are quite different from those of the adult society of which it is a part. If the values of the young are not in conflict with the values, or at least the ideals, of their elders, those values are sufficiently different that a great deal of suspicion and animosity has been produced. This phenomenon is not unique in world history nor is it unique to our country today. Some of the hypotheses advanced to explain the phenomenon are reasonable in accounting for at least part of it, but none of the alleged causes is demonstrable. And discussion is often obfuscated by those who hasten to blame the march of events on some convenient enemy. The only hard fact that we have to grasp is the breadth of the unrest which gives rise to the protest.

It seems also safe to assert that whatever the causes of unrest may be, it is only a meager few of them which are in any way amenable to change by educators or by lawyers who represent and advise educators. Black students, for example, who may be so justly offended by the subtle forms of racism which abound in our society, are not likely to be calmed in any lasting way by any action which a school or university might take. The specific issues raised by protesting black students tend to be occasions, not causes, for protest. Similarly, much of the unrest of the New Left seems to be directed toward the military and the war. Students protesting recruiting activities by certain companies or the Defense Department are surely much less concerned with the alleged impropriety of the university's hospitality to such organizations than they are attracted to an opportunity to express their attitude toward the war and the military. The problems of classified research or course credits in ROTC are simply occasions for protest; the animus is not directed toward the educational institution itself, but the institution is made to stand as a surrogate target for protest which might be more directly expressed on the steps of the Pentagon. It is vain to suppose that the institution can respond in some way that will provide durable relief from the friction. The best that can be hoped for is a papering over or an avoidance of occasions for protest, so that the ferment remains at tolerable levels.

## The Goals of the University

In considering the ways in which the pressures of unrest can be alleviated, it is necessary to give some hard thought to the essential goals of our institutions. Precisely what is it that we are trying to preserve? An administrator or lawyer who approaches the problems of these conflicts with the idea that every aspect of the current mode of institutional operation is equally sacred may find himself taking stands on issues which are indefensible or not worth defending, expending power and influence without meaning or any constructive result. If it is true that we are dealing with a whole generation that is restless, and that all students are to some degree distrustful, then our capacity to influence their actions is limited. We must focus that capacity to control in directions most central to the mission of the institution. This is a time for reappraisal and perhaps a time for shedding burdensome tasks and functions with which the educational process has been freighted by an unthinking public.

### Dispensable Functions

One function that I would expect most institutions to deem dispensable is the function of the moral disciplinarian. To some extent, of course, educational institutions cannot avoid the role of moralizers for the community; indeed, some discipline is essential to other functions of education. This is especially so for primary and secondary schools. But there has been a tradition which has caused many institutions to go further, to pursue moral discipline as a goal in itself. Doubtless there will always be a place for institutions primarily devoted to this concern. Some boarding schools for the young may well regard discipline as their primary reason for being. But most institutions, particularly those dealing with relatively mature young people, will do well to minimize the number of instances in which they find it necessary to apply disciplinary controls.

In this connection, I am reminded of a conversation I had some years ago with an English schoolmaster. I reported to him that discipline in our public schools was becoming a tough problem for many teachers and inquired whether the same was true in his school. He emphatically denied that he had any problems in controlling his students because boys dislike corporal punishment as much today as ever. On the other hand, he conceded, something was going on in his community because in recent years he had found a growing number of parents who asked him to give their sons a good caning because of difficulties at home. There is also the improbable story of the mother of the University of Chicago student who flew from California to congratulate the Chancellor for punishing her son; it was, she reported, the first time in the boy's life that anyone had stood up to him. It has to be recognized that the educational system cannot be primarily devoted to the task of standing up to young men who have never been stood up to before, unless that is to be their only mission. My schoolmaster friend is surely headed for trouble if he begins to use his cane in support of parents who have trouble dealing with feisty sons. He will do well to put as little strain on his system as he can, if he wishes to preserve it. And he may find it wise to do even less caning, if he is to pursue other objectives. Education will have to adapt to a permissive world.

Another function of educational institutions which I would expect many to find dispensable is the function of creating status. While we are still in the process of emerging from the period in which learning was a luxury, the credentials of learning have now become a necessity for many. This is not only a source of distraction to students, many of whom seem to be more interested in the effect than the substance of education, it is also a cause of resentment and an occasion for student protest. It is difficult to imagine an educational system which fails to recognize and reward excellence, but it behooves us to recognize that the conferring of honors is not the essence of the process and is a tradition that now serves some undesirable results. What was intended as a system of incentives has become a system for relieving diverse employers and admissions officers of colleges and universities of the necessity of exercising independent judgment. It has become a means for chaining young people to the expectations of those who have gone before. Educational institutions are sometimes called to exercise greater power over individuals than they are equipped to exercise. It may be wise and even necessary for many of our institutions to make changes that will prevent the overuse or misuse of the power of granting or withholding rewards as a mindless means of coercing the behavior of restless young people.

## Limitations of the University

These are examples of a broader principle, which is that educational institutions must respect the limits of their utility as instruments of social change. In times of stress and awareness of the need for social change, it is tempting to use every possible tool at hand. The urge to use schools and universities is fortified by a long tradition of claims which have been made by educators for a least a century. Our growing budgets have long been justified by assertions that education was the magic instrument for the improvement of society. I have seen a recent public opinion poll which places education far ahead of religion, business and government as a source for the changes that have been accomplished in this century. Perhaps the public is right in that assessment; I am scarcely one to say that our legislators have been misappropriating public funds for education. But some of our present troubles may be traceable to an inflated view of the possibilities—to an excess of promise. Part of what our students are telling us is that we have not delivered; they are insisting now on putting the vaunted capacities of education to work on what they perceive to be better causes. It is time now to confess to the faults of overpromise and underperformance, and to try to persuade those who wish to set out to perform new miracles that our educational institutions cannot bear so much strain. All of the universities in America could not together, I think, bring instant peace and prosperity to Asia or even to Detroit. But they can do damage to their own small capability as contributors to such causes if they overextend and fail to respect their natural limitations.

When I refer to natural limitations I am speaking primarily of the need of educational institutions for a measure of autonomy, which must be impaired by involvement in controversial social matters. Effective creative teaching cannot exist in a closely supervised situation. The changing winds of politics are a substantial threat to the teaching functions. Yet this kind of frustration of purpose is sure to result when schools are thrust into social controversy. If schools are the primary instrument of social change, then those affected by change must fight for control of the educational process. The resulting struggles are necessarily harmful to the process. Thus, one form of retrenchment seems to be in order: educational institutions should seek to remove themselves from the vortex of policy-making activity.

### The Classical Ideal

Engagement in the politics of social change is destructive to an institution of what is called "higher learning" because it is inconsistent with the idea. If we assume the classical ideal of the university as a place of inquiry, an enclave in which it is permissible and even encouraged to challenge basic premises and to think unthinkable thoughts, it becomes clear that the kind of involvement in social causes which many students are advocating and which we have sometimes practiced in the past is an unfortunate diversion.

I am not prepared to say that all institutions for young adults ought to be universities in the classical model. There may be places, for instance, for institutions which serve quite different kinds of purposes. But if, indeed, your institution purports to be and is attempting to be an institution that maintains a tradition of inquiry and a tradition of challenging basic premises, then it is important to maintain the cloistered structure. The university cannot become an active agent for social change without impairing its function as a device for conducting inquiry.

I am not saying that there is no place in the classical university for scholars who have made up their minds and are ready for action. There may even be a need for some individuals of that kind, but their actions ought to be individual and carefully framed to involve the institution as little as possible. An institution that long shelters a dominant group of social activists of whatever stripe does so at the expense of the spirit of inquiry. An institution which has a discernible position on disputed public issues has surrendered at least a portion of its ideal character as a university.

For this reason, I think it fair to say that universities should get out of the business of conferring special favors on the Reserve Officers Training Corps. They should also get out of the business of war research. In times past, when these activities were not objects of inquiry and dispute, it may have been tolerable to engage in them, although I am not prepared to say that they were ever desirable. But in the present state of our national affairs the university cannot shelter these activities without thereby taking a position, an institutional position, on public issues and thus abandoning its mission as a center of openminded inquiry into all such questions. I am prepared to give the same reason for withholding the university imprimatur from legal clinics which are primarily devoted to social service. However desirable such clinics may be, and I believe they are very desirable if not essential, they have no place in a classical university unless the clinical operation can avoid publicly disputed issues. A university has no business organizing a rent strike, however oppressive the landlords may be; neither has a university any proper business filing school desegre- gation cases, however outrageous the violation of the fourteenth amendment may be. This is not a reason for foreclosing all clinical work from law schools, or for preventing students and professors from engaging in such controversial professional work outside the cloister. But a university that is true to its classical function must be hospitable to oligarchs as well as democrats. I have disclosed my own favoritism for the classical idea of a university. I do not say that all institutions for young adults should pretend to be universities. There is certainly a variety of other institutions which pursue other goals, particularly those institutions which exist to give a narrower, more practical training to individuals and which are not committed to the ideal of impartial hospitality to all ideas. Such institutions may be better agents for social change than universities. Perhaps they can react to student protest in quite a different way.

It is not a part of my purpose to persuade you that my idea of the classical university is even sound. I advance the idea simply to illustrate that the nature of the issues worthy of confrontation depends on the institutional goals jeopardized by the situation. As the jeopardy increases, the need for precision is increased. There may be times—perhaps we have seen some—in which the institu- tion must try to use force to resist its destruction. There may be times when it is appropriate to follow the example of President Everett of Harvard. Probably many of you recall his response to an alumnus who protested the admission to the college of a former slave. President Everett explained that if, as the alumnus pre- dicted, all the alumni of Harvard should withdraw their support, and all the students should withdraw, then all the remaining resources of the university would have to be devoted to the education of the young black. It may now be necessary to direct a similar utterance to some of our restless and unhappy young people who, however righteous they may be, must be prevented from destroying the institutions which are their own best hope.

Important as it is to make this necessity understood, it is equally important to avoid making such firm stands at the wrong time and place. It is appropriate to ask whether the specific issue in dispute is really worth struggling about. I do not suppose that my few remarks here will qualify you as educational philosophers, even if I were qualified to attempt that task. Presumably, most of you are not educational policymakers, but it is surely an appropriate aspect of your professional work as lawyers to assure that a sensible educational judgment has been made before resort is had to the law of confrontations. Educators, as much as any other clients, are quite capable of losing their bearings in time of stress.

# The University's Response to Disruptive Behavior

## Robert L. Knauss*

## The Challenge of Disruptive Behavior

This is not the place to discuss various reasons why there is student disruption, but it may be worth emphasizing that tranquility on a campus is not in itself a virtue. Academic communities cannot, and should not, stand apart from the problems besetting our society. It is particularly true today when there exists widespread discontent with many of our present national priorities. Demonstrations and confrontations on campus must be viewed as a complex social phenomenon.

Some appear to be intentionally destructive and negative; others, however, are manifestations of deep, sometimes profoundly moral discontent arising out of social injustice, dubious foreign policy, and in some cases unresponsiveness within our educational institutions themselves. Broad indiscriminate acts of oppression from within or outside our colleges and universities will not eliminate the causes of discontent, and they will surely punish the innocent as well as the guilty.[1]

While I realize judicial structures within the university play some role, I think in the vast majority of instances the judicial

---

\*  Professor of Law, The University of Michigan Law School, Ann Arbor, Michigan.

1.  *See* STATEMENT OF CAMPUS DISRUPTION, issued by the Michigan Council of State College Presidents, May 20, 1969.

approach to student protests is inadequate. The university community does not lend itself to judicial proceedings. Students and faculty do not make particularly good judges or jurors. Few are equipped to fill these roles adequately. Faculty and administrators on judicial bodies may find themselves in the dual role of prosecutor and judge. Increasingly, lawyers are present during proceedings and it is difficult for judges without legal training to control the hearings. The problems relating to privacy of a student's records are more serious than they would be in a civil proceeding. Confidential information, frequently including psychiatric reports, is placed in the hands of untrained judges. The ultimate penalty available within the university community, that of expulsion, can often have much more serious consequences to a student than a typical penalty he would receive in a civil court. The seriousness is compounded currently because of the threat of the draft to suspended male students. Frequently nonstudents are involved and remain immune from all academic sanctions.

On a broader basis it should be recognized that serious disruptions within an academic community, particularly those involving large groups of students, represent political problems more than judicial problems. I think perhaps that the tools and techniques of labor mediation and arbitration may have more to offer than a judicial approach.

The real challenge to the academic community should be to channel the energies of those involved. The presence of a potential disruption on a campus should be a challenge to find ways of utilizing the situation as a creative educational experience. The approach should not be to repress the activity, but if the problem is real and the motives legitimate, the emphasis should be to sustain the activity. For example, a few years ago a potentially serious confrontation and strike on the campus of The University of Michigan was channeled into what became the first university "teach-in" on the question of our involvement in Viet Nam. Very recently it has been reported that Amherst College devoted two full days away from classes to the discussion of some of the broad policy problems that are currently serving as the background of student unrest. Recently M.I.T. had a day of discussion on the question of military research. In both instances there was no threat, no confrontation which forced the faculty and administration officials to seek such meetings. They did not wait for a disruptive protest to occur but voluntarily searched for ways to channel energies into positive programs.

As a final preliminary matter, I think it is important to be aware of the limitations of a university's response to disruptive behavior. Confusion arises when parties believe that the establishment of the system of rules or an internal judicial structure is going to be effective to keep students out of buildings. In determining the response of a college or university to disruptive acts of individuals or groups, the distinction must be made between (a) what immediate action can be taken to prevent the continuation of the illegal activity, and (b) as a completely separate matter, what should be the nature of the discipline and/or the penalties to be invoked against those involved in any wrongdoing. The alternatives available to the academic community in dealing with existing disruption include (1) negotiation, which basically involves patience in an attempt to isolate the incident—this patience and negotiation is coupled with a threat of later sanctions; (2) the use of campus or outside police activity; and (3) the use of court injunction either with or without later police action to enforce it.

The extent of a sanction to be imposed on the students involved is a separate matter. Here the college or university may: (1) discipline within the academic community through any established judicial procedure; (2) file complaints for criminal actions or contempt of court proceedings; and (3) bring civil actions for restitution and damages. The other speakers will be talking in detail about the mechanics of these various alternatives. I'm afraid no one will be able to give much in the way of concrete advice as to which alternative to use at any particular time. The best I can offer is that each incident must be looked at independently prior to determining which alternative should be used. Those responsible for making decisions must be flexible and weigh numerous factors. I think most members of the academic community would agree that intentional acts of physical coercion or violence cannot be tolerated. I think they would also agree with the statement that all appropriate means to protect institutional facilities and the rights and safety of all members of the academic community should be used. This does not mean, however, that merely because you do not call the police you are "tolerating" illegal behavior. You may make a decision to deal with the immediate situation without outside intervention, and yet at a later point institute criminal and civil action as well as internal disciplinary actions against those involved.

## The Role of Student Involvement

Why student involvement? It has become a cliche in any discussion of student unrest to profess a desire for student involvement in decisionmaking. Government spokesmen in their recent statements urging faculty and administration to have "more backbone" have almost always coupled their remarks by calling for student participation. In a recent *New York Times Magazine* article entitled "When, if Ever, Do You Call in the Cops?"[2] as diverse persons as the President of Harvard Board of Overseers, a New York police inspector, Norman Mailer and student members of the SDS disagreed completely on when police should come on campus, but all professed the virtue of student involvement.

I think there are a variety of functions and goals for student involvement. Not all are consistent or are urged from the same

2.   *When, if Ever, Do You Call in the Cops?*, NEW YORK TIMES MAGAZINE, May 4, 1969, p. 34.

motivations. I suppose the broadest concept is to compare student involvement in university decisionmaking to the current pattern of community control in the model cities program and various other community development projects. In order for such programs to be accepted in the community, they are providing for representation of the poor and of the black community on policy boards.[3] I think the same pressures give rise to the proposition that the students themselves must be represented in the making of decisions that control them, that involve them. This does not mean the decisions are going to be any better. In fact they may not be as good, but hopefully, the decisions are more likely to be respected.

A more positive argument can be made that student input will in many instances improve the quality of decisions. This is based on the principle that in most cases feedback from the consumer does help the decisionmaking process. I think it is true that most academic institutions are underadministered, compared to similar government or business units. Those responsible for decisions often have little time for planning or innovation. Student involvement (and faculty involvement) can provide valuable talent to the administration.

As a separate matter, it is argued that involvement in decisionmaking is educational for the students. I think it is, but it can often be carried to an extreme. We have some students in The University of Michigan who seem to be majoring in university decisionmaking. They spend more time on these efforts than on any other. I am afraid we may have some faculty doing the same thing.

As a tactical matter, every administration, every faculty, must have close contact with the student population. Perhaps the important reason for having student involvement is to be able to maintain the confidence of the majority of students when there is

---

3. *See* Nathan Glazer, *For White and Black, Community Control is the Issue*, NEW YORK TIMES MAGAZINE, April 27, 1969, p. 36.

a dispute, and to isolate the minority. At least in theory, if you have acted in good faith with the majority of students you are able to accomplish such isolation. One of the real advantages of student involvement is getting the most active students to become part of the system instead of operating outside the system. In some measure, I credit the success we have had at Michigan in avoiding serious disruption to the circumstance that many of the activist students, members of splinter groups of SDS, have been involved in the student government. They have been involved in the system, working within the system, rather than feeling frustrated because the normal channels of communication were denied to them. There is currently a need at many schools for positive efforts to bring black students into the system of normal student organizations.

Let me add one more comment on the need for student involvement. At our Law School commencement activities, Mr. George A. Spater, who is President of American Airlines, spoke on the role of the corporation. One of the things he described was the so-called Hawthorne effect, as it related to employee productivity. The reference stems from a series of studies of employees on production lines, made several years ago. A research team made an investigation which resulted in improvements in the lighting. Productivity increased. In a similar production line the research team recommended reducing the lighting. Again, productivity increased. After mulling over these results, the somewhat startling conclusion was that employees are people. The principal factor which increased productivity was the fact that the employee thought somebody cared about him. There is an analogy here to the efforts of university faculty and administrators to know and understand students. Productivity may be increased if we show some interest.

## How Much Student Involvement?

Where can the students be plugged into the system? Paul Carrington said that he thought academic communities should not judge morals. Broadly speaking, we used to call this kind of activity parietal rules—visitation rights, hours in the dormitories and other aspects of personal living habits. At this university we have delegated the primary authority for this kind of rulemaking to the students. There is faculty and administration input. We attempt to counsel and give the kind of advice that we expect students to give us in the academic areas. But within the university residence halls, for example, the students make their own rules as to visitation rights, by vote of the students in the particular dormitory or hall. These rules are then enforced by student judiciaries in those halls. I am not saying that every institution represented at this seminar should adopt such a policy. The character of the particular institution and its students should substantially determine any decision about the role of the students. Who are the students? Where do they come from? What is the relative maturity? We are talking about The University of Michigan where 45 percent of our students live in private apartments, outside the dormitory system. The majority of our students are over 21. In these circumstances, should the university impose more rules on a student merely because he happens to be in a dormitory rather than in an apartment? On the other hand, because we are a state university, and also because it is sound policy, we have attempted to give notice to the parents, particularly the parents of incoming freshmen, about the current rules in the various residence halls. I might add that we have some residence halls that impose relatively rigorous rules. The parents are given notice, and if they want their daughter to go to a residence hall with a stricter set of rules and standards, the opportunity is there. The burden is on the parents to make the decision. Basically, the University's approach has been that the students make their own rules on their personal living habits. Obviously the students are subject to the rules and laws of the community but no additional outside rules are enforced by the administration or faculty.

The rules of conduct that directly concern the operation of the university pose a different kind of problem. In this category would be rules against disruption, rules against interference with teaching, rules against seizure of buildings and others of a similar nature. Although these are conduct rules, they are different from the earlier group that I mentioned because there is clearly an interest of faculty and administration. At the same time there is a much greater likelihood that any rules are going to be enforced if the students have a role in their formation. If there is consent to the rules on the part of those to be governed—the students—the university is in a stronger position in respect to compliance and enforcement.

The University of Michigan has had an ad hoc committee for the past 14 months trying to develop some new Regental bylaws to establish a university council to propose rules of conduct that would apply to all members of the university community. This council would be made up of faculty and administration members and students. The council would only propose rules for passage. The proposed rules would then have to be adopted by students through the Student Government Council, the faculty through the Faculty Assembly, and not vetoed by the Board of Regents. It is recognized that all elements of the university community have an interest in rules relating to conduct which affects the operation of the University. The kind of rules we are contemplating may be fairly general at first, prohibiting violent and intentional interference with individuals and with property. They may also deal with more specific matters, such as setting up ground rules for demonstrations. The structure of the organization is quite flexible.

One of the more serious difficulties we have had in drafting the bylaws has been the question of the autonomy of the various schools and colleges within the University. We found that rule-making created not only student-faculty disputes, but also disputes arising from the concern of the faculty in a school or college that their rights were going to be taken away by a university rulemaking group. The governing faculties of the schools and colleges argue that if behavior or conduct involves academic concerns then only they should make and enforce the rules—not an all-university body, and not students. One of the things that the proposed bylaws attempt to do is to specify in some detail the academic areas under the control of the governing faculty of a school or college. These include course and curriculum content; levels of competence for grades, degrees and continued enrollment; and personal scholastic honesty. What, if any, other behavioral standards are of primary concern to the faculty?

President Fleming[4] mentioned the growing attitude that what happens off the campus normally does not concern the university. But if a student is convicted as a child molester, should the School of Education be able to determine that this kind of behavior is so closely tied to their degree program or licensing function that it should be a basis for withholding a degree? It is not an easy question, and we spent substantial time trying to draft delegations of authority and responsibility over behavior of this type—behavior that could be directly related to the academic needs.

As indicated by the preceding discussion, as one moves from general rulemaking governing behavior to student involvement in the academic area, controversy increases. However, it is in the academic areas where, in the last three years, there has been the place of greatest movement. There has been literally a revolution on this campus and, I would guess, on many campuses. There has been relatively little publicity on this, but student participation— not control but important involvement—in deciding matters strictly academic has undergone a dramatic change. In many of

---

4.    *See* page 4 *supra.*

our schools and colleges students sit on almost every faculty committee. In the School of Social Work there are students on the curriculum committee, the admissions committee and the finance committee. In the Law School we recently made changes which put students on almost every major faculty committee with the exception of the personnel committee, where a dual committee structure was established. Students are voting members of these committees. There is criticism that faculties are giving away control over academic life by these actions. It should be remembered that in every instance the faculty has voting control of the committee, and final decisions are of the faculty itself, not the committee.

In the area of student involvement in general university policy decisions, no set pattern has emerged. In general, students are being appointed on a regular basis to ad hoc committees which are established to study a particular problem. In addition, students are members of various standing committees of the Senate Assembly, which is the representative body of the full Faculty Senate.

Currently a broader basis of student involvement is being proposed for the Office of Student Services. This office, which basically provides various services to students, contains the offices of housing, counseling services, health service, financial aids, religious affairs and student organizations. The new bylaws propose establishing an executive committee made up of half faculty, half students, to advise the Vice President of Student Services; and within that office it is proposed that each of various directors will have a similarly constituted executive committee dealing with the matters enumerated above.

## Selection of Student Representatives

A great deal of time has been wasted because faculty and administration have been unwilling to delegate the appointing power to the legitimate student government organizations. It is true that often the elected student government group may not be completely representative. But if there is a legitimate student government and a democratic election process, with recall and referendum, then giving the organization some authority will, hopefully, improve its quality.

The group within the university or in a school or college which is designated to appoint student members to faculty committees often becomes a much more important organization in the eyes of the students. Gaining a seat on a governing body with such power increases in status. We had the most heavily contested election in recent Law School history last year, largely because our Lawyers Club government was finally in a position to do something. Graduate and professional students have taken a more active interest in the university Student Government Council. In the past, the university student government organization has been largely dominated by the undergraduate schools. Now the organization has been given more responsibility, particularly in the appointing capacity, and the general interest of the students has increased.

It is desirable in many instances to designate the kind of student you want appointed, particularly in a very large university. Frequently the structure of the committee will designate that students be appointed from specific departments, or that two graduates and two undergraduates be appointed. When students were appointed to a new health service committee, the student government was requested to appoint at least one married student with dependents.

There is frequently a problem of the autonomy of the various student groups. For example, the Engineering Council in this school is a very active student group, but the relationship between that group and the university Student Government Council, which is the all-university student group, is not particularly close. How do you designate which group has authority in various areas? We have taken the approach that on academic matters which concern the particular department or college, the appointing power and the decisionmaking belongs within the school or college. After all, this is the place where student voices are going to have the most influence. On problems involving the whole university, the decision must be made by the central student government.

I believe that if you are going to put any students on a committee, you should certainly have more than one and you should usually have at least three. In our current situation, if only one is to be appointed he is likely to be a radical; if two are appointed, the second student will probably be a Black Student Union member; you need at least three students to get the majority student view expressed. Placing students in these numbers on committees does not mean that such students represent "the student view." This is not any more true than to say that a couple of faculty members represent "the faculty view." If you want to get a representative view of student opinion you need to use some survey technique or referendum.

## Other Aspects of Avoiding Confrontation

A number of universities have established the academic ombudsman as a means of cutting through the problem of communication. There is someone fulfilling this role in about 30 universities.[5] The ombudsman at Chicago is a student; at Columbia, the ombudsman is an assistant dean; and it is reported that the position at Stony Brook has been occupied by three faculty members. The powers of the ombudsmen vary greatly in the several universities. In most instances they serve as a kind of answering service. They put people in touch with somebody else. If your normal channels of communication are working, perhaps

---

5.  *See* THE NATION, 207: 611-612, Dec. 9, 1968.

this kind of service would be of little value, but I think there is a need for this service as a minimum on most campuses.

At Michigan we are currently proposing a conciliation committee, or committee on communications, which will be made up of two students, two faculty members and an administrator. Its primary responsibilities will be to look ahead to problems that might lead to disruption and to try to open the channels of communication. It can on its own initiative try to stimulate discussion of issues. It has authority to serve with the consent of the parties as a mediator or arbitrator, or appoint outside parties to fulfill these roles. A committee of this type is going to be effective only if it has the respect of the academic community. It does not have any power of its own. I do think that it is important for some group within the academic community to try to plan ahead. It does not take any crystal ball to see some of the problems we will have next fall. For example, I think any university that has ROTC units, but does not have a student-faculty committee currently studying the problem, is itself negligent. We cannot wait until the barricades have been manned and then meet in a crisis situation to decide issues of importance.

One of the most unfortunate aspects of the recent disruptions at some universities has been the untenable burden placed on a faculty senate of meeting in a crisis situation with little or no organizational structure, prior history of action, adequate committee work or even prior agendas and resolutions. No large group of individuals can be expected to make decisions in such circumstances. Extensive planning and activity are needed in times of quiet in order that action can be taken in time of crisis. Student involvement, faculty involvement and positive leadership from administrators are the best defenses against disruptions.

# A Trial Lawyer's View
# of Student Disruption

## Richard L. Cates, Esq.*

## Introduction

I would like to relate to you my background in the law and in this specific area of concern, so that you may judge my competence to speak on this problem. I am basically a trial lawyer, litigating cases across the board, but I have a very close relationship with the University of Wisconsin. I have been a practicing lawyer in Wisconsin since 1951 and I taught the trial courses at the University for 12 or 13 years. Additionally, I have taught courses in other areas such as negligence and evidence because the regular professor was ill. I am close to the University by reason of the work that I do. I might add that I have been on the Board of Visitors, which is a nothing organization in the sense of assuming responsibility. But we do visit the University a couple of days each month. One of our visits was made shortly after the February protest at Wisconsin. We had the opportunity to listen to the police chief, the president, the chancellor, the black student protest leaders, some black students who weren't leaders, some of the black administrators and faculty. In this job we get a very good insight into university problems—from a layman's standpoint rather than from the faculty standpoint.

In October 1967 we had at Wisconsin what we refer to as the "Dow Chemical protest." The students went to the Commerce Building, massed in front of the interview rooms and refused to let

---

* Lawton & Cates, Madison, Wisconsin.

anyone in. They stayed in that position for several hours. The chancellor called the police—this was the first time that city police had been called to the campus. The police were there in riot gear for several hours before they finally went in and removed the students. A number of people were injured, unfortunately. I represented the University in federal court proceedings in which suits were instituted against the Board of Regents and various administrators in order to stop the University from imposing discipline.[1] The questions in the cases involved the constitutionality of our university regulation prohibiting disruption. A year or so later the regulation was declared to be unconstitutional by the district court because it was vague and overdrawn. Also in that lawsuit we litigated our right to discipline students on the basis of a common law doctrine of misconduct.

In order to avoid a repeat of the Dow Chemical incident at future interviewing by the CIA and the military services, we brought an action in circuit court for an injunction against the individuals who were the leaders in the Dow incident and also against the SDS. After a trial lasting several days, we secured a temporary injunction. Our law office was also responsible for trying the discipline cases against a number of students. Although I have tried many lawsuits, I have never tried any case resembling these disciplinary cases. The students came in windows, rang cowbells and blew whistles. It was a very valuable experience for all who were concerned in the cases.

At the request of the Regents, our office, in conjunction with a faculty committee, drafted new procedural rules and substantive rules which the University would use in disciplining students in the future.

I wish to make it clear that the background and experiences I have outlined do not provide me with any great insight into how student discipline problems are to be solved. I only claim com-

---

1. Soglin v. Kauffman, 295 F. Supp. 978 (W. D. Wis. 1968).

petence insofar as these questions involve the proof of facts in the trial of cases. Any assessment I make of the dimensions of the problems and possible solutions which go beyond this competence are opinions and beliefs formulated from my short exposure with the University of Wisconsin since October of 1967.

## Student Disruption and the Community

Recently we have had much disorder in Madison. This has occurred downtown and not on the campus. We have had as many as 600 students in confrontation with our police. Two weeks ago there were 400 or 500 students jamming the corridors of our courthouse to try to stop the prosecution of some of their fellow students who had been charged with disorderly conduct. Students had been denied a permit to have a block party. Following that denial there was a confrontation with police; windows were broken, fights occurred and many people were arrested. Perhaps some of those arrests were improper. In any event, thereafter the university students attempted to stop the arraignments.

The problem the universities face is vital to all concerned. It goes well beyond just an academic problem; it goes to the heart of our free society. I watch the people—ordinary people in Madison—watching the students who gather around our capitol square. These people stand quietly, watching the students waving their red flags and shaking their fists in the air, running up and down corridors. The faces of the ordinary people reflect anger, fear and hate. I walk into the courthouse and observe working men who are putting in the overhead ducts for air conditioning—men who have fought their own problems—come out and stand quiet in the hall, and they watch the students. Their faces show that they want the problem solved. I look at the people who are solving the problem and I see dire consequences. I see how the police solved the problem. I am not criticizing the police but I don't like police solutions; I don't like National Guard solutions; I don't like the legislature's solutions.

The joint finance committee of the legislative bodies held our budget to a level that does not even permit us to take care of the 12,000 increase in our enrollment next year, much less keep pace with all of the increments that have been required to be included in the budget. I know these men and I say to them, "What's the matter? Why can't you do better for the University?" and they say, "We're not going to!" It isn't a reasonable response; it's an emotional response. They are reflecting the attitude of their communities and what the people in these communities feel.

Who is going to solve the problem? Are we, by default, going to allow some right-wing fellow to impose his solution? Democracy has a difficult time, as President Fleming said, dealing with 400 or 500 people walking around in the community; but the fascist doesn't have difficulty. I fear this. The universities should understand the measure and the depth of the problem. It isn't just intellectual give and take on Viet Nam. Students see something which they consider an injustice. Whether it is injustice or not doesn't make any difference; they believe it to be and their blood runs hot. The policeman on the other side hears the profanity, suffers the spitting, and his blood runs hot. Shortly, what we have is a dangerous confrontation.

## The University is Responsible

I believe the solution has to be with the universities. At least, some effort must be made by the universities. I listened to Mr. Carrington's reasons why the universities can't do it. He says the institution is academic and not used to dealing with such matters. I don't believe that is a good answer. I don't know, for example, that it's a good answer to say that universities deal with teaching and don't deal with conduct.

If I sue a manufacturer of cheese because he pollutes a stream and drives the neighboring tenant away from his home because of the smell and the noxious odor, the manufacturer may say, "Well, I'm a cheese maker, and I don't know how to deal with stream pollution and all those things; but society is now saying, "Mister, if you're going to manufacture cheese, you have got to take care of the by-product." And I am telling you that if the University brings 33,000 students to the city of Madison, there is some responsibility on that university for the glass the students break uptown, for the people they get involved with. Maybe, when all is said and done, a university can do nothing. But I believe you who run the universities should try. In order to take this problem on, you are going to have to do certain things. You have to come to grips with the fallacious notion that you can carve up the person, dealing only with the student half, not bothering about the citizen half. If an employee does something wrong in civilian life, he suffers on his job, he suffers in his home, he suffers in his community. You don't divide this up. If a student is in trouble uptown, surely this doesn't mean that he *should not* be in trouble in the academic community. And I don't think it's a question of acting in loco parentis. At the time we were handling the cases in Wisconsin the faculty complained that we were performing the function of the parent. I say that we were trying to survive. We were trying to keep our doors open and we had the right to do that. The concept of splitting the student should be looked at long and hard. You have to give some thought to the other questions. To your claim that you are not qualified to solve the problem, I remind you that these same problems occur between labor and management. Labor and management had a lot of stress—sit-ins, lockouts—but in time solutions were had.

## Procedures

I think that universities must make use of outside agencies. It is possible that the solution in disciplinary cases is the use of an established outside agency. I believe that the role which my firm was asked to assume on behalf of the University of Wisconsin was one that only an outsider could perform sucessfully. We could disagree with the Board of Regents; we could disagree with the faculty. We could pursue the course we believed was most effective and would get the job done.

The university setting is not the best place to ensure a fair hearing in a discipline case. This is one area I know well. I know how to use the procedural devices of the law to get a fair hearing. And I know that the classroom setting is not the place for a fair hearing. In one of our cases the student asked to have his trial in a classroom. I objected, but it was allowed on the theory that he couldn't then say he didn't get "due process."

The events of the trial were anything but consistent with due process. Some 200 students were in the audience and every witness who took the stand had to perform on a stage. The students pounded and shuffled their feet. This stage setting affected the attitude of the witnesses. It affected the student who was being tried. He said things to please his friends. His attorney said things to please the student's friends. The upshot was that there was no litigation on the facts in the case. It was a circus; and it all resulted from the anxiety over due process. The proceeding carried all of the nomenclatures of due process but there was not a fair hearing. Because of the forum the boy insisted upon, the fact questions in the case were not fairly tried.

What sort of forum should hear student discipline cases? Everybody says the students should have a voice. But it is a question of finding out what the facts are. The decision as to who should sit and how large the forum is to be should be made on the basis of what will best do the job. What the procedure should be again should be determined by what will result in fact in a fair hearing. While the university may talk about the "overriding educational needs," it must be recognized that in the final analysis the concern must be for the individual. It is an extremely difficult job to secure procedural rules which result in securing a hearing which is fair in fact. To attempt to do more will probably defeat the basic purpose.

# Discussions

## Problems in Delegation
## of University Authority

**Carrington:** The creation of bodies designed for the purpose of giving students some power may encounter the problem of delegation of that power by whatever body is vested. It is at least arguable that in some universities, public schools and colleges power is reposed in the trustees or the regents or another governing body. An attempt to delegate that power to students results in a kind of default. Consequently, the actions taken or rules promulgated by such committees will be invalid because they lack appropriate official sanction. You should be aware of this possibility in exploring the suggestion that student power may provide some answers. You should be sure that such power is exercised in accordance with the governing statutes. Moreover, it might be wise to consider requiring such bodies to follow formal rulemaking procedures, similar to the procedures required in state administrative procedure acts. Then legislative hearings might indeed be appropriate and might properly be required.

My second point concerns the wisdom of publishing university rules governing numerous areas, including disciplinary and academic matters. In the past we have been somewhat lax about making such rules known; and enforcement of rules which have been gathering dust in a file for years, unknown even to faculty and administrators, may prove embarrassing.

Thirdly, is there any role for arbitration to play in a situation involving student protest? Is there any situation in which it would be appropriate for the university to seek agreement with its students on an arbitrator and an arbitration procedure to resolve a dispute? I will ask Marvin Niehuss* to comment.

# Arbitration

**Niehuss:** A university has reached a critical stage in its internal relations when it is considering the use of arbitration or other outside devices to control a situation. I am not at all sure that universities have used all of their own resources. Neither Mr. Knauss nor Mr. Carrington discussed the question of using the power of the university, after a fair hearing, to suspend or expell students for violation of reasonable and appropriate rules. That power is used very little today. It was used quite freely 10 or 15 years ago, and without too much concern over due process. One of the reasons the power is seldom used now is the recognition that the student will be subject to the draft if the university cancels his status as a student. But I share the concern which has been expressed here. If the university does not move to control these situations, outside forces will act and the autonomy of the institution, the faculty and the students will be in jeopardy. Mr. Cates is right; if institutions are going to insist that this is their business, then they must do something about it.

As Mr. Knauss indicated, some universities, including ours, have begun including students in bodies which control internal matters, including curricula and discipline. I am not entirely sanguine that the type of participation we have given thus far is going to satisfy too many of the students. Meanwhile pressures mount to impose control from the outside. It has been variously suggested that the federal government provide arbitrators, that the state provide arbitration proceedings and that arbitration be provided internally

---

* Professor of Law, The University of Michigan Law School, Ann Arbor, Michigan.

by the university. Admittedly, it is a device worth trying if it becomes clear that we cannot control student disruption through the traditional procedures of the university.

The use of outside devices such as arbitration will require serious consideration of the matter of such delegation of the powers of the governing bodies of the institutions. Mr. Carrington raised this question. There has been very little discussion of this problem in recent legal cases or anywhere else, for that matter. To what extent can a governing board, which by constitution or by statute is charged with the supervision of an institution and control of its funds, delegate important areas of that power? The cases in this area with which I am familiar had to do with questions of the power of trustees to adopt tenure plans for faculty and staff and whether the adoption of such plans limited the power of the trustees to discharge for what appeared to be adequate cause. There have been cases which held that trustees may not delegate their power to discharge for cause, though they agree by contract. It seems to me that delegation of the power to decide the relationship of the particular student to the institution is equally open to question. I believe that entering into an arbitration agreement would in effect be such a delegation of their governing powers. The same doubts arise in the matter of delegating such governing powers to the students themselves. I still hope that the universities will find ways of governing themselves, as they have done with varying degrees of success for a thousand years; and I hope that we won't have to come to arbitration.

**Carrington:** Mr. Cates, I believe there was an interesting Wisconsin case[1] on the issue of arbitration and the delegation of governing powers. Am I correct in recalling that the city of Madison entered into an arbitration agreement a few years ago to resolve a dispute involving the design of the city hall and that this was challenged

---

1.  Madison v. Frank Lloyd Wright Foundation, 20 Wis. 2d 361, 122 N. W. 2d 409 (1963).

on the ground that the city was in some way delegating its powers by agreeing to arbitrate?

**Cates:** That case involved the design of the Civic Center by Frank Lloyd Wright, but the question of such delegation of power by the city has been going on a lot longer than the student protest. We are having the same question in the employment field. Our court has, to this time, permitted arbitration in connection with a collective bargaining agreement made by the city with its employees. And the question came up in our student protest problems. The Board of Regents felt that any forum in which students were to be disciplined must have a majority of faculty members because the statute gave the Regents the authority and permitted them to give it to the faculty. We were very concerned about the composition of that forum because it works both ways. If a student is disciplined and expelled by a forum in which students have the majority, the student might question the legality of that expulsion on the ground that the forum lacked authority. We worried about that in Wisconsin.

**Knauss:** Mr. Cates made a very good case for the problems of a judicial approach within the university for solution of some of these problems. The thrust of my earlier remarks was to try to see if there is any positive way of heading off the need for this kind of activity. I clearly didn't mean to imply that it can't happen here or any place else.

What power and authority does a university have in emergency situations? If, for example, students are occupying a building or destroying property, what are the alternatives? The university can negotiate, sit and wait, threaten, call in the campus or the local police or attempt to get an injunction. If an injunctive order is obtained, the university may have to get police enforcement of the order. These are the various ways of handling the immediate emergencies. But what kind of sanctions can be used after there has been a breach of a university rule or regulation? The university may decide not to call in the police, yet later bring disciplinary actions against the students involved. This could be done by use of the university discipline procedures, bringing a civil action for damages or citing for contempt of court for violation of an injunction. All of these would come later.

Arbitration is one way to negotiate students out of a building. If you get agreement of both sides on what the rules for arbitration should be, you can use an outside arbitrator as substitute for disciplinary action or a judicial hearing. You can use an outside arbitrator to decide whether a student should be suspended or expelled.

**Carrington:** Using arbitration as an alternative to university punishment is a very different matter from using it in a dispute over university policy or rules. This would certainly raise the issue of delegation of powers, if you are suggesting the use of arbitration to formulate university policy.

**Knauss:** Let me give an example of a situation in which it could be used. A year ago tenants in housing for married students, housing owned by The University of Michigan, refused to pay rent to the University after a raise in their rent. The dispute between the Director of Housing and a group of students had continued for months. It was finally placed in the hands of a faculty-student committee which in fact acted as an arbitration board, in that both sides agreed to abide by the decision of that committee.

## A Student Judiciary

**Carrington:** Suppose that in our enthusiasm for student participation we create a student court which makes decisions about what happens to protestors and the protestors happen also to be the court. Is there any way of heading off that kind of situation? Obviously, the result would be to make the university disciplinary systems totally ineffective. The SDS is not going to punish itself for sitting in. If the SDS controls the student court, you might as well forget about academic sanctions. How do you avoid that kind of problem?

**Knauss:** This is not a hypothetical question. The situation you suggest happened at Stanford about 18 months ago. A student judiciary body refused to act in a particular case and the President of Stanford appointed an ad hoc discipline committee made up primarily of faculty members. My own view is that such power of the administration, which I think is implicit, should be made explicit in the by-laws. I think the president of an institution does have the inherent authority of discipline. A recent Supreme Court decision upheld the authority of the president of the university to discipline although there were no prior rules or regulations in effect.

**Carrington:** One kind of student judiciary may be a possible response to the problem: treat the members of the student judiciary as jurors, selecting them by lot and requiring compulsory service. This procedure would reach beyond the limits of the student political structure to get to those students who are substantially indifferent to activism and are not particularly involved. Such a tribunal could bear a good deal of heat. Moreover, it would be difficult to object to the fairness of the method of selection. I concede that there is always a possibility that the random lot of jurors might turn out to be all SDS or at least sympathizers with whatever activity is under way. I believe that risk could be assumed. If a situation arises in which the student demonstration is so popular that you can't get a jury to convict, maybe you had better take another hard look at how you got into that dilemma. I am persuaded that this device has real promise and I am not sure why it is objectionable to so many. The student politicians don't like it because they prefer to have the power that comes from selecting their own judges. Aside from that fact, I don't see any substantial objections to the idea.

**Niehuss:** It would not be accepted by the students at The University of Michigan. They demand complete control of the judicial process.

**Cates:** I think you always have to ask whether the forum that you select is capable of giving a fair trial—whether that forum is capable of making a determination on the fact. Taking students as jurists sounds fine in theory, but having a jury complicates trial proceedings. We have juries in many cases that we litigate, but on each side, hopefully, we have trained and competent counsel and a competent trial judge who is experienced in jury trial procedure because that is substantially what he does—he doesn't do probate, he doesn't do a lot of other things.

I am concerned, moreover, that selection of a jury which is all students may not always result in a fair trial. We have been handling the trial court at the University of Wisconsin for 12 or 13 years. We have jury trials for the students and the students sit as jurors. I have observed over the years that many times the basis on which the student jury decides a case has little or nothing to do with the evidence presented. Whatever the forum selected, there must be assurance that the person on trial will get a fair hearing.

# PART II

## Community

## Student • University

# 1

## Unrest on Campus*

The "silent" college generation of the 1950's has given way to a generation of student activists who have made headlines throughout the world in recent years. Campus unrest has become a major political and social factor.

## Dimensions

The National Student Association lists 71 student demonstrations as having occurred during the first two months of the academic year 1967-1968.[1] Twenty-seven of these were protests against the presence on campus of recruiters for the Dow Chemical Company, while three were movements against compulsory Reserve Officers' Training Corps programs.

As the academic year went on, the protests gathered momentum. At Colgate University, Boston University, and Trinity College the demonstrations were against "racism" in college policies. At Duke University, 1,500 students "sat down" on the main quadrangle to force the administration to pay nonacademic personnel more than the $1.15 an hour which had for some time been the going wage; under this pressure the school authorities capitulated to the extent of agreeing to raise the rate for nonacademic personnel to $1.45 an hour.[2] At Northwestern University Negro

---

* Report of the Illinois Legislative Council, February 18, 1969, prepared by James T. Mooney, Research Coordinator.

1. *Student Protests Here and Abroad*, NEWSWEEK, May 6, 1968, pp. 40-43+.

2. *Id.*

students briefly seized an administration building to give themselves leverage for the following demands: (1) all Negro student housing; (2) an official university statement on the viciousness of white racism; (3) more Negro students and faculty members; and (4) more courses in Negro literature and art taught by Negro faculty members approved by Negro students; after brief negotiations, the university conceded these points, admitting in effect that Northwestern University had hitherto been a white racist institution.

At Stanford University, the presence of a recruiter from the Central Intelligence Agency (CIA) touched off a student demonstration. At Roosevelt University in Chicago it was the refusal of the authorities to offer a full-time teaching post to Staughton Lynd, a historian who had made unauthorized trips to Red China and North Vietnam. At Southern Illinois University, the refusal of the authorities to sanction a speaking engagement by Stokeley Carmichael precipitated disturbances.

At Cornell, students asked the university to divest itself of its $5 million investment in banks that are members of the consortium making loans to South Africa. This the university refused to do, saying that the withdrawal of this consortium would remove one of the few restraining American influences on the apartheid policy of South Africa. At Princeton, student demonstrators have asked the university to (1) withdraw from the Institute for Defense Analysis (which does work for the Pentagon); (2) revise university policy to insure the readmission of graduate students who go to jail rather than submit to the draft; (3) eliminate the rules governing the visits of female guests to Princeton dormitories; and (4) permit members of the principal activist movement on American campuses today, the Students for a Democratic Society (SDS), to counsel other students on draft problems.

The Columbia University disturbance in the spring of 1968 involved some vandalism, some use of obscene language, and a few acts of theft, but no serious violence. It was, however, the most highly publicized incident of its kind that has occurred in the United States. The major student grievances appear to have been the university's decision to build a gymnasium in Morningside Heights and its involvement in the Institute for Defense Analysis (IDA). The gymnasium project involved the displacement of a number of Negro and Puerto Rican families from Harlem, and was viewed by Mark Rudd and other leaders of student revolt as the last step in a series of moves by the university to create a "respectable" white neighborhood around Columbia. The military research program (IDA) involved the University in antisubmarine warfare research, counterinsurgency research, and other activities which, in the opinion of many students, compromised Columbia's position as a searcher for and evaluator of truth. The university's participation in the development of the Strickman cigarette filter (which failed to live up to commercially made claims) had also caused some of the more idealistic students to question the purity of the administration's motives.

The insurrection at Columbia involved student takeovers of five buildings, the kidnapping of one dean for a day, and some scuffling with New York City police. In the sequel the university surrendered the gymnasium project but refused amnesty to the ringleaders of the student revolt.

The movement under way (February 1969) on the University of Chicago campus differs from its predecessors in that it is directed primarily against the faculty, which the students apparently feel acted in a highhanded way in refusing to renew the contract of Mrs. Marlene Dixon, a leftist scholar who favors Marxism and uses student-oriented teaching methods.[3] The troubles recently reported in San Francisco and at San Fernando State College seem racial in origin.[4]

---

3. Chicago Daily News, Feb. 3, 1969.

4. Sheldon Harris, *San Fernando's Black Revolt*, COMMONWEAL, Jan. 31, 1969, pp. 549–552.

## Organizations Involved

Although American student upheavals resemble in many of their outward manifestations the student uprisings that have shaken governments in France and Italy and have led Generalissimo Franco to decree martial law in Spain, most observers do not see in them any considerable trace of foreign leadership or influence—nothing more direct along these lines, in fact, than a great deal of admiration for such foreign personalities as Chairman Mao, Che Guevara, and Regis Debray. The authors that rebellious American college students read with approval—Herbert Marcuse, Norman Mailer, Paul Goodman, C. Wright Mills—are American; the loosely structured organizations of the New Left into which they have banded, if that is not too strong an expression, are American.[5]

In the vanguard of campus unrest is the SDS, Students for a Democratic Society. This group, founded in 1962, estimates its numbers at from 35,000 to 40,000, and the number of its chapters on American campuses at 250 to 300. Outside observers project its hard-core dedicated membership at about 6,000. Ideologically, it is against the war in Vietnam, against the Selective Service System, against the Central Intelligence Agency, and against the Dow Chemical Company as the producer of napalm. Tactically, it attempts to make as much trouble as it can for university and college administrators, hoping thus to paralyze the whole collegiate structure, and then the vast corporate structure which, in SDS's view, depends upon the colleges and universities as a bodily organism depends upon its digestive tract. The SDS is committed to the politics of "Participation," that is, to the proposition that as many people as possible should have a hand in the making of major political and social decisions.

Somewhat more loosely organized and anarchistic than the SDS

---

5. *Why Those Students are Protesting*, TIME, May 3, 1968, pp. 24–25.

is the "New Left" group known as the Youth International Party ("Yippies"). These are said to believe in a politics of the "absurd," which no one has succeeded in elucidating as yet. The YIP numbers only a few thousand students.

Other formations of the New Left include some of the younger faculty members in their ranks. These, more or less in the order of their numerical importance, seem to consist of the Resistance, Resist, the National Mobilization Committee to End the War in Vietnam (popularly called "Mobe"), and the New University Conference.

Parties of what is now commonly referred to as the "Old Left" are still active on American campuses. These include the Young Socialist Alliance, Progressive Labor, the W.E.B. Dubois Clubs, and Peace and Freedom Party.

In active adherents these various groupings of the left are much less numerous than the more conservative political formations on campus, the Young Republicans, for example (estimated numbers 150,000), or the Young Democrats (estimated numbers 100,000), or the conservative Young Americans for Freedom (estimated at 25,000). These more traditional groups have succeeded in arousing some opposition to militant demonstrations among uncommitted students. However, it is the consensus that the New Left groups are the more successful in persuading idealistic students and young faculty members to make common cause with them on specific campus issues. Those who join forces with the offical New Left in protest demonstrations tend to be, in the opinion of some close observers of contemporary campus movements, the brightest, most imaginative students, those most full of generous indignation at the social and political injustices that are on display at home and abroad. They have been characterized as children of permissive parents, "the babies who were picked up" (by David Riesman) but also as "our best kids" (by Noam Chomsky).

Various polls and studies indicate that a little over 25 percent of college students are sufficiently sympathetic to some of the aims of the New Left to be opposed to the Selective Service System.[6] Some 20 percent of American college students reported themselves as admiring Che Guevara more than any of the men who ran for the Presidency in 1968.

## Use of Drugs

Widespread drug use is sometimes noted as an important manifestation of current campus unrest. A recent poll indicates that no more than 5 or 6 percent of all the youth now on American campuses have ever even tried an hallucinogenic drug.[7] In colleges noted for their vocational and practical orientations, for student interests centered in sports and social activities, for the absence of serious student intellectual interests, hallucinogenic drug usage is quite rare.

In the more prestigious colleges, where intellectual life is more intense and intellectual competition keener, there is more widespread resort to drugs, but even on these campuses half of the students listed as users actually have used the drugs no more than two or three times in their lives and have no plans to continue using them.

A smaller number of students on these campuses use hallucinogenic drugs occasionally, for example over a weekend and socially, but have not organized their lives around drug use.

Finally, there is a relatively small but highly visible group of students who use drugs habitually and experiment with a number of different drugs, who have in fact made drug usage part of a

---

6. *American Youth, Its Outlook is Changing the World*, FORTUNE, Jan. 1969, pp. 68–71.

7. Kenneth Keniston, *Heads and Seekers: Drugs on Campus, Counter-Cultures and American Society*, AMERICAN SCHOLAR/38: 97–112, Winter 1968.

"turned on" ideology and a membership card into one of the college subcultures. This is the group variously called "heads," "acid heads," "pot heads."

## Causes of Unrest

Most discussions of the factors that are causing campus unrest assign some responsibility to the family and social environment from which the students come, some to the university environment they enter, and some to the larger environment that impinges upon them while they are in school, particularly the domestic turmoil exemplified by the racial question, and the foreign turmoil exemplified by the war in Vietnam.

Collegians today are largely the offspring of permissive and affluent parents. They are not under the pressure their forerunners in college were to gear their academic careers to personal achievement in a narrow field, the kind of achievement that would insure them the material success of a high paying position in industry or one of the professions. They are freer to regard the world around them, note its real and apparent social and political injustices and maladjustments, and develop a social and political consciousness. This awareness is stimulated and fed by the modern mass media, especially by television.

## Increase in Enrollments

The most noteworthy change in the environment to which today's students come is the startling increase in its size. Where 2.5 million students were in college a long generation ago, 6.5 million are there today. By 1970 the number is expected to reach 7.5 million. The 6.5 million now in attendance represent 40 percent of population between the ages of 18 and 21.[8]

---

8. Arthur Schlesinger, Jr., *Joe College is Dead*, SATURDAY EVENING POST, Sept. 21, 1968, pp. 24–25+.

With this influx of population, student activists say, colleges have become universities and universities "multiversities." The concept of a "value free" social science, it is argued, has turned the colleges and universities into mere feeders of technicians and administrators into the corporate structure for the perpetuation of the system, the "establishment"; it has also made of them, according to their student critics, accomplices of vast military and industrial complexes. From all this and from such other modern collegiate phenomena as huge lecture classes, the elevation of research and publication to a position of at least equality with teaching in the rating of faculty members, the steady trend toward abstract and specialized intellectuality in the better institutions, seem to have come feelings of alienation and powerlessness among today's students.

## Student Outlook

Turning their gaze toward the larger environment, these student activists see the United States as a monopolistic form of capitalism sustained by racism and imperialism. Racism leads in this view to the production of profitable ghettos at home; imperialism accounts for all the foreign interventions by means of which we keep our friends in power and our grip firm on the raw materials of the undeveloped and underindustrialized nations of the world.

These diatribes against American domestic and foreign policy have been the stock in trade of left wing movements since at least the turn of the century; nevertheless, they still seem to have a power over student activists somewhat out of proportion to their intrinsic logical force.

As matters now stand, that part of campus unrest which can be attributed to racial tensions, more specifically, to the civil rights movement, has become the preserve of the black power groups among the students; while the white elements are concerning themselves more and more with the war in Vietnam. Protests over the war have become noticeably more apolitical in nature, more in the style of civil disobedience and confrontation, since the defeat of Senator McCarthy's campaign for the Presidency and the lessening of the Kennedy influence. Whether rightly or wrongly, idealistic young men and women involved in student protest movements do not seem to think that they can effectively enter political life under the banner of a Johnson or a Nixon.

## Objectives

There seems little question that a very small number of those involved in campus unrest are hard-core revolutionaries who wish to turn the university into a political instrument and student disorders into a form of totalitarian harassment. A majority of the rebelling students, though, seem to want no more than that the colleges and universities of the country become "fountains of reform" rather than "perpetuators" of the status quo. The closest approach they make to overtly revolutionary action is the deference they pay to "civil disobedience," which they usually define as the right to refuse to lend oneself to what one regards as a monstrously unjust cause, even if ordered to do so by law. At the moment this doctrine has particular relevance in the matter of the draft, which some student protestors see as a legal command to support a monstrously unjust policy of genocide, *i.e.*, the Vietnamese War.

Most campus unrest has more limited objectives than an overthrow of the present social or political order or a quick end to the war in Southeast Asia. Most student rebels are probably not even bent on *cogobierno* (joint rule of the university by faculty and students). The reforms they have in mind seem confined to the campus, and take the following forms:

(1) Student membership on boards of trustees.

(2) Meaningful student participation in the choosing, retention, and dismissal of faculty members, and in the framing of curricula and course content.

(3) Student participation in the formulation of policies relating to grading, entrance requirements, examinations, and the expansion of the university's physical plant.

(4) Student control over discipline, housing, and other academic matters.

(5) Complete personal freedom for students living off campus.

(6) A marked relaxation of or end to all manner of curfews and other restrictions upon the social life of students, particularly in regard to relations between the sexes; in short, an abandonment by the university or college of the theory that it stands "in loco parentis" to its students.

(7) An end to campus ROTC whether of the compulsory or voluntary variety.

(8) An end to on-campus recruiting by Dow Chemical, the Central Intelligence Agency, or any other outside business, governmental, or industrial instrumentality.

(9) An end to or a sharp curtailment of university research contracts or other financial and scientific connections with agencies and firms whose primary purpose is profit or power and not the disinterested pursuit of truth, and

(10) An end to any policy of restricting the speakers who may be invited to appear on campus and the subjects they may discuss there.

## Reaction of College and University Administrators

Nothing in their experience of the 1950's seems to have prepared college and university administrators and trustees for the strong currents of campus unrest that have been flowing in the 1960's.

They have not on the whole been shocked or surprised into taking a hard or repressive line as a way out of the difficulties campus turmoil has caused them. The universities of Chicago and Columbia seem unwilling to grant amnesty to students who break school regulations, trespass on school property, and disrupt normal school procedures and proceedings, and the provost of the latter institution, political scientist David S. Truman, has remarked that the granting of wholesale amnesty in these cases is out of the question if it means turning over to a minority of the students the power to destroy a university. President Goheen of Princeton has told student demonstrators that violence will not be tolerated. President S. I. Hayakawa of San Francisco State College has emphasized the maintenance of order on campus perhaps a little more than most college authorities.

Overall, the reaction of the college and university administrators appears to be cautiously conciliatory. Experiments in coeducational housing and coeducational fraternities have been reported.[9] There is apparently a disposition to grant students more membership on various committees that advise and recommend university policies. On some campuses there has been a partial abandonment of the old system of competitive grading and marking. Campus curfews and rules governing visiting back and forth among boy and girl students have been eased in some places. There is a growing effort to recruit Negro students and faculty members and to institute various courses on Negro culture and history. Public school authorities must consider how their trustees and the State legislatures will view these developments, and private school authorities must give some thought to the reactions of their trustees.

## Survey of Trustees

A recent study of college trustees—an opinion sampling of more than 5,000 of them from 536 colleges and universities—indicates that they may be more willing to take up the challenge of direct

---

9. *Id.*

confrontation with the campus rebels than the administrators of higher education.[10]

Most of the trustees surveyed are of the opinion that they and not the young editors should control the content of campus newspapers.

Well over a third believe that it is reasonable to require loyalty oaths of faculty members. The same proportion held that students who have been punished by nonuniversity authorities for off-campus behavior should get the same punishment for the same behavior from the campus authorities.

A fourth of the trustees studied would screen the speakers invited to campuses by student groups and would deny faculty members freedom of expression.

The average trustee represented in this survey is white, Protestant, conservative, and well-to-do (with more than half having incomes in excess of $30,000 a year).

On balance these trustees appear to believe that colleges should be run like businesses, under a hierarchical structure with orders handed down from the top.

## Legislative Reactions

In the course of considering the bill that later became the Higher Education Amendments of 1968,[11] the U.S. Senate Committee on Labor and Welfare expressed its alarm and dismay at the mounting evidence of campus unrest. The committee did not think, however, that a policy of denying Federal assistance to students because of certain behavior specified by Federal law was the answer.[12] It recommended, instead, that Congress condemn

---

10. COMMONWEAL (Jan. 31, 1969), p. 544.
11. S. 3769, Public Law 90–575, 82 Stat. 1014.
12. U.S. Code Congressional and Administrative News (Nov. 5, 1968), pp. 5685 and 5686.

illegal student activity and urge the schools promptly to apply disciplinary measures, including the withholding of financial aid available through Federal programs. The committee also expressed the hope that the colleges and universities of the country, acting on information specially compiled for them by the U.S. Office of Education, would step up their campaigns of "high risk" recruitment. By "high risk" recruitment, the committee meant primarily the recruitment of Negroes and Mexican-Americans as college students.

The act as passed disregards the Senate committee's advice in the matter of writing Federal penalties into the law. It denies Federal aid for 2 years to any student who has committed serious offenses at the college he attends. This sanction applies to the following student aid programs: student loans under the National Defense Education Act of 1958; educational opportunity grants under the Higher Education Act of 1965; the student loan insurance program under the Higher Education Act of 1965; the college-work study program under the Higher Education Act of 1965, and any fellowship program carried on under the National Defense Education Act of 1958 or the Higher Education Act of 1965. The act further provides that nothing in it shall be construed to limit a university's disciplinary authority or the individual's right to express verbally his views and opinions.

## Illinois Bills

Six measures pending (as of February 12, 1969) in the 76th General Assembly, S.B.'s 191 and 206 and H.B.'s 71, 215, 219, and 222, would revoke the scholarships, and in one case, end the employment of those committing disorders on a university or college campus or interfering with its functioning.

One measure is aimed at what some student rebels consider an unholy alliance between institutions of higher learning and business interest. This is H.B. 98, which would severely restrict the power of the faculty members of State-supported institutions of higher learning to make outside contracts for research.

## Possible Measures of Alleviation

It seems universally agreed by those who have written on student disorders in the United States that a quick end to the Vietnam war would be the most likely eventuality to ease much of the campus discontent and unrest. This solution will obviously come as a gift of history rather than through the unilaterial action of any American legislature, State or Federal.

Along the same line the replacement of the present draft-based army by an army of volunteers would undoubtedly be viewed with intense satisfaction by many student activists.

On the State level, a certain amount of repressive action—for example, the revocation of scholarships in retaliation for illegal behavior—would clearly be constitutionally permissible. Other repressive measures—increased censorship over campus speakers being one that comes to mind—would, under recent decisions, encounter more constitutional trouble. As a practical matter, repressive measures, even comparatively mild ones, would be read by many in the university community as a declaration of war, as a sign that society was prepared to maintain the status quo at whatever the cost to student rights and in complete disregard of student feelings and opinions. There are those who would argue that a politics of confrontation, of violence and counter-violence can best be avoided through entrusting to college and university authorities the responsibility of keeping open to students the channels of legitimate protest and of introducing a greater measure of democracy into university affairs than now exists.

# 2

# The Array of Sanctions

## Tom J. Farer*

## Introduction

It would be idle for me to lay any claim to expertise in this area. Essentially I have been a spectator, though I have participated episodically in some of the problems at Columbia. I feel, therefore, rather like the Irish priest who was lecturing a group of his female parishioners about the maternal bliss associated with large families. During his lecture a rapidly aging mother of 11 children, one of whom was puling on her shoulder, turned to the woman sitting next to her and remarked wistfully, "I only wish I knew as little about it as he does."

The principal justification for seeking an expression of views from someone not engaged in administration is to perform what Mort Kaplan has called, with perhaps unnecessary obscurity, metatasks, which means really nothing more than taking a little time out to think about the broader policies and objectives which are being pursued. I know from my own experience in government that it is extraordinarily difficult for men who are dealing with daily crises to focus on the ultimate objectives of their activities. As a consequence, policy tends to be made alluvially. The outcome of the individual decisions one makes when confronting daily crises is often a very different kind of outcome, I suspect, than would have been intended if one had sat down and thought

---

\* Associate Professor, Columbia University School of Law, New York, New York.

about ultimate goals.

There are three kinds of issues here: issues of law, issues of policy, and issues of what one might call public relations. I do not use the term "public relations" in its manipulative sense; I mean it in the sense of being able to explain to infuriated legislators and alumni what your policies are, and in particular why you have in some cases decided not to apply sanctions.

In this context I want to approach what seems to me to be one of the important issues in this whole area. There is a widely held view that it is the legal, even the moral, obligation of administrators to prosecute and impose sanctions in response to every violation of university rules. I categorically reject this view: it is ahistorical; it is not consistent with the society's normal behavior; moreover, to the extent that it fails to measure the relationship between means and ends, it seems to me positively immoral.

There are all kinds of situations in which the society does not in fact prosecute violations of the criminal law. We rarely prosecute violations of the antitrust laws, even in the more vulgarly blatant cases. The electric price-fixing cases of a few years ago struck us as exceptional because they were exceptional. Indeed, most kinds of violations of business regulation laws, despite the fact that in many cases they are enforced theoretically by criminal sanctions, are simply not prosecuted. This is equally true even of violations of the most common kinds of criminal law. We do not prosecute the offender for a variety of reasons: he is a youth; he is the sole support of a large family; he has repented and is now rehabilitated; the courts are clogged; or there is little public support for the prosecution of violations of this particular crime, as was true, for example, of anticontraception laws. At its best, our system of criminal justice is not a license to administer justice arbitrarily; we assume that there has to be some reason for failing to prosecute. All I am suggesting is that there are many such reasons built into the whole system of criminal justice. Yet I have heard very few people—administrators, counsel to administrations or even members of the faculty—say this openly. It seems to me a perfectly simple point, and a point which one is capable of communicating to the persons outside of the university who are concerned with the policies that the administration pursues.

## Alternate Objectives Available to a University Administration

### To Preserve Order and Confirm Authority?

One objective is simply to preserve order and confirm the authority of the existing decisionmaking structure. In a sense, this objective is a denial of any purpose other than the maintenance of oneself in a position of power. It is not too hyperbolic to say that this can only be the objective of a dictatorship. After all, in any society where governmental power rests at least theoretically on the consent of the governed, one of the rooted assumptions is that power ought to be used to promote some socially useful objectives and not simply held or cherished for its own right. In any event, since colleges and universities are not self-supporting or profit-making institutions, at least they are compelled to advance some kind of justification for their being and for their structure.

If the consequences of the sanctioning policies adopted were, in effect, to seek to preserve order and confirm existing authority, we would certainly have to change the nature of the American university. Paradoxically, while the methods we would have to adopt to achieve that objective would fill out neatly the caricature drawn of us by the SDS, in fact we would be driven to create educational policies patterned after those which are being adopted in Communist China. A policy of maximum intimidation of students—implemented by expulsion at the first signs of discontent—would mean the exclusion of very large numbers of students from the university. Among those excluded would be a substantial portion of the kinds of students who have staffed our government and foundation bureaucracies, and to a lesser extent the business bureaucracy. A coherent and single-minded defense of the status quo would lead to a policy of educating the minimum number in the minimal way necessary to keep the economy functioning and to sustain militarily useful operations. We would simply want mass literacy for the bulk of the population, and we would select certain people to study physics, chemistry or foreign languages to the extent necessary for the purposes of the State Department, the CIA and the corporations engaged in international investment.

This change in education would quite clearly require changes in the greater society. Indeed, such a change would mark the end of functioning democracy as we know it. It might even deprive those in power of certain aesthetic pleasures, since schools of art and architecture tend to be cauldrons of dissidence and hence would probably suffer diminution if not elimination. A more serious matter from the point of view of those concerned primarily with national power is the problematical impact of this kind of change in educational policy, based upon the use of maximum sanctioning powers at the earliest possible moment, on economic growth.

I doubt that any respectable school administrator or his counsel would consciously espouse the unalloyed preservation of their power as an objective sufficient unto itself. But it is possible to push in that direction unconsciously through the alluvial accumulation of day-to-day decisions. Therefore, it is useful to look it in the face and then turn away. Moreover, clarification of the consequences of a policy of maximum sanctions facilitates an explanation to those outside the university why this is not the policy of most university administrations.

## To Maintain the University as it Exists Today?

A second possible objective would be to maintain the university as a socializing agent and training institute for functionaries in the corporate, governmental and foundation bureaucracies; as a means to its own replenishment for those purposes; as a mechanism for expediting *modest* social mobility; and as a center for promoting socially useful research. The issue in my mind is whether it is possible to continue to serve that objective without some movement toward a third objective, which I shall somewhat grandiloquently describe as "providing the larger society with an operating model of a truly democratic and civilized community." The reason I think objective two requires movement toward objective three is that many of the kind of socially sensitive and broadly educated young men who are recruited under contemporary standards, especially in government and the foundation world, insist on movement toward objective three and are unwilling to abide by the present arrangement of authority on campus. This is also true of the most disadvantaged in the society who are suddenly being recruited by most of our major universities.

## To Provide a Model Community?

What is it that the liberal, as well as the revolutionary, students object to in the status quo at the university? I think that most of the objections can ultimately be traced to an antagonism to the whole manipulative, accommodating style of administration, which is the rooted method and technique of administration in all of the major bureaucracies—educational, governmental and corporate. But is a different style really possible for the multiversity—for that gray, sprawling place with its vast tasks and vast population of students, faculty and administrators? Does the effort to increase the sense of participation, the sense that the university is a democratic and civilized community, preclude efficient and even innovative administration? Does it require government by committee, indeed, as is frequently feared, committees manned by activists of the Right and the Left? I sometimes try to convince my more radical friends that government by committee will, by its nature, never be innovative. If one really wants innovation, what one wants is a strong authority at the center, but an authority that operates openly and is subject to a reasonably limited term.

## Features of the Model Community

Let me suggest very briefly some of the changes which might lead to an enhanced sense of the university as a community.

First, all elements of the university community must be represented in the search for and the election of the principal executive officers. This is just a threshold requirement, but an important one.

Second, and possibly most critical, the chief executive officers of the university must be men of a quite different style than those who have tended to be selected for the last several decades. They must not be behind-the-scenes accommodators who see their basic constituency residing outside the university. They must be capable of providing forceful moral leadership and at the same time be committed to the notion of an open, plural university. They must, in other words, be capable of taking personal positions while at the same time insisting upon the right of all shades of opinion to be reflected in the university community. Let me give you an example of what I am *not* referring to. Normally there is little to be gained by reference to individual persons and incidents, but sometimes we must move out of the realm of the abstract and talk about particular cases, however painful they may be. After the first "bust" at Columbia, someone arranged an interview for me with a very senior official at the University, a man of high intelligence, a man enormously respected at Columbia. I knew that many students who originally had been antagonistic to the sit-ins were wild with fury after witnessing the savage beating of students and faculty by the police. As one who participated in that emotion, I said to the Columbia official that the best thing he could do for the campus to restore some sense of community was immediately to make a statement categorically condemning what the police had done. I said this after he himself had stated that the police had violated their instructions and that the barbarity was far too widespread to be attributable to the odd acts of a few eccentric police officers. Nevertheless that official refused to make a public statement until it was cleared with yet higher authority. His attitude was consistent with the bureaucratic ethic—until the boss clears it, the subordinate remains silent. I don't wish to denigrate that ethic. In ordinary times it is an essential condition for the implementation of community policy. But there are moments of moral crisis when one either transcends the conventional code or cedes the authority to govern. The failure to rise above it in this case caused Columbia additional pain and damage. That, then, is an example of the kind of style that I am *not* referring to.

Third, the university, if it is to move toward functioning as a model of democracy, must openly declare its commitment to the important social tasks of our time. Again, just to exemplify that pomposity, most of our great colleges and universities are still committed to the doctrine of elitism; that is, they are reluctant to employ any substantial portion of the available human or physical capital in education programs which are useful to the disadvantaged, who otherwise have no hope of catching up. In the name of merit, and frequently quite unconsciously, the university has until very recently participated in the virtual exclusion of certain groups from the middle and upper rungs of our socioeconomic ladder. That policy, however well based it may be in good faith, no longer enjoys a sufficiently wide measure of support, or even toleration.

## Interrelation of
## Objectives and Sanctions

If the university did become the principal institution in the society which comes close to achieving the third objective—an operating model of a truly democratic, civilized community—this would generate certain social problems. For if the organization of the university is far more democratic and more participatory in spirit than that of the institutions which students enter after graduation, the society may experience additional tensions. A student accustomed to feeling a sense of participation may find himself in a governmental hierarchy where he is forced to wait 15 years before his voice is heard in the formulation of policy. This frustrating situation can have a disabling impact on that person and ultimately on the institution which employs him. I cannot dismiss the problem, but clearly I am not prepared to resolve it. I simply throw it out as one the many conundrums we must wrestle today.

## The Spectrum of Sanctions

The sanctions which the university may apply are expulsion, suspension, probation, denial of facilities for group activities, denial of financial assistance and finally, the transfer of responsibility for the application of sanctions to the public authorities and the unqualified support of their investigative and prosecutorial efforts.

### Application of Sanctions by Public Authority

When applied to students, public sanctions are frequently, if not invariably, disproportionate, vindictive and discriminatory. This is true particularly in the method of arrest and in the sentences imposed. For that reason alone I think that the resort by the university to the public sanctioning processes raises serious moral problems, not to mention the practical problems arising from the antagonism generated among the larger student body by demonstrably discriminatory treatment.

There is no reason for administrations to acquiesce in the view that the criminal law ought to apply indiscriminately on and off campus. Certainly, it is a view which does not command universal support. In Latin American countries, for example, the immunity of the university community from the general sanctioning processes of the society is deeply rooted.

One justification for this is that, unlike the victim and his mugger, the administration must go on living with its students. Disputes within the college community resulting in law violation are in some ways analogous to the family fight. Family altercations result in innumerable violations of the criminal law, yet prosecution is rare. The society has clearly made a judgment that because the parties to the crime must live together, despite the fact that there has been a breach of public peace the state ought to step aside as gracefully as possible unless the injured party is determined to have the law enforced. There are strong analogies between that situation and the situation on the campus. In any event, the desirability of punishment by the public authority must be balanced against the required means. Where the means involve tactics which offend the sensibilities and the conscience of the university community—the use of police informers on the campus, for example—the university should not only refuse cooperation in such tactics, but should publicly expose police efforts to employ those tactics in advancing order on the campus.

In those cases where it is felt necessary to resort to the public authority, the administration must make greater efforts to make the police accountable. There are those who insist that it is now impossible to control the police, regardless of the precautions that are taken. Perhaps! But I have yet to see a university administration that has made any adequate effort to test that proposition. Surely no one will accuse the administrators of Columbia and Harvard of having exhausted the potential means for controlling the police. In both cases one sensed something of the Pontius Pilate syndrome. Among other things, the administration can place large numbers of photographers at the scene. The fact that policemen engaged in student-control operations make considerable effort to conceal their identities suggests that the threat of exposure can be intimidating. In addition, the administration might commission large numbers of faculty shadows for the police, particularly when they enter buildings. Although these measures will be resisted, I believe they should be tried. There are cases where the police have been controlled, for instance during the demonstrations at the Wallace rally in New York last year.

## Expulsion

The difficulty with the use of expulsion as a sanction is that it merely deprives the disobedient student of formal status in the university community. If he is to be physically expelled and prevented from returning to the campus and continuing in the dissident activity which was the cause of his expulsion, controls over ingress and egress at the campus must be imposed. Such controls impair the ability to carry on the university enterprise in a civilized way.

## Probation

Probation tends to be ineffective as a sanction because of the kinds of people who violate the rules of the university and the reasons for such violations. When the principal disciplinary problem was a panty raid by members of the football team, probation was a serious sanction—they couldn't play the next year. Most of those who engage in dissidence now are not concerned with being first man on the checker team. Forbidding participation in the traditional extracurricular activities through probation strikes me, then, as not a terribly fear-inducing sanction, unless it is used to destroy the functioning political action groups by characterizing them as being among the prohibited "extra-curricular" activities. This, of course, raises first amendment difficulties; hence it is not surprising that at least the more enlightened administrations have not employed the sanction of probation against dissident groups.

### Denial of Financial Assistance

The sanction of denial of financial assistance is grossly unfair. In large measure, it is really a sanction of discriminatory expulsion. It involves driving out of the university community its poorest members.

# A Functional Perspective

One of the historic functions of sanctions was the removal of the immediate threat to the society. The comparable university sanction, of course, is expulsion. I have already described the problems associated with expulsion of dissidents from the university.

A second historic function of sanctions was providing the occasion and a catalyst for rehabilitation. But can we talk about rehabilitation in the context of the university? Historically, rehabilitation was premised on a sense of guilt and on the need for guidance and training in some respectable profession. The guilt was thought to arise in part because the surreptitious crime was discovered. Student dissent which violates the law usually is open. And the student protestors, since they reject the authority of the university, are normally not suffused with pangs of guilt when they are sanctioned. In addition, protest is often an expression of indifference to or contempt for the respectable positions in society to which these students would have automatic access as university graduates. We must concede, therefore, that rehabilitation is really not one of the functions of university sanctions.

Deterrence, another traditional function, presumes a nice calculation of costs and benefits on the part of those who are contemplating violation of the law. Various kinds of sanctions may in fact deter significant numbers of students. We don't really know. But the principal student dissidents certainly do not appear to engage in the normal kind of cost accounting to which the sanctioning process has been addressed in the past.

Society's formal sanctions have also been seen as an alternative to self-help by the injured party. The analogous case on campus is to prevent confrontation between left- and right-wing students. I am not convinced that sanctions are often necessary to achieve that objective. The truth is that the more conservative students tend to be those who are most concerned about obtaining a college education in order to advance up the socioeconomic scale. Therefore, the threat to apply sanctions to the more conservative students is much more likely to be intimidating than the threat to apply sanctions against more radical students. Sanctions will thus control the right-wing students and prevent a confrontation between the two factions. I am not suggesting it is fair to impose sanctions on one and not on the other, but merely outlining the practicalities of the situation.

Sanctions may serve to reduce social anxiety by confirming the strength of public authorities. Sometimes this is put under the rubric of simple vengeance, but vengeance, with all its baggage of connotations, is not an accurate way of describing what the purpose of the sanction has been. In the context of the university, the relevant anxieties are those of members of the university community who were not involved in the violation of university rules and also those of members of the larger society in which the university is imbedded—legislators, alumni, potential givers. With respect to the external constituency, sanctions may perform the traditional anxiety-reducing function. They may be considerably less effective in relation to the internal constituency, because a ruthless application of sanctions has tended to radicalize a large body of the academic community.

## Applications of Sanctions: Due Process

There are two dimensions to the due process issue in the

application of sanctions. One involves rulemaking and the other adjudication. We must talk about due process both in terms of how one makes the rules of discipline and the related sanctions and how one imposes those sanctions and rules.

All of the larger groups and shades of opinion ought to be represented in the rulemaking body. In addition, there ought to be an opportunity for individual participation in the shaping of the important rules of the university. Oral participation is preferable, but if that is not possible, then at least all should be allowed some kind of reasoned and systematic written presentation. Indeed, at a state school I can imagine the courts eventually moving to the position that hearings of some kind are mandatory. I would be prepared to argue that. If the District of Columbia Insurance Commissioner cannot adopt rules governing insurance companies located in the District without a hearing, why should the administration of a state-run educational institution be able to adopt rules which will affect vital rights without some kind of a hearing? I think there is a legal as well as a prudential and moral case to be made.

With respect to adjudication, one of the issues which has bothered us at Columbia is whether all of the old informality must be jettisoned—the quiet chat with the dean. I believe there is a case to be made for the old informality. The very formal kind of adjudicative process at all levels is not consistent with the sense of a close-knit community. The solution we have adopted at Columbia is that the court of the first resort—the place where you go for your preliminary hearing—is the dean's office. If the student doesn't appear because he feels that due process requires a more formal setting for the application of rules, I don't think he ought to be obligated to appear. Rather, the failure to appear ought to be regarded as nothing more than a plea of "not guilty." The student can then move up to the next level, which should be a tribunal operating under quasi-judicial, trial-like procedures.

One of the important issues at this level is: Who are one's peers?

Should students be tried only by students and faculty by faculty? I favor mixed tribunals. Students should not be judged by tribunals composed exclusively of students and members of the faculty ought not to be judged by tribunals composed exclusively of faculty members, because the entire university community must live with the result; and the method by which the tribunal applies the laws can seriously affect that community's life. If all have an interest in the outcome, then why shouldn't all be participants in the process?

The use of faculty and perhaps members of the administration in tribunals that judge students has a second merit in that it tends to promote consistency in the application of sanctions. Consistency does not require mixed tribunals at the trial level, if the rules permit appellate bodies to revise penalties either up or down.

For similar reasons, I favor mixed tribunals to judge members of the faculty. That would not be clearly inconsistent with the principle of judgment by one's peers, for a growing proportion of faculty members are more oriented to the values and sensibilities of the student generation than to those of their older colleagues.

Another procedural possibility is a system of appeal to a body which includes one or more distinguished members of the broader community. Such members might be selected by vote of the student and faculty members of the highest appellate body. A distinguished judge or educator with no involvement in the particular conflict might contribute to a more enlightened judgment.

In conclusion, I would like to assure you that despite the very substantial difficulties in the universities, I see this time as one of great hope. My own generation—I was in school in the 50's—viewed the world with a bovine indifference and regarded injustice with what can only be described as monumental patience. This generation of students has compelled us to confront the gap between the promise and the reality of American life and to begin to bridge that gap. Perhaps it is inevitable that powerful states should pursue imperial policies. Perhaps it is inevitable that vulgar but rich men and the institutions they dominate should pollute our air and our water and our public life. This generation of students has rekindled my belief that these things are not inevitable. This time of trouble may in retrospect seem a time when vast hopes began to stumble towards the beginning of their realization. We, as the representatives of the older generations, should perhaps contemplate the possiblity that the responsibility for our contemporary troubles lies not so much in our students as in ourselves.

# 3

# The School in Court

## John P. Holloway, Esq.*

## Introduction

Student unrest is so prevalent today as to need no introduction. It might be refreshing, therefore, to look backward in time to the "good old days." I was able to locate the *Discipline Journal* of the University of Colorado for the years from 1921 to 1948. The *Journal* reflects an average of somewhat less than ten cases of minor discipline each year and a similar number of major discipline cases each year. The entries are from four to ten lines long, written in the finest of Spencerian penmanship. A random selection of entries illustrates typical punishments and attitudes of the university officials toward procedural due process. I shall read a few of the entries, to re-create the flavor of days long past. We find the following:

Dateline February 11, 1925: Miss W copies from Miss X in a regular midterm examination in French IB. Miss W denied this to Mrs. Y, but subsequently admitted it to Dean Z. She was suspended for the remainder of the winter quarter.

Dateline February 27, 1925: Mr. Y admitted taking university property, and Mr. Z, his roommate and an older man, very manfully insisted that he was more to blame than Mr. Y. Both men behaved delightfully, and the committee voted a minimum punishment, which was suspension for one week in both cases. The moral of the story appears to be that it paid to confess.

---

*     Resident Legal Counsel, University of Colorado, Boulder, Colorado.

Dateline March 16, 1928: On March 16 it was decided to suspend Mr. Y for one week because he had appropriated one-half gallon of rubbing alcohol from the women's gymnasium. The alcohol was found in a search of Mr. Y's room in connection with another discipline case.

Under major discipline entries we find the following examples:

Dateline February 16, 1926: Present on major discipline were Dean A, Dean B, Dean C, Professor D and Dean E, Chairman. I suspect that in 1926 these individuals must have comprised the full complement of deans. On the statements of both Mr. H and Miss G that they were together in the sitting room of Mr. H's boarding house from approximately 9:45 p.m. Sunday, February 7, to 4 a.m. Monday, and that Miss G did not return to her own boarding house until about 6:30 a.m., the committee decided to vote simply on the statement without any charge of sexual misconduct. It was voted that they should be suspended indefinitely, their readmission to depend on a recommendation of the discipline committee. If it had not been for the reluctance of the committee to inflict the final stigma of expulsion, the members would have considered that punishment not a bit too severe. We can earnestly hope that Miss G, at least, will never apply for readmission.

Dateline October 30, 1928: Miss A was before the discipline committee for attempting to use a book during the midterm quiz in history. The committee decided that Miss A would receive a grade of zero in the course and be placed on probation until June, automtically removing her from student activities, and that unless her grade was 3 points above the weighted average of her work to date, she would lose 25 percent of the credits earned. In a note appended, the committee was doubtful about the legality of the last requirement. Moreover, the report did not specify whether the 25 percent loss was to apply only to the current quarter or was intended to be effective for the whole year. The report notes that Dean B was later consulted about the legality of cutting credits and gave an opinion that the procedure was certainly legal.

I looked at a number of the cases in the 1940's to see if the attitude toward discipline had changed. It had not. One wonders why, since the members of the faculty were then so willing to administer discipline in this relatively unrelenting manner and often totally without due process, are they so reluctant to do so today?

## The Change in Student
## Disciplinary Procedure

### The Buttny Case

In November 1967 the University of Colorado had occasion to discipline 22 students who blockaded the placement offices to protest the presence of a CIA recruiter. The transcript of testimony before the University Discipline Committee consists of 227 pages; the record itself, exclusive of the transcript, is about two inches thick and carefully indexed with exhibits A through T. It was this material that was subsequently presented to the federal district court in the *Buttny*[1] case.

Due process was scrupulously observed in that case. The students not only had a hearing before the committee—they had an open hearing, they had a public hearing, they had a joint hearing, they had full rights of consultation, they were represented by counsel. Moreover, the matter was submitted internally for review before the Appellate Subcommittee of the Administrative Council. The Subcommittee, consisting of three senior academic deans, upheld the action taken at the hearing. The matter was reviewed by the Board of Regents and the Board upheld it.

The federal district court concluded that certainly the students had been afforded due process. The court discussed the matter in

1.    Buttny v. Smiley, 281 F. Supp. 280 (D. Colo. 1968).

great detail, indicating that the students had somewhat more than due process requires, as the institution, at the request of the students, had made something of a production out of the hearing. Nine of the students were suspended for a year, among them Buttny and McQuerrey, with the right to apply for readmission after a year. This they did and were readmitted under strict and specific terms of probation. Buttny and McQuerrey, along with others, subsequently sought to participate in the Hayakawa disruption which occurred at the University, and Buttny and McQuerrey were again called on the carpet.

As counsel for the University, I was asked what sort of hearing we must now have. Under the decided cases, I felt that simply a probation revocation type of hearing, an administrative hearing, would be sufficient, but I was overruled by the administration. By the time we were through with this second hearing, the two students were represented by nine law-trained people—four graduate lawyers, including two law professors, a political science teacher, who is a law graduate, somebody from the Lawyers's Guild and five law students. When it became apparent that we would have a preliminary hearing on a preliminary hearing on a preliminary hearing, I recommended to the Board of Regents that we must do something in-house to give the hearing committee of five laymen the guidance they would need. Consequently, we obtained the services of a retired Colorado Supreme Court Chief Justice as presiding officer. The hearing covered a span of two weeks. Instead of 227 pages of testimony, we had seven volumes of roughly 100 pages each; we had 22 exhibits, all with reference to probation revocation.

I would suggest that due process does not require carnivals of this nature. We had very much the same situation that Mr. Cates[2] had—ballons, people eating candy, one girl nursing a baby. The hearing was held in the Glenn Miller Memorial Ballroom. I think

---

2. See page 40 supra.

the University realized that it had allowed itself to be placed in a constant confrontation situation, where it was moved from a small room to a large room, to a larger room, and ultimately the demand was made that the hearing be held in our large auditorium. Discipline hearings involve the students affected and the institution; they should not be conducted as a sort of educational or recreational experience for the student body.

The changes in the manner of student discipline have happened almost overnight. As late as 1960 the University of Colorado Board of Regents received, from a select committee of faculty, a report containing these statements:

The courts of law have steadfastly declined to specify details concerning the general requirements of fair play. They have taken the position that if certain requirements are met, the university may suspend, expel, or otherwise discipline its students with the exercise of disciplinary discretion being nonreviewable by the courts. Hence, few, if any, universities in the United States pattern disciplinary procedures after judicial procedures.

These observations were correct in 1960; scores of law review articles affirm that these statements generally represented the law of that time. Courts were loathe to interfere with university and college discipline, basing their reluctance on a broad application of the principle of in loco parentis. I found only two early cases requiring a hearing in an academic situation. One was a 1723 King's Bench case,[3] which held that it was contrary to natural justice to deprive a master of his academic degrees without notice or hearing. The other was a Pennsylvania county court case[4] of 1887, which indicated that in dismissal cases the student had to be given some type of adversary hearing. Other than these two cases, the courts generally refused to get into the situation because of the in loco parentis concept.

---

3. The King v. Chancellor of the Univ. of Cambridge, 2 Raym. Ld. 1334, 92 Eng. Rep. 370 (K.B. 1723).

4. Commonwealth ex rel. Hill v. McCauley, 3 Pa. C.C.R. 77 (1887).

## The Dixon Case

Probably the one single law review article, the one single statement in legal literature which brought about the change in student discipline by the university, was Warren Seavey's comment in his article in the *Harvard Law Review*[5] in 1957. His comment was addressed to *People ex rel. Bluett v. Board of Trustees of University of Illinois.*[6] In that case the court upheld the dismissal of a student for cheating. Although she was given a hearing before her dismissal, she was not told of the evidence against her or who her accusers were, nor was she allowed to give evidence in the mandamus proceeding which she brought. Some of Seavey's observations are now legendary:

> It is shocking that the officials of a state educational institution, which can function properly only if our freedoms are preserved, should not understand the elementary principles of fair play. It is equally shocking to find that a court supports them in denying to a student the protection given to a pickpocket . . . .

> On the other hand, if a professor is dropped under similar circumstances, not only is he given protection by the courts, but the associations of professors apply all their effective extralegal pressures against the offending institution, even though the latter may not have violated its contract. These same professors, so careful in protecting the interest of their fellows, are in fact fiduciaries for their students and should be the first to afford to their students every protection.[7]

---

5. Seavey, *Dismissal of Students: "Due Process"*, 70 HARV. L. REV. 1406 (1957).

6. 10 Ill. App. 2d 207, 134 N.E.2d 635 (1956).

7. Seavey, *supra* note 5, at 1407. Professor Seavey, incidentally, may be the father of the "fiduciary theory" for student-institution relationships.

These words set the scene for what came later. The article was noted in the *Dixon*[8] case, and it has been referred to rather consistently throughout the literature.

At the same time that the courts were using the in loco parentis concept to justify their hands-off policy, a judicial attitude prevailed that higher education was a privilege, not a right. The *Dixon* case was the pioneer case which brought about a change in this concept. That case involved the summary dismissal of students who participated in a civil rights demonstration. The case still represents the most current judicial thinking on the requirements for due process in student disciplinary proceedings which involve either expulsion or dismissal. In order to reach the conclusion which the court in the *Dixon* case considered just, it was necessary to hold that higher education was no longer a question of privilege but a question of right for a student who had matriculated and been accepted by the institution. Moreover, such a student could be separated from the institution for disciplinary reasons only if he were afforded the fundamentals of due process.

The fourteenth amendment says that no state shall deprive any person of life, liberty or property without due process of law. The deprivation suffered by a student expelled certainly is not of life and it is not of liberty; so the *Dixon* case held, in effect, that the right to a higher education and the right to remain affiliated with the institution unless separated from it according to due process was a right of property. The court in the *Dixon* case said, in substance, that the student should have notice and that the nature of the hearing could vary, depending upon the circumstances of the case. In other words, not every discipline case requires a full-dress hearing. But the court stated that in every case the rudiments of an adversary proceeding may be preserved without encroaching upon the interests of the college, and the court then

---

8.  Dixon v. Alabama State Bd. of Educ., 294 F.2d 150 (5th Cir.), *cert. denied*, 368 U.S. 930 (1961).

proceeded to outline those fundamentals:

> In the instant case, the student should be given the names of the witnesses against him and an oral or written report on the facts to which each witness testifies. He should also be given the opportunity to present to the Board, or at least to an administrative official of the college, his own defense against the charges and to produce either oral testimony or written affidavits of witnesses in his behalf. If the hearing is not before the board directly, the results and findings of the hearing should be presented in a report open to the student's inspection. If these rudimentary elements of fair play are followed in a case of misconduct of this particular type, we feel that the requirements of due process of law will have been fulfilled.[9]

The *Dixon* case completely changed the concept of discipline in institutions of higher education. It had theretofore been inquisitorial as contrasted with adversary. The student appeared before the appropriate dean, who then acted as judge, jury and prosecutor. And the system was inquisitorial, whether the student appeared before one person or a committee. To change this arena from inquisitorial to adversary is a big step for an organization so highly structured that one is constantly amazed that it moves at all. Nevertheless, the institutions began to fall into line, some so reluctantly that the courts were ordering students reinstated until the schools saw fit to fulfill the fundamental requirements of due process. Since 1961, numerous federal cases have dealt with this question. One of the more interesting discussions of the question of right as opposed to privilege is found in *Knight v. State Board of Education.*[10] In answer to the argument that the interest the students have in attending the state university is a mere privilege, the court said:

9.    294 F.2d at 159.

10.    200 F. Supp. 174 (M.D. Tenn. 1961).

The Court cannot resist the conclusion in the present case that to describe the interest of the plaintiffs in continuing their educations at Tennessee A & I University as a privilege rather than a right, although perhaps accurate for some purposes, is a mere play upon words insofar as the present case is concerned.[11]

Following these federal cases, a number of cases have begun to appear in the state courts. Notable among the state court cases is *Goldberg v. Regents of University of California,*[12] which dealt with the free speech movement. In my opinion, the *Goldberg* case is of equal importance with the *Dixon* case.

## Specifics of Procedural Due Process

The court in the *Buttny* case chose to comment on the specifics of procedural due process—the acts which met the concept of fairness required in the circumstances. The court noted that no particular procedure is required, but four elements of justice must be present: adequate notice of charges, a reasonable opportunity to prepare, an orderly hearing consistent with the nature of the case, and a fair, impartial decision.[13] The procedure followed by the University of Colorado authorities was then examined in detail in the opinion and held to be sufficient to meet the requirements of procedural due process.

The court examined the rules of the University under which the disciplinary action was taken and observed that, while they were not in form specifically prohibitory, neither were they so vague and uncertain as to be open to a declaration of invalidity. The rules in question have since been made more specific. I had been

---

11.  *Id.* at 178.

12.  248 Cal. App. 2d 867, 57 Cal. Rptr. 463 (1967).

13.  281 F. Supp. at 288.

concerned that the rule we relied on in the *Buttny* case, *i.e.*, interfering with the right of others, might be attacked as obscure and inadequate to give sufficient notice because it was tucked into a rule forbidding hazing, and "Hazing" was the title of the rule.

Discovery was requested by the students in the *Buttny* case and it was granted. We considered it a reasonable request and felt it should be answered. We applied traditional concepts in the practice of law and tried the case exactly on that basis. Discovery, however, has been limited in some of the cases. In the *Wasson*[14] case faculty evaluations of students' performance and behavior were excluded.

The courts have gone into the question of how much time must be afforded between the receipt of the charges by the student and the date of hearing. In the *Jones*[15] case it was two days, and in the *Esteban*[16] case ten days.

Much emphasis has been placed on the matter of individual as opposed to collective charges. The *Buttny* case discusses the problem in great detail.

Does the institution need to advise students as to their right to counsel? The *Buttny* case said it was not necessary, but in *Madera v. Board of Education,*[17] where the right to counsel was denied by a board of education, the administrative decision was reversed by the court.

The graduate students in the *Buttny* case were given a stiffer punishment than the undergraduates. In answer to the argument of the students that since they all did the same thing they should

---

14. Wasson v. Trowbridge, 382 F.2d 807 (2d Cir. 1967).

15. Jones v. State Bd. of Educ., 279 F. Supp. 190 (M.D. Tenn. 1968), *aff'd*, /407 F.2d 834 /(6th Cir. 1969).

16. Esteban v. Central Mo. State College, 277 F. Supp. 649, 651 (W.D. Mo. 1967).

17. 267 F. Supp. 356 (S.D.N.Y. 1967), *rev'd*, 386 F.2d 778 (2d Cir. 1967), *cert. denied*, 390 U.S. 1028 (1968).

get the same punishment, the court pointed out that the age distinction made, *i.e.*, by year in school as well as age, was logical and valid. The court saw no reason why the criminal law distinction between juveniles and adults should not be applicable by analogy. The Zanders[18] case discusses this question in detail.

Institutions which have closed hearings are confronted with a practical political problem within the institution—the accusation that these are star chamber proceedings. I suggest that a room appropriately designed to provide a fair and impartial hearing and which would admit twenty or thirty people fulfills not only the legal requirements but all practical considerations. The vast majority of students being disciplined want closed hearings. But for the militant activists, an open hearing is a tremendous opportunity for confrontation and a show. The institution should not be gulled into such a carnival hearing on the basis of what is politically feasible at the time.

Possible conflicts occur on the role of the disciplining body. The commingling of decisional and prosecutorial functions has been the subject of discussion in three cases.[19] *Buttny* and *Zanders* discuss the matter of appeal in these cases. The *Due*[20] case stated that a transcript of a hearing is unnecessary, but one wonders how the case can be reviewed in a judicial proceeding if no transcript of the administrative proceeding is made.

There is now a significant body of law dealing with self-incrimination.[21] Where students have sought an injunction

18. Zanders v. Louisiana State Bd. of Educ., 281 F. Supp. 747 (W.D. La. 1968).

19. Wasson v. Trowbridge, 382 F.2d 807 (2d Cir. 1967); Wright v. Texas So. Univ., 277 F. Supp. 110 (S.D. Tex. 1967); Jones v. State Bd. of Educ., 279 F. Supp. 190 (M.D. Tenn. 1968), *aff'd*, 407 F.2d 834 (6th Cir. 1969).

20. Due v. Florida A. & M. Univ., 233 F. Supp. 396 (N.D. Fla. 1963).

21. Grossner v. Trustees of Columbia Univ., 287 F. Supp. 535 (S.D.N.Y. 1968); Goldberg v. Regents of Univ. of Calif., 248 Cal. App. 2d 867, 57 Cal. Rptr. 463 (1967); Furutani v. Ewigleben, 297 F. Supp. 1163 (N.D. Cal. 1969).

postponing expulsion hearings until after criminal trials are had, it is clear that the courts do not consider such hearings a threat to the fifth amendment right against self-incrimination, since the fifth amendment right can be invoked in the later criminal actions.[22]

# Current Problems and
# Suggested Remedies

## Ancillary Sanctions

It is apparent that the biggest question now confronting institutions of higher education is not the individual's rights vis-à-vis the institutions, but the rights of group control. The disciplinary weapons of probation, suspension and expulsion will not in any way be effective in controlling the hard-core militants. They will remain on the campuses and continue to lead the marches and the demonstrations. We have also discovered that they find various ways to obtain university financial support while they demonstrate, including passing the hat among the faculty—an exercise which is surely inappropriate. One of Mr. Buttny's friends, collecting rent and food money for that gentleman, approached a member of the University Discipline Committee which suspended him.

I would propose, then, three ancillary sanctions: denial of employment, denial of financial aid, and provisions inserted in the contract for university housing asserting that suspension or expulsion for violation of university rules and regulations terminates the lease. In the drafting of such university rules and regulations it should be provided that these sanctions may be imposed only if done at the time sentence itself is imposed.

The *Buttny* case also stands for the *inherent* power of institu-

---

22.   Furutani v. Ewigleben, *Supra* note 21.

tions to discipline. I would not recommend, however, that institutions rely on inherent power. I feel very strongly that the institution has an obligation to submit in advance to the students those rules and regulations which it expects them to fulfill, and that such rules should be unequivocal and as specific as possible. Sooner or later, when properly tested, the inherent authority concept will fail.

## Injunctive Relief

The university may, as a plaintiff, seek equitable relief through the traditional remedies of injunction and the temporary restraining order. The elements which entitle the plaintiff to equitable relief—irreparable injury not compensable in money damages and the lack of an adequate remedy at law—can easily be shown in describing the harm done to a university by disruptive behavior such as we have today.

Many states have adopted rules of civil procedure which provide that an injunctive order or order granting a temporary restraining order is binding on the parties to the action, their officers, agents, employees and attorneys, and upon those persons in active concert or participation with them who receive notice of the order by personal service or otherwise. The legal questions, therefore, seem to resolve themselves into four categories: (1) What is meant by persons in active concert or participation; (2) What is meant by notice? (3) What are the constitutional implications? (4) What about jurisdiction?

### Persons Affected by Injunctive Order; Notice

In general, the courts have said, with reference to persons in active concert or participation, an injunction cannot apply to control the conduct of persons who act independently and whose rights have not been adjudged according to law. But one who knowingly aids, abets, assists, or acts in active concert with a person who has been enjoined, and in so doing violates the injunction, can be held in contempt, even though he was not named in the order or served with process in the suit in which the injunction was issued, or served with a copy of the process or of the injunction.[23] The law today is fairly clear that the person charged with contempt must have some definable relationship with the person named in the injunction before conviction will lie. It was not always so limited. An early federal case, *Chisholm v. Caines*,[24] upheld an injunction against a trespass, in which the order was directed at a named defendant and "all persons whomsoever." The contempt defendants had not been parties to the injunction suit and had not acted in concert with the injunction defendant, but merely trespassed on the plaintiff's land, with knowledge of the decree, in pursuit of their own interests. However, a later case in the Second Circuit in 1930, *Alemite Manufacturing Co. v. Staff*,[25] *per* Judge Learned Hand, held that the only persons subject to contempt were those who abetted the injunction defendant in his violation of the decree and those who were legally identified with him, such as his agents. Judge Hand's position was followed in the famous *Chase National City Bank*[26] case and subsequently written into the federal rules.

In *Lance v. Plummer*,[27] a case decided in the Fifth Circuit in 1965, a Negro civil rights group obtained an order enjoining certain businesses and organizations in St. Augustine, Florida, from harrassing and intimidating Negroes seeking service. Lance, an unpaid deputy sheriff, was not a named defendant, but he was found in contempt of court for using profanity and threateningly

---

23. *See, for example*, Royal News Co. v. Schultz, 230 F. Supp. 641 (E.D. Mich. 1964).

24. 67 F. 285 (C.C.D.S.C. 1894).

25. 42 F.2d 832 (2d Cir. 1930).

26. Chase Nat'l City Bank v. City of Norwalk, 291 U.S. 431 (1934).

27. 353 F.2d 585 (5th Cir. 1965), *cert. denied*, 384 U.S. 929, *reh. denied*, 384 U.S. 994 (1966).

following certain Negroes seeking accommodations at a hotel. The Court of Appeals for the Fifth Circuit, sustaining Lance's contempt conviction, found that adequate evidence supported the finding that Lance was a person in active concert or participation. The order of the court complained of on appeal sought to bind all persons receiving actual notice, whether or not they fell within the class of parties to the action. However, the findings of the district court clearly showed that its order adding Lance as a defendant was justified. His conduct was in active concert or participation with the named defendant; he was doing acts allegedly complained of as being carried on by the named defendant. The appellate court went on to say that during the period when Lance committed the acts in question the admitted nexus between Lance and a person named in the injunctive order clearly warranted the determination of the trial court that Lance was subject to the terms of the injunction as being in active participation with the named defendant.

*Evers v. Birdsong*[28] is another case particularly worthy of comment. Charles Evers, a Negro civil rights leader, attempted to present certain grievances to the administration of Alcorn A & M College. In his initial attempt to stage a march on the president's house, his marchers were halted at the college entrance by security officers. The marchers surged through the officers and 235 of them were arrested. Evers then filed a class action in the federal district court and obtained a temporary restraining order, allowing 200 persons to march on the campus. This march was carried out without mishap, and the president of the college submitted to the trustees the grievances presented by the marchers. Subsequently, Mr. Evers and certain other named plaintiffs led a continuous harrassment of the college, resulting in the destruction of several buildings and the disruption of college activities, including commencement activities. The college filed an answer and counter-

---

28.   287 F. Supp. 900 (S.D. Miss. 1968).

claimed for an injunction and damages. The federal district court dismissed the plaintiff's suit and the college's claim for damages, but stated with reference to the injunction:

This authority is delegable to the school president and his officials, who must be given wide discretion in anticipating and preventing interruptions in the classroom and student activities for which the school is operated . . . . School campuses are not public in the sense of streets, courthouses, and public parks, open for expressions of free speech by the public. . . .

The right of free speech, assembly or protest, has never been so judicially enlarged as to permit disruption at a school and destruction of its property. It would seem more logical to assume that it is the duty of school officials to protect students from such disruptions related above, and for law officials of the state to protect its property from destruction.

The Court finds that plaintiff's action should be dismissed, and that upon defendant's counter action, plaintiffs and their class, described above, should be permanently enjoined and restrained from inciting, leading, participating in or counseling any marches, demonstrations or disturbances on the campus of Alcorn College.[29]

The class of persons who may be enjoined is very broad indeed; and, of course, all persons against whom contempt proceedings can be successfully brought need not be named. If a person has actual notice, regardless of source, that his conduct has been enjoined, he can be held in contempt for violating the injunction.

## Constitutional Questions

Constitutional implications are constantly raised by the student activists. The question may become: What will be the result if the university obtains an injunction against activity which is ul-

---

29. *Id.* at 905.

timately determined to be protected activity under the first amendment? In other words, is the unconstitutionality of the injunction a defense in a contempt proceeding? This is a very close question. The leading case is *Walker v. City of Birmingham*.[30] The *Walker* case affirmed, in a 5–4 decision, the principle that although the breadth and vague language of the injunction may be questioned on constitutional issues, persons enjoined cannot bypass orderly judicial review of the injunction before disobeying it. An injunction is thus a very effective tool for the school administration. And review of a contempt proceeding is practically limited to whether or not the court had jurisdiction to enter it.

## Jurisdiction

I can conceive of no situation where the university can go into the federal court as a plaintiff except in the District of Columbia. The institution would have to resort to a substitute plaintiff to obtain the diversity necessary to federal jurisdiction. Ordinarily, then, universities must apply to state courts for injunctive relief.

## Summary Suspension

Can the university summarily suspend a student? *Stricklin v. Regents of University of Wisconsin*,[31] per Judge Doyle, held that an interim suspension, even if just a few days, could not be imposed without a preliminary hearing. I respectfully submit that in the light of the Bluefield College case, *Barker v. Hardway*[32] the *Stricklin* decision is not the law. Summary suspension was upheld in the *Barker* case, as the students were engaged in violent and destructive interference with the rights of others. The *Stricklin*

---

30. 388 U.S. 307 (1967), Brennan, J., joined by Warren, Ch. J., and Douglas and Fortas, JJ., dissenting.

31. 297 F. Supp. 416 (W.D. Wis. 1969).

32. 283 F. Supp. 228 (S.D.W. Va.), *aff'd per curiam*, 399 F.2d 638 (4th Cir. 1968), *cert. denied*, 394 U.S. 905 (1969).

decision would appear to be tacitly overruled, as the *Barker* case upholds the right to summarily suspend and have a later hearing. In the *Barker* case incidentally, the students were charged with harassment and intimidation of the president of the school.

## Legislation

Colorado has enacted legislation[33] directed at campus disorders. To my knowledge this is the first such bill to be enacted. Every one of the acts declared to be unlawful in the bill has been considered by the courts as sufficient grounds for expulsion or suspension of students from the institution.

A new section has been added to the California Penal Code[34] to deal with the removal of nonstudents from campuses in the specified circumstances. That statutory provision has been upheld in *People v. Agnello.*[35]

The array of remedies or tools available to the institution in student conflict cases may, therefore, be summarized as: (1)

---

33.  H.B. 1016: Concerning crimes and punishments, and prohibiting certain trespass upon the property of and the interference with the peaceful conduct of institutions of higher education.
Be it enacted by the General Assembly of the State of Colorado:
Section 1. Declaration of purpose.—The general assembly, in recognition of unlawful campus disorders across the nation which are disruptive of the educational process and dangerous to the health and safety of persons and damaging to public and private property, establishes by this act criminal penalties for conduct declared in this act to be unlawful. However, this act shall not be construed as preventing institutions of higher education from establishing standards of conduct, scholastic and behavioral, reasonably relevant to their lawful missions, processes, and functions, and to invoke appropriate discipline for violations of such standards.
Section 2. Interference with members of staff, faculty, or students of institutions of higher education—trespass—damage to property—misdemeanors—penalties.—(1) (a) No person shall, on the campus of any community college, junior college, college, or university in this state, hereinafter referred to as "institutions of higher education", or at or in any building or other facility owned, operated, or controlled by the governing board of any such institution of higher

institutional discipline leading to probation, suspension or expulsion; (2) injunctive relief from the courts; and (3) prosecution under criminal trespass laws or special criminal laws such as Colorado's Campus Disorder Bill.

The injunctive procedure route has special merit for colleges and universities in that it allows them to take the initiative and control the proceedings at their discretion, which is not always possible when cases are turned over to a district attorney for criminal prosecution. A temporary order can usually be obtained ex parte, and civil contempt hearings are immediately held without the delays usually encountered in criminal trials. Convictions are usually not bondable, *i.e.*, the offender is jailed or fined on the spot and appeal is usually limited. Convictions of civil contempt, incidentally, do not go on the students' records as in the conviction of a crime or felony.

Other advantages of proceedings to secure injunctions in cases of student disorders are: (a) public declaration by the courts of

education, willfully deny to students, school officials, employees, and invitees:

    (b)    Lawful freedom of movement on the campus;

    (c)    Lawful use of the property, facilities, or parts of any institution of higher education; or

    (d)    The right of lawful ingress and egress to the institution's physical facilities.

    (2)    No person shall, on the campus of any institution of higher education, or at or in any building or other facility owned, operated, or controlled by the governing board of any such institution, willfully impede the staff or faculty of such institution in the lawful performance of their duties, or willfully impede a student of such institution in the lawful pursuit of his educational activities, through the use of restraint, abduction, coercion, or intimidation, or when force and violence are present or threatened.

    (3)    No person shall willfully refuse or fail to leave the property of, or any building or other facility owned, operated, or controlled by the governing board of any such institution of higher education upon being requested to do so by the chief administrative officer, his designee charged with maintaining order on the campus and in its facilities, or a dean of such college or university, if such person is

the unlawful nature of the acts by the disrupting students; (b) the favorable public reaction; (c) the imposition of restraint upon the disrupting students by a nonuniversity governmental entity; and (d) the furnishing of an excuse to cease disruption to students who are looking for an excuse to return to class.

The disadvantages of proceeding to secure injunctions are: (a) the injunction is not self-enforcing; (b) the local sheriffs are required to serve copies of the injunction; (c) enforcement of the injunction is through complicated contempt proceedings which, in criminal contempt situations, result in the arrest of student offenders by law officers, which could have been accomplished by the enforcement of criminal laws rather than via the injunction route; (d) unless the university is prepared to enforce the injunction through contempt proceedings, the law may be actively flouted by students who know the university will be reluctant to proceed by the institution of contempt actions; (e) an improvidently secured injunction can have the effect of polarizing resistance to university discipline.

---

committing, threatens to commit, or incites others to commit, any act which would disrupt, impair, interfere with, or obstruct the lawful missions, processes, procedures, or functions of the institution.

(4) Nothing in this section shall be construed to prevent lawful assembly and peaceful and orderly petition for the redress of grievances, including any labor dispute between an institution of higher education and its employees, or any contractor or subcontractor or any employee thereof.

(5) Any person who violates any of the provisions of this section shall be deemed guilty of a misdemeanor and, upon conviction thereof, shall be punished by a fine not to exceed five hundred dollars, or imprisoned in the county jail for a period not to exceed one year, or by both such fine and imprisonment.

Section 3. Effective date—applicability.—this act shall take effect on the first day of the first month following its passage, and shall apply only to violations of the act alleged to have occurred on or after such date.

Section 4. Severability.—If any provision of this act or the application thereof to any person or circumstances is held invalid, such invalidity shall not affect other provisions or applications of the act

The ultimate solution is to be prepared to use all three remedies for the serious disruptions, starting with institutional discipline, which I still believe to be the most effective, followed by, or in connection with, the injunction and/or criminal prosecution under a workable but reasonable criminal law. I submit in closing that Colorado's statute meets these criteria.

which can be given effect without the invalid provision or application, and to this end the provisions of this act are declared to be severable.

    Section 5. Safety clause.–The general assembly hereby finds, determines, and declares that this act is necessary for the immediate preservation of the public peace, health, and safety. [Approved Feb. 25, 1969, effective March 1, 1969.]

34.  West's Ann. Pen. Code, §602.7:

    (a)  In any case in which a person who is not a student or officer or employee of a state college or state university, and who is not required by his employment to be on the campus or any other facility owned, operated or controlled by the governing board of any such state college or state university, enters such campus or facility, and it reasonably appears to the chief administration officer of such campus or facility or to an officer or employee designated by him to maintain order on such campus or facility that such person is committing any act likely to interfere with the peaceful conduct of the activities of such campus or facility or has entered such campus or facility for the purpose of committing any such act, the chief administrative officer or officer or employee designated by him to maintain order on such campus or facility may direct such person to leave such campus or facility, and if such person fails to do so, he is guilty of a misdemeanor.

    (b)  As used in this section:

    (1)  "State university" means the University of California, and includes any affiliated institution thereof and any campus or facility owned, operated or controlled by the Regents of the University of California.

    (2)  "State college" means any California state college administered by the Trustees of the California State Colleges.

    (3)  "Chief administrative officer" means the president of a state college or the officer designated by the Regents of the University of California or pursuant to authority granted by the Regents of the University of California to administer and be the officer in charge of a campus or other facility owned, operated or controlled by the Regents of the University of California.

35.  66 Cal. Rptr. 571 (1968).

# 4

# The Student in Court

## Richard A. Lippe, Esq.*

I am honored to be with such a distinguished group of panelists, including Professor Van Alstyne, who was writing about this subject long before most of us were thinking about it.

In May 1968 a conference similar to this one was held in Denver at which Edward Schwartz, then president of National Student Association, expressed the view that conferences convened to discuss the legal rights of students were not particularly useful because they focused on the wrong questions. Included in his comments was the following statement:

> For the past two years, many of the people at this conference have been meeting almost bimonthly to rehash a set of familiar issues concerning student rights. We acknowledged at these meetings our general agreement on the nature of due process; we recounted the latest instance of the elimination of a campus speaker ban; we debated whether student political organizing should remain free from administrative control; we took a peek at the rising incidence of spying on the campus; and, in general, we patted ourselves on the back and agreed that higher education is making progress in these areas.[1]

---

\*     Lippe & Ruskin, Mineola, New York.
1.     45 DENVER L.J. 525 (1968).

Mr. Schwartz went on to say that these were the concerns of so-called "procedural liberals" and were an unfortunate substitute for consideration of the real issues confronting the academic community today: student participation in the decisionmaking structure of the university and the role that the university should play in the society. He concluded his comments by making a prediction:

In the coming year, you will be met with a new round of campus protests—no doubt as serious, if not more serious, than those which you faced this spring. Some of you will become skillful counterinsurgents, others of you will learn how to use the police, and a few of you may lose your jobs. Nevertheless, however adept you become in handling tactics, the protests will not end until you become adept at accepting change.[2]

# The Lawyer's Role
# and the Direction of
# the Student Movement

Our firm first became involved in the field of student legal rights when we were retained by the student government at the State University of New York at Stony Brook in July of 1968. Several days later, an editorial in *Newsday,* a Long Island daily, commented favorably as follows:

The standard impulse of the rebellious college student is to picket, stage a march or hold a sit-in and if that doesn't work—to riot. Yet, there seems to be a more peaceful, if unusual, way for students to present their demands: Hire a lawyer . . . .

The idea seems to be an improvement over the more

---

2. *Id.* at 532.

violent methods of protest. Riots and sit-ins disrupt collegiate life without producing meaningful progress. Reasoned discussion often leads to a solution. It may be less fun than a sit-in, but in the end it is apt to accomplish more.[3]

I think it is clear from the events of the last several months that our hopes as reflected in this editorial were overly optimistic and that Mr. Schwartz was right. The major problems confronting universities today relate to overall questions of social and educational policy that cannot be dealt with effectively by affirmative legal action. For this reason, the lawyer's representation of students can be a rather frustrating and difficult experience.

Still, a lawyers's traditional role should not be underestimated. Through the representation of students in criminal proceedings and the assertion of procedural rights, the lawyer can help create a "protected" atmosphere within which students can meaningfully assert themselves. Moreover, the attorney does have a role to play with respect to these broader questions of social and educational policy. By initiating test cases, drafting proposed legislation and guiding students through a maze of conflicting institutional relationships, the lawyer can help focus public interest and initiate a dialogue on the important issues.

During the past decade, public interest and pressure has been a motivating force behind many of the reforms adopted by our institutions and where necessary, as in the reapportionment area,[4] the United States Supreme Court has taken a broad view of its powers and responsibilities. The apparent conservative trend in our society, however, suggests that public opinion may now impede meaningful reform of our institutions of higher education, and progress through the courts, if any, will be labored and arduous.

I suspect that what is going to occur, and what is in fact already occurring, is that students will engage in collective activity anal-

---

3.   Newsday, July 31, 1968.
4.   Baker v. Carr, 369 U.S. 186 (1962).

ogous to that of labor unions. Robert Powell, current president of the National Student Association, stated at the Denver conference that the form which student activity will take in the future will be organized union activity with collective bargaining.[5] What is occurring today is comparable to what occurred in the early 1900's, with one significant difference. The early union sit-ins and protests took place over working conditions and wages. Today's students are perhaps more selfless and are concerned with the quality and direction of American life. I do not condone today's violence or disregard of law. Nevertheless, we must recognize that many students are willing to risk serious personal consequences because of their commitment to a more just and humane society.

In my opinion, collective activity and negotiations by student "unions" constitute the wave of the future. It is here that the attorney can play an invaluable role in helping to formulate proposals and in guiding ensuing negotiations.

Unfortunately, our experience indicates that school administrators are less than enthusiastic over this prospect. At Stony Brook, the administration was visibly upset when we suggested that student grievances be resolved through collective bargaining and was unwilling to even use the term "negotiation." What was offered as an alternative was the establishment of another advisory committee. At the State University of New York at Binghamton, the undergraduates wanted to retain us to advise them with respect to the development and implementation of a governance proposal. The faculty, however, was concerned that the proceedings might become adversary in nature.

This attitude on the part of college officials is most unfortunate. Our experience has convinced us that it is in the best interest of both the students and the university to resolve their difficulties through discussion and negotiation.

Current case law suggests that students have a better chance of

---

5.   See Comment, 45 DENVER L.J. 669, 673 (1968).

securing "rights" through negotiation with school officials than through court action. It is also clear that universities must resolve these issues through internal discussion and negotiation if they are to avert the threat of encroachment from the outside. The federal government has already passed legislation affecting the aid colleges may give to students convicted of crimes which disrupt the administration of the institution.[6] A number of similar bills were introduced in the New York legislature during the 1969 session.[7] Police invasions of schools are not uncommon and political figures have increasingly made statements concerning the actions that college officials should take to end present difficulties.

In discussing the role of the attorney and the direction of the student movement, it is also important to recognize that one of the major concerns of today's student is the relationship between the university and society. James Ridgeway in his recent book, *The Closed Corporation*,[8] describes in detail the financial support received by universities from government sources[9] and the inter-relationship that exists between the university and other institutions in society. For this reason, students feel that the university is an active part of the social milieu and has a responsibility to take a clear position by word and deed with respect to the critical issues facing the nation.

At a joint meeting of the Eastern Association of College Deans and Advisers of Students with the National Association of Student Personnel Administrators held in December of 1968 in Atlantic City, New Jersey, Dr. Mason W. Gross, President of Rutgers, in an

---

6. Higher Education Amendments of 1968, 82 Stat. 1014, § 504.

7. *See* page 133 *supra*, notes 6, 7.

8. JAMES RIDGEWAY, THE CLOSED CORPORATION (Ballantine Books, Inc., 1969).

9. *Id.* at p. 5. According to Ridgeway, "80 percent of MIT's funds are estimated to come from the government. Columbia and Princeton get about 50 percent of their money from Washington."

address entitled "The Changing Concept of the College Student," suggested that universities, as institutions, must begin to take clear positions on many of today's important issues, including Viet Nam and the urban crisis. According to Dr. Gross, much of today's college unrest is due to a credibility gap between students and college officials which can be eliminated only by the officials taking such action.

This student concern, beyond affecting the actions of college officials, may well express itself in useful collective activity. For example, the student government at the State University of New York at Buffalo has retained our firm to initiate an action to enjoin the construction program of the State University. The students contend that the contractors have been hiring workers from unions which discriminate in their admissions policy.

In this manner the student government is acting much like a social action organization. Although it might at first seem that such collective activity is far removed from the academic process, I suggest that it is a vital educational experience, and that students by their involvement in such issues substantially broaden their knowledge and also make an important contribution to society.

## Traditional Legal Theories
## As Applied to Student Rights

The traditional legal theories used in dealing with questions of student legal rights have been discussed extensively in the literature.[10] Generally speaking, these theories may be grouped into three categories:

(a) The concept that the college stands in loco parentis and

---

10. *See* 45 DENVER L.J. 612 (1968). The articles and accompanying footnotes in this volume also set forth an abundant number of case and article citations.

therefore has the power to control the conduct of the student much as a parent would do.

(b) The concept that the college has inherent authority to determine the rules and regulations under which it will operate and that student is therefore subject to such rules and regulations.

(c) The concept that the college and the student have a contractual relationship in which the school agrees to furnish the student with an education and the student agrees to pay for such education and abide by the school's regulations.

The docrines of in loco parentis and inherent authority are not useful fictions to support the expansion of student legal rights. By their general nature such theories tend to buttress the authority of college officials, and, in fact, were designed to serve this function. The contract theory, however, permits some latitude and can be used as a basis for extending student rights. Recently, there has been introduced the fiduciary theory—the idea that the school is a fiduciary vis-à-vis the student and that such relationship determines the respective rights and responsibilities of the college and its students.[11] This theory represents an attempt to broaden the rights of students by placing the responsibility of a fiduciary on the university, but to my knowledge no case has yet been decided on this basis.

Courts use such theories as legal characterizations to subsume their conclusions with respect to the relationship they believe should exist between the college and the student in a particular factual situation.[12] For this reason, it is useful to consider the manner in which traditional legal arguments may be used in the assertion of student legal rights.

---

11. *See* Goldman, *The University and the Liberty of Its Students—A Fiduciary Theory*, 54 KY. L.J. 643 (1966).

12. *See* United States District Judge Johnson's discussion in Moore v. Student Affairs Committee of Troy State Univ., 284 F. Supp. 725 (M.D. Ala. 1968).

The contract theory, in particular, lends itself to effective use. A recent case, *Drucker v. New York University*,[13] decided by the Civil Court of the City of New York, is a good example. In this case a student resigned six days before the term opened and two days after paying his registration fee. The school's 55-page bulletin specified that such fees were not refundable upon withdrawal or dismissal. The student sued to recover his registration fee and the court upheld his position, concluding that the provisions of the bulletin were not effectively brought to the attention of the student and, therefore, the requisite consent was absent. In addition, the court held that the school's retention of the money was illegal, since the sum represented a penalty rather than liquidated damages.

My firm has been faced with several nonlitigated situations where general principles of contract law applied. One such problem arose in connection with the acute lack of housing on the Stony Brook campus. During the summer of 1968, the school wrote all prospective sophomores stating that none of those who registered for dormitory rooms would be "tripled." Upon arriving in September many sophomores found that they had been "tripled" and requested our advice. It was our opinion that the school had breached its contract and could be held liable for any additional cost incurred by students for renting rooms comparable to those for which they had registered. Our position was made known to the school officials, who then provided the sophomores with suitable accommodations.

A second situation which arose at the beginning of the school year concerned a student who had transferred to Stony Brook as a geology major. To his dismay, he was told at registration that all geology courses were filled. The student had already terminated his enrollment at his former school and had to attend Stony Brook or forego a year of college. When our advice was requested, we

13.   293 N.Y.S. 2d 923 (Civ. Ct. 1968).

took the position that the school was in breach of its agreement with the student and could be held liable for monetary damages or compelled to permit the student to register for geology courses. Again, the matter was resolved in an amicable and satisfactory manner.

A very important source of student rights which must be carefully examined is the entire structure of rules and regulations governing the operation of the college. State schools, in particular, are likely to be subject to several levels of such restrictions. For example, the units of the State University of New York are subject to statutory provisions, regulations adopted by the State University Trustees (a state-wide supervisory board), rules passed by the local council (nine-member councils appointed by the Governor for each unit of the state university), and by the internal policies, rules and regulations adopted by the several university constituencies—administration, faculty and students.

Interestingly enough, our first controversy regarding student legal rights arose in this context. When we were first retained by the student government at Stony Brook, a check was issued to us on which the administration stopped payment. It was the school's position that it had final authority to approve the expenditure of student government monies obtained from student activity fees. We called the attention of the school's chief financial officer to the regulations passed by the State University Trustees which confer on the student government the right to assess, collect and disburse such funds. Several days later a new check was issued.

Another situation involved the school's internal regulations and the theory of inherent authority. In this instance we represented a nonstudent youth who was charged with criminal trespass and loitering by the security police at Stony Brook.[14] During the day our client practiced in a band with several students in preparation

---

14.  People v. Dick (Index No. BR88/69 cr)(6th Dist. Ct. Suffolk Cty., 1969) (no opinion).

for a function that was to take place on campus. On one such occasion a resident assistant asked that he leave, since he did not have a guest pass. He refused and the campus security police were called and arrested him.

At trial, the prosecution's position was that the school had inherent authority to police the campus and could prohibit nonstudents from access to the campus. We took the position that the school regulation which permitted a nonstudent to be on campus if in the company of a student governed. In addition, we maintained that our client was on the campus for a proper purpose. The court upheld our contentions and dismissed the criminal charge.

A third situation involved the parking regulations in effect at Stony Brook. The New York Education Law empowers a nine-member local council appointed by the Governor to make regulations governing the conduct and behavior of students. The parking regulations in effect at the school are somewhat unrealistic in view of the very limited parking areas available. In the course of our investigation into the parking problem, we learned that parking regulations that had been in effect at the university for six years prior to the fall of 1968 were never passed by the local council but rather were adopted by the school's president. We now have under advisement a suit against the school for reimbursement of all the illegal parking penalties that were assessed during the six-year period.

Another example involved the adoption of parietal rules governing hours at the State University of New York at Binghamton. A regulation of the State University Trustees permits the local council to pass regulations only "after consultation . . . with representatives of . . . students in promulgating or in reviewing and

---

15.   8 N.Y.C.R.R. §500.2(a).

ratifying regulations on student conduct."[15] This provision is designed "to encourage, maintain, and assure adequate communication with and participation by . . . students at the respective campuses . . . ."[16] In spite of these provisions, however, parietal hour restrictions were adopted after students received two days' notice of a hearing on them during final exams. Our opinion was requested with respect to the validity of parietal hour restrictions, and it was our advice that such restrictions were invalid for a number of reasons, including a failure to comply with the regulations of the State University Trustees.

These examples indicate that there are traditional legal arguments that may be used effectively in the vindication of student legal rights. It is obviously necessary to consider the constitutional dimensions of any problems that arise in this area. It should be recognized, however, that courts in general have not been receptive to any unique arguments which in their views tend to undermine the authority of school administrators. In these situations the advocate is far better off grounding his claims on traditional legal theories.

## Traditional First Amendment Freedoms as Applied to Student Legal Rights

Several of the other speakers will be discussing this topic. For this reason I will explore it only briefly, and instead focus on what I consider to be several emerging problem areas.

It should be noted that recent court decisions have rather uniformly upheld student exercise of traditional first amendment

---

16. *Id.*

freedoms[17] and have made clear that public universities are bound by the standards of procedural due process.[18] Even these so-called traditional constitutional rights, however, raise sophisticated issues which require a delicate balance between student and institutional needs. These issues include the public-private distinction, the elements of procedural due process and the degree to which the exercise of first amendment freedoms may validly impinge on otherwise legitimate university interests. These and similar issues will arise constantly during the balance of this conference.

# Evolving Problems
# in the Area of
# Student Legal Rights

## The Right of Privacy

The students' assertion of a right of privacy challenges most directly the concept that the university stands in loco parentis to its students, and that it may adopt any regulations reasonably necessary to exercise effective supervision and discipline over them. This view of the university's role vis-à-vis its students has its antecedent in the apprentice system and, as Dr. Mason Gross has observed, reflects the Renaissance notion that the university is

---

17. See Stricklin v. Regents of Univ. of Wisconsin, 297 F. Supp. 416 (W.D. Wis. 1969) (student may not be temporarily suspended without hearing); Dickey v. Alabama State Bd. of Educ., 273 F. Supp. 613 (D. Ala. 1967) (student's right to express himself in school publications); Hammond v. South Carolina State College, 272 F. Supp. 947 (D.S.C. 1967) (student's right to assemble and protest in an orderly and nonviolent manner concerning matters of school policy); Brooks v. Auburn Univ., 296 F. Supp. 188 (M.D. Ala. 1969) (University attempt to prevent Rev. William Sloane Coffin from speaking on campus against draft invalid political censorship that violates students' first amendment rights).

18. Dixon v. Alabama State Bd. of Educ., 294 F.2d 150 (5th Cir.), cert. denied, 368 U.S. 930 (1961).

responsible for educating the whole man.[19]

These concepts, however, are inconsistent with today's facts when one considers the mean age of American college students, the relative impersonality of the college institution and the competing interests of such an institution.[20] As one court has observed, "[T]he doctrine of 'In Loco Parentis' is no longer tenable in a university community . . . ."[21]

Moreover, one of the major functions of a public college is to afford an alternative educational opportunity to those of lesser means. It presents very serious dangers to permit the government to use this financial leverage to dictate standards of personal and moral conduct.

Furthermore, a public university is an administrative unit of the state in much the same manner as any other governmental subdivision of the state. In *Marsh v. Alabama*,[22] the Supreme Court held that the residents of a company-owned town were entitled to the protection of the fourteenth amendment. In so holding, the court recognized that the company-owned town was, for all practical purposes, a municipal unit of government regulating the everyday activities of its residents. Similarly, a university bears this governmental relationship to its students and may no more regulate the private affairs of such students than a municipality may regulate the private affairs of its constituents.[23]

---

19. Address by Dr. Mason Gross, "The Changing Concept of the College Student," December 6, 1968, joint meeting of Eastern Assoc. of College Deans and Advisers of Students with Nat. Assoc. of Student Personnel Admin.
20. Van Alstyne, *The Student As University Resident*, 45 DENVER L.J. 582, 591 (1968).
21. Buttny v. Smiley, 281 F. Supp. 280, 286 (D. Colo. 1968).
22. 326 U.S. 501 (1946).
23. *See* People v. Ware, N.Y.L.J., July 11, 1968, p. 1, col. 4 (Cty. Ct. Montg. Cty., N.J., 1968) (city cannot dictate what man wears); Breen v. Kahl, 296 F. Supp. 702 (W.D. Wis. 1969) (public high school regulation forbidding long hair violates fourteenth amendment); Illinois v. Fries, 37 U.S.L.W. 2683 (Sup. Ct., Ill., 1969) (State statute requiring motorcyclists to wear protective head gear unconstitutional).

For these reasons, it is my judgment that university regulation of personal conduct in nonacademic areas is so peripherally related to the academic interests of the university that any substantial encroachment on the personal freedom of the student may be held unconstitutional as the law of student legal rights evolves.

The student's right of privacy also requires consideration of the authority of noneducational officials. Such officials should be deemed to have no more power with respect to college students than with respect to any other class of private citizens. This is the obvious implication of the Supreme Court decision holding that minors are entitled to the protection of procedural due process in juvenile delinquency proceedings.[24] The fact that educational authorities might be held to have some leeway in their actions toward students in certain restricted circumstances does not necessarily mean that such power or authority may be delegated to noneducational officials.

## The Dormitory

Conflicting student and institutional interests must be reconciled when a student's right of privacy in a dormitory room is involved. To my knowledge, only two cases directly raise this problem. In *Moore v. Student Affairs Committee of Troy State University*[25] the court upheld a state university's suspension of a student based on evidence introduced at a disciplinary hearing which had been obtained during a warrantless search of the student's dormitory room by the school officials. In *People v. Cohen,*[26] the court in a criminal proceeding ruled inadmissible evidence which was obtained by a warrantless police search of a student's dormitory room at a private college. The police had been accompanied by school officials who were concerned about drug

---

24.  *In re* Gault, 387 U.S. 1 (1967).

25.  284 F. Supp. 725 (M.D. Ala. 1968).

26.  52 Misc. 2d 366, 292 N.Y.S.2d 706 (1st Dist. Ct., Nassau Cty., 1968).

use and had requested a police survey. In so holding Judge Burstein stated:

> It has been argued that a student impliedly consents to entry into his room by University officials at any time . . . . [E]ven if the doctrine of implied consent were imported in this case, the consent is given, not to police officials, but to the University and the latter cannot fragmentize, share or delegate it . . . .
>
> University students are adults. The dorm is a home and it must be inviolate against unlawful search and seizure. To suggest that a student who lives off campus in a boarding house is protected but that one who occupies a dormitory room waives his Constitutional liberties is at war with reason, logic and law.[27]

These two cases when read together suggest that college officials may conduct reasonable searches of dormitory rooms without obtaining a search warrant as part of their disciplinary authority[28] but that such power may not be delegated to police officers whose activities are governed by the strict standards of the fourth amendment, including its requirement for a warrant.

It would seem to me, however, that officials of schools deemed to be "public" should be bound by fourth amendment standards and required to obtain a search warrant prior to searching a dormitory room. From the student's point of view it makes little difference if his privacy is invaded by a police officer or a college official. Furthermore, it can hardly be argued that college discipline should take priority over effective law enforcement.

The warrant requirement is designed to insure that an independent judicial officer not involved in the situation will make the

---

27.   292 N.Y.S.2d at 709, 713.

28.   Such authority would seem to be held by the college officials of any college deemed to be "private" within the meaning of the fourteenth amendment unless considered to be against public policy.

determination as to whether there is probable cause to infringe on an individual's privacy. A college official desiring to conduct an administrative search of a student's dormitory room is likely to be just as "involved" as a police officer and, therefore, should be subject to the warrant requirement.

The Supreme Court has already held the fourth amendment's warrant requirement applicable to administrative enforcement of housing regulations by municipalities,[29] and its rationale in these cases certainly extends to a public college's search of dormitory rooms.[30] The different needs of college authorities and the police can certainly be reflected in the standards evolved to govern the issuance of such warrants.[31]

The Supreme Court had an opportunity to clarify these problems in the case of *Overton v. People of New York*.[32] In this case a high school principal allowed the police access to a student's locker. The police found drugs, and the student was convicted on this evidence.

The New York courts found that the police officers's search warrant was invalid but upheld the search on the ground that the principal had delegated his authority to search the locker to the police. The Supreme Court accepted certiorari, vacated the judgment and remanded the case to the New York courts for

---

29. Camara v. Municipal Court of San Francisco, 387 U.S. 523 (1967); See v. City of Seattle, 387 U.S. 541 (1967).

30. *But see* United States v. Donato, 269 F. Supp. 921 (E.D. Pa. 1967), *aff'd*, 379 F.2d 288 (3d Cir. 1967) U.S. officials have right to search employee's locker in U.S. Mint) and United States v. Grisby, 335 F.2d 652 (4th Cir. 1964) (military authorities may search living quarters of marine).

31. *See* Comment, *Camara and See: Accomodation Between the Right of Privacy and the Public Need*, 47 NEB. L. REV. 613 (1968).

32. 20 N.Y.2d 360, 283 N.Y.S.2d 22 (1967), *judgment vacated and remanded*, 393 U.S. 85 (1968), *reargument scheduled*, 23 N.Y.2d 869, N.Y.S.2d    (1969).

determination as to whether the principal had acted under duress. If the New York courts find such duress existed, then the case will be decided on this basis. But if it is determined that no duress exists, the Supreme Court may well provide guidance on a number of issues concerning a student's right of privacy.

## The Use of Undercover Agents

The greatest threat to the privacy of students is the now commonplace and indiscriminate use of undercover agents on campus. In addition, this practice is also inconsistent with the concept of academic freedom and has a chilling effect on the exercise of first amendment rights by all members of the academic community, thus seriously affecting the relationship existing among members of such community.

For more than a year undercover agents have posed as students on the Stony Brook campus. Students have told me that they are afraid to speak on their own telephones and that they view one another with suspicion. Faculty members have stated publicly that they are inhibited in their classroom presentations and in their relationships with students. This surveillance has distorted the entire educational process and has produced an atmosphere of fear and apprehension. From what I read, this problem is not unique to Stony Brook.

Certainly, there is some outer boundary beyond which police surveillance cannot go without violating the due process clause of the United States Constitution. For example, I am confident that a court would not permit a criminal prosecution to proceed on the basis of evidence obtained by police by placing hundreds of undercover agents throughout a community, keeping such community under constant surveillance to find evidence of criminal activity, and inducing the children of the residents of such community to inform on their parents. Yet, in many respects this is an accurate description of what has occurred on the Stony Brook campus.

Beyond some fundamental notion of due process, the indiscriminate use of undercover agents on campus may well constitute a search within the meaning of the fourth amendment. The job of an undercover agent on campus is to search out a student with drugs, buy them from him and retain the evidence. Is this not really a search? If this is so, then undercover agents may only be placed on campus pursuant to search warrants issued by independent judicial officers on probable cause.

The law governing the use of informers and undercover agents has just recently begun to evolve. Traditionally, the use of undercover agents was not considered a search within the meaning of the fourth amendment on the theory that the agent is admitted to the presence of the suspect by his own doing and at his own risk.[33]

*Massiah v. United States*[34] was the first case which indicated there might be some change in the law regarding the use of undercover agents. In the *Massiah* case two individuals were arrested, indicted, and then let out on bail. One chose to cooperate with the police and a radio receiver was put in his car. The informer then elicited statements from Massiah which were transmitted over the radio receiver. These statements were put into evidence by government agents at trial. The Court held that such procedure was violative of the Constitution and that the evidence so obtained was not admissible. The purported ground of the Court's decision was that defendant was improperly questioned in the absence of counsel. It appears, however, that the right to an attorney had nothing to do with the legality of the procedures employed, and that the Court was concerned with the kind of use that was made of an undercover agent.

The next case to deal with this problem was *United States v.*

---

33. On Lee v. United States, 343 U.S. 747 (1952).

34. 377 U.S. 201 (1964).

*Hoffa.*[35] In this case James Hoffa was convicted of attempting to influence jurors. The evidence introduced at trial was based on information supplied by an informer who was a frequent visitor at Hoffa's hotel suite. There was some dispute in the factual record as to whether the government had planted the informer, but the majority of the Supreme Court took the position that it didn't make any difference. Whether the informer was planted or not, the defendant had admitted the person to his presence and confided in him. For this reason, Hoffa's constitutional rights were not violated.

The Court's holding in this case reverts to the traditional doctrines governing the use of undercover agents. Chief Justice Warren dissented, however, stating that the *Massiah* case was intended to place some limitations on the use of undercover agents:

> An invasion of basic rights made possible by prevailing upon friendship with the victim is no less proscribed than an invasion accomplished by force . . . .
>
> At this late date in the annals of law enforcement, it seems to me that we cannot say either that every use of informers and undercover agents is proper or, on the other hand, that no uses are. There are some situations where the law could not adequately be enforced without the employment of some guile or misrepresentation of identity . . . . However, one of the important duties of this Court is to give careful scrutiny to practices of government agents when they are challenged in cases before us, in order to insure that the protections of the Constitution are respected and to maintain the integrity of federal law enforcement.[36]

Despite the decision reached in the *Hoffa* case, several decisions have now placed limitations on the use of undercover agents.

---

35. 385 U.S. 293 (1966).

36. *Id.* at 314-315.

These cases rely on *Katz v. United States*,[37] which held that a listening device placed on a public telephone booth by police without first obtaining a warrant constituted an unlawful search in violation of the fourth amendment. The facts in *Katz* did not involve the use of an undercover agent. The Court's opinion, however, speaks broadly and suggests that a person has the right to exclude "the uninvited ear" from infringing on his privacy.

In *United States v. White*[38] the defendant was convicted of possession and the sale of narcotics as a result of the testimony of a federal narcotics agent who heard the defendant make incriminating statements which had been transmitted by an electronic device hidden under an informer's clothes. The court, relying on the *Katz* case, held that the agent's testimony was inadmissible since no prior search warrant had been obtained authorizing this procedure. Similarly, in *United States v. Jones*[39] the court held inadmissible electronic recordings of statements elicited from defendant by an informer cooperating with the police when no warrant had been secured.

The decisions in both of these cases distinguish the *Hoffa* case, which they cite as standing solely for the proposition that an informer may testify as a witness to conversations and dealing with a defendant and, therefore, under *Katz v. United States*, the product of an electronic communication obtained by planting a device on an informer is inadmissible unless a search warrant is first obtained.

In my judgment, however, this is not a meaningful or sensible distinction. In either situation, the suspect's right of privacy is equally infringed upon. Moreover, the electronic recording is, in fact, more reliable than the testimony of the undercover agent. Therefore, these cases are really inconsistent with *Hoffa*, applying

---

37.  389 U.S. 347 (1967).
38.  405 F.2d 838 (7th Cir. 1969).
39.  292 F. Supp. 1001 (D.D.C. 1968).

instead the rationale of *Massiah*.

The holdings of these cases do not make illegal the use of an undercover agent. They merely require that a search warrant be first obtained. Such a requirement will not significantly impair law enforcement. It will insure that an independent judicial officer will make a determination as to the necessity and extent of use to which an undercover agent may be put. The needs of law enforcement and the considerations relevant to the protection of an individual's privacy will be balanced as standards evolve for the issuance of search warrants for undercover agents. For this reason, the use of undercover agents should be considered a search and brought within the framework of the fourth amendment.

## Other Issues Involving Right of Privacy

*Confidentiality of Student Records.* Very little has been written concerning the confidentiality of student records and the case law is rather sparse. It has been suggested that many of the legal issues involving student records can be resolved by viewing them as public records.[40]

Such records, however, present several important problems which cannot and should not be resolved in this legalistic fashion. These problems may be summarized in the following questions: What information must a student furnish to the school? Does a student have a proprietary interest in any such information which permits him to determine whether and to whom such information shall be made available? Is the school limited in the kind of information that it may include in the student records? Does a student have a right to notice of any entry that will be placed on his record? Does a student have a right to a hearing to contest the accuracy or relevance of that which is proposed to be entered on his record?

---

40. Strahan, *Should Colleges Release Grades of College Students to Draft Boards?*, 43 NO. DAK. L. REV. 721 (1967).

As these questions suggest, entries made in student records can become of great importance, and school administrators should, therefore, take great care in establishing and operating a record system. It is also important that lawyers raise many of these issues so that the law governing the confidentiality of student records may begin to reflect the relevant consideration.

*Confidentiality of Student Communications.* No legal privilege is provided in New York or elsewhere for private communications between a student and members of the faculty and administration. This has created a serious problem at Stony Brook where a number of faculty members have been subpoenaed by the grand jury and questioned concerning activities on campus. At least one faculty member has refused to answer and been held in contempt of court.

This kind of investigative activity can have a very damaging impact on a college's educational and social environment. It is crucial to the learning process that students feel completely free to communicate with all members of the university community. For this reason, it is my opinion that a privilege should be established by legislation for student communications made to faculty and members of the administrative staff.

It should be noted, however, that student communications are privileged if made to a doctor, lawyer or certain other professionals where such professional privilege is provided for by state law. Such privilege has no particular relation to the academic community, but rather is available to all persons who take advantage of it.

*A Student's Fifth Amendment Right.* Although not entirely clear, it is my understanding that a student at a public college may be disciplined or expelled for refusing to testify at a disciplinary hearing. This is consistent with a number of cases which hold that a public pupil employed may be dismissed for refusing to answer questions relating to the conduct of his job.[41]

41.   Beilan v. Board of Public Educ., 357 U.S. 399 (1958); Nelson v. County 362 U.S. 1 (1960).

Nevertheless, some uncertainty is created by the Supreme Court's decision in *Spevack v. Klein*,[42] which holds that a lawyer may not be disbarred for refusing to provide information concerning his professional behavior. The only distinction which seems to exist in this case is that an attorney is a private rather than a public employee—a distinction which does not seem meaningful to me. Moreover, a recent case sheds doubt on the continuing validity of *Spevack*[43] and it would appear that if a student refuses to furnish information to the school concerning his conduct as a student, the school may validly suspend or expel him.

In any event, it is clear that if a student does furnish information to a public school for disciplinary purposes, such information may not be used against him in a subsequent criminal proceeding. The Supreme Court has held that public employees may not have used against them in a criminal proceeding evidence which they had to furnish in order to retain their jobs.[44] The same rationale is certainly applicable to students who furnish information to a public college in conjunction with a disciplinary proceeding.[45] It is not clear, however, whether this same protection is available to a student attending a private college.

### The Student Government as a Legal Entity

My earlier comments suggested that student collective activity will become increasingly common. It is interesting to note that New York law encourages this development by requiring that student representatives be consulted prior to the adoption of any rule or regulation at the several units of the State University of

---

42. 385 U.S. 511 (1967).
43. *See* Uniformed Sanitation Men Ass'n, Inc. v. Commissioner of Sanitation, 392 U.S. 280 (1968) (concurring opinion).
44. Garrity v. New Jersey, 385 U.S. 493 (1967).
45. *See* Furutani v. Ewigleben, 297 F. Supp. 1163 (N.D. Cal. 1969).

New York,[46] and also by authorizing student governments on campuses of the State University to establish, collect and disburse student activity fees.[47]

Student government, to be effective, must have financial independence and the right of participation in decisionmaking on campus. The regulations and policies of the State University Trustees ensure that these conditions will exist.

Collective student activity by its very nature raises a number of difficult legal questions. What is the legal status of student government? What powers does it possess? May student government sue or be sued in its own name? May student government invest its monies? What is the tax status of student government? Is student government liable on its contracts? Is student government responsible for libelous articles published under its auspices? Can individual students be held liable for the actions of student government? May the school or individual members of the faculty or administration be held liable for the actions of student government?

Our firm has already faced many of these problems while representing the student government at Stony Brook. Businessmen have questioned us concerning the enforceability of contracts with the student government in view of the fact that most of its officers and members are less than 21 years of age. Banks have questioned us concerning the legal status of the student government when it wanted to open bank accounts. Brokerage firms have raised innumerable questions when the student government attempted to invest its funds.

Our firm has rendered the opinion that under New York law the student government at Stony Brook is a nonprofit unincorporated association. This term refers to a "society or body of individuals, formed for social, political, moral, religious, benevolent, protective

---

46. 8 N.Y.C.R.R. §500.2.
47. 8 N.Y.C.R.R. §302.14.

or mutual purposes, or to promote some public, scientific or educational object . . . and not for purposes of trade or direct pecuniary profit."[48]

As an unincorporated association, certain questions concerning student government are answered. For example, its property is held by all students as joint tenants, and when a student graduates and ceases to be a member, his interest passes to the remaining students. In this manner continuity is ensured.

Moreover, under New York law neither a nonprofit unincorporated association nor its membership can be held liable for one member's act undertaken on behalf of the association unless such act has been authorized or ratified by specific action of the entire membership. Thus, the New York Court of Appeals has held that neither a union nor its membership could be held liable for a libelous article published by a union committee with responsibility for such publication since such articles were not specifically authorized or ratified by the individual members of the union.[49]

The fact is, however, that our opinion concerning the legal status of the student government at Stony Brook may not prove particularly helpful when other issues arise where age normally is determinate, i.e., enforceability of a contract, legal ability to sue or be sued. Similarly, our characterization of the student government is not particularly helpful when questions arise involving its relationship to other persons or instrumentalities at the school.

One way to avoid these problems may be to incorporate the student government.[50] The more inflexible corporate form,

---

48.   3 N.Y. Jur., Associations and Clubs, §1, p. 338.
49.   Martin v. Curran, 303 N.Y. 276 (1951).
50.   Such incorporation should take place in a state which does not require directors to be 21 or over. Otherwise, the student government will probably be forced to vest control in nonstudents. Moreover, the student government should be incorporated as a nonprofit or membership corporation. This may be relevant in regard to potential tax liability and, in any event, the provisions governing business corporations are completely irrelevant to the operation of a student government.

however, is not really suited to the informal manner in which a student government functions. Nevertheless, a corporation as a separate legal entity may choose whomever it desires to act as its agent without respect to age, and this may enable the student government to avoid a number of perplexing legal problems.

To my knowledge none of these problems have yet been discussed in the literature or dealt with by court decision. Under current law, there may well be no readily ascertainable answers, and therefore, legislation might well be required.

## Conclusion

The preceding discussion has analyzed a number of important issues involving the legal rights of students. Nevertheless, the major problems confronting our universities relate to significant questions of social and educational policy.

These issues do not lend themselves to resolution through the assertion of student legal rights. They can be resolved only through discussion and negotiation among all elements of the university community. Any satisfactory result must achieve a delicate balance among student, faculty and institutional needs.

# 5

# Problems of Dual Jurisdiction
# of Campus and Community

## Edward C. Kalaidjian*

The recent and prospective intrusion of the community into the administration of institutions of higher education has a great potential for harm. Such community action has already taken several forms.

## Statutes

In New York, the legislature this term amended the Education Law by adding Article 129-A,[1] which requires colleges to adopt

---

\*    Thacher, Proffitt, Prizer, Crawley & Wood, New York, New York.

1.    N.Y. Educ. Law §6450 (McKinney 1969 Supp.). Regulation by colleges of conduct on campuses and other college property used for educational purposes

     1.    The trustees or other governing board of every college chartered by the regents or incorporated by special act of the legislature shall adopt rules and regulations for the maintenance of public order on college campuses and other college property used for educational purposes and provide a program for the enforcement thereof. Such rules and regulations shall govern the conduct of students, faculty and other staff as well as visitors and other licensees and invitees on such campuses and property. The penalties for violations of such rules and regulation shall be clearly set forth therein and shall include provisions for the ejection of a violator from such campus and property, and in the case of a student or faculty violator his suspension, expulsion or other appropriate disciplinary action. Such rules and regulations shall be filed with the regents and the commissioner of education not later than ninety days after the effective date of this act. All amendments to such rules and regulations shall be filed with the regents and the commissioner of education not later than ten days after their adoption.

rules and regulations "for the maintenance of public order on college campuses" and to establish a program for the enforcement of the rules. The required rules, which are to apply to students, faculty, staff and visitors, are to provide penalties including "ejection of a violator" from the campus and, in the case of faculty and students, suspension, expulsion and other disciplinary action. The rules are required to be filed with the Regents and the Commissioner of Education before a college or university may be eligible to participate in the new $20.1 million program of state aid for colleges.

A proposed amendment to Article 129-A,[2] which has passed both houses of the legislature, would also require colleges to enforce their rules as a further condition of eligibility for state aid.

This legislation raises several questions: (1) What does "maintenance of public order on college campuses" mean? Obviously, it deals with occupation of buildings or disruption of classes or other university functions. But would the statute outlaw noisy or disorderly outdoor demonstrations, activities which have generally been regarded as within the traditional latitude of campus expression? (2) How will enforcement proceedings under the required rules mesh with existing provisions relating to discipline of tenured faculty members or with the grievance machinery applicable to unionized college employees? (3) Will provisions for "ejection of violators" from the campus limit the essential discretion of university officials in determining when and in what circumstances the police should be summoned to the campus?

---

2. If the trustees or other governing board of a college fails to file the rules and regulations within the time required by this section such college shall not be eligible to receive any state aid or assistance until such rules and regulations are duly filed.

3. Nothing contained in this section is intended nor shall it be construed to limit or restrict the freedom of speech nor peaceful assembly.

§ 2. This act shall take effect immediately. [Approved and effective April 21, 1969.]

2. A.6901, vetoed by Governor Nelson A. Rockefeller, May 26, 1969.

By involving the state in the disciplinary rules and procedures of institutions of higher learning, this statute increases the possibility that a private university's disciplinary proceedings may be held to be "state action" subject to the fourteenth amendment of the United States Constitution on the principles stated in *Burton v. Wilmington Parking Authority*[3] and *Simkins v. Moses H. Cone Memorial Hospital.*[4] This may no longer be a matter of great moment, of course, in view of the efforts by many private universities to provide the simple fundamentals of due process mandated for state universities in *Dixon v. Alabama State Board of Education.*[5]

Enactment of the proposed amendment to Article 129-A which specifically requires enforcement of the rules as a condition for receiving state aid might reasonably be regarded as creating improper pressures on those presiding at the hearings of misconduct cases.

The New York Legislature has passed three other pieces of legislation bearing on the administration of colleges and universities:

(1) Education Law §634,[6] passed by the legislature at the last session and now before the Governor, would deprive state scholarship or financial aid to students convicted of any felony or misdemeanor, such as criminal trespass, unlawful assembly, etc., in which the accusatory document alleges that the offense was committed on a campus.

(2) Penal Law §240.22,[7] also passed by the legislature and forwarded to the Governor, defines a new crime, aggravated disorderly conduct for the disruption of normal functions of a college or university occurring on or within 500 feet of the campus, as a Class A misdemeanor. The offense would be punishable by a sentence not to exceed one year.

---

3.    365 U.S. 715 (1961).
4.    323 F.2d 959 (4th Cir. 1963).
5.    294 F.2d 150 (5th Cir. 1961).
6.    S.524, vetoed by Governor Nelson A. Rockefeller, May 26, 1969.
7.    A.6877, vetoed by Governor Nelson A. Rockefeller, May 26, 1969.

(3) The legislature also enacted amendments to the New York Penal Law[8] making unauthorized possession of firearms on a campus a Class A misdemeanor or, if the person involved has previously been convicted of any crime, a Class D felony. This same legislation makes a person guilty of criminal trespass in the first degree when, in the course of committing such a crime, he possesses or knows that another participant possesses explosives, deadly weapons or firearms and has accessible ammunition therefor.

Legislation concerned with and about the administration of colleges and universities has also been introduced this session in Congress. H.R. 10,074 would require a suspension of federal assistance to institutions of higher education which experience disorders and fail to take appropriate protective measures within a reasonable time. It would also require the termination of financial assistance to teachers, instructors and lecturers guilty of violation of any law in connection with such a campus disorder. H.R. 10,571 would establish a Federal Higher Education Mediation and Conciliation Service.

The state legislation and proposed federal legislation above

---

8.    N.Y. Penal Law (McKinney 1969 Supp.). Section 1. Subdivision ten of section 265.05 of the penal law is hereby renumbered to be subdivision eleven and a new subdivision ten is hereby inserted to read as follows:
    10.    Any person who knowingly has in his possession a rifle, shotgun or firearm in or upon a building or the grounds, used for educational purposes, of any school, college or university without the written authorization of such educational institution, is guilty of a class A misdemeanor, and he is guilty of a class D felony if he has previously been convicted of any crime.
    § 2. Paragraph three of subdivision a of section 265.20 of such law is here amended to read as follows:
    3.    Possession of a pistol or revolver by a person to whom a license therefore has been issued as provided under section 400.00; provided, that such a license shall not preclude a conviction for the offense defined in subdivision ten of section 265.05.
    § 3. Section 140.05 of such law is hereby amended to read as follows:

would materially increase the participation of the community in the management of institutions of higher education and have the potential of significantly restricting the traditional self-government of campus communities.

## Community Action Without Statutory Authorization or Request

Without a formal complaint from campus authorities, several district attorneys have filed criminal charges against disruptive students and outsiders. Recently *The New York Times* reported independently initiated criminal cases resulting from disruptions at Cornell University and Brooklyn College. These actions may result from public dissatisfaction with recent cases in which universities initiated criminal charges against large numbers of students but subsequently requested the court to withdraw the charges.

Institutions of higher education must be made aware that the community will move into any vacuum created by vacillation or ineffectiveness in college and university disciplinary procedures.

---

§ 140.05.  Criminal trespass in the fourth degree

A person is guilty of criminal trespass in the fourth degree when he knowingly enters or remains unlawfully in or upon premises

Criminal trespass in the fourth degree is a violation.

§ 4.  Section 140.10 of such law is hereby amended to read as follows:

§ 140.10  Criminal trespass in the third degree

A person is guilty of criminal trespass in the third degree when he knowingly enters or remains unlawfully in a building or upon real property which is fenced or otherwise enclosed in a manner designed to exclude intruders.

Criminal trespass in the third degree is a class B misdemeanor.

§ 5.  Section 140.15 of such law is hereby amended to read as follows:

§ 140.15  Criminal trespass in the second degree

A person is guilty of criminal trespass in the second degree when he knowingly enters or remains unlawfully in a dwelling.

Unless institutions of higher education marshall all the intellectual and educational resources at their command to restore and maintain conditions conducive to their educational purposes, the community will assume that function and the results may be catastrophic to higher education.

## When Criminal and Disciplinary Proceedings are Pending

As an aftermath of disruptive demonstrations, students have increasingly been charged simultaneously with violations of the criminal law of the state and with violations of university rules resulting from the same act. In the typical case, a student who has been identified as a participant in the occupation of a building may be named as a defendant in a criminal trespass action and may also be charged by his university with violation of the campus rule forbidding building occupations or other forms of disruptions. In several such cases, students have sought unsuccessfully to enjoin the college from proceeding with its disciplinary hearing until the

---

Criminal trespass in the second degree is a class A misdemeanor.

§ 6. Such law is hereby amended by adding thereto a new section, to be section 140.17, to read as follows:

§ 140.17    Criminal trespass in the first degree

A person is guilty of criminal trespass in the first degree when he knowingly enters or remains unlawfully in a building, and when, in the course of committing such crime, he:

1.    Possesses, or knows that another participant in the crime possesses, an explosive or a deadly weapon; or

2.    Possesses a firearm, rifle or shotgun, as those terms are defined in section 265.00, and also possesses or has readily accessible a quantity of ammunition which is capable of being discharged from such firearm, rifle or shotgun; or

3.    Knows that another participant in the crime possesses a firearm, rifle or shotgun under circumstances described in subdivision two.

Criminal trespass in the first degree is a class D felony.

§ 7. This act shall take effect on the first day of September next

criminal action has been adjudicated. In support of their injunction applications, the students have asserted that unless the college
disciplinary proceeding is stayed, they must testify in their own
defense or risk suspension or expulsion by remaining silent; if they
testify at the college hearing, they claim their testimony will be
used against them in the subsequent trial of the criminal action.

Several grounds for denying the students' motions for stays of
college disciplinary hearings have been given by the courts. In
*Goldberg v. Regents of University of California*,[9] the earliest of
the cases, the court noted that university rules and community
criminal statutes do not serve the same ends and recognized the
university's interest in the swift conclusion of disciplinary proceedings. The federal court for the Southern District of New York
was presented with the same issue in *Grossner v. The Trustees of
Columbia University*.[10] Judge Frankel, who heard the application,
commented in his opinion that the simultaneous pendency of an
administrative proceeding and a criminal action involving the same
event does not require that the administrative proceeding be
stayed. For an analogy, the court noted that a motor vehicle
commissioner authorized to suspend a driver's license for speeding
need not wait the outcome of a negligent homicide prosecution
before considering administrative action. It is noteworthy that in
*Grossner* the plaintiffs took the position that the university did
not even have the right to call the alleged violators before the dean
for the purpose of ascertaining whether the accused admitted or
denied the charge of misconduct or wished to stand mute. In
either of the latter two events, that is, a denial or refusal to
respond to the charge, a hearing was the next step.

In *Furutani v. Ewigleben*[11] a California federal court, denying
the students' application to enjoin a college's disciplinary proceed-

succeeding the date on which it shall become a law. [Approved May 2,
1969, effective Sept. 1, 1969.]

9. 248 Cal. App. 2d 867, 57 Cal. Rptr. 463 (1967).

10. 287 F. Supp. 535 (S.D.N.Y. 1968).

11. 297 F. Supp. 1163 (N.D. Cal. 1969).

ing, pointed out that if the plaintiff students were obliged to testify in the college proceeding to avoid expulsion, their testimony could be excluded in the subsequent criminal trial based upon the decision of the United States Supreme Court in *Garrity v. New Jersey*.[12] In the *Garrity* case certain New Jersey police officers testified in an Attorney General's investigation of irregularities to which no immunity statute was applicable. Under a New Jersey statute, the police officers would have been subject to removal from office if they had invoked the fifth amendment when questioned in the investigation. Subsequently, the police officers involved were tried for conspiracy to obstruct the administration of the traffic laws. At their trial the testimony which they had given in the Attorney General's investigation was received in evidence against them and they were convicted. The Supreme Court reversed on the ground that the officers' testimony in the Attorney General's investigation should not have been received in evidence.

Describing the police officers' predicament, the Court stated they were confronted with a choice "between the rock and the whirlpool." The Court concluded:

> We now hold the protection of the individual under the Fourteenth Amendment against coerced statements prohibits use in subsequent criminal proceedings of statements obtained under threat of removal from office, and that it extends to all, whether they are policemen or other members of our body politic.[13]

The *Furutani* case extends this principle to testimony which might be given by a student in a college disciplinary proceeding.

In concluding the discussion of the issue arising from the simultaneous pendency of criminal and university charges based upon the same act, I might mention that Columbia University's

---

12.   385 U.S. 493 (1967).

13.   *Id.* at 500.

rules permit a student facing both criminal and university charges to defer the university proceedings by taking a special leave of absence from the university until the criminal case is resolved.

## The Use of Police in Disruptive Demonstrations on Campus

### The Psychological Factor

Most university communities look with disfavor upon the use of police to terminate a building occupation. There are several reasons for this: (1) Historically, the police have been associated in the American experience with the use of force to repress social actions by underprivileged groups, such as labor unions. (2) In the more recent past the police have been associated in the public mind with repression of the black civil rights movement in the South. Further, during the Democratic National Convention in Chicago in 1968, millions of people witnessed on television the behavior of the Chicago police in the streets of that city. (3) The New Left movement, which operates extensively on symbolic issues and actions, has exploited the symbol of police brutality by applying to policemen such terms as "fascists," "pigs" and other expletives.

As a result of these and other conditions, the police are associated in the campus mind with unreasoning force and brutality. This psychological factor increases the likelihood that the use of police will result in violence and that escalation of campus strife may be expected as an aftermath to a police bust.

### The Escalation Factor

Experience in the use of police to terminate a campus building occupation indicates that the use of excessive force is likely to occur and may be inevitable in the interaction between police and, emotionally charged demonstrators at the point of confrontation.

Even when policemen are most carefully briefed beforehand, the hysteria and defiance they encounter in clearing a building tend to spur them to commit the very excesses which they were cautioned against. The sight of students emerging from an occupied building with police-inflicted wounds or the sight of policemen using clubs on students in open areas adjacent to the occupied buildings naturally stirs feelings of revulsion in the minds of viewers. As a result, members of a campus community who have previously supported neither the objectives nor the means employed by the radical movement are stirred to sympathize with and support the movement.

This phenomenon is precisely what occurred at Columbia during the police actions which occurred on the campus in 1968. Despite diligent efforts by University officials to minimize the possibility of police excesses, in the heat of the action numerous instances of excessive force occurred in the plain view of hundreds of people. While many of these onlookers had not previously lent any active support to the symbolic issues involving the construction of the new gymnasium in Morningside Park or the University's relatively insignificant association with the Institute for Defense Analysis, the spectacle of what many viewers regarded as police brutality had an instantaneous radicalizing effect. In consequence of the two police actions SDS generated broad support by the exploitation of the police brutality issue. This support sufficed to sustain an SDS-led strike which caused the suspension of many classes for the balance of the term of several weeks and the cancellation of final examinations in some courses.

## When to Call the Police

The decision to call in the police will be controversial whenever it is made. However, several factors should enter into the judgment.

### The Time Element

The longer an unlawful occupation of a building lasts the more likely it is to acquire de facto legitimacy. Permitting a building occupation to continue is also likely to increase not only the number of participants but also their moral certainty of the righteousness of their cause. This may not be true in every case but it was the experience at Columbia in the spring of 1968.

### Campus Opinion During Initial Stages

Generally speaking, the occupation of a building may be terminated with minimum use of police force at the initial stages when the occupants' confidence quotient is lowest. However, university officials often find that campus support for the use of police at the early stage of a building occupation cannot be marshalled. Many campus groups will believe that, given a little time for negotiations, the occupants can be coaxed out peacefully.

### Threats From Other Campus Groups

One of the most compelling factors in deciding when to call in the police is the threat of widespread campus fighting between the demonstrators and groups of students who oppose the objectives and means of the building occupiers. When this threat of physical violence is imminent, the use of police becomes both necessary and justifiable.

### Communication With the Campus Community

While a building or buildings are being occupied, it is of the utmost importance that university officials maintain the fullest communication with interested faculty and student groups about the progress of negotiations and the status of campus conditions. When the time to call the police comes, elements of the informed campus may, nonetheless, withhold their support for the use of police, but they are less likely to be alienated if they understand the conditions which led to the calling of the police.

If open communication to numerous segments of the campus has been effective, it may also achieve a second important purpose of isolating and withdrawing support from those occupying campus buildings.

## Minimizing the Risk of Police Action

There are numerous measures which may be taken to reduce the possibility that police action will get out of hand. First, the course of action should be planned with the police. University officials should attend the briefings at which the police are instructed by their superior officers concerning the conduct of operations. During the briefing officials should define clearly for the police the outdoor areas of the campus which are to be cleared. If they don't, the police may expand the operations beyond the immediate campus areas adjacent to occupied buildings. Police should be instructed to take violators from the building to the police vans by the shortest campus route to minimize the possibility of confrontations with sympathizers while the violators are being led away. In typical cases campus entrances to occupied buildings will be barricaded from within by the occupants, and the campus area in front of the buildings is likely to have drawn a large crowd of the sympathetic and the curious. University officials should provide the police with accurate building plans showing all means of entering the building, including any underground passageways or utility tunnels. University observers should be stationed at each of the occupied buildings to identify violators as they are removed from the building. Notice to the occupants to vacate the buildings should be read over a bull-horn as a requisite to any subsequent criminal trespass action.

Notwithstanding all of these precautions and others which

experience might indicate, the use of police to terminate a building occupation should be recognized as a last resort measure when other means have failed. The police operation carries with it the very real possibility of broadening support for the radical movement, polarizing campus opinion, and radicalizing previously uninvolved persons.

## The Privacy of Student Quarters

In evaluating the dormitory resident's fourth amendment rights, it does not matter whether the relationship between the institution and the student be characterized as in loco parentis or contract. Perhaps the relationship should be termed academic in that it is based upon the peculiar and occasionally competing interests of the college and the student. At any rate, the student has the right to be free of unreasonable search and seizure. A tax-supported public college may not compel a waiver of that right as a condition of admission.

Conversely, the institution has an obligation to promulgate and to enforce reasonable regulations designed to maintain discipline over students and to foster a campus environment conducive to educational purposes. In part, the right of school authorities to search and the right of a dormitory resident to privacy depend on whether the college authorities have reasonable grounds to believe that a student is using his dormitory room for an illegal purpose or one which would seriously interfere with campus discipline. The standard of "reasonable cause to believe," sufficient to justify a search by college administrators for evidence of suspected violations of law, is lower than the constitutionally protected criminal law standard of "probable cause." This is so because of the special obligations of the institution to maintain discipline.

On these principles, the courts have upheld the validity of searches conducted by academic authorities either without a search warrant or in the company of police whose search warrant was invalid.[14]

Most colleges and universities have in effect a regulation by which the college reserves the right to enter dormitory residents' rooms for inspection purposes, and the reserved right of inspection includes not only the room but the personal baggage or property of the occupant.

## Privacy of Student Records and Communication

Several privileges are or may be applicable to student records and confidential communications:

**The Educator-Student Relationship.** In New York State, the educator-student relationship, of itself, is not the basis of any legal privilege protecting the confidentiality of private communications between a student and a dean or his staff or a faculty member. There may be sound reasons for creating such a statutory privilege, based on the need for candid communication on subjects affecting the student's welfare and education.

**The Physician-Patient Privilege.** This privilege attaches to confidential communications between a doctor and his patient, provided the information was necessary to enable the physician to treat the patient. This privilege would be applicable to university medical and dispensary records. It should be noted that New York Public Health Law §3304(2) destroys the physician-patient privilege as to communications about narcotics.

**The Psychologist-Patient Relationship.** In New York, confiden-

---

14. Moore v. Students Affairs Comm., 284 F. Supp. 725 (M.D. Ala. 1968); People v. Overton, 20 N.Y.2d 360 (1967). Both of these cases contain excellent discussions of the problem and citations of pertinent authorities.

tial communications between a registered psychologist and a patient are privileged to the same extent as confidential communications between an attorney and his client. This privilege would attach to communications between a college or university psychologist and a student about a problem of concern to the student.

**Social Worker-Client Privilege.** Confidential communications between a duly registered social worker and his client in the course of professional employment are privileged to the extent provided in the New York Civil Practice Law and Rules §4508. This privilege would be available to a university-employed social worker.

**The Chaplain's Privilege.** A privilege attaches to confidential communications in the form of a confession by a student to a college or university chaplain as long as the confession was made to the chaplain in his professional capacity as a spiritual adviser.

Before it releases to any governmental or private agency any information on file concerning matters of student discipline or matters which might tend to incriminate or to degrade a student, the university department or office involved should consult the university counsel. A college or university may divulge nonprivileged information from its records without incurring legal liability provided the following circumstances are present: the information is furnished in response to a proper request; the person requesting the information has a genuine interest in the subject matter and a need for the information; the institution gives no more information than is requested; and the information is furnished in good faith and not with the intent of causing damage to the person inquired about.

## Handling the Nonstudent Problem

In a large urban university such as Columbia we are required to contend with many varieties of nonstudents: former students suspended as a result of the disruptions of spring 1968; dropouts from Columbia and Barnard; neighborhood dissidents, white and black; high school students recruited by SDS; and students from other colleges and universities in the area. Some of the principal leaders of the SDS this year are students who were suspended because of their activities in the spring of 1968. SDS' most recent tactic, after their own efforts to disrupt the Columbia campus in spring 1969 fizzled, has been to try to recruit masses of black and white city high school students to occupy buildings in support of the demand for open admissions. SDS has also sought to recruit demonstrators from the Morningside Heights and Harlem neighborhoods to protest the University's purchase and closing of rundown apartment buildings in the vicinity of the campus. Fortunately, SDS has not been successful in assembling large or effective groups of high school students or community residents, and it cannot be said that either high school kids or community residents have been a serious problem at Columbia this year.

Nonstudents, particularly suspended students and dropouts, are not subject to university disciplinary rules since they are not members of the campus community. Consequently, the only method of dealing with them is through criminal charges or through the use of injunctions, for violations of which criminal contempt charges will lie. As some of you may know, so far in 1969 Columbia has successfully used the injunction in dealing with students and nonstudents. It was first used in connection with a sit-in by a group of black students and nonstudents in the Columbia College Admissions Office on April 14 and 15. This group vacated the premises as soon as their attorneys were provided with copies of the injunction. On April 17, a group estimated to exceed 200 students and nonstudents occupied Philosophy Hall in an SDS-sponsored sit-in. That group vacated the premises less than an hour after the University's injunction was served in the building. Finally, on April 30 and May 1, Fayerweather Hall and Mathematics Hall, both large university academic buildings, were occupied by an estimated 200 or more SDS members and their friends, both students and nonstudents. They refused to leave when warned that they were violating the injunction against disruptive demonstrations. However, as soon as they heard that the court had signed a writ of body attachment, directing the sheriff of the City of New York to bring them before the court on charges of criminal contempt, they scurried from the building after covering their faces with cloths to conceal their identities. The University is now prosecuting criminal contempt charges against the first group of identified demonstrators. Many of them are nonstudents.

## Occupation of Off-campus Buildings

Colleges and universities that own business or residential real estate adjoining their campuses are likely to experience, or to have experienced already, SDS-sponsored occupations of portions of such properties. As a large owner of real estate on Morningside Heights, Columbia has had several such episodes. We have found that these off-campus apartment occupations are simpler to terminate because they do not draw large crowds of spectators. Since the apartments are located on city streets, the police can effectively seal off the area around the building without encountering large numbers of defiant students. It has been Columbia's experience that an announcement to the occupants that they will be charged with criminal trespass unless they leave the premises forthwith has succeeded in bringing about a peaceful vacating. The use of injunctions in connection with off-campus building sit-ins has not thus far been necessary.

## Conclusion

The extreme public concern over student disruptions of university life and over violence and lawlessness is causing the community to intervene in the traditionally autonomous operation of institutions of higher education. This intervention is often uninformed and politically motivated. It has the potential for damaging American institutions of higher education more seriously and more permanently than the disruptive acts which have initiated it.

# 6

# Panel Discussion — I

## Injunctions

**Carrington:** We have received a number of questions directed to problems involving the use of injunctions. The first one: What is the situation of a university or college seeking an injunction against a trespass which has not yet occurred? Suppose we are going to have an ROTC parade next week. We know that students are going to try to disrupt the parade and we would like to enjoin them. Is there any prospect of getting such an injunction?

**Holloway:** Yes. As a matter of fact, the courts have been rather liberal in granting them. The college may simply allege that they have reason to suspect that certain things are about to take place, and that if they do, the college has reason to suspect that specific harm will result.

I might add that sometimes the tables are turned and students bring suit first. Then the institution can, of course, counterclaim, as Alcorn A. & M. did in the *Birdsong*[1] case.

Fred Gray, who was counsel in the *Dixon*[2] case, has just handed me a late opinion showing how successful counterclaims can be. It is *Scott v. Alabama State Board of Education,*[3] dated May 14, 1969. There may be some new law in it, too, in that two or three charges that Alabama State College made in suspending the three plaintiffs are found to be vague and the court orders the students reinstated. This charge, for example, was held to be vague:

---

1. Evers v. Birdsong, 287 F. Supp. 900 (S.D. Miss. 1968).
2. Dixon v. Alabama State Bd. of Educ., 294 F.2d 150 (5th Cir.), *cert. denied*, 368 U.S. 930 (1961).
3. The opinion, which has not yet been reported as this volume goes to press, is reprinted in Appendix H.

"Willful refusal to obey a regulation or order of Alabama State, such refusal being of a serious nature and contributed to a substantial disruption of the administration and operation of the College, March 29 – April 8, 1969."

A charge that a student "through verbal exhortations and/or threats and/or intimidation prevented or discouraged other Alabama State students from attending classes, March 31–April 7, 1969," was said to be ambiguous and vague. The court observed that "exhortation" in normal usage would be used to describe speech that might well be constitutionally protected. The three students were ordered reinstated pending, if the college desires, a further specification of the charges and another hearing.

To get back to my point about counterclaim, Alabama State counterclaimed for injunctive relief in this case and got it—got, in fact, a very broad injunction ordering the students whose dismissals or suspensions were upheld to forthwith leave the premises they had been occupying and to leave the campus. Failure to do so could result in contempt proceedings.

**Carrington:** I will address this question to Professor Van Alstyne. Does the trend toward the use of injunctions, particularly anticipatory injunctions, against demonstrations obviate the need for drawing rules with the kind of specificity that you suggested?

**Van Alstyne:** I don't think it obviates the need for specificity unless, of course, the university is content to rely exclusively on the civil process and is indifferent to any desire to reserve a prerogative separately to take disciplinary action against the students. If it wants to transfer fully to the civil authorities responsibility for policing this area, I suppose the injunctive remedy is a reasonably promising one. Then, however, the injunction is subject to certain serious restrictions of its own. Though the issue has not been raised, I think it is possible that the injunction issued against certain demonstrations is itself challengeable on constitutional grounds if issued in an ex parte proceeding, yet there may have been opportunity at least to serve process on the other side and have them appear in argument. There is a Supreme Court decision in which an injunction secured by a municipality to prevent a downtown demonstration was violated. The people were then cited for contempt and they successfully defended the contempt citation on the basis that given the first amendment nature of their conduct, they had been denied procedural due process in the issuance of the injunction. Again, the injunction can be very limited in time. You simply can't have, in an ex parte proceeding, an injunction which lasts indefinitely. The injunction is a serviceable alternative, highly useful in some circumstances, especially to frighten the students into leaving buildings. But to suggest that it is an adequate substitute for adequate campus rules and an adequate student judiciary is a wishful thought.

**Carrington:** I want to ask Mr. Cates and Mr. Kalaidjian whether, from their experiences, they have found the injunction an effective way to clear out a building. What do you think, Mr. Cates?

**Cates:** At Wisconsin we sought injunctive relief following a demonstration against job interviews by Dow Chemical.[4] We went to court, made allegations and gave proof that we expected similar demonstrations when the CIA and the military came on campus to recruit, and we got an injunction. I don't know that the injunction proceedings were responsible, but we *were* able to conduct those interviews. Protests at the interviews were lawful and did not obstruct or interfere with the rights of others. Again, I don't know that the proceeding itself caused this, but I do believe that when you seek an injunction and name individuals, you put the spotlight on people. They can't evade their individual responsibility in the matter and hide behind a group. Litigation is a device our society offers us to fight things out. Just being involved in litigation has an effect on the litigants themselves, whether the case means anything to outsiders or not. The parties are put into a setting and a

4.   *See* Appendix F, *infra.*

scene foreign to their experience. Litigation makes the man pay a price—if he wants to run around with a group of other people and try to break the law, then he has got to go through this proceeding. Just going through the proceeding takes its toll. Given the proper circumstance, this is an effective tool for the institution.

**Kalaidjian:** It must be realized that the injunction is not a cure-all for everybody's academic problems. The use of the injunction must be approached very carefully. In the fall of 1968 we at Columbia made a policy decision not to seek recourse to an injunction for frivolous reasons, but to reserve it for activity so serious as to create an imminent peril of widespread disruption or interference with university activities. Having made that decision, we also decided that even when such conduct was imminent we would not seek an injunction anticipatorily, but would wait until there had been an occurrence. An advantage of this approach is that when the institution *does* seek an injunction the campus knows it is necessary and that it is not intended as a menacing or restrictive ploy.

So that we could move quickly once something had occurred, we prepared standby papers. Based on our experience, we could almost predict what we would have to say and who we would have to name as defendants, so about all we left blank was the day of the occurrence and the name of the building where it would happen. The result was that when the school was put to the test this spring—when various groups sought to probe to see whether they could repeat last year's riots—we were ready. The first instance occurred on April 14, when a group of black students and nonstudents conducted a sit-in in the admissions office. Notices of admission were due out in a few days, and the admissions people were pressed to get them out on time. It took us only about five hours from the time the sit-in started until we had the signature of a judge on a temporary restraining order. Within another hour and a half, on the advice of their counsel, 14 or 15 sitters-in had left the office. Of course, we were very pleased about that. We hadn't obtained the injunction for the purpose of getting contempt charges, but for the purpose of clearing the admissions office and restoring its function immediately, and in this case it worked.

But I did not regard this as a very significant test of the efficacy of the injunction; the number was too small, and SAS—the Student Afro-American Society—not SDS, was involved. And at Columbia, at least, SDS is really bent on demonstrating its ability to impair the institution in some way. On two subsequent occasions SDS tried to stage large sit-ins involving at least 200 students. The first was in Philosphy Hall. We got an injunction and within an hour SDS voluntarily left the building. At that point I began to think that the injunction had some efficacy at Columbia.

The final test came on April 30 and May 1 when there was an SDS-sponsored sit-in of 200 people at Fayerweather and Mathematics Halls. The previous injunction was still in effect; the students were warned that their conduct in this sit-in was in violation of that injunction and that they were subjecting themselves to prosecution for contempt. We went to the court and obtained a show cause order requiring the students in the buildings to come to court and show cause why they shouldn't be punished for contempt. The sheriff was authorized to serve the students in the building, but if he couldn't, he was to use a bullhorn and read it to the demonstrators in each building. Of course, the sheriff couldn't get in. The following morning when the order was returnable in court, none of the sitters-in appeared. Thereupon I presented, and the court signed, an order for the issuance of a writ of body attachment commanding the sheriff to apprehend those in the buildings and bring them before the court to answer a charge of contempt.[5] An SDS representative in court telephoned the

---

5.   The complaint and supporting documents and the order in this case, Trustees of Columbia University v. Students for a Democratic Society, are reprinted in Appendix G.

campus, and almost before the ink was dry on the order, the students were scurrying from the building with rags over their faces in an effort to conceal their identity.

When I got back to the campus about 40 minutes later, an interview with an SDS leader was in progress on WKCR, the university radio station. The reporter asked him why the SDS people obeyed the injunction. The student's reply was very interesting. He said, "Well, the injunction escalates the risk of conducting a sit-in. It is no longer a question of simply violating university rules, or even of being subjected to charges of criminal trespass, which may later be withdrawn. It brings us into confrontation with the court."

So I would say, based on our experience at Columbia, that the injunction has proved to be an effective tool for crisis management, but I would not recommend it be used lightly every time some administrator feels put upon by a sassy student or a dirty word or some other minor irritant.

**Carrington:** From your point of view as counsel for students, Mr. Lippe, do you have any comment?

**Lippe:** I would like to make clear that student governments are not necessarily adverse to some of the things we are talking about now. Student governments are not usually controlled by the SDS.

I think that the explanation given by Mr. Kalaidjian is one reason why injunctions are effective, but there may be another reason, too, depending on the sophistication of the students involved. At Buffalo, for example, an injunction was effective in one case this spring because it brought home to a number of people involved in a demonstration what really was going on, and how they could get into difficulties with the law. Some of the demonstrators were only friends or girl friends of the people really involved, and they chose to leave when confronted with an injunctive order. Similarly, at Stony Brook this year 300 people had occupied the library overnight. We, as the student government counsel, were called and arrived about five minutes before some

200 police were to enter the building and arrest all the students. We were given an opportunity to go into the library and speak with our clients. An hour and a half later, 279 of the students left the building voluntarily. Only 21 remained and were arrested, and even these gave themselves up outside so there wouldn't be any violence. We spoke to many of the students afterward and asked them why they had left, because we really didn't know. They said they left because when someone they trusted told them what the potential consequences of their actions were, they understood what they were getting into and they didn't want to get into it. So, depending upon the nature of the people involved, the injunction can be effective not only as a threat, but also as a symbol to bring home to the kids what they may be getting themselves into.

Further, from the point of view of the institution and the students, using an injunction is a far more effective way of dealing with problems than using the police. I do have a couple of caveats, however. In drafting your injunctions don't use language so broad that it raises problems similar to the problems we talked about regarding the specificity of regulations. A too-broad prohibition gives enormous discretion to administrators with respect to future activities and could be vulnerable to legal attack as having a chilling effect on first amendment freedoms. Such injunctions also raise the hackles of the students, who don't know what, if anything, they can do subsequently.

**Carrington:** The next question I will direct to Mr. Kalaidjian. If the college or university is a little lax in enforcing an injunction, can a public official seek enforcement?

**Kalaidjian:** It is theoretically possible. If a college or university, having procured an injunction, simply allowed it to be flouted, the court would be greatly concerned because a willful violation of a court order is not an offense against the litigant, it is an offense against the court. Therefore, the court itself might feel obliged to take measures to ensure enforcement of an injunction it had granted.

## Sanctions

**Carrington:** Professor Farer, several people are interested in your position, which seemed to start from the proposition that there are a number of situations in which it is wise not to invoke sanctions against students, and they ask under what circumstances is it appropriate to use sanctions? You did not address yourself to the affirmative proposition in your remarks and there are those who would like to hear you do so.

**Farer:** That seems a perfectly reasonable request. I am not sure that I can respond to it successfully in terms of laying down one or two or three rules. There are obviously a number of things about which all of us would agree. I assume we would agree that the use of personal violence against any member of the academic community is simply outside the bounds of tolerance and would justify calling the police. The same would be true of major damage to property, as arson. But those are the easy cases. For the most part debate is centered around the question of calling the police to remove people from buildings—those people who are in one way or another obstructing the use of university property. That is a much more difficult question. I presume we are talking also about the broader question of sanctions as such, not just the police. Recently there was a violation of the rules in Columbia Law School where we have not the slightest intention of seeking sanctions. I think we are right. The black student group had been engaged in more or less informal, even desultory discussion over the past year with an ad hoc faculty group about a number of issues. Members of the black student group felt that the faculty group did not formally represent the faculty, which was true, and that we weren't making any progress, which is debatable. In any event, they decided to have a study-in. It was a most artful demonstration. It was very close to examination time. Students drifted into the library, took seats, gathered their books around them, put up several signs announcing that they were conducting a study-in and then studied-in. Indeed, some of us thought it set an excellent example for other members of the student body. The only violation of the rules was that they stayed overnight, and the Dean maintained the library as an open area throughout the night. One colleague was very resentful that steps were not being taken to identify the students and to impose sanctions. These students honestly felt that the faculty had not talked with them about real issues. Their purpose was not revolutionary; indeed, they raised questions about our educational enterprise which we should have raised ourselves a few years ago. The outcome was a commitment on both sides to reexamine some of our assumptions in the area. I think it was settled amicably. That demonstration was used for what is one of the primary appropriate purposes of any act of civil disobedience—perhaps the only reason—to engage all interested parties in a constructive dialogue about certain values which are shared by them. I use this illustration to respond to the categorical assertion one hears frequently: the rule of our society is that sanctions must be imposed whenever the law is violated. I suggest that is not the rule of our society. One can point to an infinite number of cases where we accept the fact that sanctions will not be imposed. To impose such a rule is ahistorical and ignores the objectives of the institution.

**Van Alstyne:** I want to enter a modest dissent from that view. There is a degree of circularity in the proposition that because society frequently does not live up to its own aspirations it is therefore proper that it not do so in this case. You said that frequently antitrust violations are not prosecuted, frequently executive decisions are made not to pursue a known violation of the law, and this argues from what is for me a very doubtful *is* to a *therefore it ought to continue to be so.* I suggest that there is another way of looking at this: that the law may be enforced but you take the circumstances of the conduct more properly into account, not in executive discretion to apply or withhold the law, but in the appropriate sanction to be applied once the law has followed its course. Perhaps I am quite mistaken about this, but in your own case, for instance, I'm sure we are each persuaded that such a mild transgression, with no doubt sufficient cause, requires no significant punishment or no punishment at all. I am a bit troubled about the use of executive discretion, however, to pick and choose among known law violators as to the subjects of prosecution itself. I realize it takes place all the time, but I really was of the opinion that there is a fairly widely shared sentiment that this encourages a kind of subliminal denial of equal protection—some are favored because of the executive sympathy with their case and are not prosecuted, whereas others are disfavored and they are prosecuted. We might be better off with a uniform application of the law; the differences in transgression then assert themselves in the choice of sanctions or no sanctions. It may simply be a reprimand and that is all.

**Carrington:** Would your analysis lead you to make a record of the fact that these young men held a study-in?

**Van Alstyne:** I think that is part of the problem of the application of sanctions but not a part of the decision as to whether or not there might be a disciplinary proceeding. Part of my difficulty is that I don't know who has the omniscience to decide when a neutrally-framed rule, whether it is a college regulation or a state statute, is meant not to be applied to this man. Perhaps there is a kind of common law and custom in the background, Tom, I don't know; but I find it a much harder question than you do.

**Farer:** I don't know that I find it an easy question; and of course, as any good lawyer would, you have structured the argument in such a way that you naturally want to be successful in it. If I thought that the nature of my argument was that since there *is* a gap between the aspiration of the society and its realization it ought to be accepted—if that were in fact my argument—I would leave the battlefield in tatters. I don't think that is the nature of my argument. What I am suggesting is not merely that society arbitrarily and invidiously fails to enforce its laws, but that the society accepts the fact that there should be deviations from the uniform enforcement pattern in some cases. Now what are some of those cases? One area I suggested was the area of family relationships. I think we often don't prosecute the husband who beats up his wife, or the wife who beats up her husband, for quite good reasons. Neither one of them wants to see the sanctions of society imposed, and if it were recorded it might be more difficult for the husband to obtain a job to support his wife more adequately. All I am saying, then, is that there are some cases in the society where we recognize that the sanction ought not be imposed, that there is always a burden on the prosecutor to justify it, and that there are good reasons and bad reasons. In the antitrust area, frequently the reasons are corrupt reasons, I quite agree. On the other hand, the reasons may be that the corporation in question is prepared to modify its policies and to save the government the considerable expenditure involved in obtaining a court order which would get it to modify its policies in precisely the same way. The funds can be used more effectively in other places. Therefore, it seems to me that the philosophy is built into the society. It is not a reflection of the gap between justice and its realization; it is part of the sense of justice of the society—a quite different notion.

## The Student Press

**Carrington:** We have some questions on the problem of the student press. Is it necessary to provide the university facilities to student organizations who insist on publishing profanity?
**Farer:** That is not the one that particularly interests me. If you mean profanity as defined by the Supreme Court, hard-core obscenity which can be banned under existing constitutional

restrictions, the answer is quite simple. The problem is different if you are talking more colloquially about obscenity and raise the larger issue of what happens when students print things in their newspapers which offend large numbers of your most generous benefactors. The Law School at Columbia has had this problem recently with the Law School newspaper, which is published not only with the support of the school but with the help of a small fund provided by our alumni. I think that it is legitimate to ask for some measure of fairness in the reporting of a newspaper, at least to the extent that it is supported by the university. I regard this as roughly analogous to the fair allocation of time requirement for radio and television. Any kind of censorship of the editorial position of the newspaper offends me profoundly and raises, at least in the state universities, important first amendment questions. But it may be possible to achieve the functional equivalent of a fair presentation of a news story by requiring alternative representations of what occurred. If the dean wants to put a statement in the newspaper describing his version of a certain kind of confrontation, I think he has that right, as long as he doesn't take up an inordinate amount of space. The notion of fair allocation of time to present opposing views on important controversial issues should be imposed on college newspapers and perhaps ought to be contemplated more broadly, although it does raise serious constitutional questions.

**Carrington:** We have a bill pending in the Michigan legislature proposing that any university administrator failing to adopt standards of decency for university publications will be guilty of a misdemeanor. Most legislation of this kind is invalid, I suppose, but it emphasizes the current interest in the character and the quality of school publications.

**Van Alstyne:** May I comment? You get different legal answers under different arrangements. For instance, it would seem to me to make a considerable difference if the students are compelled to subscribe to the campus newspaper. In that circumstance there may be, by analogy, an abuse of first amendment freedoms, in that the fees required of them as a condition of remaining in good standing in the school are used by the editorial board of the paper to propagandize in favor of a certain view, *i.e.*, the ideology that characterizes the editorial tone of that particular paper. If the newspaper is wholly financed by the university and is part of its journalistic laboratory, this would seem to give it a greater proprietary control. The school is not attempting merely to use a so-called claim of governmental force to regulate the press, but it is deciding, rather, how it elects to spend its own money in developing this auxilliary enterprise as part of its program in journalism. It is a very different situation if the student newspaper is an independent corporation which supports itself by advertising, even though much of the advertising comes from the university under a contract reserving them the right to use a certain space every day to publish notices of general interest to the campus. The degree of possible control by the university scales way down in that circumstance, especially if other kinds of magazines and newspapers are also permitted to be distributed on campus, which I suspect might be constitutionally compelled. One can answer the question as to the extent of university control only by bearing in mind the different relationships possible. The *Joint Statement on Rights and Freedoms of Students*[6] commends the financial severing and the rendering independent of the student press. To avoid both the perniciousness and the inevitable responsibility of censorship by the administration whenever it has a primary financial responsibility for the paper, financial independence would seem to be the most civilized resolution wherever it's possible. The institution then deals with the paper by contract, as it would with a downtown paper. Then, of course, the paper becomes subject to state laws respecting libel or obscenity or whatever—responsible in the same way as any other paper.

---

6.  *See* Appendix A.

**Lippe:** This matter has come up at Stony Brook, and that is one of the reasons why the students have chosen to finance their own paper. This also answers the question raised yesterday with respect to the financial responsibility of the institution itself for potential libel.

**Carrington:** What is the consequence of having the university's name on the front of a newspaper? Does that give it any kind of responsibility or leverage in dealing with the contents of the newspaper?

**Van Alstyne:** I think it may give the school both, to the extent that it acquiesces in that representation, but the policy recommendation is clear—the student newspaper ought not make any pretense of representing the institution in the views it presents or the character of the stories it carries. Indeed, that is a further recommendation of the *Joint Statement:* the student press is not to make any claim, indeed, should disavow that it represents the university in its editorial position or otherwise.

**Lippe:** At least two court cases have, in dicta, dealt with the problem. They strongly suggest that if the student newspaper claims to represent the university and to present the university's point of view, they might be subject to discipline, under appropriate regulations.

**Van Alstyne:** On the other hand, I don't think that the university should take the position that providing accommodations or some financial backing for the newspaper gives the university the right of censorship. The university should take the position of the owner of a radio station—to provide equal time or space, even though the university may not be compelled to do so. The university should think of the newspaper as simply a kind of receptacle in which the various positions on campus can be reflected; the university provides no more than the air waves, the printing press or whatever it may be. That should be the relationship.

## Incorporation of Student Organizations

**Carrington:** There is a question for Mr. Lippe regarding student organizations: Can a student organization be incorporated? And if so, what are the consequences of that?

**Lippe:** Generally, you *can* incorporate a student organization. In New York, for example, you can proceed in one of two ways: You can incorporate it as a membership corporation, in which case you might require the consent of the Department of Education; or you can request a charter from the Regents, the overall authority for regulation of education which has the power to charter educationally related corporations.

But as a practical matter, as I mentioned earlier, I don't believe any state in the country permits corporate directors to be under 21 years of age. This means that the incorporation procedure is not available in most situations. Corporate law would require students to surrender control of the organization to directors over 21, and they won't want to do that.

**Carrington:** However they are organized, when student organizations seek to bring suit, what kind of standing problems do they encounter? In a suit to stop a building project, for example, what kind of a class are they representing? I take it it is not a taxpayer's suit.

**Lippe:** First let me say that we, as counsel for the student councils at Stony Brook, have not yet initiated such a suit, but I think in the state university construction situation which I mentioned, the argument that the students have standing to sue is very tenuous. However, in other situations where the student government has a more direct interest—for example, where the suit involves school policies which apply across the board to all students—the standing argument is stronger. If you are willing to accept the concept that the student government is an unincorporated association, much like a union, then it would be governed by the standing laws applicable to such groups. But I think that ultimately the standing question really depends on the nature of the claim being brought. The student government was one of the plaintiffs in a successful parking suit at Stony Brook in which we obtained a restraining order. The standing issue was not raised, but if it had been I think that the court probably would have found the student association had standing, since the school's policy of impounding automobiles affected all students.

## Subpoena of Student Records

**Carrington:** Mr. Kalaidjian, what do you do when you receive a subpoena asking for all the records you may have bearing on the activities and careers of certain named students?

**Kalaidjian:** When a university official gets such a subpoena he obviously has to call in counsel to review the records and see whether any of them fall in any of the classical privileges against disclosure. If they do, naturally those records would not be produced in response to the subpoena. If the files contain information that might be incriminatory or tend to degrade the student, the university might itself contest the subpoena, or suggest to the student that he, as the litigant, should contest it.

**Van Alstyne:** Customarily, subject to rather narrow exceptions, that subpoena will have to be honored. I think the university might try to resist by all means, as perhaps some have failed to do. But the real lesson, it seems to me, is not as to the policy of the university in making its records available; it is rather in its policy of making the records. The suggestion I mean to imply is that a university should not record anything which is not really essential to its academic purposes. If that practice is followed, the university has less worry about the subpoena process and less mistrust on the part of its students as well.

**Lippe:** Because of this danger, I think due process absolutely demands that a student be informed of what might be put on his record and given an opportunity to contest the validity of the notation. Substantial harm could be done later by such records, if the institution makes the records of students available to potential employers.

**Kalaidjian:** This raises a philosophical problem. Whether we like it or not, we all make our record as we go through life. I don't think that students ought to expect their university to cover their tracks. There is no walking away from what we do, there is no absolution through concealment, and I think that students should realize that they have to live with their acts.

**Carrington:** I have another question for you, Mr. Kalaidjian: What is the wisdom or propriety of asking for faculty and student participation in the decision to call the police?

**Kalaidjian:** We have provision for that at Columbia. The rules currently provide that representatives of the university rulemaking committee consult with the president about the decision to call the police in certain circumstances. The more support available, or if not support, the more understanding of the reason why the police are called, the better it is for all. Having the president consult with other campus elements helps to create some understanding of what was in the mind of the official when he took the action.

## University Counsel for Students

**Carrington:** Would it be useful or desirable or sound policy for a university or college to provide funds to establish a permanent relationship with counsel to represent students? Mr. Lippe, would you speak to that?

**Lippe:** I think it presents some very grave difficulties because of the attorney-client relationship. For example, our firm is on a strict retainer with the student government. The legal questions we direct ourselves to depend upon the wishes of the student government. If individual students call us, we instruct them to take their inquiries to the student government, which then determines whether we utilize our efforts in that particular situation. If the administration provided the funds for the attorney, it would create an awkward situation, because the university would have to make those decisions as to the individual. Even if the university were to say that such decisions could be made by the student government, it would create a bit of conflict for the attorney who is being paid by the university. The direct relationship is more sensible. The fee should not be paid by the university, because the attorney may in many cases be opposing the institution. In those schools where the administration makes a certain amount of money available to student government as part of its financial support, I suppose the university could provide funds for an attorney as well, without creating any big problem.

## Civil Liability of the University

**Carrington:** I have a question for Mr. Niehuss: What would be the civil liability of university officials who are alleged to be negligent in permitting counter-protest? Suppose we have a dispute between factions and damages for injuries are sought on the allegation that the university officials were negligent in failing to prevent or subdue the conflict.

**Niehuss:** I don't know the answer. You are suggesting that the university might be held accountable for having failed to call in police or their own security forces. I know of no case involving the issue. Columbia students, I believe, sued the trustees for creating a too liberal atmosphere at Columbia. We had a demonstration at Michigan which blocked a Navy recruiter and persons wishing to talk to him and counter-demonstrators appeared, trying to force their way in. One of the latter claimed that one of the protestors had assaulted him and he wanted to call the police, but that someone in the university administration had discouraged the idea. The student then threatened to sue someone for depriving him of protection. He apparently reconsidered.

# PART III

## Constitutional Considerations

# 7

# How Private are Private Institutions of Higher Education?

### William M. Beaney*

## Traditional Distinctions —
## Public and Private Institutions

Essentially, the problem in comparing the powers and duties of private and public institutions of higher learning with respect to their students is that the subject has not yet commanded sufficient attention by the courts to provide us with firm answers to the questions we would like to have answered. The law in this area is in a state of becoming, and the qualities of a prophet, rather than those of a scholar, are called for.

As commentators have pointed out, it is clearly possible for the courts to impose restrictions on private universities arising from the law of contracts, or from that body of ever-changing legal principles—the law of torts.

For although both private and public institutions have a penchant for including in their regulations sweeping assertions of their power to suspend or expel students on whatever grounds they find convincing, modern courts might well regard the contractual relationship as one of adhesion, and read in reasonable rules limiting arbitrary dismissals of students.

Similarly, students might claim tortious injury, where their education is interrupted and their reputation damaged by allegedly unfair suspension or dismissal, or an invasion of privacy or trespass

---

* Professor of Law, University of Denver College of Law, Denver, Colorado.

might be basis for a suit arising from an institutional intrusion into student rooms, lockers, etc.

Yet it must be recognized that the sparse record of court decisions in the past suggests that these common law avenues have not appealed to many students, and the generous treatment by courts of institutional claims of autonomy has resulted in even fewer successful claims.

Nevertheless, we should keep in mind the potentialities of these common law remedies, which may be used against private institutions as the courts are called upon to adjudicate more and more claims, *if* the courts refuse to treat private institutions as "public" with respect to their treatment of students.

The distinction between the two types of institutions, on the surface at least, is that public educational institutions, like all other governmental entities at the state level, are bound by the guarantees of the fourteenth amendment, and in our context, especially the equal protection of the laws and the due process of law clauses and implementing congressional enactments. The national government is similarly inhibited by the fifth amendment due process of law clause, which, by a legerdemain so familiar to lawyers, can be made to do service for an equal protection clause, as we learned in the 1954 school segregation cases.

Private persons, groups, associations, corporations, and, ostensibly, private educational institutions, do not appear to be limited by these constitutional limitations, though the public policy of a community, expressed through statutes, may ban discriminatory acts, and, in various other ways protect individuals against undesirable behavior by private persons. But, in the absence of such legislatively expressed policy, does the Constitution of the United States impose any limitations on "private" acts that, if deemed acts of the state, would infringe one or more constitutional provisions, or one or more acts of Congress designed to protect individuals against deprivation of their constitutional rights?

## Judicial Restrictions
## on Private Entities

The answer, simply stated, is that the courts have treated the conduct of a private entity as though it were public, when certain vital rights have been adversely affected by that conduct. Let me briefly cite some of the leading cases before dealing with the specific problem of the private colleges and universities. In *Marsh v. Alabama*[1] a town wholly owned by a private corporation was viewed by the Court in a 6–3 decision as though it were a typical municipality. Hence, Jehovah's Witnesses could not be punished under a state trespass law for distributing literature contrary to the wishes of the town's management. Justice Black, for the majority, rejected the contention that the town managers were in a position analogous to that of a homeowner. "The more an owner, for his advantage, opens up his property for use by the public in general, the more do his rights become circumscribed by the statutory and constitutional rights of those who use it . . . ,"[2] was Justice Black's broad explanation of why the public function of the privately owned town made the owner amenable to the Constitution. Another illustrative decision is *Shelley v. Kraemer*,[3] where the Supreme Court, 6–0, held unenforceable by the courts a covenant in a property deed restricting use and occupancy to the white race. Though the discriminatory action of the individual property holder was not in itself state action, the effort to enforce his purpose through a court order, the only way such a covenant would be effective, involved the state in the discriminatory behavior, and thus violated the equal protection clause. In *Barrows v. Jackson*[4] the same principle was invoked to prevent a suit by

1.    326 U.S. 501 (1946).

2.    *Id.* at 506.

3.    334 U.S. 1 (1948).

4.    346 U.S. 249 (1953).

one covenantor against another for damages for breach of covenant. Three later cases should be mentioned. In the first,[5] the Supreme Court held that the discriminatory policy of a private owner of a restaurant occupying leased space in a public parking authority violated equal protection of the laws. The Court also invalidated on the same ground an effort to substitute private trustees for the city of Macon, Georgia, in order to continue what for years had been a city-maintained segregated park, as provided in the will of a white donor.[6] The nature of the function and the close identification of the city and park for many years were cited as justifying the classification. Finally, in the 1968 decision in *Food Employees Local 590 v. Logan Valley Plaza, Inc.*[7] the Court held, 6–3, that the private owners of a shopping center could not prevent the exercise of a first amendment right of picketing private stores located in the center, citing *Marsh v. Alabama,* and stressing the public-like nature of modern shopping centers and the severe limitation of first amendment rights that would result if they were declared off-limits to protestants and pickets.

In summing up, these noneducational decisions seem to turn on whether private individuals or groups are endowed by the state with powers or functions governmental in nature, as in *Evans, Marsh* and *Logan Valley,* or the state is to some significant extent a participant in, or has a close relation to, the private activity, as in *Burton, Shelley, Barrows* or *Terry v. Adams,*[8] where a state had delegated an important aspect of the elective process to a private political association in a futile effort to avoid the accusation of state discrimination in voting. In both situations the affected person must raise an important constitutional claim.

-----

5.    Burton v. Wilmington Parking Authority, 365 U.S. 715 (1961).

6.    Evans v. Newton, 382 U.S. 296 (1966).

7.    391 U.S. 308 (1968).

8.    345 U.S. 461 (1953), *reh. denied,* 345 U.S. 1003 (1953).

## Constitutional Restrictions
## on Private Schools

When we try to discover when private colleges and universities may be treated as public with respect to constitutional guarantees for students, we have a limited number of cases, and the weight of opinion seems to support the position that at least for some purposes the "privateness" of institutions relieves them of constitutional obligations that inhibit state-supported institutions. A familiar formulation, although dictum, is set forth in *Zanders v. Louisiana State Board of Education:*

> [S]tudents in private schools do not have the same protected rights as those in public institutions concerning disciplinary proceedings because the constitutional reach of the Fourteenth Amendment clearly extends to State action but not to private action.[9]

Yet for reasons that I will advance later, I have considerable difficulty in accepting these decisions as reflecting the final position of the courts. Let me attempt a brief summary.

One of the most forthright statements denying a distinction between public and private institutions is in *Guillory v. Administrators of Tulane University,* where Judge J. Skelly Wright said, "[O]ne may question whether any school or college can ever be so 'private' as to escape the reach of the Fourteenth Amendment .... [A]dministrators of a private college .... do the work of the state, often in the place of the state. Does it not follow that they stand in the state's shoes?"[10] Yet, this is but dictum, since Judge Wright held that Tulane was in reality a public institution in its origin and development, and even in the modern era had sufficient ties to the state to render its actions "state actions."

---

9.   281 F. Supp. 747, 757 (W.D. La. 1968).

10.  203 F. Supp. 855, 858–59 (E.D. La. 1962), *judgment vacated in part,* 212 F. Supp. 674 (E.D. La. 1962).

Hence, a racially discriminatory admission policy could not stand. In a per curiam opinion, the University of Tampa, which considered itself a private institution, was found to have a sufficiently "public" nexus to inhibit racial discrimination in admissions (a surplus city building had been made available to the university's founders and city land had been leased to the institution).[11]

In other cases, the courts have refused to hold private institutions "public." Columbia University was not sufficiently "public," said a district judge in a suit for an injunction to bar disciplinary action against student leaders of the 1968 spring riots and building seizures,[12] to make its acts "under color" of state law, since the state did not participate in any significant way in Columbia affairs, and higher education was not a "public" function in the eyes of the law. The court did drop the cryptic comment that ". . . action in some context or other by such a university as Columbia would be subject to limitations like those confining the state."[13] After all, this was a case where the petitioners were claiming a first amendment right of expression manifest through seizure of buildings and disruption of the normal activities of the university. In a different context—perhaps racial discrimination in admissions or refusal to permit constitutionally approved forms of expression—a different result would follow.

In the University of Denver sit-in case,[14] the Tenth Circuit Court of Appeals held that institution to be private, in spite of significant tax benefits on property used for both educational and commercial purposes. Hence, the procedural guarantees of the fourteenth amendment were not applicable to student disciplinary proceedings.

---

11.  Hammond v. University of Tampa, 344 F.2d 951 (5th Cir. 1965).
12.  Grossner v. Trustees of Columbia Univ., 287 F. Supp. 535 (S.D.N.Y. 1968).
13.  *Id.* at 549.
14.  Browns v. Mitchell, 409 F.2d 593 (10th Cir. 1969).

Finally, there is the recently reported decision of the prestigious Second Circuit Court of Appeals in *Powe v. Miles*.[15] The facts are important and should be kept in mind. Alfred University is a small, private liberal arts university incorporated in 1857. In 1948 as part of a massive effort by the State of New York to develop a more substantial and coordinated statewide system of higher education the state asked Alfred to assume control of the New York State College of Ceramics, a state institution fully supported by the state. Alfred accepted the obligation to operate Ceramics, which was physically adjacent to its own campus, with the state agreeing to contribute annually an amount sufficient to cover all of Ceramics' direct costs, plus a portion of Alfred's total overhead, representing in all approximately 20 percent of Alfred's total financial income. The students of Alfred, including the Ceramics college, were governed by the same President, Dean of Students and regulations of conduct, took classes throughout the institution, and, except that Ceramics students concentrated in Ceramics while the remainder of Alfred's students only occasionally took courses in Ceramics, they were indistinguishable members of a single institution. But then came the day of the ROTC review and presentation of awards. Almost as if they perceived the potentialities of a future lawsuit, *three* Ceramics students and *four* Alfred students in the Liberal Arts College, holding signs protesting ROTC activities, the war in Vietnam, and asserting various demands, marched onto the field, and, unlike other demonstrators, refused to withdraw upon request and by their interference with the proceedings violated previously announced university regulations concerning demonstrations. The seven demonstrators, having been suspended, brought suit against Alfred's President and the University. Wielding a fine legal scalpel, the court determined that Alfred vis-à-vis its Ceramics students was a "public" institution. Alfred remained a private institution, however, as to its non-

---

15.   407 F.2d 73 (2d Cir. 1968).

Ceramics students. The Alfred non-Ceramics students were not protected by the fourteenth amendment—the Ceramics students were. I should quickly add that, fortunately, the procedures applied by Alfred to its Ceramics students were found to meet constitutional requirements, the court stressing that only the essential elements of due process, and not the refinements associated with cases in courts of law, were required of universities in disciplining students.

What are we to make of this curious situation in law? What are the practical lessons to be drawn from the present posture of legal doctrine?

Arguably, the courts can find a private institution to be "public" on the basis of benefits bestowed on an institution, contractual and other ties, or the similarity of its functions to that of public institutions *if* the courts choose to do so. When will courts choose to do so is the crucial question that remains. I suggest that courts will weigh the substantiality of the claim against the institution and the relevance and significance of the challenged institutional policy or act in the light of a private institution's announced purposes and educational program and decide which should prevail. Let me be more specific. A private institution with announced sectarian views may discriminate in admissions against those of other views—it may not be permitted to discriminate on racial grounds. A private institution may be permitted to enforce a well-advertised code of conduct for students. It may not normally act in such a way that it deprives students of their basic constitutional rights, though an exception may be recognized for sectarian institutions. A private institution may discipline students who violate its rules, but is it free to have ambiguous or overly general rules, and is it free of requirements of fairness, of due process, in the procedures used in suspending or expelling students? The justification for private colleges and universities has been their ability to provide valuable social services that otherwise would have to be established and supported by the state. In addition, they provide numerous options and opportunities for experimentation and special purposes that are desirable in a free, pluralistic society. Military, religious and other special function institutions enrich the educational sector of our society, but racial discrimination, denial of basic constitutional rights, or expulsion without fair procedures are indefensible attributes of "private" or "public" institutions. Private institutions, in short, must be able to justify their "privateness" in the future, and not regard it as an adequate basis for a short-hand negative response to student claims that receive constitutional protection in comparable public institutions of higher learning.

# 8

# The Constitutional Protection
# of Protest on Campus

## William W. Van Alstyne*

## The Joint Statement

The principal burden of my address is to provide a brief description of evolving constitutional law limitations on the authority of public universities to curtail forms of political expression on campus and to suspend or expel students by summary procedures. Because no other notice in this meeting has yet been taken of it, however, I want to begin by drawing your attention to a wholly extralegal document which may be of considerable practical importance on most campuses quite aside from its congruence with constitutional law. The document is the *Joint Statement on Rights and Freedoms of Students.*[1]

The *Joint Statement* originated in a standing committee of the American Association of University Professors in 1960. A final draft to the Association's satisfaction was finally devised in 1965. At that point it became a joint project, and it is the joint nature of the enterprise which suggests that the *Statement* may be extremely influential from campus to campus, because of its broad cross-sectional support. The *Statement* represents the declared policy not merely of the professoriat or the A.A.U.P. with its 90,000 members representing roughly one-third of all full-time faculty in accredited institutions of higher learning in the United States; it is the policy position of the Association of American

---

\*     Visiting Professor, Stanford University Law School. Professor of Law, Duke University Law School, Durham, North Carolina.
1.     54 A.A.U.P. Bull. 258 (1968), reprinted as Appendix A, *infra.*

Colleges, an administrative organization exclusively representing more than 900 institutions; it is the policy statement of the National Association of Student Personnel Administrators, representing several thousand deans, and of the National Association of Women Deans and Counselors, as well as the National Student Association (which these days enjoys a far more savory reputation than when SDS was not in the field as a rival on the Left). It is, I believe, this uniquely representative character of the *Joint Statement* which may secure its practical importance from place to place. Even if my remarks, which attempt to identify the standards of the *Joint Statement* with those of the fourteenth amendment as a matter of constitutional demand, should be proved inaccurate, or even if I have incorrectly anticipated the flow of judicial decisions and misjudged their degree of shared hostilities to student unrest—even so, the *Statement* is bound to have considerable influence as a bargaining point. Copies of the *Statement* can be secured through any of the organizations named above. Most of my remarks will dovetail with portions of that *Statement* quite precisely. Some sections of the *Statement*, moreover, have already been favorably adverted to by federal district courts on at least three occasions;[2] in at least one district court case[3] the *Joint Statement* position was adopted as essentially a

---

2. *See, e.g.*, Marzette v. McPhee, 294 F. Supp. 562 (W.D. Wis. 1968); Stricklin v. Regents of Univ. of Wisconsin, 297 F. Supp. 416 (W.D. Wis. 1969); Scoggin v. Lincoln Univ., 291 F. Supp. 161, 174 (W.D. Mo. 1968): "Adoption and compliance with the standards recommended to educational institutions by qualified persons from within their own ranks, undoubtedly would tend to keep the problems of student discipline on the campus and out of the courts. ... Institutions that have adopted and followed disciplinary procedures comparable to those recommended in the Joint Statement consistently have had their impositions of discipline sustained by the courts."

3. Stricklin v. Regents of Univ. of Wisconsin, *supra* note 2, at 420: "The standard embodied in my March 14 opinion, obviously, is the standard contained in the 'Joint Statement' quoted above. It is a fair and reasonable standard, entitled to recognition as an essential ingredient of

correct statement of fourteenth amendment demands. The sections of the *Statement* congruent with recent federal decisions include the statement of policy with regard to the prerogative of the students to support political causes on campus by any orderly means;[4] their prerogative to be critical through the student press, albeit a university-financed press;[5] their prerogative to invite guest speakers without restriction in the nature or content of such speeches or the political affiliations of the speakers;[6] and the procedural safeguards and specificity of rules which meet the standards of procedural due process.[7]

The *Joint Statement,* unlike the Constitution, makes no distinction between the public and the private institution, and I suppose the reason is self-evident: as a matter of sound educational instinct it is difficult to rationalize a distinction in terms of fundamentally fair standards. If it is true as a general proposition that legal counsel ought to be admitted to a student disciplinary proceeding to assure some modicum of fairness (though the extent of his

the procedural due process guaranteed by the Fourteenth Amendment."

4. *See, e.g.,* Tinker v. Des Moines Independent Community School Dist., 393 U.S. 503 (1969) (nondisruptive wearing of protest armbands on campus and even in classrooms is protected by the first amendment); Burnside v. Byars, 363 F.2d 744 (5th Cir. 1966) (nondisruptive wearing of protest buttons on campus and in classrooms is protected by the first amendment); Hammond v. South Carolina State College, 272 F. Supp.947 (D.S.C. 1967) (peaceful student demonstrations on campus protected by first amendment against vague, overly broad, and standardless regulation). *See also,* Lucas, Comment, 45 DENVER L.J. 622 (1968).

5. *See, e.g.,* Dickey v. Alabama State Bd. of Educ., 273 F. Supp. 613 (M.D. Ala. 1967); Pickering v. Bd. of Educ., 391 U.S. 563 (1968).

6. Brooks v. Auburn Univ., 296 F. Supp. 188, 195 (M.D. Ala. 1969), quoting approvingly the following which corresponds closely to the position of the *Joint Statement*: "The college may generally regulate the appearance of invited guest speakers only to an equivalent extent as may a civil polity regulate public facilities that are otherwise suitable as meeting places. It may establish neutral priorities (for example, giving preference to a regular academic event over an invitation to a guest

participation may be subject to the discretion of the hearing board), it is hard to determine why it is less true when the instutution is not technically a public one and, therefore, not technically required by the due process clause of the fourteenth amendment to accept that proposition. Indeed, the distinction between public and private institutions at least in matters of *procedure,* it may be suggested, seems much more difficult to argue as an original proposition than differences between public and private institutions in respect to the content of the substantive rules. Where students may in fact have a meaningful choice among colleges whose substantive rules reflect differing academic life styles, due regard for the values of pluralism in higher education should restrain us from condemning one or another institution and from seeking to bring each into colorless conformity with all others. Except in respect of freedom of speech, belief, critical inquiry, and access to untrammeled opinion, where it may fairly be suggested that an institution lacking these qualities falls short

---

speaker sought to be scheduled for the same time). It may require that the sponsoring organizations submit sufficient information to enable university officials to provide an orderly means of allocating facilities. It may oblige the speaker to assume full responsibility for any violation of law involved in his own conduct. It probably may require a statement that the views presented are not necessarily those of the institution or of the sponsoring group. But it may neither proceed by rules that are vague or that reserve unchecked discretion to censor, nor may it screen speakers according to their political affiliation, their subject matter, or their point of view." Snyder v. Bd. of Trustees of Univ. of Illinois, 286 F. Supp. 927 (N.D. Ill. 1968); Dickson v. Sitterson, 280 F. Supp. 486 (M.D.N.C. 1968); Student Liberal Action Fed'n v. Louisiana State Univ., Civ. No. 68-300 (E.D. La., Feb. 13, 1968); Stacy v. Williams, No. WC. 6725-K (N.D. Miss. Jan. 14, 1969); Danskin v. San Diego Unified School Dist., 171 P.2d 885 (1946), 28 Cal. 2d 536; Buckley v. Meng, 230 N.Y.S.2d 924 (Sup. Ct. 1962); East Meadow Community Concerts Ass'n v. Bd. of Educ., 18 N.Y.2d 129, 219 N.E.2d 172, 272 N.Y.S.2d 341 (1966), *reaff'd after remand,* 19 N.Y.2d 605, 224 N.E.2d 888, 278 N.Y.S.2d 393 (1967 *per curiam*). *See also,* Lucas, *supra* note 3; Pollitt, *Campus Censorship: Statutes Barring Speakers from State Educational Institutions,* 42 N.C.L. REV.

of academic freedom in any sense, there may be room enough in higher education for a variety of standards of a substantive kind (*e.g.*, diversity in social regulations), within reasonable degree.

The same position is more difficult to carry, however, in respect to procedural due process. If it is reasonable that the standards of an institution ought to be registered with sufficient clarity—that students know well in advance of committing themselves to a course of conduct whether what they propose to do is forbidden or is permitted—then it does not jar the notion of pluralism in higher education to require that the same standard apply within private institutions. Again, the *Joint Statement* makes no distinction. I can make none on educational grounds. I doubt whether, in the long run, the courts are going to make much of the distinction. Professor Beaney[8] discussed the fading distinction between the public and the private institutions for fourteenth amendment purposes. While some of the recent decisions have surprised me in their relative conservatism,[9] the fading character

---

179 (1963); Van Alstyne, *Political Speakers at State Universities: Some Constitutional Considerations*, 111 U. PA. L. REV. 328 (1963).

7. *See* note 2, *supra*; Esteban v. Central Mo. State College, 277 F. Supp. 649 (W.D. Mo. 1967), 290 F. Supp. 622 (W.D. Mo. 1968); Marzette v. McPhee, 294 F. Supp. 562 (W.D. Wis. 1968); Schiff v. Hannah, 282 F. Supp. 381 (W.D. Mich. 1966); Dixon v. Alabama State Bd. of Educ., 294 F.2d 150 (5th Cir.), *cert. denied*, 368 U.S. 930 (1961); Knight v. State Bd. of Educ., 200 F. Supp. 174 (M.D. Tenn. 1961).

8. *See* page 171 *supra*.

9. *See, e.g.*, Grossner v. Trustees of Columbia Univ., 287 F. Supp. 535 (S.D.N.Y. 1968); Greene v. Howard Univ., 271 F. Supp. 609 (D.D.C. 1967) (but pending outcome on appeal, the court of appeals issued a temporary restraining order reinstating the students, Civ. No. 1949-67, D.C. Cir., Sept. 8, 1967); Parsons College v. North Central Ass'n, 271 F. Supp. 65 (N.D. Ill. 1967); Guillory v. Administrators of Tulane Univ., 203 F. Supp. 855 (E.D. La. 1962), *judgment vacated in part*, 212 F. Supp. 674 (E.D. La. 1962). In Powe v. Miles, 407 F.2d 73 (2d Cir. 1968), Judge Friendly held that Alfred University was subject to the fourteenth amendment in respect to one of its colleges but not as to another part of its operation. Assuming that courts may make distinctions of "state action" in the different facilities or programs within a

of the distinction is a trend I expect to see continued. With the trend toward heavy federal supplements to private institutions, given the so-called quasi-public nature of education itself, the constitutional distinction is almost certain to continue its decline for most significant purposes.[10] But even as a pragmatic matter, most private institutions which want to rest on the legal privacy of their corporate prerogatives are resting on the proverbial frail reed, under the circumstances.

# Minimum Procedural Guarantees of the Constitution

## Qualifications

The constitutionally evolving minimum procedural guarantees of the fifth amendment and the fourteenth amendment due process clauses by definition apply thus far only to governmentally assisted bodies. Thus, the ensuing discussion is perhaps irrelevant to any university which is technically private for constitutional purposes. At the same time, even in the area of

---

given institution, it would appear inevitable that the rules and regulations applicable to the whole of the university would, as a practical matter, have to be uniform and in accordance with fourteenth amendment requirements.

10. *See e.g.,* Judge Wright's Opinion in the "first" Guillory case, *supra;* Commonwealth v. Brown, 370 F. Supp. 782 (E.D. Pa. 1967), *aff'd,* 392 F.2d 120 (3d Cir. 1968), *cert. denied,* 391 U.S. 921 (1968); Sweetbriar Institute v. Button, Civ. No. 66-C-10-L (W.D. Va. 1967); Food Employees Local 590 v. Logan Valley Plaza, Inc., 391 U.S. 308 (1968); Evans v. Newton, 382 U.S. 296 (1966); Burton v. Wilmington Parking Authority, 365 U.S. 715 (1961); Eaton v. Grubbs, 329 F.2d 710 (4th Cir. 1964); Terry v. Adams, 345 U.S. 461 (1953). Cohen, *The Private-Public Legal Aspects of Institutions of Higher Education,* 45 DENVER L.J. 643 (1968); Note, *Private Government on the Campus— Judicial Review of University Expulsions,* 72 YALE L.J. 1362 (1963). American Communications Ass'n v. Douds, 339 U.S. 382, 401 (1950) ("When authority derives in part from Government's thumb on the scales, the exercise of that power by private persons becomes closely

contracts, there are a few court decisions respecting private institutions which have tried to and have begun to read into the field of private university student contracts a concept of unconscionability, a concept which tends to set aside boilerplate clauses in student handbooks reserving almost unilateral, total prerogative to modify rules or to compose ad hoc grounds for expulsion and other sanctions. With regard to the private institution, where the relationship is, strictly speaking, still contractual and not constitutional, there is a very modest trend, even in the common law courts, to second-guess the intrinsic rock-bottom fairness of such boilerplate clauses.[11] I mention this in passing merely as an eminently practical matter. Traditionally, of course, knowledgeable house counsel serving the interests of his college clients would almost routinely put into the contract, or the handbook that is incorporated by reference into that contract, this large reservation of authority. It could always be used to fall back upon in case of subsequent litigation and friction between the student and university. I suggest that the boilerplate provisions in the field of private higher education, rather than being especially serviceable to the institution, may now be positively destructive; that is to say, such a provision may void the effort to discipline under it, when something a little bit more specific, a little less rugged, would have been sustained by the courts.

The concept of procedural due process is not a frozen thing. It does not refer to a single fixed style of procedure. The general observation of the Supreme Court has been that the quality of the procedure must be directly proportioned to the gravity of the harm which may befall the individual whose guilt is ascertained

---

akin, in some respects, to its exercise by Government itself.")

11.  *See* Drucker v. New York Univ. 293 N.Y.S.2d 923 (Civ. Ct. 1968) (tuition refunded in spite of contrary provision which student had not in fact seen but which was expressly incorporated by reference into his contract of matriculation). For further discussion, *see* Van Alstyne, *The Student as University Resident,* 45 DENVER L.J. 582, 583-84 note 1 (1968).

pursuant to that procedure. The degree of procedural due process is a function of the seriousness of the offense, to put it in a more direct manner. If all that can happen at the terminus of a given dispute between a student and a counselor or a dean is an oral reprimand or the temporary suspension of some social privilege, not even the most ambitious, intrusive federal court will require a quasi-judicial proceeding to be had before allowing the dormitory manager or the appropriate dean or someone else to dispose of such disputes with great informality. Thus, my remarks on a stepped-up concept of procedural due process apply only to those kinds of offenses which can result in substantial jeopardy to the student's academic career. Expulsion is the most obvious such jeopardy and suspension might well qualify also.

Certain offenses for which there is no suspension may, in the long term, have much more invidious consequences and, therefore, should require the kind of procedure I will outline. Such an offense might have grave consequences because the published determination of guilt carries with it a degree of stigma damaging to the ensuing career of the student. For example, an allegation and a finding that the student had committed an act of homosexuality may result only in referral to a psychiatrist or something of that sort; but such a finding noted on the student's permanent record subsequently to be made available to inquiring third parties—prospective employers and the like—is at least as damaging as suspension for a term. The procedural due process to be outlined, which will seem unreasonably demanding to some and which is not uniformly supported by current federal court decisions, is, therefore, intended to be applicable only to the grave cases.

Further, nothing in the system I mean to outline need displace the effort by the university, in the first instance, to dispose of alleged violations by highly informal process, so long as there is an opportunity reserved to the student to insist upon a de novo hearing, if he is in disagreement with the integrity of the finding or the appropriateness of the discipline sought to be imposed in the very informal proceeding. The outcome of such a de novo hearing, however, must be totally unprejudiced and uninfluenced by whatever may have transpired between the student and the administration in the informal proceeding. While there is nothing in the system of due process which says that a university need dispense with attempts at informal reconciliation, this single cautionary note should be sounded. The desire of the university to economize or to preserve its style of intimacy with the student, in a more affirmative sense, by trying even grave offenses by mere informal interview with an appropriate official as a first step, is a sustainable enterprise if, but only if, nothing that transpires there carries over to a subsequent hearing in the event the student is dissatisfied with the result. Otherwise, the formal hearing serves no protective function. To the extent that information which the student may have disclosed in the counseling situation may be used against him in the formal situation, the formal hearing itself becomes quite a useless enterprise and its legitimacy is in question.

With all of the caveats mentioned above, an essential outline of evolving standards is fairly simple to provide. I have tried to do so in pieces published in the *Denver Law Journal*,[12] the *U.C.L.A. Law Review*[13] and the *Florida Law Review*.[14] (Consequently, I propose to avoid the waste and further duplication of footnotes for supporting documentation which may be found in those articles and in notes 2–7 *supra*.)

## Requirements of Procedural Due Process

The first step in due process has to do with the necessity for or

---

12. Van Alstyne, *The Student as University Resident*, 45 DENVER L.J. 582 (1968).
13. Van Alstyne, *Procedural Due Process and State University Students*, 10 U.C.L.A. L. REV. 368 (1963).
14. Van Alstyne, *The Judicial Trend Toward Student Academic Freedom*, 20 FLA. L. REV. 290 (1968).

degree of clarity of rules. The authority of the university to discipline students based upon no rules whatever but upon a claim of an inherent authority to maintain order or to police minimum conditions of civilized conduct on campus has already been discussed in this seminar.[15] In civil society, of course, action taken by the state in the absence of any law forbidding conduct with sufficient clarity that reasonable men may know in advance what is forbidden would be held flatly to deny due process. Indeed, it involves the concept of an ex post facto law. And to the extent that there is no rule published in advance by the university and available to inform a student of what he is forbidden to do, and he discovers only after he has committed himself to a course of action that it is now declared to have been wrongful, the procedure has the unsavory flavor of an ex post facto law. Several of the courts have nonetheless sustained expulsion proceedings based upon the claim of inherent authority. To the best of my knowledge, this has occurred only in cases where the nature of the student's conduct, actually established in a fair hearing, was such that no reasonable student could have imagined that the conduct would not be punishable or that it was permitted—cases involving arson or the physical and long-term occupation of buildings or the willful destruction of property. In such situations, a claim that there was no rule giving advance warning that the act might be subject to discipline sounds entirely enfeebled and, in fact, quite dishonest. There is still some sense in the traditional lawyer's distinction—denigrated by professors in criminal law these days— between a kind of *malum in se* and *malum prohibitum.* To the extent that the conduct in question is of a serious nature, one cannot get terribly exercised about the claim of surprise, the ex post facto claim. But the *malum prohibitum* concept, it may be suggested, should advise one that there are numerous areas, given the heterogeneity of faculties and student bodies, where people

---

15. *See* page 94 *supra.*

may reasonably question whether something is permitted or forbidden. If the university draws from any substantial geographic area, any control of dress style, for example, should be set out in crisp and specific rules published and accessible to students. Such matters as class attendance and rules of social behavior should be spelled out in preexisting rules, if such conduct is to be appropriately subject to discipline.

Additionally, I should not wish to be misunderstood as commending a system of campus justice which presumes to operate upon a claim of inherent authority, substantially without rules. Indeed, I do not agree with those courts which rely upon such devices, nor do I think that the ex post facto quality of certain exercises of inherent authority exhaust the objections against it. The absence of regularly adopted, reasonably clear rules encourages at least three other difficulties. First, but not least as a practical consideration, it invites dispute and controversy which could be avoided; not all students or faculty will readily assume the legitimacy of this sort of power nor are many likely to agree, except in the most extreme case, whether the conduct was of such a kind that those engaging in it should have expected to be punished. After all, we are more accustomed to plan our affairs on a presumption that that which is not prohibited is permitted, rather than the more totalitarian opposite. Second, the claim of inherent power is readily subject to abuse; one cannot help but suspect that it may sometimes result in denials of equal protection, *e.g.*, that a raucous campus demonstration to celebrate a football game will not incur sanctions but a demonstration no less disruptive, directed to a less popular political issue, may suddenly bring forth the use of inherent power to punish. It is true that the presence of a clear published rule is itself no guarantee against its unequal application, of course, but surely it is better by significant degree than to permit a university administration to compose a rule ad hoc, when its determination to do so must inevitably be influenced by its sympathy with or hostility to the particular

conduct in question. Third, even within the precincts of a
university there may be wisdom in opting for a system of
legislative due process, *i.e.*, an arrangement where the formulation
of rules is not exclusively the business of those who also decide
when a particular charge shall be brought. A claim of inherent
authority neglects the salutary separation of functions and powers,
however, and lends itself to additional criticism on that account.

## The Priority of First Amendment Freedoms

The growing magnitude of one exception almost swallows up
the claim that the university can ever act on the basis of its
inherent authority. That exception seems to exist in the field of
first amendment freedoms: freedom of speech, freedom of peaceable assembly, freedom to petition government, including the
public institutional government, for redress of grievances. A very
large pattern of Supreme Court decisions in this area imposes a
spectacular degree of precision and narrowness and specificity in
rulemaking. A rule which is even marginally broader than it
constitutionally may be under the first amendment demands is in
peril of being held void on its face, even though the conduct
involved in the case where the challenge to the rule arises is
conduct which the institution clearly could have proscribed had
the rule been drawn with a becoming specificity and clarity. Even
the very guilty man who has misbehaved in a substantially harmful
manner and gone well beyond protected first amendment rights
may sometimes get free under the doctrine that the rule or the
statute is void on its face for vagueness or overbreadth. There are
no less than six federal district court decisions[16] so holding.

16. Soglin v. Kauffman, 295 F. Supp. 978 (W.D. Wis. 1968); Snyder v. Bd.
of Trustees of Univ. of Illinois, 286 F. Supp. 927 (N.D. Ill. 1968);
Dickson v. Sitterson, 280 F. Supp. 486 (M.D.N.C. 1968); Hammond v.
South Carolina State College, 272 F. Supp. 947 (D.S.C. 1967); Stacy v.
Williams, No. WC. 6725-K (N.D. Miss. 1969); Student Liberal Action
Federation v. Louisiana State Univ., Civ. No. 68-300 (E.D. La., Feb. 13,

Indeed, one from South Carolina[17] applied precisely to this point. It was provided by rule that a demonstration could not be held on campus without the prior consent of the president of the institution. Though the particular demonstration was highly disruptive—this was one on the Orangeburg State College campus shortly before the so-called Orangeburg Massacre—the students suspended under the rule were reinstated by federal court. The court simply held the rule void on its face because it capriciously entrusted arbitrary discretion to the president, giving him freedom to pick and choose among demonstrations without any listing of criteria to control his judgment. The reason for this amazing result—amazing to laymen, at least—is simply that freedom of speech and freedom of peaceable assembly are regarded by the Supreme Court not merely as constitutionally protected but constitutionally precious, constitutionally important things that society must not discourage. The presence of the vague, the ambulatory, the standardless or the overly extensive rule, the mere presence of the published rule, it is felt, tends to produce a chilling effect even with regard to the protected areas of speech. To the extent that the rule seems to forbid even those demonstrations which would be constitutionally protected, the students are discouraged by the presence of the rule from conducting even the legitimate form of protest. Thus, one who has conducted the illegitimate protest can utilize the objection that the rule is void on its face. I am suggesting that to the extent the institution relies on the rule, certainly in the first amendment area, in the protest area, it must not rely on a boilerplate position; it must have very narrow, very specific, very precise rules that go no further in the control of demonstrations on campus than the substantive law of the first

---

1968); Buckley v. Meng, 230 N.Y.S.2d 924 (Sup. Ct. 1962). *See also* Keyishian v. Bd. of Regents (and cases cited therein), 385 U.S. 589 (1967).

17.   Hammond v. South Carolina State College, note 16 *supra*.

amendment entitles the university to reach under those circumstances. Assuming the requisite specificity of the rule, among those things which are now required to discipline for any grave offense, I would list the several items discussed below.

A student must not only be charged pursuant to a specific rule, but must be charged with some kind of specific notice of the alleged misconduct, alleged to violate the rule itself. The charge must be placed in ample time before any hearing, of course, to insure that he has reasonable opportunity to prepare for the hearing.

While a majority of the courts so far examining the question have held that even a public institution need not permit a student to be represented by retained counsel,[18] either as counsel or simply as an adviser, at least two courts have held to the contrary.[19] This is an evolving area. Indeed, until 1961 there was no federal decision holding that the quality of procedural due process applied to public university students at all.[20] Thus, competent house counsel reading precedents in 1960 could say that there were no demands. Competent counsel reading them today could still say that counsel is not required under the majority rule, but he would not be reading trends. The presence of counsel in an advisory role is an emerging trend. To the best of my knowledge, those universities that have permitted counsel to

18. *See, e.g.,* Barker v. Hardway, 283 F. Supp. 228 (S.D. W.Va. 1968), *aff'd per curiam,* 399 F.2d 638 (4th Cir. 1968), *cert. denied,* 394 U.S. 905 (1969).

19. *See* Esteban v. Central Mo. State College, 277 F. Supp. 649 (W.D. Mo. 1967), 290 F. Supp. 622 (W.D. Mo. 1968); Goldwyn v. Allen, 54 Misc. 2d 94, 281 N.Y.S.2d 899 (Sup. Ct. 1967); Madera v. Bd. of Educ., 267 F. Supp. 356 (S.D.N.Y. 1967), *rev'd,* 386 F.2d 778 (2d Cir. 1967) (on grounds that the hearing was not essentially disciplinary or penal, but more in the nature of counseling to determine the appropriate school in which petitioner should be placed), *cert. denied,* 390 U.S. 1028 (1968).

20. Dixon v. Alabama State Bd. of Educ., 294 F.2d 150 (5th Cir.), *cert. denied,* 368 U.S. 930 (1961). *See also* Knight v. State Bd. of Educ., 200 F. Supp. 174 (M.D. Tenn. 1961).

participate in hearings have not found it unduly awkward, time-consuming or expensive. As a practical matter, the university will ordinarily have to put counsel on the other side as well. The informality of proceedings in which the commission both hears and adjudicates and really informally prosecutes by asking the questions and bringing in the witnesses, probably cannot long endure once retained counsel represents the students. An intermediate position at those universities having law schools, a position which probably will continue to be acceptable to the federal courts, is to supply a senior law student as counsel for a student charged with an offense. The quality of the advice of such counsel would probably be regarded by the courts as substantial enough to assure the minimum rights of the student charged: the opportunity to testify, the opportunity to hear witnesses and demand that the hearing committee decide the matter exclusively on the basis of what is presented in the hearing (a standard administrative law requirement) and probably the opportunity to cross-examine. Occasionally a court has said that cross-examination is not itself indispensable. The Court of Appeals for the Fifth Circuit took the position that in the absence of an opportunity to cross-examine, the student at least would have to be given the names of all witnesses who appeared against him plus a resumé of all things to which those witnesses testified, in order to put him in a suitable position to respond.[21]

In regard to the question of trial by one's peers, it is suggested that the sixth amendment notion of trial by jury in that sense is unlikely to be important. The students have a calm and rational policy claim for some representation of their own peers on the hearing boards, but I do not anticipate a federal court decision to that effect.

---

21. Dixon v. Alabama State Bd. of Educ., 294 F.2d 150 (5th Cir.), *cert. denied*, 368 U.S. 930 (1961).

In regard to Mr. Farer's[22] suggestion that a mixed tribunal, representative of the cross sections of the university community—administration, faculty and students—seems highly desirable as a matter of policy, even to judge matters affecting the faculty, I must say that I am professionally embarrassed. As a matter of law, no doubt the academic career of tenured members of the faculty may be put in jeopardy before a committee composed in part of students, but under the standards of the A.A.U.P., which are policed by its censure of noncomplying institutions, the academic career of a faculty member who has tenure may not be placed in jeopardy before a committee in which students have any role at all. The honeymoon on representative tribunals stops there, however selfish it may outwardly seem.

Thus far no university proceeding has been regarded as sufficiently criminal in character that a student could justly claim the privilege against self-incrimination. There is, however, the crossover problem referred to earlier[23]—the very practical problem of the student who is involved or alleged to be involved in a demonstration and also arrested on a downtown charge. I quite agree that the university need not suspend its proceeding on the basis that the information thus required of the student might be used to his inconvenience in the downtown prosecution. I agree also that if it is a state university putting the student on trial, and he is obliged to discuss the transaction or risk losing the case on campus, nothing he discloses may be admitted in evidence downtown or even used to furnish a further lead for investigation of that charge.[24]

22. See page 80 supra.

23. See page 93 supra.

24. This may be an overstatement. The Supreme Court has held, however, that inculpatory statements made by a public employee under threat of being fired unless he answers questions immediately related to his employment may not subsequently be introduced into evidence against him in a criminal prosecution. See Gardner v. Broderick, 392 U.S. 273 (1968); Garrity v. New Jersey, 385 U.S. 493 (1967). Arguably,

Some students in the private universities will complain, but so far as I know there is no restriction on the use, in the criminal proceeding, of information forceably required to be given by the student on campus, if the institution is private rather than public. There may exist, to this extent, a remnant of the silver-platter doctrine—the notion that the state is not involved in the act of compelling self-incrimination, because that is done by an institution which is by definition not a state university. The state does not induce it and does not solicit it, and the information is not acquired by the state in any improper way. Thus, while the private institution may go ahead with its hearings in this situation, the students can raise a very considerable grievance that the procedure is unfair, because that information can, in all likelihood, still be used against them downtown.

## Mass Disruptive Behavior — Due Process Problems

With regard to the new style of protest involving such large numbers of people, it would appear that the deliberate processes of the kinds of hearings one is inclined to outline are simply not feasible. They present new problems, one of which is the use of interim emergency suspension, a technique that has been actively considered and sometimes employed at a number of campuses— San Francisco State, San Jose and recently at Stanford, which has had an interminable series of demonstrations this spring.

If the elaborate system one is inclined to outline is genuinely

---

therefore, a state university may coerce self-incriminatory statements from a student to determine his continuing eligibility to remain on campus but the state could not subsequently utilize such statements against him in a regular criminal prosecution. *See* Furutani v. Ewigleben, 297 F. Supp. 1163 (N.D. Cal. 1969).

required in each case, the time consumed between the alleged infraction and the processing of these many cases permits the students to remain on campus until a decision of guilt has been reached in the deliberative process; in the meantime they may repeat the disruptive behavior. If they are arrested, they may post bail and come back to campus and continue the disruption. Thus, there is a felt urgency for some power of interim suspension. Yet, since the suspension is made without any hearing, there would seem again to be a procedural due process objection. Is the student suspended on the basis that he is guilty of violating the valid disruptive conduct rules? That does not seem plausible, for there has been no hearing to determine that. If that is the rationale of the suspension, it is probably enjoinable immediately in a federal court. If there is a rationale, it can only be that there is sufficient reason to suppose that the continuing presence of the student on campus, after he is charged under the rule but pending the outcome of the hearing on the merits of the charge, constitutes a substantial hazard to the property or to the other members of the university community. That reasoning will be respected by the courts, up to a point. But a recent federal court decision[25] suggests that the interim suspension is sufficiently serious to require that the student must be given an opportunity within three days, roughly, to appear before someone to provide assurance that his presence on campus pending his hearing is not in fact, and will not in fact be used as a threat of disorder. In short, even with the power of emergency suspension, one must build in a brief informal hearing so that a student may reasonably satisfy someone that in fact his presence, pending an outcome of a fair hearing for an alleged violation of the rules, will not be disruptive. On such a rationale, a number of students at the University of Wisconsin

---

25. Stricklin v. Regents of Univ. of Wisconsin, 297 F. Supp. 416 (W.D. Wis. 1969). *See also* Marzette v. McPhee, 294 F. Supp. 562 (W.D. Wis. 1968).

were suspended for only three weeks pending a hearing. They were reinstated by federal order on the grounds that with no opportunity to test the basis of the interim suspension itself, they had been denied procedural due process as required by the fourteenth amendment.

There is another practical problem in disciplining students for mass disruptive behavior. In the mass situation, where the means of identifying the participants and getting evidence against them is so lacking, even the most conscientious tribunal tries to make do with a kind of second-rate form of evidence. Such a situation has been recently reviewed by the federal court in San Francisco.[26] The case involved the many hundreds of San Francisco State University students allegedly involved in the disruption there. As there were not enough witnesses, not enough photographs, not enough firsthand evidence to make the case, the hearing committee at the university relied in each case upon the police record of arrest as sufficient to establish disruptive conduct in violation of the rule, in the absence of any evidence to the contrary offered by the student. A number of students were put on probation and some were suspended. They proceeded to the federal district court, before Judge Zirpoli. He has recently ordered their reinstatement on constitutional grounds.[27] The basis for the order is very straightforward: the mere recordation by a police officer that he placed Mr. X under arrest at a given time and place does not by itself show, even by substantial evidence, that Mr. X was violating the disruptive conduct rule of the university. It is consistent with the known information, for instance, that he was a spectator at the time, or a passerby at the scene, or was there trying to render aid to someone else. The evidence by itself is not enough. This is a final kind of constitutional caveat—given the procedural integrity of the hearing board and the regularity of its rules, ultimately all

---

26.   Wong v. Hayakawa, No. 50983 (N.D. Cal., April 24, 1969).

27.   *Id.*

must be backed by some form of written record containing substantial evidence, considered as a whole, that the material elements of the campus rule have in fact been violated. That is a rather stringent test to meet, in view of the mass civil disobedience on campus, but it seems, nonetheless, to be an emerging constitutional demand.[28]

---

28.  An exceptionally comprehensive and useful article which appeared too late for earlier reference in this conference is: *Wright, The Constitution on Campus*, 22 VAND. L. REV. 1027 (1969).

# 9

## Panel Discussion — II

### Freedom of Expression

**Carrington:** Professor Van Alstyne, to what extent is demonstration which employs obscene language, amplified by bullhorn, constitutionally protected?

**Van Alstyne:** Very little. The question really is lifted from the *Goldberg*[1] case. That case was the deteriorated end of the free speech movement, as I recall. It then became the filthy speech movement. Large groups of students were holding four-letter spellouts over loudspeaking systems. They were disciplined and sought reinstatement on first amendment grounds.

The most recent Supreme Court opinion,[2] quite properly in my judgment, scaled down the offense of obscenity, or the use of obscenity under circumstances where it may be made an offense by a state or by a community or by a university, to a "time, place and manner" common sense standard. The recent decision reversing the conviction of an individual merely for possessing obviously obscene matter seems to me to indicate the so-called real nature of obscenity. The real nature, now, is largely aesthetic. It is the use of certain kinds of expository styles under circumstances where the speaker must know that the use of the words will be repugnant to other people who are unwilling auditors. Thus, it would seem that punishability of obscenity has now become largely a function of

---

1.  Goldberg v. Regents of Univ. of Calif., 248 Cal. App. 2d 867, 57 Cal. Rptr. 463 (1967).

2.  Stanley v. Georgia, 394 U.S. 557 (1969).

the time and place and manner of its use. The *Goldberg* court in this respect is probably correct. The deliberate use, before a captive audience, of obscene language that offends their sensibilities may appropriately be made the subject of discipline without violating first amendment standards. That is the essence of the offense. It becomes a harder case if the obscenity is printed in the student underground press, which one must volunteer to read. It becomes a bit more awkward to say that we should be able to forbid the use of obscenity in such a publication, even though the consuming public knows in advance the nature of the publication, since it has appeared on campus before and they must volunteer to be offended. The answer is not clear. It's possible that some courts will allow the control to extend that far, but I think it is doubtful on policy grounds.

**Carrington:** What of the students who choose simply to sit on the front steps of the administration building, leaving a small corridor for people to get through and not closing the building altogether? Is that conduct constitutionally protected?

**Van Alstyne:** One has to take it in three steps. I will answer you directly and then give you the three steps. If the case were exactly that way, I think a fine argument could be made that the activity was protected. The three steps or three elements involved in the determination are these:

If we have a seemingly neutral rule which simply said there must be no assembly of any kind within 100 yards of the administration building or any other academic building, the rule is not on its face an anti-speech regulation. The rule appears to separate the protection of free speech from the place where speech may take place. Free speech is not infringed. Fair enough. The perplexity of that point of view is, however, that none of us—as Eric Sevareid observed when Mr. Justice Black made this distinction in his interview on CBS—none of us thus far has discovered a way of inventing a platform in the air, because our ability effectively to reach an audience can't be separated from some prerogative to choose a place from which to speak. Thus, the majority of the Supreme Court has not accepted the distinction—a flat distinction that says so long as the regulation is not anti-speech on its face, not directed to the prohibition of expression, but is merely a neutral ban on assemblies of any type for any purpose on public property, it is enough. The Supreme Court has said it is not enough. The justification must be that under the particular circumstances the style of communication rises above the level of mere inconvenience or petty annoyance, and is at least in substantial conflict with the accomplishment of other legitimate uses to be made of the property. Thus, clearly congestive picketing, clearly disruptive or raucous demonstrations, clamorously interfering with classes, blocking access, are clearly subject to prohibition by a university as they are by responsible state law.

The usual test in this field is really that the manifestation of expression, in terms of the style and the manner of communication, must rise above the level of mere inconvenience or annoyance to be subject to regulation. Once it does, a rule may properly be invoked. There is one possible exception. I have perhaps overstated the protection of the first amendment to that extent— to the extent that the university may restrict or forbid any form of picketing or assembly or even handbilling, in very limited places, leaving many alternatives in meaningful forms free for peaceful demonstration on campus. To be specific, I think it not unlikely that a court would uphold a flat ban on picketing inside academic buildings, even as against a particular picketing that happened to occur in a corridor at a time when there was no class in session, so that in point of fact it turned out not to be disruptive. But the restriction is so marginal, given alternative forms and given the administrative inconvenience of having to make ad hoc decisions, that limited restrictions of certain kinds of inside facilities would seem to be tolerable. If you were to expand this ban, on the other hand, to forbid even handbilling or the distribution of leaflets within the student union, I would suspect that that regulation is subject to constitutional reproach. The student union is a central traffic area—a place where people mix and can readily be reached through the peaceful distribution of leaflets. This is largely a matter of trading off interests, of balancing the vitality of the first amendment conduct against competing interests, legitimate interests, to be served on campus.

## Search of Student Quarters

**Carrington:** I will ask Mr. Kalaidjian to what extent the university should feel inhibited in conducting a search of rooms for firearms or a search for women. What kind of information do you need to conduct such a search, and under what circumstances can you use the results?

**Kalaidjian:** The rule seems to be that a university authority requires less information to render a search reasonable than would be required to get a warrant. As a practical matter, however, the business of search has to be done most judiciously. I don't believe university people ought to be popping in and out of rooms indiscriminately. They must have some very substantial grounds for believing that something very serious is going on in the room to justify it as a matter of policy and law.

**Van Alstyne:** The *Joint Statement* provision on student privacy and circumstances for search sets essentially the same standards that the federal courts have used under the fourth amendment with regard to private citizens; that is to say, no particular distinction is made because the university may own the property. In our judgment that is no more worthy a consideration for an intrusion into privacy than the fact that the state owns public housing. Such state ownership does not justify fishing expeditions into the tenants' apartments. There are, so far as I know, only two federal court decisions. The more impressive one out of Alabama, decided by Judge Johnson, does suggest that the fourth amendment applies. Students have a constitutional right to privacy even in a college-owned dormitory, but quite rightly, something less than the degree of probable cause required of a policeman will suffice. Nonetheless, there must be some specific reason to suppose that a rather grave offense has taken place or is taking place, or that the evidence of that offense can be secured in the student apartment. This development of the law is less than a year old. Until a year ago, comfortable counsel might have said, "Why, it's outrageous! There is no such thing as a student right to privacy; we have this form that every student signs, consenting to search of his apartment." I assure you that such consent is absolutely worthless in this area. It has no more validity today than the act of a public housing authority in coercing such consent from a tenant and then relying upon it for a fishing expedition search. That practice has already been thrown out by the federal court.

**Lippe:** I believe that the whole area of requirement of warrants may well insert itself in here, apart from the reasonable circumstances of the particular search. Many of you are probably familiar with the cases decided by the Supreme Court in the housing inspection area, especially *See v. Seattle*.[3] In that case it was clear that a warrant was required even in the administrative type of search in which a municipality wanted to make spot checks in a whole area. A warrant is now required in those situations, although the nature of the evidence that must be brought before the judge for the issuance of the warrant will vary, depending upon the need of the municipality and the kind of infringement on the individual's privacy. *People v. Overton*[4] allowed a search by police officers of a student's high school locker and narcotics were found. The judgment in that case, upheld in the New York courts, has now been vacated by the Supreme Court and the case sent back to the New York courts for

---

3.    387 U.S. 541 (1967).
4.    51 Misc. 2d 140, 273 N.Y.S.2d 143, 20 N.Y.2d 360 (1967).

reconsideration. Unfortunately, the Court seems to be implying that the consent of the high school principal to the search was under duress and thus invalid. Apparently the Court is trying to avoid the issue of search in an educational institution. However, there is a good chance that that case will go right back up again. If so, the Supreme Court may be forced to give an answer on that issue.

## Mass Hearings

**Carrington:** One question for Professor Van Alstyne: If you have 100 offenders, is there any way of getting them all into one hearing and getting the matter cleaned up with efficiency and dispatch?

**Van Alstyne:** I feel somewhat diffident about this. There certainly is no legal impropriety in holding a joint trial, and I don't believe that even with the assistance of counsel the student could constitutionally insist upon a separate trial, despite the possibility that a kind of prejudice may occur because of testimony in one part of the trial that relates to another student. Stanford has had a number of such trials. Most recently, a group of about 65 students were tried at one time. This procedure was made more feasible because the group agreed to be represented by three law students, doing away with the possible disruption of having individual attorneys.

I wanted to say something about the demand for a public trial. It seems to me that the trial, having been made public, then sets the scene for further disruption, completely undermining the fair and essential function of an orderly hearing. Surely there is no legal requirement for a public trial in the sense of a massive amphitheater for the amusement of the spectators. The provision for public trial in the sixth amendment is not for the edification of the public—it is for the protection of the accused. That function is adequately served if there are permitted in the hearing room two or three neutral outside observers. I think there is wide misunderstanding here. Universities frequently invite really enormous distress because their hearing tribunals can't possibly cope with a disruptive audience. They are under no commitment whatever to stage these hearings as carnival spectacles.

## Due Process for High School Students

**Carrington:** Professor Van Alstyne, would you distinguish between college students and high school students with respect to the concepts of procedural due process?

**Van Alstyne:** I would not. It is a bit unclear as to whether the courts will make that distinction, but I think the inclination is against it. You can make quite a different case on the substantive side, depending in part on the age of the person involved. At some point, every one of us is going to admit that at some lesser age it is appropriate for some third party to take a degree of supervisory responsibility over that young person that you would regard as singularly officious and inappropriate in the context of higher education. I yield to that thought, perhaps, at a different level than each of you would. To put it specifically, I have no doubt that a high school may police styles of social behavior and that they may have rules forbidding or permitting students to belong to social clubs of a rather exclusive and snobbish form. These are younger people and the case for in loco parentis is more compelling in some areas of life. With regard to protected forms of political discussion, the distinction begins to fade out against the axioms of the Constitution.

On the procedural side, I don't understand the basis for making the distinction. To be sure, if a high school student is genuinely being counseled and assisted and there is no prospect of a penalty—the school counselor is without any disciplinary authority and without any obligation to report the student's remarks to the principal—the greatest informality is highly desirable. No one wishes to impose the adversary process on that relationship. But if the student may be thrown out of the high school for the balance of the year, losing a year's work in high school, I don't know on what basis rational men more willingly dispense with fundamentally fair modes of determining guilt and the appropriateness of given penalties at the high school level than the college level. The degree of damage done to the high school student by mistake in fact or mistake in judgment may be every bit as great as the loss of a year to the college student suspended.

## Special Purpose Public Institutions

**Carrington:** I have a question for Mr. Beaney who, in his formal remarks, discussed the idea that the courts may regard the actions and policies toward students of private institutions differently from those of public institutions because of the "special purpose" private institutions may have. Is it not possible that a public institution could also have a special purpose somewhat like those you suggest?

**Beaney:** I think it is very difficult to conceive of a public institution with an academic program so special that it could violate constitutional mandates in any way. In any professional school, of course, it is perfectly rational and within the Constitution to set certain prerequisites for admission and then certain rules as to professional behavior while a student. But beyond that, I don't know. Are you asking whether a public military institution can say "Ye who enter here abandon all rights"?

**Carrington:** Yes; that's the idea.

**Beaney:** I would hate to have the case of defending the state on that one.

**Lippe:** Perhaps West Point, for example, can set much more stringent regulations about the dress of its students than could another public institution which doesn't have the same kind of special purpose.

**Carrington:** And whether it is a public or private institution doesn't matter?

**Lippe:** In a situation like West Point's there is a different balance because of the special purpose.

**Kalaidjian:** The Court of Appeals for the Second Circuit decided a case involving this point.[5] The question in the case was whether a student at the U.S. Merchant Marine Academy was entitled to be represented by counsel in a disciplinary proceeding. As I recall, the court held that due process did not include representation by counsel. But that holding necessarily implies that even a special purpose academy is subject to the constitutional mandates of due process if it is operated as a public institution.

**Holloway:** The court in that case held that the student had not had a fair hearing, and one reason was the fact that one of the hearing officers was, in effect, also a prosecutor. The court held that the individual who assembled that data for the purpose of presenting the case to the disciplining body could not also sit as a member of the body. I think that case is support for some of the principles that Mr. Lippe has been urging.

## Applying Criminal and Administrative Sanctions

**Carrington:** Is there any problem of double jeopardy in applying both criminal and administrative sanctions to the same individual for the same offense, Mr. Kalaidjian?

**Kalaidjian:** There is no legal prohibition against it. There is a problem in a policy sense, as to the extent to which it is reasonable to punish a student twice for the same thing. For instance, if he has been sentenced to jail for 15 days for criminal trespass, is it then reasonable for his university, for the same act, to suspend him for a term or two? That is a policy question.

---

5.    Wasson v. Trowbridge, 382 F.2d 807 (2d Cir. 1967).

# APPENDIXES

# A

## JOINT STATEMENT ON
## RIGHTS AND FREEDOMS OF STUDENTS

*In June, 1967, a joint committee, comprised of representatives from the American Association of University Professors, U.S.* National Student Association, Association of American Colleges, National Association of Student Personnel Administrators, and National Association of Women Deans and Counselors, met in Washington, D.C., and drafted the Joint Statement on Rights and Freedoms of Students *published below.*

*The multilateral approach which produced this document was also applied to the complicated matter of interpretation, implementation, and enforcement, with the drafting committee recommending (a) joint efforts to promote acceptance of the new standards on the institutional level, (b) the establishment of machinery to facilitate continuing joint interpretation, (c) joint consultation before setting up any machinery for mediating disputes or investigating complaints, and (d) joint approaches to regional accrediting agencies to seek embodiment of the new principles in standards for accreditation.*

*Since its formulation, the Joint Statement has been endorsed by each of its five national sponsors, as well as by a number of other professional bodies. The endorsers are listed below:*

*U.S. National Student Association*
*Association of American Colleges*
*American Association of University Professors*
*National Association of Student Personnel Administrators*
*National Association of Women Deans and Counselors*
*American Association for Higher Education*
*Jesuit Education Association*
*American College Personnel Association*
*Executive Committee, College and University Department, National Catholic Education Association*
*Commission on Student Personnel, American Association of Junior Colleges*

## Preamble

Academic institutions exist for the transmission of knowledge, the pursuit of truth, the development of students, and the general well-being of society. Free inquiry and free expression are indispensable to the attainment of these goals. As members of the academic community, students should be encouraged to develop the capacity for critical judgment and to engage in a sustained and independent search for truth. Institutional procedures for achieving these purposes may vary from campus to campus, but the minimal standards of academic freedom of students outlined below are essential to any community of scholars.

Freedom to teach and freedom to learn are inseparable facets of academic freedom. The freedom to learn depends upon appropriate opportunities and conditions in the classroom, on the campus, and in the larger community. Students should exercise their freedom with responsibility.

The responsibility to secure and to respect general conditions conducive to the freedom to learn is shared by all members of the academic community. Each college and university has a duty to develop policies and procedures which provide and safeguard this freedom. Such policies and procedures should be developed at each institution within the framework of general standards and with the broadest possible participation of the members of the academic community. The purpose of this statement is to enumerate the essential provisions for student freedom to learn.

## I. Freedom of Access to Higher Education

The admissions policies of each college and university are a matter of institutional choice provided that each college and university makes clear the characteristics and expectations of students which it considers relevant to success in the institution's program. While church-related institutions may give admission preference to students of their own persuasion, such a preference should be clearly and publicly stated. Under no circumstances should a student be barred from admission to a particular institution on the basis of race. Thus, within the limits of its facilities, each college and university should be open to all students who are qualified according to its admission standards. The facilities and services of a college should be open to all of its enrolled students, and institutions should use their influence to secure equal access for all students to public facilities in the local community.

## II. In the Classroom

The professor in the classroom and in conference should encourage free discussion, inquiry, and expression. Student performance should be evaluated solely on an academic basis, not on opinions or conduct in matters unrelated to academic standards.

### A. Protection of Freedom of Expression

Students should be free to take reasoned exception to the data or views offered in any course of study and to reserve judgment about matters of opinion, but they are responsible for learning the content of any course of study for which they are enrolled.

### B. Protection against Improper Academic Evaluation

Students should have protection through orderly procedures against prejudiced or capricious academic evaluation. At the same time, they are responsible for maintaining standards of academic performance established for each course in which they are enrolled.

## C. Protection against Improper Disclosure

Information about student views, beliefs, and political associations which professors acquire in the course of their work as instructors, advisers, and counselors should be considered confidential. Protection against improper disclosure is a serious professional obligation. Judgments of ability and character may be provided under appropriate circumstances, normally with the knowledge or consent of the student.

## III. Student Records

Institutions should have a carefully considered policy as to the information which should be part of a student's permanent educational record and as to the conditions of its disclosure. To minimize the risk of improper disclosure, academic and disciplinary records should be separate, and the conditions of access to each should be set forth in an explicit policy statement. Transcripts of academic records should contain only information about academic status. Information from disciplinary or counseling files should not be available to unauthorized persons on campus, or to any person off campus without the express consent of the student involved except under legal compulsion or in cases where the safety of persons or property is involved. No records should be kept which reflect the political activities or beliefs of students. Provisions should also be made for periodic routine destruction of noncurrent disciplinary records. Administrative staff and faculty members should respect confidential information about students which they acquire in the course of their work.

## IV. Student Affairs

In student affairs, certain standards must be maintained if the freedom of students is to be preserved.

### A. Freedom of Association

Students bring to the campus a variety of interests previously acquired and develop many new interests as members of the academic community. They should be free to organize and join associations to promote their common interests.

1. The membership, policies, and actions of a student organization usually will be determined by vote of only those persons who hold bona fide membership in the college or university community.

2. Affiliation with an extramural organization should not of itself disqualify a student organization from institutional recognition.

3. If campus advisers are required, each organization should be free to choose its own adviser, and institutional recognition should not be withheld or withdrawn solely because of the inability of a student organization to secure an adviser. Campus advisers may advise organizations in the exercise of responsibility, but they should not have the authority to control the policy of such organizations.

4. Student organizations may be required to submit a statement of purpose, criteria for membership, rules of procedures, and a current list of officers. They should not be required to submit a membership list as a condition of institutional recognition.

5. Campus organizations, including those affiliated with an extramural organization, should be open to all students without respect to race, creed, or national origin, except for religious qualifications which may be required by organizations whose aims are primarily sectarian.

## B. Freedom of Inquiry and Expression

1. Students and student organizations should be free to examine and discuss all questions of interest to them, and to express opinions publicly and privately. They should always be free to support causes by orderly means which do not disrupt the regular and essential operation of the institution. At the same time, it should be made clear to the academic and the larger community that in their public expressions or demonstrations students or student organizations speak only for themselves.

2. Students should be allowed to invite and to hear any person of their own choosing. Those routine procedures required by an institution before a guest speaker is invited to appear on campus should be designed only to insure that there is orderly scheduling of facilities and adequate preparation for the event, and that the occasion is conducted in a manner appropriate to an academic community. The institutional control of campus facilities should not be used as a device of censorship. It should be made clear to the academic and large community that sponsorship of guest speakers does not necessarily imply approval or endorsement of the view expressed, either by the sponsoring group or the institution.

## C. Student Participation in Institutional Government

As constituents of the academic community, students should be free, individually and collectively, to express their views on issues of institutional policy and on matters of general interest to the student body. The student body should have clearly defined means to participate in the formulation and application of institutional policy affecting academic and student affairs. The role of the student government and both its general and specific responsibilities should be made explicit, and the actions of the student government within the areas of its jurisdiction should be reviewed only through orderly and prescribed procedures.

## D. Student Publications

Student publications and the student press are a valuable aid in establishing and maintaining an atmosphere of free and responsible discussion and of intellectual exploration on the campus. They are a means of bringing student concerns to the attention of the faculty and the institutional authorities and of formulating student opinion on various issues on the campus and in the world at large.

Whenever possible the student newspaper should be an independent corporation financially and legally separate from the university. Where financial and legal autonomy is not possible, the institution, as the publisher of student publications, may have to bear the legal responsibility for the contents of the publications. In the delegation of editorial responsibility to students the institution must provide sufficient editorial freedom and financial autonomy for the student publications to maintain their integrity of purpose as vehicles for free inquiry and free expression in an academic community.

Institutional authorities, in consultation with students and faculty, have a responsibility to provide written clarification of the role of the student publications, the standards to be used in their evaluation, and the limitations on external control of their operation. At the same time, the editorial freedom of student editors and managers entails corollary responsibilities to be governed by the canons of responsible journalism, such as the avoidance of libel, indecency, undocumented allegations, attacks on personal integrity, and the techniques of harassment and innuendo. As safeguards for the editorial freedom of student publications the following provisions are necessary.

1. The student press should be free of censorship and advance approval of copy, and its editors and managers should be free to develop their own editorial policies and news coverage.

2. Editors and managers of student publications should be protected from arbitrary suspension and removal because of

student, faculty, administrative, or public disapproval of editorial policy or content. Only for proper and stated causes should editors and managers be subject to removal and then by orderly and prescribed procedures. The agency responsible for the appointment of editors and managers should be the agency responsible for their removal.

3. All university published and financed student publications should explicitly state on the editorial page that the opinions there expressed are not necessarily those of the college, university, or student body.

## V. Off-Campus Freedom of Students

### A. Exercise of Rights of Citizenship

College and university students are both citizens and members of the academic community. As citizens, students should enjoy the same freedom of speech, peaceful assembly, and right of petition that other citizens enjoy and, as members of the academic community, they are subject to the obligations which accrue to them by virtue of this membership. Faculty members and administrative officials should insure that institutional powers are not employed to inhibit such intellectual and personal development of students as is often promoted by their exercise of the rights of citizenship both on and off campus.

### B. Institutional Authority and Civil Penalties

Activities of students may upon occasion result in violation of law. In such cases, institutional officials should be prepared to apprise students of sources of legal counsel and may offer other assistance. Students who violate the law may incur penalties prescribed by civil authorities, but institutional authority should never be used merely to duplicate the function of general laws. Only where the institution's interests as an academic community are distinct and clearly involved should the special authority of the institution be asserted. The student who incidentally violates institutional regulations in the course of his off-campus activity, such as those relating to class attendance, should be subject to no greater penalty than would normally be imposed. Institutional action should be independent of community pressure.

## VI. Procedural Standards in Disciplinary Proceedings

In developing responsible student conduct, disciplinary proceedings play a role substantially secondary to example, counseling, guidance, and admonition. At the same time, educational institutions have a duty and the corollary disciplinary powers to protect their educational purpose through the setting of standards of scholarship and conduct for the students who attend them and through the regulation of the use of institutional facilities. In the exceptional circumstances when the preferred means fail to resolve problems of student conduct, proper procedural safeguards should be observed to protect the student from the unfair imposition of serious penalties.

The administration of discipline should guarantee procedural fairness to an accused student. Practices in disciplinary cases may vary in formality with the gravity of the offense and the sanctions which may be applied. They should also take into account the presence or absence of an honor code, and the degree to which the institutional officials have direct acquaintance with student life in general and with the involved student and the circumstances of the case in particular. The jurisdictions of faculty or student judicial bodies, the disciplinary responsibilities of institutional officials and the regular disciplinary procedures, including the student's right to appeal a decision, should be clearly formulated and communicated in advance. Minor penalties may be assessed informally under prescribed procedures.

In all situations, procedural fair play requires that the student be informed of the nature of the charges against him, that he be given a fair opportunity to refute them, that the institution not be arbitrary in its actions, and that there be provision for appeal of a decision. The following are recommended as proper safeguards in such proceedings when there are no honor codes offering comparable guarantees.

## A. Standards of Conduct Expected of Students

The institution has an obligation to clarify those standards of behavior which it considers essential to its educational mission and its community life. These general behavioral expectations and the resultant specific regulations should represent a reasonable regulation of student conduct, but the student should be as free as possible from imposed limitations that have no direct relevance to his education. Offenses should be as clearly defined as possible and interpreted in a manner consistent with the aforementioned principles of relevancy and reasonableness. Disciplinary proceedings should be instituted only for violations of standards of conduct formulated with significant student participation and published in advance through such means as a student handbook or a generally available body of institutional regulations.

## B. Investigation of Student Conduct

1. Except under extreme emergency circumstances, premises occupied by students and the personal possessions of students should not be searched unless appropriate authorization has been obtained. For premises such as residence halls controlled by the institution, an appropriate and responsible authority should be designated to whom application should be made before a search is conducted. The application should specify the reasons for the search and the objects or information sought. The student should be present, if possible, during the search. For premises not

controlled by the institution, the ordinary requirements for lawful search should be followed.

2. Students detected or arrested in the course of serious violation of institutional regulations, or infractions of ordinary law, should be informed of their rights. No form of harassment should be used by institutional representatives to coerce admissions of guilt or information about conduct of other suspected persons.

## C. Status of Student Pending Final Action

Pending action on the charges, the status of a student should not be altered, or his right to be present on the campus and to attend classes suspended, except for reasons relating to his physical or emotional safety and well-being, or for reasons relating to the safety and well-being of students, faculty, or university property.

## D. Hearing Committee Procedures

When the misconduct may result in serious penalties and if the student questions the fairness of disciplinary action taken against him, he should be granted, on request, the privilege of a hearing before a regularly constituted hearing committee. The following suggested hearing committee procedures satisfy the requirements of procedural due process in situations requiring a high degree of formality.

1. The hearing committee should include faculty members or students, or, if regularly included or requested by the accused, both faculty and student members. No member of the hearing committee who is otherwise interested in the particular case should sit in judgment during the proceeding.

2. The student should be informed, in writing, of the reasons for the proposed disciplinary action with sufficient particularity, and in sufficient time, to insure opportunity to prepare for the hearing.

3. The student appearing before the hearing committee should have the right to be assisted in his defense by an adviser of his choice.

4. The burden of proof should rest upon the officials bringing the charge.

5. The student should be given an opportunity to testify and to present evidence and witnesses. He should have an opportunity to hear and question adverse witnesses. In no case should the committee consider statements against him unless he has been advised of their content and of the names of those who made them, and unless he has been given an opportunity to rebut unfavorable inferences which might otherwise be drawn.

6. All matters upon which the decision may be based must be introduced into evidence at the proceeding before the hearing committee. The decision should be based solely upon such matters. Improperly acquired evidence should not be admitted.

7. In the absence of a transcript, there should be both a digest and a verbatim record, such as a tape recording, of the hearing.

8. The decision of the hearing committee should be final, subject only to the student's right of appeal to the president or ultimately to the governing board of the institution.

# B

## GENERAL ORDER
## ON
## JUDICIAL STANDARDS OF PROCEDURE
## AND SUBSTANCE

### IN REVIEW OF

### STUDENT DISCIPLINE IN TAX SUPPORTED
### INSTITUTIONS OF HIGHER EDUCATION

The recent filing in this Court of three major cases for review of student discipline in tax supported educational institutions of higher learning has made desirable hearings by this Court en banc in two such cases, namely Civil Actions No. 16852–4 (Western Division) and No. 1259 (Central Division). These hearings were desirable to develop uniform standards to be applied in the two civil actions and to ensure, as far as practicable, that the future decisions in similar cases in the four division of this Court would be consistent.

Because of the great interest in student discipline and because of the violence which has occurred in the educational institutions recently, counsel for all interested tax supported institutions, counsel for any privately supported educational institution,

225

counsel for the American Civil Liberties Union, the Attorney General of Missouri, and counsel for any officially elected or recognized student government or faculty association, were afforded an opportunity to file briefs and address oral agrument to the federal questions of substance and procedure presented by cases involving student discipline. After consideration of the briefs and arguments this Court en banc does hereby

ORDER that hereafter, until further Order of the Court en banc, in the absence of exceptional circumstances, the judicial standards of procedure and substance, enunciated in the attached Memorandum, be treated as applicable to cases in this Court wherein questions involving disciplinary action of students in tax supported institutions of higher learning are presented; provided, however, that in any civil action, the jurisdiction and powers of the individual judge to whom the case is assigned are not affected hereby; and provided further, that no party to an action be precluded from submitting and requesting therein a decision *de novo* inconsistent with these standards.

September 18, 1968

> (s) William H. Becker, Chief Judge
> (s) John W. Oliver, District Judge
> (s) William R. Collinson, District Judge
> (s) Elmo B. Hunter, District Judge

# MEMORANDUM ON JUDICIAL STANDARDS
## OF
## PROCEDURE AND SUBSTANCE
## IN REVIEW OF

## STUDENT DISCIPLINE IN TAX SUPPORTED
## INSTITUTIONS OF HIGHER EDUCATION

### Definitions

"Education" as used herein means tax supported formal higher education unless the context indicates another meaning.

"Institution" and "educational institution" as used herein mean a tax supported school, college, university, or multiversity.

"Mission" as used herein means a goal, purpose, task, or objective.

### Introductions

The number of actions for review of student disciplinary action has been increasing in this and other courts as shown by the cases in this Court and the reported cases.[1]

---

1.  Esteban et al. v. Central Missouri State College et al. (W.D.Mo., 1967), 277 F.Supp. 649; Esteban, et al. v. Central Missouri State College (W.D.Mo.), 290 F.Supp. 622; Scoggin et al. v. Lincoln University et al. (W.D.Mo.), 291 F.Supp. 161; Barker v. Hardway (C.A.4, 1968), 399 F.2d 638, affirming (S.D.W.Va., 1968) 283 F.Supp. 228; Madera v. Board of Education of City of New York (C.A.2, 1967), 386 F.2d 778, reversing (S.D.N.Y., 1967) 267 F. Supp. 356; Dixon v. Alabama State Board of Education (C.A.5, 1961), 294 F.2d 150, reversing (M.D.Ala., 1960) 186 F.Supp. 945; Moore v. Student Affairs Committee of Troy State University (M.D.Ala., 1968), 284 F.Supp. 725; Zanders v. Louisiana State Board of Education (W.D.La., 1968), 281 F.Supp. 747; Buttny v. Smiley (D.Colo., 1968), 281 F.Supp. 280; Dickson v. Sitterson (M.D.N.C., 1968), 280 F. Supp. 486; Jones v. State Board of Education of and for the State of Tennessee (M.D.Tenn., 1968), 279

These cases reflect rapid development and much controversy concerning appropriate procedural and substantive standards of judicial review in such cases. Because of the importance in this district of clearly enunciated reliable standards, this Court scheduled hearings in the second *Esteban* case and in the *Scoggin* case for the purpose of hearing arguments and suggestions of the parties and of interested amici curiae on the standards which would be applied regardless of the judge to whom the cases are assigned by lot. This was done for the purpose of uniformity of decision in this district.

The following memorandum represents a statement of judicial standards of procedure and substance applicable, in the absence of exceptional circumstances, to actions concerning discipline of students in tax supported educational institutions of higher learning.

## Relations of Courts and Education

Achieving the ideal of justice is the highest goal of humanity. Justice is not the concern solely of the courts. Education is equally concerned with the achievement of ideal justice. The administration of justice by the courts in the United States represents the people's best efforts to achieve the ideal of justice in the field of civil and criminal law. It is generally accepted that the courts are necessary to this administration of justice and for the protection of individual liberties. Nevertheless, the contributions of the modern courts in achieving the ideals of justice are primarily the products of higher education. The modern courts are, and will continue to be, greatly indebted to higher education

F.Supp. 190; Dickey v. Alabama State Board of Education (M.D.Ala., 1967), 273 F.Supp. 613; Hammond v. South Carolina State College (D.S.C., 1967) 272 F.Supp. 947; Due v. Florida A. and M. University (N.D.Fla., 1963), 233 F.Supp. 396.

for their personnel, their innovations, their processes, their political support, and their future in the political and social order. Higher education is the primary source of study and support of improvement in the courts. For this reason, among others, the courts should exercise caution when importuned to intervene in the important processes and functions of education. A court should never intervene in the processes of education without understanding the nature of education.

Before undertaking to intervene in the educational processes, and to impose judicial restraints and mandates on the educational community, the courts should acquire a general knowledge of the lawful missions and the continually changing processes, functions, and problems of education. Judicial action without such knowledge would endanger the public interest and be likely to lead to gross injustice.

Education is the living and growing source of our progressive civilization, of our open repository of increasing knowledge, culture and our salutary democratic traditions. As such, education deserves the highest respect and the fullest protection of the courts in the performance of its lawful missions.

There have been, and no doubt in the future there will be, instances of erroneous and unwise misuse of power by those invested with powers of management and teaching in the academic community, as in the case of all human fallible institutions. When such misuse of power is threatened or occurs, our political and social order has made available a wide variety of lawful, non-violent, political, economic, and social means to prevent or end the misuse of power. These same lawful, non-violent, political, economic and social means are available to correct an unwise but lawful choice of educational policy or action by those charged with the powers of management and teaching in the academic community. Only where erroneous and unwise actions in the field of education deprive students of federally protected rights or privileges does a federal court have power to intervene in the educational process.[2]

## Lawful Missions of Tax Supported
## Higher Education

The lawful missions of tax supported public education in the United States are constantly growing and changing. For the purposes of this analysis, it is sufficient to note some of the widely recognized traditional missions of tax supported higher education in this country. Included in these lawful missions of education are the following:

(1) To maintain, support, critically examine, and to improve the existing social and political system;

(2) To train students and faculty for leadership and superior service in public service, science, agriculture, commerce and industry;

(3) To develop students to well rounded maturity, physically, socially, emotionally, spiritually, intellectually and vocationally;

(4) To develop, refine and teach ethical and cultural values;

(5) To provide fullest possible realization of democracy in every phase of living;

(6) To teach principles of patriotism, civil obligation and respect for the law;

(7) To teach the practice of excellence in thought, behavior and performance;

---

2. These principles are not applicable where influences outside the educational community seek to impose unlawful and irrelevant conditions on the educational institution. Cf. Dickson v. Sitterson (M.D.N.C.) 280 F.Supp. 486, in which the legislature of North Carolina attempted by statute to limit protected free speech in the facilities of the University of North Carolina.

(8) To develop, cultivate, and stimulate the use of imagination;

(9) To stimulate reasoning and critical faculties of students and to encourage their use in improvement of the existing political and social order;

(10) To develop and teach lawful methods of change and improvement in the existing political and social order;

(11) To provide by study and research for increase of knowledge;

(12) To provide by study and research for development and improvement of technology, production and distribution for increased national production of goods and services desirable for national civilian consumption, for export, for exploration, and for national military purposes;

(13) To teach methods of experiment in meeting the problems of a changing environment;

(14) To promote directly and explicitly international understanding and cooperation;

(15) To provide the knowledge, personnel, and policy for planning and managing the destiny of our society with a maximum of individual freedom; and

(16) To transfer the wealth of knowledge and tradition from one generation to another.[3]

3. In addition to standard encyclopedic treatises some authoritative statements of the missions of tax supported education may be found in the following works and documents: Report of Commissioners Appointed To Fix The Site of The University of Virginia found in Crusade Against Ignorance—Thomas Jefferson on Education, (Teachers College Columbia University 1961), 114—118; Cremin, The Genius of American Education (Vintage Books 1966); Higher Education for American Democracy: The Report of President's Commission, I. Establishing the Goals, (Washington Government Printing Office 1947); The Student Personnel Point of View, (American Counsel on Education, Washington, D. C., 1938 Revised 1949); Einstein, Out of My Later Years, (Philosophical Library, New York 1950) 31; Gardner, Ex-

The tax supported educational institution is an agency of the national and state governments. Its missions include, by teaching, research and action, assisting in the declared purposes of government in this nation, namely:

To form a more perfect union,

To establish justice,

To insure domestic tranquility,

To provide for the common defense,

To promote the general welfare, and

To secure the blessing of liberty to ourselves and to posterity.

The nihilist and the anarchist, determined to destroy the existing political and social order, who direct their primary attacks on the educational institutions, understand fully the missions of education in the United States.

Federal law recognizes the powers of the tax supported institutions to accomplish these missions and has frequently furnished economic assistance for these purposes.

The genius of American education, employing the manifold ideas and works of the great Jefferson,[4] Mann, Dewey and many

---

cellence: Can We Be Equal and Excellent Too? (Harper and Bros., New York 1961); Dewey, Democracy and Education, (Appleton Century Crofts, New York 1950); Mueller, Student Personnel Work on Higher Education (Houghton Mifflin, Boston 1961) 4–10; Hatch and Stefflre, Administration of Guidance Services, (Prentice-Hall, Inc. 1965, 2 ed., Englewood, N. J.) 3–16.

4. Thomas Jefferson, the earliest and greatest advocate of tax supported higher education and the unequalled defender of personal liberty, reported in his correspondence on an early instance of a student riot at his creation, the University of Virginia, in these words:

From letter of August 27, 1825, to Ellen W. Coolidge:

"Our University goes on well. We have passed the limit of 100 students some time since. As yet it has been a model of order and good behavior, having never yet had occasion for the exercise of a single act of authority. We studiously avoid too much government. We treat them as men and gentlemen, under the guidance mainly of their own discretion. They so consider themselves, and make it their pride to acquire that character for their institution. In short, we are as quiet on that head as the experience of six months only can justify. Our other living authorities, has made the United States the most powerful nation in history. In so doing, it has in a relatively few years expanded the area of knowledge at a revolutionary rate.

With education the primary force, the means to provide the necessities of life and many luxuries to all our national population, and to many other peoples, has been created. This great progress has been accomplished by the provision to the educational community of general support, accompanied by diminishing interference in educational processes by political agencies outside the academic community.

If it is true, as it well may be, that man is in a race between education and catastrophe, it is imperative that educational institutions not be limited in the performance of their lawful missions by unwarranted judicial interference.

---

professors, too, continue to be what we wish them. Mr. Gilmer accepts the Law chair, and all is well."
From letter of October 13, 1825, to Joseph Coolidge, Jr.:
"The news of our neighborhood can hardly be interesting to you, except what may relate to our University, in which you are so kind as to take an interest. And it happens that a serious incident has just taken place there, which I will state to you the rather, as of the thousand versions which will be given not one will be true. My position enables me to say what is so, but with the most absolute concealment from whence it comes; regard to my own peace requiring that,—except with friends whom I can trust and wish to gratify with the truth.

"The University had gone on with a degree of order and harmony which had strengthened the hope that much of self government might be trusted to the discretion of the students of the age of 16 and upwards, until the 1st instant. In the night of that day a party of fourteen students, animated first with wine, masked themselves so as not to be known, and turned out on the lawn of the University, with no intention, it is believed, but of childish noise and uproar. Two professors hearing it went out to see what was the matter. They were received with insult, and even brick-bats were thrown at them. Each of them seized an offender, demanded their names (for they could not distinguish them under their disguise), but were refused, abused, and the culprits calling on their companions for a rescue, got loose, and withdrew to their chambers. The Faculty of Professors met the next

## Obligations of a Student

Attendance at a tax supported educational institution of higher learning is not compulsory. The federal constitution protects the equality of opportunity of all qualified persons to attend. Whether this protected opportunity be called a qualified "right" or "privilege" is unimportant. It is optional and voluntary.

The voluntary attendance of a student in such institutions is a voluntary entrance into the academic community. By such voluntary entrance, the student voluntarily assumes obligations of performance and behavior reasonably imposed by the institution of choice relevant to its lawful missions, processes, and functions. These obligations are generally much higher than those imposed on all citizens by the civil and criminal law. So long as there is no

---

day, called the whole before them, and in address, rather harsh, required them to denounce the offenders. They refused, answered the address in writing and in the rudest terms, and charged the Professors themselves with false statements. Fifty others, who were in their rooms, no ways implicated in the riot and knowing nothing about it, immediately signed the answer, making common cause with the rioters, and declaring their belief of their assertions in opposition to those of the Professors. The next day chanced to be that of the meeting of the Visitors; the Faculty sent a deputation to them, informing them of what had taken place. The Visitors called the whole body of students before them, exhorted them to make known the persons masked, the innocent to aid the cause of order by bearing witnesses to the truth, and the guilty to relieve their innocent brethren from censures which they were conscious that themselves alone deserved. On this the fourteen maskers stepped forward and avowed themselves the persons guilty of whatever had passed, but denying that any trespass had been committed. They were desired to appear before the Faculty, which they did. On the evidence resulting from this enquiry, three, the most culpable, were expelled; one of them, moreover, presented by the grand jury for civil punishment (for it happened that the district court was then about to meet). The eleven other maskers were sentenced to suspensions or reprimands, and the fifty who had so gratuitously obtruded their names into the offensive paper retracted them, and so the matter ended.

invidious discrimination, no deprival of due process, no abridgement of a right protected in the circumstances, and no capricious, clearly unreasonable or unlawful action employed, the institution may discipline students to secure compliance with these higher obligations as a teaching method or to sever the student from the academic community.

No student may, without liability to lawful discipline, intentionally act to impair or prevent the accomplishment of any lawful mission, process, or function of an educational institution.

## The Nature of Student Discipline
## Compared to Criminal Law

The discipline of students in the educational community is, in

---

"The circumstances of this transaction enabled the Visitors to add much to the strictness of their system as yet new. The students have returned into perfect order under a salutary conviction they had not before felt that the laws will in future be rigorously enforced, and the institution is strengthened by the firmness manifested by its authorities on the occasion. It cannot, however, be expected that all breaches of order can be made to cease at once, but from the vigilance of the Faculty and energy of the civil power their restraint may very soon become satisfactory. It is not perceived that this riot has been more serious than has been experienced by other seminaries; but, whether more or less so, the exact truth should be told, and the institution be known to the public as neither better nor worse than it really is"

From letter of November 14, 1825, to Ellen W. Coolidge:

"My Dear Ellen,—In my letter of October 13 to Mr. Coolidge, I gave an account of the riot we had had at the University and of its termination. You will both, of course, be under anxiety till you know how it has gone off. With the best effects in the world, having let it be understood from the beginning that we wished to trust very much to the discretion of the students themselves for their own government. With about four-fifths of them this did well, but there were about fifteen or twenty bad subjects who were disposed to try whether our indulgence was without limit. Hence the licentious transaction of which all but the case of irrevocable expulsion, a part of the teaching process. In the case of irrevocable expulsion for misconduct, the process is not punitive or deterrent in the criminal law sense, but the process is rather the determination that the student is unqualified to continue as a member of the educational community. Even then, the disciplinary process is not equivalent to the criminal law processes of federal and state criminal law. For, while the expelled student may suffer damaging effects, sometimes irreparable, to his educational, social, and economic future, he or she may not be imprisoned, fined, disenfranchised, or subjected to probationary supervision. The attempted analogy of student discipline to criminal proceedings against adults and juveniles is not sound.

In the lesser disciplinary procedures, including but not limited to guidance counseling, reprimand, suspension of social or academic

---

I gave an account to Mr. Coolidge; but when the whole mass saw the serious way in which that experiment was met, the Faculty of Professors assembled, the Board of Vistors coming forward in support of that authority, a grand jury taking up the subject, four of the most guilty expelled, the rest reprimanded, severer laws enacted and a rigorous execution of them declared in future,—it gave them a shock and struck a terror, the most severe as it was less expected. It determined the well-disposed among them to frown upon everything of the kind hereafter, and the ill-disposed returned to order from fear, if not from better motives. A perfect subordination has succeeded, entire respect towards the professors, and industry, order, and quiet the most exemplary, has prevailed ever since. Every one is sensible of the strength which the institution has derived from what appeared at first to threaten its foundation. We have no further fear of anything of the kind from the present set, but as at the next term their numbers will be more than doubled by the accession of an additional band, as unbroken as these were, we mean to be prepared, and to ask of the legislature a power to call in the civil authority in the first instant of disorder, and to quell it on the spot by imprisonment and the same legal coercions provided against disorder generally committed by other citizens from whom, at their age, they have no right to distinction."

All the foregoing quotations are found in The Writings of Thomas Jefferson, Library Edition, The Thomas Jefferson Memorial Association, Washington, D. C., 1904, Volume 18, pp. 341–348.

privileges, probation, restriction to campus and dismissal with leave to apply for readmission, the lawful aim of discipline may be teaching in performance of a lawful mission of the institution.[5] The nature and procedures of the disciplinary process in such cases should not be required to conform to federal processes of criminal law, which are far from perfect, and designed for circumstances and ends unrelated to the academic community. By judicial mandate to impose upon the academic community in student discipline the intricate, time consuming, sophisticated procedures, rules and safeguards of criminal law would frustrate the teaching process and render the institutional control impotent.

A federal court should not intervene to reverse or enjoin disciplinary actions relevant to a lawful mission of an educational institution unless there appears one of the following:

    (1)    a deprival of due process, that is, of fundamental concepts of fair play;

    (2)    invidious discrimination, for example, on account of race or religion;

    (3)    denial of federal rights, constitutional or statutory, protected in the academic community; or

    (4)    clearly unreasonable, arbitrary or capricious action.

---

5.    Brady and Snoxell, Student Discipline in Higher Education, American Personnel and Guidance Association, 1965; Williamson, Student Personnel Services in Colleges and Universities, McGraw Hill, 1961, pp. 141–212; Mueller, Student Personnel Work in Higher Education, Houghton, Mifflin, Boston, 1961, pp. 352–355; Hatch and Stefflre, Administration of Guidance Services, Prentice-Hall, Inc., 1965, 2d ed., Englewood, N. J., pp. 16–27; Williamson and Foley, Counseling and Discipline, McGraw Hill, New York, 1949, pp. 1–49; Baaken, The Legal Basis For College Student Personnel Work, 2d ed. 1968, The American Personnel and Guidance Association, Washington, D.C.; Callis, Educational Aspects of In Loco Parentis, 8 Journal of College Student Personnel, 231–233, July 1964; Cf. Van Alstyne, Student Academic Freedom and Rule Making Powers of Public Universities, 2 Law in Transition Quarterly 1; Developments in the Law—Academic Freedom, 81 Harvard Law Review 1045–1159.

## Provisional Procedural and
## Jurisdictional Standards

In the absence of exceptional circumstances these standards are applicable.

### Jurisdiction

1.  Under Sections 1343(3), Title 28, and 1983, Title 42, U.S.C., and also in appropriate cases under Sections 2201, 1331(a) or 1332(a), Title 28, U.S.C., the United States District Courts have jurisdiction to entertain and determine actions by students who claim unreasonably discriminatory, arbitrary or capricious actions lacking in due process and depriving a student of admission to or continued attendance at tax supported institutions of higher education.

### Nature of Action

2.  The action may be
    (a)  Under Section 1983, an action at law for damages triable by a jury;
    (b)  Under Section 1983, a suit in equity; or
    (c)  Under Section 1983 and Section 2201, a declaratory judgment action, which may be legal or equitable in nature depending on the issues therein.

### Question of Exhaustion of Remedies

3.  In an action at law or equity under Section 1983, Title 42, U.S.C., the doctrine of exhaustion of state judicial remedies is not applicable. The fact that there is an existing state judicial remedy for the alleged wrong is no ground for stay or dismissal.[6]

---

6.  Monroe v. Pape, 365 U.S. 167, 81 S.Ct. 473, 5 L.Ed.2d 492; Damico v.

Ordinarily until the currently available, adequate and effective institutional processes have been exhausted, the disciplinary action is not final and the controversy is not ripe for determination.

## Right to Jury Trial

4.   In an action at law under Section 1983, the issues are triable by jury and equitable defenses are not available.

## Trial of Equitable Actions

5.   In an equitable action by a court without a jury under Section 1983, equitable doctrines and defenses are applicable.

    (a)   There must be an inadequate remedy at law.

    (b)   The plaintiff must be in a position to secure equitable relief under equitable doctrines, for example, must come with "clean hands."

## Question of Mootness

6.   In an action at law or equity under Section 1983, Title 42, U.S.C., to review severe student disciplinary action, the doctrine of mootness is not applicable when the action is timely filed.[7]

---

California, 389 U.S. 416, 88 S.Ct. 526, 19 L.Ed.2d 647; McNeese v. Board of Education, 373 U.S. 668, 83 S.Ct. 1433, 10 L.Ed.2d 622.

7.   Cf. Carafas v. La Vallee, 391 U.S. 234, 88 S.Ct. 1556, 20 L.Ed.2d 554 (1968), overruling Parker v. Ellis, 362 U.S. 574, 80 S.Ct. 909, 4 L.Ed.2d 963 (1960), and Sibron v. State of New York, 392 U.S. 40, 88 S.Ct. 1889, 20 L.Ed.2d 917 (1968), qualifying St. Pierre v. United States, 319 U.S. 41, 63 S.Ct. 910, 87 L.Ed.1199 (1943).

## Provisional Substantive Standards
## in Student Discipline Cases
## Under Section 1983, Title 42

1.  Equal opportunity for admission and attendance by qualified persons at tax supported state educational institutions of higher learning is protected by the equal privileges and immunities, equal protection of laws, and due process clauses of the Fourteenth Amendment to the United States Constitution. It is unimportant whether this protected opportunity is defined as a right or a privilege. The protection of the opportunity is the important thing.

2.  In an action under Section 1983, issues to be determined will be limited to determination whether, under color of any statute, ordinance, regulation, custom or usage of a state ("state action"), a student has been deprived of any rights, privileges, or immunities secured by the Constitution and laws of the United States.

3.  State constitutional, statutory, and institutional delegation and distribution of disciplinary powers are not ordinarily matters of federal concern. Any such contentions based solely on claims of unlawful distribution and violation of state law in the exercise of state disciplinary powers should be submitted to the state courts. Such contentions do not ordinarily involve a substantial federal question of which the district court has jurisdiction under Section 1983. This rule does not apply, however, to actions based on diversity jurisdiction under Sections 1331, 1332 or 2201, Title 28, U.S.C.

4.  Disciplinary action by any institution, institutional agency, or officer will ordinarily be deemed under color of a statute, ordinance, regulation, custom or usage of a state ("state action") within the meaning of Section 1983, Title 42, U.S.C.

5. In the field of discipline, scholastic and behavioral, an institution may establish any standards reasonably relevant to the lawful missions, processes, and functions of the institution. It is not a lawful mission, process, or function of an institution to prohibit the exercise of a right guaranteed by the Constitution or a law of the United States to a member of the academic community in the circumstances. Therefore, such prohibitions are not reasonably relevant to any lawful mission, process or function of an institution.

6. Standards so established may apply to student behavior on and off the campus when relevant to any lawful mission, process, or function of the institution. By such standards of student conduct the institution may prohibit any action or omission which impairs, interferes with, or obstructs the missions, processes and functions of the institution.

    Standards so established may require scholastic attainments higher than the average of the population and may require superior ethical and moral behavior. In establishing standards of behavior, the institution is not limited to the standards or the forms of criminal laws.

7. An institution may establish appropriate standards of conduct (scholastic and behavioral) in any form and manner reasonably calculated to give adequate notice of the scholastic attainments and behavior expected of the student.

    The notice of the scholastic and behavioral standards to the students may be written or oral, or partly written and partly oral, but preferably written. The standards may be positive or negative in form.

    Different standards, scholastic and behavioral, may be established for different divisions, schools, colleges, and classes of an institution if the differences are reasonably relevant to the missions, processes, and functions of the particular divisions, schools, colleges, and classes concerned.

8. When a challenged standard of student conduct limits or

forbids the exercise of a right guaranteed by the Constitution or a law of the United States to persons generally, the institution must demonstrate that the standard is recognized as relevant to a lawful mission of the institution, and is recognized as reasonable by some reputable authority or school of thought in the field of higher education.[8] This may be determined by expert opinion or by judicial notice in proper circumstances. It is not necessary that all authorities and schools of thought agree that the standard is reasonable.

9. Outstanding educational authorities in the field of higher education believe, on the basis of experience, that detailed codes of prohibited student conduct are provocative and should not be employed in higher education.[9]

    For this reason, general affirmative statements of what is expected of a student may in some areas be preferable in higher education. Such affirmative standards may be employed, and discipline of students based thereon.

10. The legal doctrine that a prohibitory statute is void if it is overly broad or unconstitutionally vague does not, in the absence of exceptional circumstances, apply to standards of student conduct. The validity of the form of standards of student conduct, relevant to the lawful missions of higher education, ordinarily should be determined by recognized educational standards.

11. In severe cases of student discipline for alleged misconduct, such as final expulsion, indefinite or long-term suspension, dismissal with deferred leave to reapply, the institution is

---

8. Cf. Van Alstyne, Student Academic Freedom and Rule Making Powers of Public Universities: Some Constitutional Considerations, 2 Law in Transition Quarterly 1, 1. c. 23–25.

9. Brady and Snoxell, Student Personnel Work in Higher Education (Houghton-Mifflin, Boston, 1961) p. 378.

obligated to give to the student minimal procedural requirements of due process of law.[10] The requirements of due
process do not demand an inflexible procedure for all such
cases. "But 'due process' unlike some legal rules, is not a
technical conception with a fixed content unrelated to time,
place and circumstances."[11] Three minimal requirements
apply in cases of severe discipline, growing out of fundamental conceptions of fairness implicit in procedural due
process. First, the student should be given adequate notice
in writing of the specific ground or grounds and the nature
of the evidence on which the disciplinary proceedings are
based. Second, the student should be given an opportunity
for a hearing in which the disciplinary authority provides a
fair opportunity for hearing of the student's position,
explanations and evidence.[12] The third requirement is that
no disciplinary action be taken on grounds which are not
supported by any substantial evidence.[13] Within limits of
due process, institutions must be free to devise various types
of disciplinary procedures relevant to their lawful missions,
consistent with their varying processes and functions, and
which do not impose unreasonable strain on their resources
and personnel.

10. Dixon v. Alabama State Board of Education (C.A.5) 294 F.2d 150,
cert. den. 368 U.S. 930, 82 S.Ct. 368, 7 L.Ed.2d 193 (1961); Esteban
v. Central Missouri State College (W.D.Mo., 1967) 277 F.Supp. 649.
11. Cf. concurring opinion in Joint Anti-Fascist Refugee Committee v.
McGrath, 341 U.S. 123, 71 S.Ct. 624, 95 L.Ed. 817; Cafeteria and
Restaurant Workers Union v. McElroy, 367 U.S. 886, 81 S.Ct. 1743, 6
L.Ed.2d 1230, l. c. 1236.
12. The first two requirements are supported by Dixon v. Alabama State
Board of Education, supra, and Esteban v. Central Missouri State
College, supra.
13. Cf. Thompson v. City of Louisville, 362 U.S. 199, 80 S.Ct. 624, 4
L.Ed.2d 654, l. c. 659. In citing the *Thompson* case there is no
intention to require adherence to the judicial exclusionary rules of
evidence.

There is no general requirement that procedural due process in student disciplinary cases provide for legal representation, a public hearing, confrontation and cross-examination of witnesses, warnings about privileges, self-incrimination, application of principles of former or double jeopardy, compulsory production of witnesses, or any of the remaining features of federal criminal jurisprudence.[14] Rare and exceptional circumstances, however, may require provision of one or more of these features in a particular case to guarantee the fundamental concepts of fair play.

It is encouraging to note the current unusual efforts of the institutions and the interested organizations which are devising and recommending procedures and policies in student discipline which are based on standards, in many respects far higher than the requirements of due process. See for example the Joint Statement on Rights and Freedoms of Students, 54 A.A.U.P. Bulletin No. 2, Summer 1968, 258, a report of a joint committee of representatives of the U.S. National Students Association, Association of American Colleges, American Association of University Professors, National Association of Student Personnel Administrators, National Association of Women's Deans and Counselors, American Association of Higher Education, Jesuit Education Association, American College Personnel Association, Executive Committee, College and University Department, National Catholic Education Association, Commission on Student Personnel, American Association of Junior Colleges; and the University of Missouri, Provisional Rules of Procedure In Student Disciplinary Matters.

Many of these recommendations and procedures represent wise provisions of policy and procedure far above

---

14. Dixon v. Alabama State Board of Education, supra; Madera v. Board of Education of City of New York, supra.

the minimum requirements of federal law, calculated to ensure the confidence of all concerned with student discipline.

The excellent briefs and arguments, including those of amici curiae, have been of great assistance in the preparation of this memorandum.

# C

## THE BOARD OF HIGHER EDUCATION OF THE CITY OF NEW YORK

RESOLVED, That the Board of Higher Education in compliance with Chapter 191 of the Laws of 1969, hereby adopt the following rules and regulations for the maintenance of public order on college campuses and other college property used for educational purposes.

## Rules and Regulations for The Maintenance of Public Order Pursuant to Article 129A of the Education Law

The tradition of the university as a sanctuary of academic freedom and center of informed discussion is an honored one, to be guarded vigilantly. The basic significance of that sanctuary lies in the protection of intellectual freedoms: the rights of professors to teach, of scholars to engage in the advancement of knowledge, of students to learn and to express their views, free from external pressures or interference. These freedoms can flourish only in an atmosphere of mutual respect, civility and trust among teachers and students, only when members of the university community are willing to accept self-restraint and reciprocity as the condition upon which they share in its intellectual autonomy.

Academic freedom and the sanctuary of the university campus extend to all who share these aims and responsibilities. They cannot be invoked by those who would subordinate intellectual freedom to political ends, or who violate the norms of

247

conduct established to protect that freedom. Against such offenders the university has the right, and indeed the obligation, to defend itself. We accordingly announce the following rules and regulations to be in effect at each of our colleges which are to be administered in accordance with the requirements of due process as provided in the Bylaws of the Board of Higher Education.

With respect to enforcement of these rules and regulations we note that the Bylaws of the Board of Higher Education provide that:

THE PRESIDENT. The president, with respect to his educational unit, shall:

"a.   Have the affirmative responsibility of conserving and enhancing the educational standards of the college and schools under his jurisdiction:

"b.   Be the advisor and executive agent to the Board and of his respective College Committee and as such shall have the immediate supervision with full discretionary power in carrying into effect the bylaws, resolutions and policies of the Board, the lawful resolutions of any of its committees and the policies, programs and lawful resolutions of the several faculties;

"c.   Exercise general superintendence over the concerns, officers, employees and students of his educational unit * * *."

## I. Rules

1. A member of the academic community shall not intentionally obstruct and/or forcibly prevent others from the exercise of their rights. Nor shall he interfere with the institution's educational process or facilities, or the rights of those who wish to avail themselves of any of the institution's instructional, personal, administrative, recreational, and community services.

2. Individuals are liable for failure to comply with lawful

directions issued by representatives of the University/college when they are acting in their official capacities. Members of the academic community are required to show their identification cards when requested to do so by an official of the college.

3. Unauthorized occupancy of University/college facilities or blocking access to or from such areas is prohibited. Permission from appropriate college authorities must be obtained for removal, relocation and use of University/college equipment and/or supplies.

4. Theft from or damage to University/college premises or property, or theft of or damage to property of any person on University/college premises is prohibited.

5. Each member of the academic community or an invited guest has the right to advocate his position without having to fear abuse, physical, verbal, or otherwise from others supporting conflicting points of view. Members of the academic community and other persons on the college grounds, shall not use language or take actions reasonably likely to provoke or encourage physical violence by demonstrators, those demonstrated against, or spectators.

6. Action may be taken against any and all persons who have no legitimate reason for their presence on any campus within the University/college, or whose presence on any such campus obstructs and/or forcibly prevents others from the exercise of their rights or interferes with the institution's educational processes or facilities, or the rights of those who wish to avail themselves of any of the institution's instructional, personal, administrative, recreational, and community services.

7. Disorderly or indecent conduct on University/college-owned or -controlled property is prohibited.

8. No individual shall have in his possession a rifle, shotgun or firearm or knowingly have in his possession any other dangerous instrument or material that can be used to inflict bodily harm on an individual or damage upon a building or the grounds

of the University/college without the written authorization of such educational institution. Nor shall any individual have in his possession any other instrument or material which can be used and is intended to inflict bodily harm on an individual or damage upon a building or the grounds of the University/college.

## II. Penalties

1. Any student engaging in any manner in conduct prohibited under substantive Rules 1–8 shall be subject to the following range of sanctions as hereafter defined in the attached Appendix: admonition, warning, censure, disciplinary probation, restitution, suspension, expulsion, ejection, and/or arrest by the civil authorities.

2. Any tenured or non-tenured faculty member, or tenured or non-tenured member of the administrative or custodial staff engaging in any manner in conduct prohibited under substantive Rules 1–8 shall be subject to the following range of penalties: warning, censure, restitution, fine not exceeding those permitted by law or by the Bylaws of the Board of Higher Education, or suspension with/without pay pending a hearing before an appropriate college authority, dismissal after a hearing, ejection, and/or arrest by the civil authorities. In addition, in the case of a tenured faculty member, or tenured member of the administrative or custodial staff engaging in any manner in conduct prohibited under substantive Rules 1–8 shall be entitled to be treated in accordance with applicable provisions of the Education Law or Civil Service Law.

3. Any visitor, licensee, or invitee, engaging in any manner in conduct prohibited under substantive Rules 1–8 shall be subject to ejection, and/or arrest by the civil authorities.

# Appendix

**Sanctions Defined:**

A.    ADMONITION. An oral statement to the offender that he has violated university rules.

B.    WARNING. Notice to the offender, orally or in writing, that continuation or repetition of the wrongful conduct, within a period of time stated in the warning, may be cause for more severe disciplinary action.

C.    CENSURE. Written reprimand for violation of specified regulation, including the possibility of more severe disciplinary sanction in the event of conviction for the violation of any university regulation within a period stated in the letter of reprimand.

D.    DISCIPLINARY PROBATION. Exclusion from participation in privileges or extracurricular university activities as set forth in the notice of disciplinary probation for a specified period of time.

E.    RESTITUTION. Reimbursement for damage to or misappropriation of property. Reimbursement may take the form of appropriate service to repair or otherwise compensate for damages.

F.    SUSPENSION. Exclusion from classes and other privileges or activities as set forth in the notice of suspension for a definite period of time.

G.    EXPULSION. Termination of student status for an indefinite period. The conditions of readmission, if any is permitted, shall be stated in the order of expulsion.

H.    COMPLAINT TO CIVIL AUTHORITIES.

I.    EJECTION.

RESOLVED, That a copy of these rules and regulations be filed with the Regents of the State of New York and with the Commissioner of Education.

RESOLVED, That these rules and regulations be

incorporated in each college bulletin.

Adopted by the Board of Higher Education
June 23, 1969, Calendar No. 3(b)

# D

## INTERIM RULES — COLUMBIA UNIVERSITY

### Resolution

Adopted By The Faculty
on Sept. 12, 1968
on Motion of the

## Joint Committee on Disciplinary Affairs

The Faculty hereby approves and endorses the attached *Interim Rules* relating to Rallies, Picketing and Other Mass Demonstrations. We urge all members of the University community to abide by these rules, and to cooperate in their implementation, until more permanent arrangements can be devised.

The Faculty also recommends that the President and the Trustees take the following actions, which we consider essential to the maintenance of an orderly campus community and the application of internal discipline:

(a) Urge the Courts to dismiss criminal charges against students charged only with criminal trespass on either April 30 or May 22;

(b) Make clear that the Joint Committee on Disciplinary Affairs (or any successor body on which elected faculty and student representatives have majority representation) has final authority in imposing University discipline.

(c) Indicate that they will accept petitions from students or faculty and respond directly to such petitions within a reasonable time.

Affirmative actions on the foregoing are essential for the creation of a proper environment within which University discipline can be carried out. We request that the President report to the Faculty on these matters at the earliest possible date.

The Faculty requests that the Executive Committee make prompt arrangements for the election of student members to the Joint Committee, the elections to be completed not later than October 30, 1968. Faculty members of the Joint Committee will stand for election at the meeting of the Faculty. Faculty vacancies shall be filled by the Executive Committee, and administrative vacancies shall be filled by the President. The Joint Committee shall continue to exercise appellate authority over all disciplinary proceedings and shall make such supplementary rules as may be required to facilitate the processing of such cases.

The Faculty requests the Executive Committee to constitute a new permanent body, containing substantial representation for faculty, students and administrators, to formulate rules to govern behavior on the Columbia campus and to establish an appropriate disciplinary structure for the University. This body also shall have full authority to revise the Interim Rules Relating to Rallies, Picketing and Other Mass Demonstrations. It is the opinion of the Joint Committee that the new body should consist of faculty members, elected by the Faculty (40 per cent); students, elected by the student bodies of the various schools and divisions of the University under procedures prescribed by the Executive Committee after consultation with student groups (40 per cent); and administrators, elected by the Council of Deans and Directors (20 per cent). Since it is a matter of greatest urgency that the Interim Rules, and other rules governing behavior and discipline, shall be subject to continuing review and revision, the Executive Committee is requested to give this matter a high priority and to constitute the new rulemaking body at the earliest possible date. In order to provide guidance for this new body, the Executive Committee shall arrange for an early poll on the Interim Rules in order to ascertain the view of students.

The Faculty requests the Executive Committee to make arrangements to provide legal assistance to students proceeded against in University disciplinary proceedings for violations of University regulations who seek such assistance.

The Faculty requests the Executive Committee to make arrangements for the appointment of faculty and student observers to observe the conduct of police and demonstrators, and to separate spectators from the police action in the event of police intervention to terminate a demonstration.

The Faculty recommends that the Executive Committee initiate preparation of codes of conduct for members of the University community other than students and that the policies governing such conduct be made public when available.

## Interim Rules Relating
## To Rallies, Picketing and
## Other Mass Demonstrations

Rallies, picketing and the circulation of petitions have an important place in the life of the university. They are a vital part of the democratic process, a means by which protests may be registered and attention drawn to new directions possible in the evolution of our community. In the context of a responsive administration and responsible faculty such activities can form an effective part of constructive relations between student, faculty and administration.

At the same time, it must be recognized that picketing and other mass demonstrations conducted without reasonable restraint, especially during this critical period of institutional revision can have detrimental consequences for the University community. First, they may prevent large numbers of teachers and students from pursuing the instructional and scholarly activities which attracted them to the University. Second, such demonstrations can provide an environment in which highly reprehensible individual acts can be committed—such as the burning of research papers, the rifling of files, the destruction of University property, the infliction of violence. Third, if the University is incapable of terminating such demonstrations as get out of hand, it becomes likely that police intervention will ensue, which brings in its wake a whole series of repugnant consequences. Fourth, the course of a demonstration is difficult to predict and seemingly minor lawless acts may pave the way for more egregious assaults upon the University.

One of the principles goals of the present period of University restructuring is the creation of effective means of communication between students, faculty and administration. To permit attainment of this and the other goals of restructuring it is necessary that some reasonable restraints be imposed on the place and manner in which picketing and other demonstrations are conducted.

## Regulations

Picketing and other demonstrations are hereby declared to be in violation of University regulations if participants:

    (a)    Gather in such fashion as to physically hinder entrance to, exit from, or normal use of a University facility;

    (b)    Create a volume of noise that prevents members of the University from carrying on their normal activities (use of bull-horns or sound amplification equipment must be subjected to particularly careful control under the enforcement procedures described hereafter);

    (c)    Employ force or violence, or constitute an immediate threat of force or violence, against persons or property;

(d)   Congregate or assemble within University buildings in such fashion as to disrupt the University's normal functions or violate the following rules:

1.   No group may be admitted into a private office unless invited, and then not in excess of the number designated or invited by the occupant. Passage through reception areas leading to private offices must not be obstructed.

2.   Corridors, stairways, doorways and building entrances may not be blocked or obstructed in violation of the regulations of the New York City Fire Department or of the University. Clear and unimpeded passageway must be maintained at all times. For this purpose the Proctor may set a limit on the number of picketers or demonstrators who will be permitted in such areas.

3.   Rooms in which instruction, research or study normally take place may be occupied only when assigned through established University procedures.

4.   Any noise which interferes with the work or study of persons in a building will not be permitted.

5.   Buildings must be cleared at the normal closing time for each building unless other arrangements are approved in advance.

[ These five   limitations   are   substantially   those proposed in the "Student Life Report."]

The Proctor shall be informed of the time and place of demonstrations in advance of any public announcement of plans for a demonstration. He may prescribe only such limitations on the areas in which demonstrations are held as are reasonably necessary to avoid physical harm or physical conflict between groups of demonstrators. He should also advise students as to whether their planned demonstration is consistent with these rules.

Decisions of the Proctor as to numbers of indoor demonstrators and as to the area in which a demonstration is held (as set forth above) shall be binding unless and until they are reversed or modified on appeal to the Joint Committee.

## Enforcement

The President shall designate a University official who will have principal authority for enforcement of these rules (hereafter referred to as the Delegate).

*Comment:* Upon constitution of the new faculty-student-administration rulemaking body referred to in the Joint Committee's accompanying resolution, the President shall consult with this body concerning the person named as Delegate, and he shall be satisfactory to both.

Should any member of the University believe that an assembly or other demonstration violates the rules listed above, he may notify the Office of the President by calling the Security Office. The President's Delegate shall proceed to the site of the gathering and determine if the stated rules have been violated. (In this and in all subsequent instances, the Delegate may act through an agent or representative.) If the Delegate finds that the assembly violates the rules, he shall prescribe modifications in the conduct of the assembly and allow a reasonable time for making the necessary adjustments. If the assembly fails to make the prescribed adjustments, the Delegate shall rule that the assembly is thenceforth unlawful and shall order immediate termination. Participants and spectators who fail to disperse shall be liable to University discipline as described below and the Delegate shall warn them of that fact.

*Comment:* The Delegate is given the initial task of determining whether a demonstration is unlawful or not. With respect to most situations, the rules themselves provide reasonably clear guidelines. In doubtful situations, the Delegate's judgment should be respected. However, the Delegate's decision is always subject to review in subsequent disciplinary proceedings and an adverse declaration by the Delegate does not make a lawful demonstration unlawful. By the same token, a belief by a student that the Delegate has made a mistake does not make an unlawful demonstration lawful, or exonerate or excuse the student, if the Delegate has properly declared that the demonstration is unlawful.

Students who engage in repeated demonstrations of a similar character after a declaration that the first demonstration was unlawful and a warning that penalties would ensue if it was not terminated, need not be given additional declarations or warnings. Such a series of unlawful demonstrations may be regarded as a single unlawful demonstration if similar in character. A warning is not necessary if a demonstration is a deliberate and obvious violation of the rules (as determined by a disciplinary tribunal in the subsequent disciplinary proceeding).

*Comment:* This paragraph is concerned with two problems. First, demonstrations of a "hit and run" character are made unlawful after the first determination and warning. Students who engaged in improper picketing at one location and desisted upon warning by the Delegate would expose themselves to disciplinary sanctions if they resumed the same kind of activity at a different location or at a later time. Second, demonstrations which are deliberate and obvious violations—e.g., blockading a University official in his office—would not be excused because the action was completed prior to a declaration of illegality.

Any student engaged in a demonstration declared unlawful

by the Delegate must, upon request, identify himself to anyone who identifies himself as the Delegate or his agent.

If a demonstration is not ruled unlawful, but spectators are committing violations of these rules, the Delegate shall order the spectators to conform to the rules or to disperse and shall assure that participants in the lawful demonstration are not subjected to disciplinary sanctions. Moreover, no demonstration, lawful or unlawful, justifies an unlawful counter-demonstration.

Should students find themselves subject to criminal penalties, they shall nevertheless be subject to University disciplinary proceedings for violations of these rules. University disciplinary proceedings shall go forward without regard to extramural proceedings, except that a student facing both criminal and University charges relating to the same underlying facts may elect to defer the University proceedings by obtaining a special leave of absence from the University until the criminal case is resolved. While criminal proceedings cannot be avoided in all instances, it should be emphasized that the primary means for dealing with problems of student behavior should be University discipline.

*Comment:* Neither the constitutional privilege against self-incrimination nor the prohibition against double jeopardy prevents a University from bringing disciplinary proceedings against students charged with violations of the criminal law relating to the same set of facts. *Grossner* v. *Trustees of Columbia University,* 287 F.Supp. 535 (S.D.N.Y. 1968); *Goldberg* v. *Regents of University of California,* 57 Cal.Rep. 463 (1957). With respect to the privilege against self-incrimination, the provisions of the rules permitting students to withdraw until related criminal proceedings are resolved, is probably more generous than the law requires. See *Oleshko* v. *New York State Liquor Authority,* 29 A.D. 2d 84 (First Dept. 1967), aff'd men., 21 N.Y. 2d 778 (1968). In general, a defendant in a civil proceeding is not entitled to have the proceeding stayed pending the resolution of related criminal proceedings. See, e.g., *United States* v. *American Radiator & Standard Sanitary Corp.*, 388 F.2d 201 (3d Cir. Dec. 18, 1967), cert. denied, ____ U.S. ____ (1968). Any other result would mean that a student could delay or escape University discipline simply by engaging in conduct sufficiently serious to warrant criminal sanctions.

## Disciplinary Proceedings

The Delegate shall endeavor to identify students who have participated in an unlawful demonstration and shall institute disciplinary proceedings against such students. The Delegate shall notify the student in writing of the charge against him, citing these rules and including a copy. Simultaneously, the Delegate shall notify the chairman of the appropriate disciplinary tribunal, convened in accordance with the Joint Committee's report of May 9, 1968. The chairman shall direct the student to appear before the tribunal at the earliest practicable date. A student who fails to appear before the disciplinary tribunal, as directed, shall be suspended unless he has theretofore requested and is granted a postponement. In lieu of appearing before the tribunal, the student may elect to settle his case by agreement with his Dean; the settlement agreed upon shall be certified to the disciplinary tribunal.

In proceedings before a disciplinary tribunal, the charge of violation of these rules shall be presented by the Delegate. The student shall have the right to be advised by counsel of his own choosing and to present evidence in his own behalf, but counsel shall not participate in the proceedings without the permission of the tribunal. The student is not required to give evidence against himself. A transcript of the proceedings shall be made. While it is essential that the proceedings be fair and orderly, it is not requisite that strict rules of evidence be applied in all instances or that all the rules governing the conduct of judicial proceedings be applied. The proceedings shall be open to the public unless the student elects to have a closed hearing; the tribunal also may close the hearing on the ground that the spectators are disrupting the proceedings. Subject to the requirements previously stated as to the review hereafter provided, each tribunal shall be free to shape its own procedures, including the adoption of reasonable standards to govern the behavior of counsel.

> *Comment:* While tribunals are given the authority to control participation of counsel in the proceeding, tribunals are also obligated to proceed in a fair manner. Thus, if in any case the Delegate were to be represented by a person with legal training, obviously the student also should be permitted full representation. And tribunals should be receptive to claims that special circumstances require that counsel participate on a particular point. The Joint Committee will review all assertions of unfairness in cases appealed to it, and will continue to review the proper role of counsel in University disciplinary proceedings.

Schools may convene more than one disciplinary tribunal if several are necessary to dispose of disciplinary charges expeditiously. In the event hearings before a disciplinary tribunal are not held promptly, the Joint Committee will designate a panel of its members to act in lieu of the disciplinary tribunal. (These members shall then be excluded in appellate review of the panel's decision.)

Alternates shall be selected to serve in lieu of members of disciplinary tribunals who may be unavailable. Students charged with violations shall be accorded an opportunity to challenge any member of the tribunal for cause. If the challenged member does not disqualify himself, the remaining members of the tribunal shall pass on whether the challenged member shall be disqualified.

The student shall be presumed innocent and the burden of proving a violation shall rest upon the Delegate. However, the

Delegate may establish a violation, in the absence of contrary evidence, by showing (a) that the demonstration was unlawful, and (b) that the student has been reasonably identified as one of those present at the scene of the demonstration. In the event of a conflict in the evidence, a violation by the student must be established by a clear preponderance of the evidence.

Decisions of the tribunal shall be by majority vote.

Participants in unlawful demonstrations should be subjected to disciplinary sanctions appropriate to the offense. While each case must be judged on its individual facts, the following general guidelines are provided:

(1)　For initial offenses of a minor nature, the student should be placed on disciplinary probation for one or more semesters. Minor offenses are those which involve no injury to person or property, and no serious or prolonged disruption of University functions.

(2)　For repeated offenses of a minor nature, or an offense by a student on disciplinary probation, the student should be censured or suspended. Censure exposes the student to expulsion for a subsequent offense and becomes a part of his record as long as he remains a student in the University.

(3)　For offenses of a major nature, the student should be suspended or expelled. Major offenses are those which involve injury to person or property, or disrupt one or more University functions to a significant extent or for a prolonged period.

(4)　Students remain responsible for their individual conduct. Individual acts of violence, and individual violations of other University regulations, remain subject to disciplinary sanctions, even though the actions of the group may conform to these rules.

(5)　In any case in which the penalty of suspension has been determined, the student should be given the opportunity to withdraw from the University if he so requests.

*Comment:* In judging the appropriateness of this sanction, several factors deserve mention:

1. This document constitutes a general warning that the sanction of suspension will be imposed in certain cases so that no participant in an unlawful demonstration can claim that he did not realize the seriousness of his misconduct.

2. A further warning of the imposition of sanctions is generally prescribed in these procedures for terminating unlawful demonstrations.

3. This document also constitutes a considered judgment as to the proper limits of activities designed to assert grievances and protest injustice. Thus, in the usual case the motives or objectives of participants will not be held to constitute a justification for their behavior or a reason for not imposing the penalty of suspension if otherwise warranted.

## Appeals and Special Procedures

The Joint Committee will entertain appeals by the student from decisions of the tribunal on any ground. Appeals by the Delegate will also be entertained, but only on the following two grounds: (a) procedural error amounting to fundamental unfairness, or (b) gross disparity of penalties.

*Comment:* The Joint Committee gives great weight to the decisions of disciplinary tribunals. In the usual case, it would intervene only to assure that proceedings are fairly conducted, i.e., that both the student and the Delegate have an opportunity to present their case fairly. Thus, both the student and the Delegate may appeal on the basis of procedural error amounting to fundamental unfairness. While the student may appeal on other issues—insufficiency of evidence to support the decision, undue severity of penalty—the Delegate is limited to the sole additional ground of gross disparity of penalties. This ground is essential to assure that serious inequities do not result in the case of students similarly situated. Without this ground of appeal, it would be necessary to substitute a single centralized hearing tribunal for the disciplinary tribunals in each school.

It is contemplated that procedures for the imposition of penalties will be expeditious. However, no penalty shall enter into force until the student has exhausted his appellate rights. Appellants have five working days in which to file an appeal. Extensions may be granted at the discretion of the Joint Committee. The appeal should contain all arguments and evidence to be presented, as the Joint Committee may choose not to conduct oral argument on such an appeal, but may rely on written briefs by the student and the Delegate and on the transcript of any hearings held in the case at issue. Each party shall have an opportunity to comment upon any appeal by the other party. The sanctions decided upon should take effect no earlier than the date of exhaustion of all appellate rights.

In addition to hearing appeals, the Joint Committee will respond to inquiries about the rules or its procedures.

In the event that the Delegate suspects that a student has committed an act of violence of such magnitude that his continued presence on campus would endanger the University community, the Delegate shall direct that the student appear before the Joint Committee. If, after hearing the Delegate and the student, the Joint Committee concludes that the continued presence of the student on the campus poses a substantial threat to life or property, the student shall be suspended pending resolution of disciplinary charges against him. These charges shall be presented to a disciplinary tribunal at the earliest practicable time agreeable to the student. If the student is exonerated, the suspension shall be expunged from his record.

## Police Intervention

Disorderly demonstrations on campus, if not terminated by University personnel, may lead to the deplorable consequences of police intervention. In the event that such intervention appears unavoidable, these procedures shall be followed:

If students refuse to terminate a demonstration declared unlawful by the Delegate, the President must determine in consultation with the Executive Committee of the Faculty whether the police shall be called. If the President, together with a majority of a panel established by the Executive Committee (which will be available to the President at all times), agree that the demonstration is a violation of these rules, that it poses a serious threat to the orderly functioning of the University, and that it cannot be promptly terminated without police intervention, the police shall be called to terminate the demonstration and the demonstrators shall be warned of that fact. It is recommended that if the police are called after the President consults with the Executive Committee, neither the President nor the members of the Executive Committee shall attempt to negotiate with demonstrators about their demands.

*Comment:* The role of the Executive Committee shall be assumed by the proposed faculty-student-adminstration rule-making committee as soon as possible after that committee is constituted.

The President has the primary duty of protecting lives and property on the campus. Nothing in this section shall prevent the President from asking for police assistance in order to counter acts of violence, destruction of property, or other violations of law. But if the President is unable to consult with the panel of the Executive Committee, or to obtain its concurrence, the special procedures set forth below shall not apply.

If a demonstration is terminated in accordance with the consultation procedures outlined above, each student arrested by the police in the course of terminating the demonstration shall be notified in writing: (a) that he is charged with a violation of these rules; (b) that his arrest constitutes evidence sufficient to establish a violation of these rules in the absence of contrary evidence; and (c) that he will be suspended from the University in seven days unless, prior to that time, he obtains a ruling from his dean, the disciplinary tribunal of his school, or a panel of the Joint Committee, that he was not a participant in an unlawful demonstration (all such rulings being subject to appeal to the Joint Committee). If a student testifies or presents other evidence denying his participation in an unlawful demonstration, he shall be exonerated unless a clear preponderance of the evidence establishes a violation. If a student is unable to obtain the requisite ruling, his suspension shall go into effect at the stated time, unless the student is not accorded a hearing despite prompt application to both a disciplinary tribunal and the Joint Committee. Suspension from the University under these procedures shall be for one year from the beginning of the semester in which the suspension was initially imposed.

## THE JOINT COMMITTEE
## ON DISCIPLINARY AFFAIRS

Quentin Anderson, Chairman

Thaddeus W. Borun

Pearl Chesler

Howard McP. Davis

Mark Flanigan

Andrew Gaspar

William Goldfarb

William K. Jones

Peter B. Kenen

Julian M. Miller

Frank Motley

Chester Rapkin

Richard C. Robey, Executive Secretary

Steven Schwarz

Daniel Weingrad

John Wellington

Eric D. Witkin, Vice-Chairman

# E

Order Granting Permanent Injunction.

## QUEENS COUNTY, NEW YORK
## SUPREME COURT
## SPECIAL TERM, PART III

### Justice Agresta

BOARD OF HIGHER EDUCATION OF THE CITY OF N.Y. v. STUDENTS FOR A DEMOCRATIC SOCIETY*—This action for a permanent injunction

"1. Restraining and enjoining each and all of the defendants and all other persons receiving notice of this injunction from congregating or assembling within or adjacent to or threatening to congregate or assemble within or adjacent to any of the plaintiff's academic or administrative buildings, recreation rooms or athletic facilities or in any corridors, stairways, doorways and entrances thereto on the campus of Queensborough Community College, in such manner as to disrupt or interfere with normal functions conducted by plaintiff in such place or to block, hinder, impede or interfere with ingress to or egress from any such properties by plaintiff's faculty, administrators, students, employees or guests thereat;

"2. Restraining and enjoining each and all of the defendants and all other persons receiving notice of this injunction from creating or broadcasting or threatening to create or broadcast on plaintiff's Queensborough Community College campus or in the

---

\*    Order granting a permanent injunction in Board of Higher Education of the City of New York v. Students for a Democratic Society, printed in the NEW YORK LAW JOURNAL, June 12, 1969.

streets adjacent there, any loud or excessive noise that hinders, impedes, prevents or interferes with the conduct of normal activities by members of the College community;

"3. Restraining and enjoining each and all of the defendants and all other persons receiving notice of this injunction from employing force or violence, against persons or property on plaintiff's Queensborough Community College campus;

"4. Restraining and enjoining each and all of the defendants and all other persons receiving notice of this injunction from threatening to do or inciting or counselling others or conspiring with others to do any of the above mentioned acts; and

"5. Granting plaintiff such other relief as may be proper." was tried before me at Special Term, Part III. Plaintiff, Board of Higher Education of the City of New York, governs and administers Queensborough Community College (hereinafter called Queensborough). Defendants Auerbach, Tivoli, Raps, Kanin, Brown, Wininger, Reed, Spiller and Moore are duly-enrolled students at Queensborough; defendants Faigelman, McDonald and Silberman, at the time of the institution of this action, were non-tenured members of the instructional staff at Queensborough; defendant Leslie Joyce Silberman is the wife of Professor Silberman; defendant Students for a Democratic Society, Queensborough Community College Chapter, is a chartered campus organization; and defendant Ad Hoc Faculty-Student Coalition to End Political Suppression is an unchartered organization on the campus of Queensborough.

The events that have given rise to this action are but another manifestation of the unrest on our college campuses today. The facts that I have adduced after a seven-day trial can be summarized as follows:

On April 18, 1969, shortly after noon, an authorized outdoor rally was held on the Queensborough campus and immediately thereafter many of the participants in that rally entered the Library-Administration Building and began a "sit-in" on the fourth floor. Thereafter, at about 9 P.M. on April 18, 1969, the president of Queensborough informed the students that they were subject to arrest on criminal trespass charges in the second degree and at about 9 P.M. over 100 members of the New York City Police Department, Tactical Patrol Force, assembled near the campus. On or about that time, the buildings were vacated.

On April 21, 1969, an order to show cause was signed by a justice of this court made returnable on April 23 which provided, inter alia, that pending the hearing of the motion for a temporary injunction defendants, and all other persons receiving notice of the injunction, should cease from activities which tended to "disrupt or interfere with normal functions" on the campus.

Thereafter on April 21, shortly after the noon hour, anywhere from 400 to 600 people re-entered the Library-Administration Building and "sat-in" in the lounge area located on the fourth floor. At about 5:30 P.M., service of the order to show cause, which contained the temporary restraining order, was made on those who had occupied the lounge. They left the Library-Administration Building but returned at 7:15 P.M. and at that time the "sit-in" began in earnest and was to last until May 7.

After hearing voluminous testimony by Kurt Schmeller, president of Queensborough Community College, his assistant, Miss Eleanor Pam, and testimony by many members of the faculty and many of the defendants, I make the following findings which are material and necessary on the question of whether an injunction should issue.

I find that those who "sat-in" on the fourth floor of the Library-Administration Building remained there after the normal closing hours of the building even though they were requested to remove themselves and that their motivation for sitting in in the building was their being informed that an English professor, the defendant Donald Silberman, would not be reappointed for the following year.

I find that during the "sit-in," the students used loud

amplification systems, played guitars and generally disrupted the work being carried on in the other offices on the fourth floor, which included the president's office, the registrar's office, the bursar's office and the admissions office.

I find that even though the students made an effort to keep the area clear and to keep it clean, cigarette butts often could be found on the floor and there were burns in the carpet. Furthermore, at certain times during the course of the "sit-ins," administration personnel were abused by profanities. The certificate of occupancy for the fourth floor area, which was used by those who "sat in," limited occupation to 100 people, the number of people normally employed on that floor, and I find that at times this number was exceeded by the participants alone, particularly during performances by well-known entertainers brought in by the organizers of the "sit-in" to "entertain" during the course of the occupation of the fourth floor. This excessive number of people caused building violations to issue against the university.

On April 28, 1969, a decision of a justice of this court continued the temporary restraining order which, inter alia, restrained defendants from disrupting or interfering with the normal functions of the university and from employing force or violence against persons or property on the campus. However, despite this order, the "sit-in" continued and by May 1 substantial destruction of university property occurred. At that time, the participants of the "sit-in" were apprised that the police were assembling to physically remove them from the buildings and some of the participants piled office furniture in the stairways, ripped out telephones and caused substantial other destruction of university property.

The fundamental question presented is whether this court has the power to issue the injunction sought. I hold that this court does have that power and that a permanent injunction, limited in its terms as indicated below, shall issue for the following reasons:

The proven conduct of the defendants constitutes, among

other wrongs, a continuous trespass. It is beyond dispute in this jurisdiction that a court of equity, under certain circumstances, has jurisdiction to enjoin a continuous trespass (Coatsworth v. Lehigh Valley RR., 156 N. Y. 451; Wheelock v. Noonan, 108 N. Y. 179; Poughkeepsie Gas Co. v. Citizen Gas Co., 89 N. Y. 493; Garvey v. L.I. RR., 159 N. Y. 323; Van De Carr v. Schloss, 277 App. Div. 475; see, also, the following treatises: 4 Pomeroy Equity Jurisprudence, 5th ed., sec. 1357; 1 High on Injunctions, 4th ed., sec. 697; 43 C. J. S. 2d, sec. 57, at p. 521). As was stated by Mr. Justice Chase, "Where a trespass is of a continuous nature, a person has a right to invoke the restraining order of a court of equity to prevent the same and in an action for that purpose the court can, and should, grant all the relief that the nature of the action and the facts demand" (Sadlier v. City of New York, 185 N. Y. 403, 413). The facts which guide the court are (1) the irreparability of the injuries; (2) the inadequacy of the remedy at law and (3) whether injunctive relief will avoid a multiplicity of actions (Williams v. N. Y. Central RR., 16 N. Y. 97, and 1 High on Injunctions, sec. 697).

There can be no question that defendants have caused irreparable injury both to the facilities of their college and to its normal educational and administrative procedures and that the remedy at law is inadequate in that a multiplicity of law actions will be needed to give plaintiff a remedy and that such a remedy would, in reality, afford no relief against continued disruption of the campus facilities. The mere fact that a permanent injunction has never before sought in this jurisdiction against such activities does not defeat plaintiff's application (see Mendenhall v. School District No. 83, 90 Pac. 773). The rule as set forth in a leading treatise is "It is not a fatal objection to the granting of an injunction that the use of the writ for the particular purpose for which it is sought is novel" (43 C.J.S. 2d, 429; see, also, Unity Contract Bridge Club v. Wallender, 187 Misc. 23). The extension of the doctrine of injunctive relief against continuous trespass to this novel situation constitutes the adaptation of a traditional remedy to a new situation which, of course, is in the best tradition of equity jurisprudence. It is this ability of our law to so adapt that has made it survive over the centuries.

Defendants contend, however, that injunctive relief does not lie because (1) a public facility is involved and (2) equity will not enjoin criminal acts. This court does not agree with the first contention. In County Court of Harrison v. West Virginia Air Service (132 W. Va. 1), the Supreme Court of Appeals of West Virginia, in an action by the county as the owner of a public airport to restrain the defendant lessee from the further use of the airport after its lease had expired, held that where an injunction is sought against one who trespasses on a public facility there is even greater reason for its issuance than when private facilities are involved. This court agrees with the reasoning of that opinion.

Defendants also contend that because a public university is involved here, its students as members of the public somehow possess the right to "occupy its facilities." A similar contention was presented to the court in People v. Martinez (43 Misc. 2d 94), which was a criminal action against four defendants who entered police headquarters to see the Police Commissioner of the City of New York and sat on the floor of the public corridors and refused to leave when requested. The court stated at page 97:

"The Police Headquarters building was thus property owned by the City of New York. 'Property is ownership; the unrestricted and exclusive right to a thing; the right to dispose of a thing in every legal way, to possess it, to use it, and to exclude every one else from interfering with it' (Black's Law Dictionary, Third Edition, p. 1447). A public building is one 'belonging to or used by the public for the transaction of public or quasi public business' (Black Law Dictionary, ibid. p. 1460).

"The words 'public property' and 'public building,' as interpreted by the defendants in their brief are ill-defined. Their meanings may not be distorted into an exercise in semantics. The public owns such property only in a very broad and general sense. The deed to such property is not in the name of each individual citizen in this city, either as joint tenants or tenants in common. The title to Police Headquarters is in a municipal corporation known as the City of New York. Such so-called public building, especially one which houses so vital a functioning department as the Police Department, may not be used in a manner which suits the whim or caprice of every citizen, without reducing our government to chaos (Bi-Metallic Co. v. State Board of Equalization of Colorado, 239 U.S. 441, 36 S. Ct. 141, 60 L. Ed. 372). There is no blanket right to every citizen in his use of this type of property. The rights of others must always be considered (Johnson v. May, 189 App. Div. 196, 204, 178 N.Y.S. 742, 748).

"In a comparable situation, the Appellate Division, Third Department said: 'School buildings are not public places in the sense that the use thereof may be demanded as a matter of right by any individual or organization as a forum for public or private discussions' (Ellis v. Allen, 4 A. D. 2d 343, 344, 165 N.Y.S. 2d 624, 626)."

Nor does this court agree with defendants' second contention, i.e., that this court has no power to enjoin the acts because "equity will not enjoin the commission of a crime." In the landmark case of People ex rel. Bennette v. Laman (277 N.Y. 368) the Court of Appeals of this state stated at pages 376, 381 and 384:

"That a court of equity will not undertake the enforcement of the criminal law, and will not enjoin the commission of a crime is a principle of equity jurisprudence that is settled beyond any question. There can equally be no doubt that the criminal nature of an act will not deprive equity of the jurisdiction that would otherwise attach (Cranford v. Tyrell, 128 N.Y. 341; Davis v. Zimmerman, 91 Hun. 489, 492; Matter of Debs, 158 U.S. 564, 593). Whether or not the act sought to be enjoined is a crime, is immaterial. Equity does not seek to enjoin it simply because it is a crime; it seeks to protect some proper interest. If the interest sought to be protected is one of which equity will take cognizance, it will not refuse to take jurisdiction on the ground that the act which invades that interest is punishable by the penal statutes of the State. Equity does not pretend to punish the perpetrator for the act; it attempts to protect the right of the party (here the People) seeking relief, and to prevent the performance of the act or acts, which here may injure many. * * * We have pointed out that the fact that a criminal penalty is imposed for the performance of such acts will not deprive equity of its jurisdiction. In equity the court will consider the criminality of the act only to determine whether, under the particular circumstances, equitable intervention is necessary to give adequate protection to the interest invaded or whether justice will be best served by relegating the parties to the criminal court. * * * They allege facts showing that the acts of defendant imperil the health of the people of the community, and will continue to cause irreparable injury to the health of the people and perhaps to their lives. The relators invoke only the ordinary powers of a court of equity. The power of the court to restrain acts which are dangerous to human life, detrimental to the public health and the occasion of great public inconvenience and damage is one that is possessed by all courts of equity (Health Dept. v. Purden, supra). Enough has been shown here, which if proven upon the trial, will warrant the issuance of an injunction" (see also Lanvin Parfums, Inc., v. Le Dans, Ltd., 9 N.Y. 2d 516). Here, too, the acts sought to be enjoined constitute a danger to human life and property and occasion "great public inconvenience" and the interest sought to be protected is one of which equity takes cognizance. Accordingly, equitable jurisdiction attaches even though defendants' acts may be incidentally criminally punishable."

Defendants' final contention is that somehow their activities on this campus were and are constitutionally protected and, therefore, equity may not enjoin them. Such a contention, i.e., that one is privileged to disrupt a college campus was put to rest in Hutt v. Brooklyn College of the City of N.Y. (an unpublished opinion of the United States District Court, Eastern District, New York, dated Dec. 28, 1968) where the court stated:

"That the state may, in some cases, constitutionally punish conduct intended to express an idea or point of view, is not open to question. See, e.g., United States v. O'Brien, U.S. 88 S. Ct. 1673 (1968). The Supreme Court has often rejected the proposition that 'people who want to propagandize protests or views have a constitutional right to do so whenever and however and wherever they please * * *' Adderley v. Florida, 385 U.S. 39, 48, 87 S. Ct. 242, 247 (1966); Cox v. Louisiana, 379 U.S. 599, 85 S. Ct. 476 (1965). The admitted facts of this case indicate a willful trespass on College property, the exclusion of administrative personnel of the College and an intentional refusal by the plaintiffs to end their seizure and adverse holdings of College property after being warned that they faced suspension or dismissal and even arrest for violating the rules of the College and the New York State trespass laws. Even assuming that the aforesaid conduct does combine 'speech' elements with 'nonspeech' elements, nothing in the First Amendment forbids the State (or College authorities) from disciplining students who prevent others from access to College facilities. See Buttny v. Smiley, 281 F. Supp. 280 (D. Colo. 1968). A reasonable balancing of interests must reserve to the State (and the College) the power to preserve its facilities for their intended uses. The right to communicate does not include the right to confiscate. (see, also, Grossner v. Trustees of Columbia University of the City of N.Y., 287 F. Supp. 535)."

Accordingly, this court is of the opinion that an injunction is to issue which is to be perpetual against defendants Students for a Democratic Society, the Ad Hoc Faculty-Student Coalition to End Political Suppression and Leslie Joyce Silberman and, as against defendants Donald J. Silberman, Faigelman, MacDonald and the student defendants, is to last until such time as they are no longer, as the case may be, faculty members or students at Queensborough Community College. The defendants and all others receiving notice of this injunction are enjoined from:

(1) Congregating or assembling within or adjacent to any of the plaintiff's academic or administrative buildings, recreation rooms or athletic facilities or in any corridors, stairways, doorways and entrances thereto on the campus of Queensborough Community College, in such manner as to disrupt or interfere with normal functions conducted by plaintiff in such place or to block, hinder, impede or interfere with ingress to or egress from any such properties by plaintiff's faculty, administrators, students, employees or guests thereat; and

(2) Employing force or violence against persons or property on plaintiff's Queensborough Community College campus.

The issuance of such an injunction, limited to those activities which disrupt the normal activities at the College and to activities that tend to produce violence on the campus does not in any way offend any of the constitutional guarantees contained in the First Amendment of the United States Constitution. This injunction in no way proscribes or circumvents constitutionally-protected activities. This court is well aware that the right to peacefully protest and to disseminate even those views that may be abhorrent to a majority of the populace is the cornerstone upon which our Constitution rests. However, where that protest, as here, becomes violent and, in essence, deprives others of their right to pursue their studies in a relatively tranquil atmosphere, that protest can no longer be privileged or protected if society itself and the rule of law which governs it is to survive.

The foregoing constitutes the decision of this court and all matters made at the trial with regard to the action for a permanent injunction are resolved in a manner consistent with this opinion. Settle judgment.

# F

Summons and complaint for permanent injunction, filed in the case of *Wisconsin ex rel. La Follette v. Cohen,* in Dane County Circuit Court, Wisconsin.

## STATE OF WISCONSIN
## IN CIRCUIT COURT FOR DANE COUNTY

☆ ☆ ☆ ☆ ☆ ☆ ☆ ☆ ☆ ☆ ☆ ☆ ☆ ☆ ☆ ☆ ☆ ☆ ☆ ☆ ☆ ☆ ☆ ☆ ☆ ☆ ☆ ☆ ☆☆

STATE OF WISCONSIN ex rel.
BRONSON C. LaFOLLETTE,
ATTORNEY GENERAL,
                    Plaintiff,


          -v-


ROBERT S. COHEN, DAVID LEE GOLDMAN, CARLOS F. JOLY, WILLIAM SIMONS, EVAN STARK, ROBERT A. WEILAND, ROBERT B. SWACKER, ROBERT K. ZWICKER, MADISON, WISCONSIN CHAPTER, STUDENTS FOR A DEMOCRATIC SOCIETY, its Officers, Agents and All Other Persons Acting By, Through, or In Their Behalf,

                    Defendants.

☆ ☆ ☆ ☆ ☆ ☆ ☆ ☆ ☆ ☆ ☆ ☆ ☆ ☆ ☆ ☆ ☆ ☆ ☆ ☆ ☆ ☆ ☆ ☆ ☆ ☆ ☆ ☆ ☆☆

## SUMMONS

THE STATE OF WISCONSIN, TO THE SAID DEFENDANTS:
    YOU ARE HEREBY SUMMONED AND REQUIRED to

serve upon Bronson C. LaFollette, Attorney General, whose address is State Capitol, Madison, Wisconsin, an answer to the complaint which is herewith served upon you within twenty (20) days after service of this summons upon you, exclusive of the day of service, and in case of your failure so to do, judgment will be rendered against you according to the demand of the complaint.

Dated this 7th day of November, 1967.

P.O. ADDRESS        /s/ BRONSON C. LaFOLLETTE,
State Capitol,               Attorney General
Madison, Wisconsin

ARLEN C. CHRISTENSON,
Deputy Attorney General

RICHARD L. CATES,
Attorney

JOHN H. BOWERS,
Attorney

ATTORNEYS FOR PLAINTIFF,
STATE OF WISCONSIN

## STATE OF WISCONSIN
## IN CIRCUIT COURT FOR DANE COUNTY

☆ ☆ ☆ ☆ ☆ ☆ ☆ ☆ ☆ ☆ ☆ ☆ ☆ ☆ ☆ ☆ ☆ ☆ ☆ ☆ ☆ ☆ ☆ ☆ ☆ ☆ ☆ ☆ ☆ ☆☆

STATE OF WISCONSIN ex rel.
BRONSON C. LaFOLLETTE,
ATTORNEY GENERAL,
       Plaintiff,

       -v-

ROBERT S. COHEN, DAVID LEE GOLDMAN,
CARLOS F. JOLY, WILLIAM SIMONS, EVAN
STARK, ROBERT A. WEILAND, ROBERT B.
SWACKER, ROBERT K. ZWICKER, MADISON,
WISCONSIN CHAPTER, STUDENTS FOR A
DEMOCRATIC SOCIETY, its Officers, Agents and
All Other Persons Acting By, Through, or In Their
Behalf,
       Defendants.

☆ ☆ ☆ ☆ ☆ ☆ ☆ ☆ ☆ ☆ ☆ ☆ ☆ ☆ ☆ ☆ ☆ ☆ ☆ ☆ ☆ ☆ ☆ ☆ ☆ ☆ ☆ ☆ ☆☆

### COMPLAINT

COMES NOW, Bronson C. LaFollette, Attorney General of Wisconsin, Arlen C. Christenson, Deputy Attorney General, Richard L. Cates and John H. Bowers, Attorneys, for and in behalf of the State of Wisconsin, being duly authorized so to do, and respectfully allege:

1. Bronson C. LaFollette is the Attorney General of the State of Wisconsin and is the chief legal officer of the State.

The University of Wisconsin, (hereinafter the University) established in the City of Madison, by Section 36.01 Wis. Stats., pursuant to Article 10, Section 6, of the Wisconsin Constitution, is governed by a Board of Regents, consisting of nine members, appointed by the governor by and with the consent of the Senate, and one member, ex officio, the State Superintendent of Public Instruction.

2. The University at Madison is composed of eleven schools and colleges with a faculty of 4,187 members (full-time equivalent). The student enrollment on the Madison campus is 33,000. The University employs 4,767 civil service employees. The Madison campus is comprised of 560 acres with approximately 95 buildings devoted to classrooms and other educational functions.

The Government of student affairs and student conduct is, by delegation from the Regents, vested in the Faculty.

3. Each of the following above named defendants is a student at the University. Defendant, Robert S. Cohen resides at Route #1, Oregon, Wisconsin; Defendant, David Lee Goldman resides at 313 North Livingston Street, Madison, Wisconsin; Defendant, Carlos F. Joly resides at 523 West Washington Avenue, Madison, Wisconsin; Defendant, William Simons resides at 550 West Mifflin Street, Madison, Wisconsin; Defendant, Evan Stark resides at 4337 Melford Street, Madison, Wisconsin; Defendant, Robert A. Weiland resides at 544 West Main Street, Madison, Wisconsin; Defendant, Robert B. Swacker resides at 35 North Mills Street, Madison, Wisconsin; Defendant, Robert K. Zwicker resides at 404 North Frances Street, Madison, Wisconsin; the defendant, "Students for a Democratic Society" (hereinafter S.D.S.), is an unincorporated organization, with student members, on the University Campus.

4. This action is brought by the State of Wisconsin by its attorney general at the request of the governor of the State of Wisconsin, pursuant to Sections 14.12 and 280.02, Wis. Statutes.

5. The defendants are persons who are students at the University and who individually and collectively purport to be leaders of groups of students and various other persons who act individually and in concert under the name and style of unincorporated associations of individuals, and ad-hoc committees and

organizations, for the purpose of protesting by public demonstration, on the University campus, policies and decisions of the government of the United States of America and the University of Wisconsin. Demonstrations are made against certain job placement interviews, involving the use of University facilities by governmental and military organizations and private corporations, under rights guaranteed to said students by the Constitution of the United States and of this state.

6. Pursuant to its responsibility and authority as an educational institution, the University, as is customary in institutions of higher learning throughout the United States maintains a full-time staff to carry out an effective program of career information and placement service, including interviews for job placement upon graduation. The program is described in Faculty Document 121, March 8, 1967, annexed hereto and marked Exhibit "A" and made a part hereof with the same force and effect as though set out in full. The faculty policy on placement adopted by the faculty on March 8, 1967 is as follows:

(Ex. "A"– pp. 6–7)

"The Committee on Placement Services recommends that the Madison Campus Faculty approve the following "Policy Statement" adopted by the Committee on January 19, 1967:

"The essential function of University Placement Services is to provide a comprehensive career advisory and placement service for the students of the University. The services include arranging for them to meet on campus with a wide range of representatives to learn of current and projected employment and educational opportunities.

The policy of the University Placement Services with respect to campus interviews is to permit at appropriate times any bona fide employer or higher education or professional school representative to meet with interested students in university facilities when available for purposes of exchanging voluntarily such information as may be relevant.

This information exchange is an essential first step in mutual assessment of opportunities and applicant's interest and qualifications and in many instances leads to specific offers.

The *representative* should be an employee of or authorized agent for the organization scheduling the visit: government, business, industry, education, social agency—wherever legitimate employment or educational opportunities exist. Employment agencies or representatives operating on a fee basis are not scheduled.

A *student* is defined as one who is currently enrolled at the University of Wisconsin. Students and alumni of other institutions of higher learning who have the requested educational qualifications may be permitted to see visiting employer representatives. However, where time is a factor, priority is given first to current student and then alumni of this University.

This policy is in accord with Chapter 11 (11.09 and 11.10) statement on use of facilities approved by the Faculty on December 12, 1966, 'that facilities of the University are primarily for University purposes of instruction, research and public service.' "

7. Pursuant to its responsibility to carry out career information and placement service, the University from time to time schedules placement interviews at various locations on the campus. The students are informed of this program through the Student Handbook published by the University by publication of placement schedules in the Campus Newspaper and by notices placed upon bulletin boards at various places on the campus. The importance of the program and the extent of its use by the students is shown by the report of the faculty, Faculty Document 121 (Exhibit A):

(Ex. "A", P.5)

"Taking the second semester of 1965—66 and the first semester of 1966—67 we can present an approximate year's volume and extent of activity, as follows:

Total individual student involvement: 3,445

Total student interviews: 19,269

Total organizations with scheduled interviews on campus (schools, colleges, libraries, social agencies, gov't, business and industry). 1,939

To round out the figures some 3500 students were involved in some 20,000 interviews with about 2000 organization representatives. Of course there is some overlap with students who interview both semesters, and organizations likewise. But in general over half of the graduating students interview in the course of their life on campus."

8. Pursuant to its career information and placement service, the University has, in the past, scheduled placement interviews with various branches of the military services, the Central Intelligence Agency of the United States, the Dow Chemical Corporation and numerous other organizations. Such placement interviews were scheduled on the University campus for February 22, 23, and 24, 1967 with the Dow Chemical Company; with the Central Intelligence Agency in April of 1967; with the Dow Chemical Corporation October 17—20, 1967.

9. The defendants, and others, have from time to time chosen as the method of their protest an action in concert by a number of persons, which has come to be described as "protest demonstrations" or "student protests".

10. In May of 1966, student protesters staged a nine day sit-in against the University's involvement in the students' relationships with the selective service system. In October of 1966, United States Senator Edward Kennedy attempted to give a speech on the campus, but could not effectively do so as a consequence of "organized heckling" from student and non-student protesters. In December 1966, student protesters heckled and physically surrounded and blocked representatives of the

United States Marine Corps who were on the campus recruiting, in an effort to force the University to discontinue the recruiting activity. There were no pre-demonstration statements or threats to block entrances or other students from access to University offices or recruiters or from hearing Senator Edward Kennedy's speech before these protests. No injury, property damage or arrests resulted from these protest demonstrations.

11. Placement interviews with the Dow Chemical Company were scheduled for February 20–24, 1967. On February 16, 1967, a news item appeared on the front page of the Daily Cardinal, the student newspaper, reporting that the defendant, S.D.S., planned a massive sit-in against the Dow interviews. It was reported that S.D.S., planned to block all entrances and that the protest would continue until the Dow interviews were terminated before their scheduled completion. The threatened protest demonstration was staged during the week of February 20–24, 1967. Access to classrooms, offices and study rooms were blocked; classrooms and offices were occupied, and administrative personnel and employees could not work. The demonstration was marked by threats and fear of physical harm to persons, property damage, and loud, abusive and obscene language. Seventeen students and two non-students were arrested for disorderly conduct. The disorderly conduct cases are still pending in the Wisconsin courts.

12. During various stages of the week long protest described in paragraph 11 herein, the number of demonstrating protesters varied from 15 to upwards of 500 persons. During the various stages of this protest, the protesters assembled and demonstrated at various places on the campus. Some of the protesters staged an overnight sit-in in the halls and corridors of Bascom Hall.

13. On April 11th and 12th, 1967, a student protest demonstration against the Central Intelligence Agency interviews on the campus was conducted in and about the Law Building. At times upwards of 200 students were involved. There was no obstruction or injuries or property damage reported and no

arrests were made.

14. The University Placement Service scheduled interviews with the Dow Chemical Corporation from October 17–20, 1967 for students desiring them. Anticipating probable protest demonstrations, the University, through the office of the Dean of Student Affairs, issued a policy statement affirming that the interviews with Dow would be conducted, re-affirming the right of all persons to peaceful assembly and expression by lawful means and giving notice that attempts to disrupt the interviews would result in discipline by the University. The statement was widely circulated and publicized on the campus. A copy of the statement is annexed hereto marked Exhibit "B" and incorporated herein by reference with the same force and effect as though set out in full.

15. Through its Office of Student Organization Advisors, the University administration made every effort to establish and maintain communications with one or more of the defendants, and others acting in concert with them, in the defendants' making of their plans for conducting protest demonstrations. The director of the Office of Student Organization Advisors, contacted one or more of the defendants and offered cooperation, guidance and assistance in explaining and communicating to the protest leaders and its membership the guidelines required to enable the University to carry on its classes and other University operations, and established by the Deans of the School of Business, the Colleges of Agriculture, Engineering and the Chairman of the Department of Chemistry in whose facilities the Dow interviews were to be conducted. Though initial communication was established, further efforts by the administration to discuss the guidelines were spurned by one or more of the defendants and others acting with them.

A copy of a letter dated October 12, 1967 to defendant, Robert B. Swacker from the Office of Student Organization Advisors, with the guidelines established by the Deans of the School of Business, the Colleges of Agriculture, and Engineering and the Chairman of the Department of Chemistry are marked Exhibits "C", "D", "E", "F", and "G", annexed hereto and incorporated herein in full by reference with the same force and effect as though set out in full.

16. On October 13, 1967, the Director of the Office of Student Organization Advisors and the Director of the Department of Protection and Security went to a meeting being held by one or more of the defendants and others acting in concert with them regarding the planned protest against the Dow interviews, and attempted to discuss and explain the guidelines for the protest which were established to enable the University to carry on its work. Their efforts were spurned by one or more of the defendants, and others acting in concert with them. The aforesaid Directors nevertheless distributed and left with one or more of the defendants for distribution, two hundred copies of an abstract of the guidelines to be in effect for the demonstration regarding the Dow interviews. A copy of that abstract is annexed hereto marked Exhibit "H" and incorporated herein in full by reference with the same force and effect as though set out in full.

17. On or about October 16, 1967, one or more or all of the defendants and others acting in concert with them distributed hand-outs to students on the campus, declaring determination to block and stop the Dow interviews. The hand-outs specifically declared that on Wednesday, October 18, 1967, the demonstrators would enter a building in which the Dow Corporation and interested students would be engaged in interviews and stop them. At least two such hand-outs were distributed; a copy of each of which is marked Exhibits "I" and "J" and is annexed hereto and incorporated herein in full by reference with the same force and effect as though set out in full.

18. The interviews between students and Dow representatives commenced on Tuesday, October 17, 1967 at the Commerce Building. Demonstrations occurred on that date without serious incident, and without attempts to block the interview.

19. The Dow interviews were scheduled to continue on Wednesday, October 18, 1967 in the Commerce Building. At about 10:45 A.M., a large group of protesters, led and participated in by one or more of the defendants marched into the Commerce Building. The protesters spread themselves through the corridor area and completely blocked the corridor with about 200 persons. Singing, stamping and yelling ensued. University Security Officers and members of the administration attempted to keep order and maintain ingress and egress through the hall and into the offices, and particularly in offices in which Dow interviews were scheduled.

20. By 11:30 A.M., October 17, 1967, the first floor hall and entrances to the main administrative offices and certain classrooms in the Commerce Building were blocked by protesters. Repeated attempts by University officials to clear the doorways and halls were resisted and failed. One or more of the defendants urged the protesters to "lock up" and block anyone trying to enter the offices. Negotiations by University officials with one or more of the defendants who were acting as protest spokesmen were unsuccessful.

21. One or more or all of the defendants, acting in concert with each other and with various other persons, on the 18th of October, 1967, intentionally denied to other students their right freely to speak with Dow Chemical Corporation representatives and intentionally incited and counseled others to do the same. To carry out that purpose, one or more or all of the defendants acting in concert with each other and with various other persons, intentionally, physically obstructed and blocked the hall and doorways of the first floor of the Commerce Building, intentionally denied to persons who desired to interview with Dow Chemical Corporation representatives their right to do so, intentionally denied to others their right of ingress and egress through the hallway, intentionally denied to other University students and other members of the University community their right to attend

and conduct classes, intentionally denied to other University students and other members of the University community their right to carry on University operations in the offices of the Commerce Building, and intentionally incited and counseled others to do all of the foregoing.

22. Despite repeated attempts by University officials to negotiate a peaceful solution to the blocking of the Dow interviews and physical blocking of the University offices and classrooms facilities, loud singing and shouting, one or more or all of the defendants acting in concert with each other and with various other persons while physically blocking the hall and doorways to offices and classrooms in the Commerce Building refused to clear the doorways to the classrooms and offices and refused to permit ingress and egress to said offices, classrooms and hallway, and refused to conduct the protest demonstration in a manner to permit the University to conduct classes and carry out its operations and to permit other members of the University community to interview for jobs, and attend classes.

23. After repeated attempts by officers of the University administration to negotiate with one or more or all of the defendants and others acting in concert with them for a peaceful termination of the defendants' intentional physical blocking of doorways to offices and classes in the Commerce Building, their intentional physical blocking and denial to others of their right of ingress and egress to offices, classrooms and the Dow interviews, their use of physical violence and obscenities and after repeated declarations by recognized law enforcement officers that the assembly was unlawful, law enforcement officers of the University and of the City of Madison, entered the Commerce Building under instructions to remove the demonstrators with a minimum possible force. The officers were met with obscenities and by aggressive physical resistance from protesters and rioting ensued.

24. As a consequence of the rioting and violence which ensued from the demonstration on October 18, 1967, forty-seven

students and three non-students of college age, and twenty-one law enforcement officers suffered personal injury. Two of the injured law enforcement officers were hospitalized for five days or more and were so seriously injured as to require corrective surgical procedures. Property damage to University facilities and equipment exceeded $1,500.00. Overtime expenses to the City of Madison for law enforcement services exceeded $7,000.00. Following the riot which ensued from the demonstrations, for the ensuing 24 to 48 hours, the University operations were partially disrupted.

25. During each of the demonstrations described herein, neither the University administration nor the police officers of the City of Madison, while acting under the direction of the University Administration had in any way interfered with the constitutional right of the defendants and others acting in concert with them to peacefully demonstrate and to peacefully and lawfully express their protest to policies of the government of the United States of America and of the Regents, Faculty and Administration of the University of Wisconsin. The University rather, has affirmatively assisted and protected the rights of all who were engaged in the demonstrations to peacefully assemble and express their protest. The University has at all times made extensive efforts to maintain communication with the defendants and others acting in concert with them to provide for reasonable guidelines which will permit the University to continue and carry on its operations and which will protect other members of the University community from intimidation, fear of physical harm, physical injury and the right of the defendants and others to peacefully assemble and demonstrate and to express their protest in a constitutional manner.

These efforts by the University administration have been spurned by one or more or all of the defendants acting in concert with others and one or more or all of the defendants have intentionally incited and counseled others to spurn said efforts by the University.

26. The defendants and each of them and others acting in concert with them have acted unlawfully and in violation of the constitutional rights of other University students and other members of the University community. In view of the overt acts of the defendants and others acting in concert with them during the recent Dow interviews, and of statements made by the defendants and others acting in concert with them following said interviews, there exists a clear and present danger that the defendants will continue their intentional physical blocking of doorways to offices and classrooms and offices, the use of physical force and obscenities and shouting to prevent the University administration and other members of the University community from carrying on its classes and other operations in protest of future interviews scheduled on the campus, and that the defendants will incite and counsel others to do the same. Evidence of said intent is an Article in the Daily Cardinal dated November 2, 1967, and a hand-out distributed on the campus on or about November 2, 1967, a copy of each of which is annexed hereto marked Exhibit "K" and "L" respectively, and incorporated herein with the same force and effect as though set out in full.

Interviews with the military services are presently scheduled for November 20–21, 1967, and with the Central Intelligence Agency on November 27–28, 1967.

27. If the defendants are permitted to continue their intentional physical blocking of offices and classrooms and other unlawful activities described herein, as an unlawful incident to what the University recognizes as a constitutional right to peacefully assemble and demonstrate and protest, it will be impossible for the security officers of the University of Wisconsin and law enforcement officers of Dane County and the City of Madison, to ensure adequate protection to the health and welfare of the University students and to other members of the University community or to ensure the protection of the property of the State of Wisconsin or to protect persons and property from the

clear and present danger of civil disturbance, injury and damage.

28. The defendants' actions during the past in connection with career placement interviews conducted on the campus by the Central Intelligence Agency, the Dow Chemical Corporation, the Armed Services, and their announced intention to continue their activities constitute a clear and present danger to the order, peace, health, safety, and welfare of the University community and to the State of Wisconsin.

29. The actions of the defendants in blocking and denying ingress and egress to the facilities of the University of Wisconsin and in inciting and counseling others to do the same, as outlined above, is an unreasonable, unwarranted and unlawful means of citizens' petition for redress of grievances or of citizens' right to assemble, to free speech, and to peacefully demonstrate and protest and constitutes a public nuisance under Chapter 268, Wis. Stats., against the peace, dignity, welfare and safety of the University community and of the State of Wisconsin, and its citizens.

30. Plaintiff states that none of the defendants or others acting in concert with them have been in the past or are now or will in the future be deprived of any of their rights as citizens of the United States, or the State of Wisconsin, or the University of Wisconsin nor any of their agents, officers or servants, without due process of law. The plaintiff and the University administration and other members of the University community recognize and defend the right of the defendants and all citizens of the United States and of this state, to peacefully assemble and to freely speak and petition for the redress of grievances and recognize that in furtherance of such rights that defendants and all citizens of the United States and this state have the additional right to conduct peaceful, reasonable demonstrations to call attention to their claims.

31. The pattern of action set forth above carried on by the defendants and each of them individually and acting in concert

with each other and with other persons, does not constitute reasonable demonstration in support of any petition for redress of alleged grievances under the Constitutions of the United States nor of this state, nor does it constitute a lawful method of assembly or of exercising their right of free speech or of demonstrating as an incident to such rights.

32. If the defendants continue unreasonable demonstrations on the University campus, a clear and present danger exists that the University operations will be physically blocked and other University students and members of the University community will be denied their right of ingress and egress to University buildings, classrooms and offices and will be denied their right to carry on and participate in career placement interviews and to conduct and participate in classroom and administrative activities and that the welfare and safety of the demonstrators and of the other members of the University community will be threatened. Unless defendants are enjoined as requested herein plaintiff will suffer irreparable injury which cannot be repaired by the payment of money damages.

33. Annexed hereto, marked Exhibits "M", "N" and "O" and incorporated herein by reference with the same force and effect as though set out in full are:

Faculty Document 122, dated March 6, 1967 (Ex. "M");
An article which appeared in the Daily Cardinal on October 12, 1967 (Ex. "N");
An article which appeared in the Daily Cardinal on October 14, 1967, (Ex. "O").

WHEREFORE, Plaintiff asks the Judgment and Decree of this Court to preserve the right which students and other members of the University community share with citizens generally, to exercise their constitutional rights, including the right of free assembly and free speech, to be free from the deliberate prevention of the right to listen, from the deliberate prevention of the right to conduct and attend classes, the deliberate prevention of the right to conduct and participate in career placement interviews and the right to be free from physical harm, and the right to carry on without disruption University operations, and for that purpose plaintiff prays for the judgment and decree of this court;

    1.    Permanently enjoining, without bond and upon hearing, the defendants and each of them individually and as members of any corporate or unincorporated association or *ad-hoc* committee or any other organization, and all persons acting by, through or in their behalf, their agents and representatives, from committing the following acts or engaging in the following conduct on the University campus:

    a.    Intentionally, physically blocking entrances to University buildings or to halls or corridors in University buildings or inciting or counseling others to do so;

    b.    Intentionally, physically blocking entrances to offices and classrooms in University buildings or inciting or counseling others to do so;

    c.    Intentionally, physically denying to other students, members of the University community, or other persons, ingress and egress to offices on the University campus or inciting or counseling others to do so;

    d.    Intentionally, physically denying to other students, members of the University community, or other persons, ingress and egress to classrooms on the University campus or inciting or counseling others to do so;

    e.    Intentionally, physically denying to other students, members of the University community, or other persons, ingress and egress to other facilities on the University campus or inciting or counseling others to do so;

    f.    Intentionally, physically restraining others from ingress and egress to University buildings, offices, classrooms or other University facilities or inciting or counseling others to do so;

g.    Intentionally shouting, singing or using obscenities in the halls, corridors or classrooms or offices of University buildings, which has the purpose or effect of preventing the carrying on of classes, job placement interviews and other University business and inciting or counseling others to do so;

h.    Intentionally threatening physical harm or violence against other students, other members of the University community or any other person or persons on the University campus and inciting or counseling others to do so;

i.    Intentionally, physically occupying or blocking offices of the University buildings which has the purpose or effect of preventing the carrying on of the University business.

2.    That this Court, to make unnecessary a multiplicity of actions by plaintiff, retain jurisdiction of the defendants and of the cause in order to give plaintiff such other full and adequate relief as may be necessary from time to time, to enter such orders and decrees as may be necessary to preserve order and protect the health, welfare and safety of the members of the University community and the University property.

3.    Plaintiff State of Wisconsin, prays for such other and further relief as the Court in its discretion deems equitable in the premises. Dated this 7th day of November, 1967.

THE STATE OF WISCONSIN


/s/ BRONSON C. LaFOLLETTE,
Attorney General

ARLEN C. CHRISTENSON,
Deputy Attorney General

RICHARD L. CATES,
Attorney

JOHN H. BOWERS,
Attorney

ATTORNEYS FOR PLAINTIFF,
STATE OF WISCONSIN

# G

Complaint, summons, order to show cause and contempt citation.

**SUPREME COURT OF THE
STATE OF NEW YORK
COUNTY OF NEW YORK**

☆ ☆ ☆ ☆ ☆ ☆ ☆ ☆ ☆ ☆ ☆ ☆ ☆ ☆ ☆ ☆ ☆ ☆ ☆ ☆ ☆ ☆ ☆ ☆ ☆ ☆ ☆ ☆ ☆

THE TRUSTEES OF COLUMBIA UNIVERSITY
IN THE CITY OF NEW YORK,
                    Plaintiff,

            -against-

STUDENTS FOR A DEMOCRATIC SOCIETY,
Columbia University Chapter, LEWIS COLE,
STUART GEDAL, MORRIS GROSSNER, ANNE
HOFFMAN, ELEANOR RASKIN, ROBERT H.
ROTH AND "JOHN DOE" NUMBERS 1 to 100,
the latter being unknown persons present in or
adjacent to Philosophy Hall, Columbia University,
in connection with the unlawful occupation of that
building,

                    Defendants.

☆ ☆ ☆ ☆ ☆ ☆ ☆ ☆ ☆ ☆ ☆ ☆ ☆ ☆ ☆ ☆ ☆ ☆ ☆ ☆ ☆ ☆ ☆ ☆ ☆ ☆ ☆ ☆ ☆

## COMPLAINT

Plaintiff by its attorneys Thacher, Proffitt, Prizer, Crawley &
Wood, complaining of the defendants, alleges upon information
and belief:

1. Plaintiff is a corporation organized by special act of the Legislature of the State of New York in 1810 with an office at its Morningside Heights campus in the Borough of Manhattan, City of New York.

2. The defendant Students for a Democratic Society, Columbia University Chapter, is an unincorporated association having no president or treasurer. Its authorized representatives registered with plaintiff are defendants Gedal, Grossner, Hoffman and Roth.

3. Defendants Gedal, Hoffman, Raskin and Roth are duly enrolled students of Columbia University or Barnard College.

4. Defendants Cole and Grossner are not known at this time to have any existing connection with plaintiff.

5. On the afternoon of April 17, 1969, defendant Students for a Democratic Society, Columbia University Chapter, certain of the other defendants, and other persons unknown to plaintiff, forcibly entered Philosophy Hall, one of the academic buildings on plaintiff's Morningside Heights campus, where they are conducting an unauthorized demonstration by occupying that building, denying access to and egress from the building and depriving plaintiff of use of the building for plaintiff's regularly scheduled classes and other academic uses.

6. Plaintiff has notified defendants and others occupying Philosophy Hall with them that their presence in the building is unauthorized and has demanded that defendants and others present in the building with them immediately vacate the premises but defendants and those occupying Philosophy Hall with them have failed and refused to comply with plaintiff's demands.

7. The unlawful occupation of Philosophy Hall by defendants and others acting with them has created an imminent peril that similar activity may spread to other buildings of plaintiff, causing a wider disruption of plaintiff's academic operations such as plaintiff suffered in late April and May 1968.

8. Plaintiff has no adequate remedy at law.

WHEREFORE, plaintiff demands a permanent injunction

1. Restraining and enjoining each and all of the defendants and all other persons receiving notice of the injunction from congregating or assembling within or adjacent to any of plaintiff's academic or administrative buildings, dormitories, recreation rooms or athletic facilities or in any corridors, stairways, doorways and entrances thereto, in such manner as to disrupt or interfere with normal functions conducted by plaintiff in such places or to block, hinder, impede or interfere with ingress to or egress from any such properties by plaintiff's faculty, administrators, students, employees or guests;

2. Restraining and enjoining each and all of the defendants and all other persons receiving notice of the injunction from creating or broadcasting on plaintiff's Morningside Heights campus or in the streets adjacent thereto, any loud or excessive noise that hinders, impedes, prevents or interferes with the conduct of normal activities by members of the University community;

3. Restraining and enjoining each and all of the defendants and all other persons having notice of the injunction from employing force or violence or the threat of force and violence, against persons or property;

4. Restraining and enjoining each and all of the defendants and all other persons receiving notice of the injunction from threatening to do or inciting or counseling others to do any of the abovementioned acts; and

5. Granting plaintiff such other relief as may be proper, together with costs and disbursements of this action.

Dated New York, New York
    April 17, 1969                                    Yours, etc.,


THACHER, PROFFITT, PRIZER, CRAWLEY & WOOD
Attorneys for Plaintiff
40 Wall Street
New York, N.Y. 10005
269-5100

STATE OF NEW YORK    )

                         : ss.:

COUNTY OF NEW YORK   )

      EDWARD B. McMENAMIN, being duly sworn deposes that he is the Secretary of The Trustees of Columbia University in the City of New York; that he has read the foregoing complaint and that it is true to the knowledge of deponent except as to those matters alleged on information and belief and as to those matters he believes it to be true. The verification is made by deponent because the Trustees of Columbia University in the City of New York is a corporation of which deponent is an officer.

Sworn to before me this             /s/ Edward B. McMenamin
17 day of April, 1969.

    /s/ Margaret K. Jennings
    Notary Public

SUPREME COURT OF THE
STATE OF NEW YORK
COUNTY OF NEW YORK

☆☆☆☆☆☆☆☆☆☆☆☆☆☆☆☆☆☆☆☆☆☆☆☆☆☆☆☆☆☆☆☆☆☆
☆
THE TRUSTEES OF COLUMBIA UNIVERSITY    ☆
IN THE CITY OF NEW YORK,    ☆
   Plaintiff,    ☆
   ☆
   ☆
   -against-    ☆
   ☆
   ☆
STUDENTS FOR A DEMOCRATIC SOCIETY,    ☆
COLUMBIA UNIVERSITY CHAPTER, et al.,    ☆
   Defendants.    ☆
   ☆
☆☆☆☆☆☆☆☆☆☆☆☆☆☆☆☆☆☆☆☆☆☆☆☆☆☆☆☆☆☆☆☆☆ ☆

AFFIDAVIT

STATE OF NEW YORK    )
            : ss.:
COUNTY OF NEW YORK    )

    RALPH S. HALFORD, being duly sworn, deposes that he is employed by plaintiff as Vice President for Special Projects and that the facts stated below are based upon his personal knowledge and upon reports which he has received in the regular course of his duties from employes and students of plaintiff. This affidavit is submitted in support of plaintiff's application for a temporary restraining order and for a preliminary injunction.

    Late in the afternoon on April 17, 1969, Philosophy Hall, one of the academic buildings on plaintiff's Morningside Heights campus was entered and occupied by a group consisting of the defendants as well as other students and outsiders whose identities are not known to deponent. The total number of persons occupying Philosophy Hall is estimated to be in excess of 100.

After defendants and those acting with them in the occupation of Philosophy Hall had entered the building, they promptly barricaded the doors at the campus entrance to the building as well as the door giving access to the building from an underground tunnel.

During the occupation of Philosophy Hall by the defendants and those associated with them, violent fist fights occurred between persons seeking to enter and occupy the building and students who attempted to prevent the occupation. Three students, Fred Lowell, Peter Sordillo and Juris Kaza, who sought to prevent defendants and those associated with them from closing the doors to Philosophy Hall were sprayed by persons unknown with a burning chemical from an aerosol can.

The occupation of Philosophy Hall by defendants and those acting with them has totally deprived plaintiff of the use of that building for numerous classes which were scheduled to be conducted therein. Professor Jacques Barzun was denied entry to the building by defendants and those acting with them when he sought to gain entrance for the purpose of conducting a scheduled seminar for Ph.D. candidates. University classes are normally held in Philosophy Hall in the evening until 11:00 p.m. Subsequent to the occupation of Philosophy Hall by defendants and those acting with them, other students who oppose the group within the building have threatened to resort to force and to batter down the doors with timbers in an effort to eject the occupants.

The current situation on plaintiff's campus, as described above, has created imminent danger of severe bodily injury to students and other persons on the campus, substantial destruction of plaintiff's property and the likelihood that other buildings may be occupied with the consequence that plaintiff may suffer again a disruption of its academic operations comparable with that which occurred exactly a year ago when four buildings and portions of a fifth were seized, police were twice called to oust the occupants therefrom and the University's normal academic operations were restricted by a student strike.

No prior application has been made for the relief requested.

WHEREFORE, deponent respectfully requests that plaintiff's application for a temporary restraining order and a preliminary injunction be granted.

/s/ Ralph S. Halford

Sworn to before me this
17th day of April, 1969.

/s/ Margaret K. Jennings
Notary Public

## SUPREME COURT OF THE
## STATE OF NEW YORK
## COUNTY OF NEW YORK

☆ ☆ ☆ ☆ ☆ ☆ ☆ ☆ ☆ ☆ ☆ ☆ ☆ ☆ ☆ ☆ ☆ ☆ ☆ ☆ ☆ ☆ ☆ ☆ ☆ ☆ ☆ ☆
☆

THE TRUSTEES OF COLUMBIA UNIVERSITY
IN THE CITY OF NEW YORK,
Plaintiff,

-against-

STUDENTS FOR A DEMOCRATIC SOCIETY,
Columbia University Chapter, LEWIS COLE,
STUART GEDAL, MORRIS GROSSNER, ANNE
HOFFMAN, ELEANOR RASKIN, ROBERT H.
ROTH and "JOHN DOE" NUMBERS 1 to 100,
the latter being unknown persons present in or
adjacent to Philosophy Hall, Columbia University,
in connection with the unlawful occupation of that
bldg.,

Defendants.

☆ ☆ ☆ ☆ ☆ ☆ ☆ ☆ ☆ ☆ ☆ ☆ ☆ ☆ ☆ ☆ ☆ ☆ ☆ ☆ ☆ ☆ ☆ ☆ ☆ ☆ ☆ ☆

## SUMMONS

*Plaintiff designates*
New York
*County as the place of trial*
*The basis of the venue is*
Plaintiff's residence

To the above named Defendants

YOU ARE HEREBY SUMMONED to answer the complaint in this action and to serve a copy of your answer, or, if the complaint is not served with this summons, to serve a notice of appearance, on the Plaintiff's Attorney(s) within 20 days after the service of this summons, exclusive of the day of service (or within 30 days after the service is complete if this summons is not personally delivered to you within the State of New York); and in case of your failure to appear or answer, judgment will be taken against you by default for the relief demanded in the complaint.

Dated, New York, New York
April 17, 1969.

THACHER, PROFFITT, PRIZER, CRAWLEY & WOOD
Attorney(s) for Plaintiff
Office and Post Office Address
40 Wall Street
New York, New York
Tel. 269-5100

At a Special Term, Part II of the Supreme Court of the State of New York, held in and for the County of New York at 60 Centre Street, New York, New York, on the 17 day of April 1969.

PRESENT:
    HONORABLE JAWN A. SANDIFER
    Justice

☆ ☆ ☆ ☆ ☆ ☆ ☆ ☆ ☆ ☆ ☆ ☆ ☆ ☆ ☆ ☆ ☆ ☆ ☆ ☆ ☆ ☆ ☆ ☆ ☆ ☆ ☆ ☆ ☆ ☆ ☆
                                                              ☆
THE TRUSTEES OF COLUMBIA UNIVERSITY                           ☆
IN THE CITY OF NEW YORK,                                      ☆
                    Plaintiff,                                ☆
                                                              ☆
                                                              ☆
            -against-                                         ☆
                                                              ☆
                                                              ☆
STUDENTS FOR A DEMOCRATIC SOCIETY,                            ☆
Columbia University Chapter, LEWIS COLE,                      ☆
STUART GEDAL, MORRIS GROSSNER, ANNE                           ☆
HOFFMAN, ELEANOR RASKIN, ROBERT H.                            ☆
ROTH and "JOHN DOE" NUMBERS 1 to 100,                         ☆
the latter being unknown persons present in or                ☆
adjacent to Philosophy Hall, Columbia University,             ☆
in connection with the unlawful occupation of that            ☆
building,                                                     ☆
                                                              ☆
                    Defendants.                               ☆
                                                              ☆
☆ ☆ ☆ ☆ ☆ ☆ ☆ ☆ ☆ ☆ ☆ ☆ ☆ ☆ ☆ ☆ ☆ ☆ ☆ ☆ ☆ ☆ ☆ ☆ ☆ ☆ ☆ ☆ ☆ ☆ ☆

## ORDER TO SHOW CAUSE

Upon the annexed summons, verified complaint, and the affidavit of Ralph S. Halford, sworn to on April 17, 1969, and sufficient reason appearing therefor, it is

ORDERED that the defendants show cause before this Court at Special Term, Part I, New York County Court House, 60

Centre Street, New York, New York, on 29th April 1969 at 10:00 a.m. why an order should not be entered herein pending the hearing and determination of the issues in this action:

1. Restraining and enjoining each and all of the defendants and all other persons receiving notice of this injunction from congregating or assembling within or adjacent to any of plaintiff's academic or administrative buildings, dormitories, recreation rooms or athletic facilities or in any corridors, stairways, doorways and entrances thereto, in such manner as to disrupt or interfere with normal functions conducted by plaintiff in such place or to block, hinder, impede or interfere with ingress to or egress from any of such properties by plaintiff's faculty, administrators, students, employees or guests;

2. Restraining and enjoining each and all of the defendants and all other persons receiving notice of this injunction from creating or broadcasting on plaintiff's Morningside Heights campus or in the streets adjacent thereto, any loud or excessive noise that hinders, impedes, prevents or interferes with the conduct of normal activities by members of the University community;

3. Restraining and enjoining each and all of the defendants and all other persons receiving notice of this injunction from employing force or violence, or the threat of force or violence, against persons or property on plaintiff's campus;

4. Restraining and enjoining each and all of the defendants and all other persons receiving notice of this injunction from threatening to do or inciting or counseling others to do any of the abovementioned acts; and

5. Granting plaintiff such other relief as may be proper; and it is further

ORDERED that pending the hearing and determination of this motion, the defendants and all other persons receiving notice of this injunction be and they hereby are restrained and enjoined:

1. From congregating or assembling within or adjacent to any of plaintiff's academic or administrative buildings, dorm-

itories, recreation rooms or athletic facilities or in any corridors, stairways, doorways and entrances thereto, in such manner as to disrupt or interfere with normal functions conducted by plaintiff in such place or to block, hinder, impede or interfere with ingress to or egress from any of such properties by plaintiff's faculty, administrators, students, employees or guests;

2. From creating or broadcasting on plaintiff's Morningside Heights campus or in the streets adjacent thereto, any loud or excessive noise that hinders, impedes, prevents or interferes with the conduct of normal activities by members of the University community;

3. From employing force or violence, or the threat of force or violence, against persons or property on plaintiff's campus;

4. From threatening to do or inciting or counseling others to do any of the abovementioned acts; and it is further

ORDERED that service of this order and the papers upon which it is made be accomplished by serving the defendants personally, and by serving the parents of those defendants who have not yet attained the age of twenty-one years by registered mail, on or before April 19th, 1969 at 4 p.m.

ENTER,
/s/ Jawn A. Sandifer
J.S.C.

No. 131A of 5/1/69
SP. I - N.Y.

## THE TRUSTEES OF COLUMBIA UNIVERSITY
## IN THE CITY OF NEW YORK
v.
## STUDENTS FOR A DEMOCRATIC SOCIETY, etc. et al.

MARKS, J.:

On April 17, 1969, upon the application of plaintiff, The Trustees of Columbia University in the City of New York, a temporary restraining order was signed by a justice of this court. The said order restrained and enjoined the Students for a Democtatic Society and certain named and un-named defendants from congregating or assembling within or adjacent to any of plaintiff's academic or administration buildings and parts thereof in such manner as to disrupt or interfere with the normal functions conducted by plaintiff. Said order further provided that the defendants and all other persons receiving notice of this injunction be and they hereby are restrained and enjoined from creating or broadcasting on plaintiff's Morningside Heights campus or in the streets adjacent thereto, any loud or excessive noise which hinders, impedes, prevents or interferes with the conduct of normal activities of members of the university community and further from employing force or violence or the threat of force or violence against persons or property on plaintiff's campus; and further from threatening to do, or inciting or counseling others to do any of the aforementioned acts.

Upon the facts as alleged in an affidavit of Ralph S. Halford, vice president for Special Projects of Columbia University, indicating that there was a wilful violation of the restraining order of April 17, 1969, an order was made directing the defendants to show cause on May 1, 1969 why they should not be punished for a criminal contempt of this court. The defendants defaulted in appearance on May 1, 1969, but this court thereafter on its own motion, vacated said default and is now deciding the issues on the merits.

Interrogatories were served upon the attorneys for defendants and they have replied to the same by alleging that to answer the questions propounded, would violate their constitutional rights and privileges, as more particularly set forth in said answers.

Full hearings were held by this court and testimony was heard from the witnesses for plaintiff and defendants and from the evidence adduced, I find that the defendants had knowledge of the terms and conditions of the restraining order of April 17, 1969. Not only was service made personally upon some of the defendants but the campus was saturated with newspaper, radio, pamphlet distribution, conversation, pronouncements and oratory and the injunctive order was headline news of the first magnitude.

I find further that the defendants participated in taking over and barricading Mathematics and/or Fayerweather Halls in direct violation of the specific terms of the restraining order. It is not necessary to relate the many individual wilful acts on the part of the defendants, from which I also find that the normal functions conducted by the plaintiff were disrupted. The disorders as testified to by Columbia witnesses, were due in no small measure to what appears to have been planned action by groups which included these defendants.

It appears that during the unlawful occupation of the said buildings, there was damage amounting to approximately twelve thousand dollars.

The defendants elected not to testify in their own behalf and the witnesses called by them have not enlightened the court on any of the issues presented in this proceeding.

I find that the claim of defendants that they were under a compulsion to answer the propounded interrogatories did not violate any of their constitutional rights.

Whether campus reform is overdue is not the subject matter

before this court. Better communication with students and reform if needed, cannot be obtained by illegal methods on the campus or by failure of respect for constituted authority. There is no place for violence in our society.

In the recent case of Walker v. The City of Birmingham, 388 U.S. 307, at pages 320, 321, where petitioners defied an injunction order and were convicted of criminal contempt, Mr. Justice Stewart, in writing for the majority opinion of the court, stated: "No man can be judge in his own case ****. This court cannot hold that petitioners were constitutionally free to ignore all the procedures of law and carry their battle to the streets. *** But respect for judicial process is a small price to pay for the civilizing hand of the law which alone can give abiding meaning to constitutional freedom".

Everyone has the right to protest, to criticize, to disagree, but when buildings are occupied illegally, then it is the sword that is being used rather than the reason of the book.

Since the court was empowered to issue the order of April 17, 1969, it is concurringly true that it cannot brook its violation. To permit nullification by wilful violation of the order would be a step towards overthrow of the courts and the removal of the bulwark of constitutional democracy. It would be the first step towards authoritarian government. If the defendants disagreed with the court order, or considered it illegal, they could have availed themselves of the remedy offered them by section 5704 CPLR. They chose not the democratic process nor the course of dignity, but a course of wilful and flagrant violation of the order of this court. To condone such action as took place would lead only to a lawless society. Since these defendants have defied the order of this court, they must be prepared to accept the penalty.

I therefore find the defendants Lewis Cole, Stuart M. Gedal, Henry M. Gehman, Michael J. Golash, Jr., Juan D. Gonzales, Thomas D. Hurwitz, Robert Henry Roth and Roger J. Taus guilty of criminal contempt and sentence each of said defendants to a term of imprisonment in the jail of the county of New York for thirty days and to pay a fine of one hundred dollars each; in case of default in the payments of said fines, until such fines be fully paid, for an additional period of ten days after the period of thirty days above mentioned shall have expired. Let warrants of commitment issue to the Sheriff of the County of New York to take these defendants into custody forthwith to effectuate the terms of the order being signed simultaneously herewith.

Dated, June 10, 1969.

/s/

J.S.C.

# H

Order Granting Injunction.

## IN THE UNITED STATES DISTRICT COURT FOR THE MIDDLE DISTRICT OF ALABAMA, NORTHERN DIVISION

☆ ☆ ☆ ☆ ☆ ☆ ☆ ☆ ☆ ☆ ☆ ☆ ☆ ☆ ☆ ☆ ☆ ☆ ☆ ☆ ☆ ☆ ☆ ☆ ☆ ☆ ☆ ☆

SYLVESTER SCOTT, ERNESTINE WILSON, LEROY W. DUNBAR, HELEN BROWN, TIMOTHY MAYS, WHEELER M. WASHINGTON, ALEXANDER S. ANDERSON, Individually and on behalf of all others similarly situated,

Plaintiffs,

-vs.-

ALABAMA STATE BOARD OF EDUCATION, GOVERNOR ALBERT P. BREWER, Ex Officio Chairman of ALABAMA STATE BOARD OF EDUCATION, Montgomery, Alabama; LEVI WATKINS, Individually and as President of ALABAMA STATE COLLEGE, Montgomery, Alabama, ROSE H. ROBINSON, Individually and as Acting Director of Student Affairs, Alabama State College, Montgomery, Alabama; SIMON W. WALKER, Individually and as Coordinator of Financial Aid, Alabama State College, Montgomery, Alabama; SAVAGE J. WHISENHUNT, Individually and as Director of Student Teaching, JOHN B. HALL, Individually and as Chairman of the Faculty Discipline Committee, ZELIA S. EVANS, Individually and as a member of the Ad

CIVIL ACTION NO. 2865-N

Hoc Faculty-Student Committee, and B. J. SIMMS,
Individually and as a member of the Ad Hoc
Faculty-Student Committee,

Defendants.

## ORDER

Plaintiffs are approximately 50 students at Alabama State College who were indefinitely suspended or dismissed from college because of their participation, along with a number of nonstudents, in events related to or growing out of "demonstrations" in and around the college dining hall from March 29, 1969, to April 8, 1969. As a result of this activity the college was closed for a period from April 7 to April 21, 1969. Plaintiffs allege that the activities for which they were suspended or dismissed from school are protected by the First Amendment to the Constitution of the United States and that, in any event, the procedures adopted by the college did not satisfy the requirements of the due process clause of the Fourteenth Amendment. Their complaint seeks injunctive relief in the form of an order of reinstatement, and damages. The jurisdiction of this Court is invoked pursuant to the provisions of 28 U.S.C. § § 1331(a) and 1343(3) and (4).

President Levi Watkins and other officials of Alabama State College filed an answer and a counterclaim in which they sought injunctive relief against continuing actions of the plaintiffs alleged to be interfering with the orderly operation of Alabama State College as an educational institution. A motion for temporary restraining order was filed simultaneously and was granted May 5, 1969, on the basis of numerous affidavits reflecting that subsequent to filing this lawsuit plaintiffs, in an attempt to promote their cause by extra-judicial means, had:

(1) Refused to quit the campus after being dismissed or

suspended as students;

(2) Intimidated students desiring to attend classes and prevented their attendance at classes;

(3) Intimidated faculty members desiring to conduct classes;

(4) Damaged college property; and

(5) Otherwise disrupted the orderly operation of Alabama State College as an educational institution.

The defendants Alabama State Board of Education and Governor Albert P. Brewer as ex officio Chairman thereof have moved to dismiss the complaint as it relates to them on the basis that primary responsibility for maintenance of order at the college rests with the college administration and that they have exercised no authority relative to the actions from which the complaint arises. This motion is due to be granted.

## I. Procedural Due Process

In the landmark case of *Dixon v. Alabama State Board of Education,* 294 F.2d 150 (5th Cir. 1961), a case also involving Alabama State College students, it was settled that due process requires notice and some opportunity for a hearing before students at a tax-supported college may be expelled for misconduct. Here, notice was given and hearings were held; the issue is whether the procedure provided satisfied constitutional requirements.

The evidence reflects that approximately 80 students were served with formal statements of charges. Each of these statements was on a form letter listing 11 charges growing out of the "demonstration." Those charges which were deemed applicable to the addressee were marked with a prominent "X." The letter advised the students that hearings would be held on April 17, 1969, at which time they would be afforded an opportunity to be heard and to present witnesses in their defense.

The hearings were later rescheduled for April 23, 1969. At that time, counsel for plaintiffs, representing some 50 of the students charged, objected to the statement of charges on the ground that the charges were unduly vague and did not advise students specifically of the acts they were alleged to have committed. When counsel's request that the charges be made more definite was denied, he and plaintiffs, on his advice, dramatically refused to participate in the hearings.

The hearings were held as scheduled before an Ad Hoc Faculty-Student Committee. This Committee heard the evidence against each student charged, made specific findings with respect to each charge, and made recommendations to President Watkins of an appropriate disposition of each case. As a result, it appears that 7 students were dismissed from the college, 43 were indefinitely suspended, 21 were found not guilty, and 3 cases were disposed of otherwise. Those who were dismissed or suspended were offered an opportunity to have their cases reviewed by President Watkins. Of those who exercised that opportunity, at least eight had their indefinite suspensions reduced to special probation.

Plaintiffs' attack in this Court on their dismissals and suspensions continues to center on the alleged vagueness of the charges. *Dixon, supra* at 158, advises that:

"The notice should contain a statement of the specific charges and grounds which, if proven, would justify expulsion under the regulations of the Board of Education."

An examination of the statement of charges reveals that some of the charges do indeed lack the specificity required to enable a student adequately to prepare defenses against them. For example, the first charge provides:

"Willful refusal to obey a regulation or order of Alabama State, such refusal being of a serious nature and contributed to a substantial disruption of the administration

and operation of the College, March 29—April 8, 1969."
That charge is rendered completely open-ended by the failure to
specify which regulation or order was involved.

On the other hand, certain of the other charges, when
viewed in the circumstances of the case, make quite clear the basis
upon which the college proposes to take disciplinary action. For
example, the second charge provides:

"Principals in the seizure, occupation, and unauthorized use of the Alabama State Dining Hall and Union
building, March 29—April 8, 1969."

Plaintiffs contend that one bad apple spoils the entire
bushel, *i.e.*, that if any of the charges against a student was
unconstitutionally vague then he was deprived of an education
without due process of law. This Court, however, cannot adopt
such a rigid and formalistic approach. *Dixon* makes clear that the
question in each case is whether the rudimentary elements of fair
play have been observed. Thus, this Court concludes that if a
student was notified and found guilty of one satisfactorily specific
charge, then his dismissal or suspension will not be held to be
procedurally inadequate on the ground of vagueness, whether or
not he was also charged with unduly vague charges. By way of
analogy, it may be observed that in the criminal law, where more
rigorous procedures are required, an appellate court will not
examine alleged errors with respect to one count of an indictment
when the appellant was also convicted and sentenced concurrently
on another count found to be or conceded to be valid. *Benefield v.
United States,* 370 F.2d 912 (5th Cir. 1966); *Mishan v. United
States,* 345 F.2d 791 (5th Cir. 1965).

An examination of the exhibits reveals that all but eight of
the dismissed or suspended students were charged with and
convicted of, *inter alia,* being principals in the seizure, occupation,
and unauthorized use of the dining hall. Of those eight remaining,
Timothy Mays was found guilty of the specific charge that he
"threatened and/or pushed an Alabama State official who was

carrying out his appropriate functions at the College Dining Hall and Union building, March 29–April 8, 1969"; Jonny F. Hall was found guilty of the specific charge that he "misappropriated and/or removed without authority Alabama State equipment and supplies, March 29–April 8, 1969"; and Marvin E. Wilson, Sandrew Marshall, and Bobby L. Cobb were found guilty of the specific charge that they "blocked entrances and/or held doors so as to deny rightful persons normal entrance and exit to the Alabama State Dining Hall March 29–April 8, 1969."

Murry A. Hardy and Joshua Booker were charged only with the willful refusal to obey a regulation or order of Alabama State College—the charge which was indicated above to be unduly vague. Leroy Dunbar was charged with the above vague charge and, in addition, with the charge that he "through verbal exhortations and/or threats and/or intimidation prevented or discouraged other Alabama State students from attending classes, March 31–April 7, 1969." That charge is also ambiguous and vague. "Exhortation" in normal usage would be used to describe speech that might well be constitutionally protected. *These three students will be ordered reinstated, pending, if the college desires, a further specification of the charges and another hearing.*

Plaintiffs have not directly challenged the adequacy of the hearings themselves. In the course of the hearing in this Court, however, they did raise some question about the impartiality of the Committee which heard the evidence. The evidence reflects that this Committee was selected in a reasonable fashion considering the emotional circumstances which tended to render nearly everyone at the college at least mildly partisan. Moreover, this Court, with the advantage of hindsight, finds that, viewed in the large, the Committee appears to have dealt fairly with the students involved.

It is also appropriate to note that plaintiffs were afforded an opportunity to be heard, to present evidence, and to be represented by counsel at the hearings. Those who on advice of counsel did not take advantage of these opportunities have waived whatever rights they may have had to them. This Court will express no opinion on whether or not that advice reflected good political judgment; it will be observed that, although plaintiffs' counsel is an able and experienced attorney, it may have been unwise legal advice. As plaintiffs' counsel knows, or should know, when one makes an objection—whether meritorious or not—in a judicial proceeding, and the objection is overruled, the only orderly and efficient procedure is to have the objection noted and to appeal to higher authority if one does not prevail. Any other procedure would afford endless opportunities for delay in unmeritorious cases by the simple tactic of making an objection and walking out if the objection is overruled. Here, the Committee was duly and legally constituted, jurisdiction had vested, and due notice of the hearing had been given.

## II. First Amendment

Having determined that the substantial majority of the dismissed and suspended students were not denied procedural due process, this Court now finds it necessary to reach the issue of whether their dismissals and suspensions violated substantive rights protected by the First Amendment. This Court again takes the view that if a student was found guilty of a specific charge of conduct not protected by the First Amendment, whether or not he is also charged with activities which might be protected, then his suspension or dismissal may stand. The issue then becomes whether the activities described by the college as "the seizure, occupation, and unauthorized use of the dining hall" and described by the students as "a demonstration" are protected by the First Amendment.

The evidence reflects, however one describes it, that these plaintiffs and other students and nonstudents, rather than the duly constituted authorities of the college, were in control of the dining hall for a period of ten days. Although the operations of the dining hall were not altogether halted, it is clear that the normal and orderly operation of the dining hall was considerably altered. Whether intended or not, one clear result of these students' actions was to deprive numerous other people, including students with contractual rights in the form of meal tickets, of the opportunity to use the dining hall. The college clearly has a right to enforce regulations which tend to prevent conduct having this effect.

The plaintiffs seem to be arguing that irrespective of the college's interest in the orderly operation of the dining hall, their conduct was protected symbolic speech because they intended by their conduct to communicate their dissatisfaction with certain conditions at the college. The Supreme Court rejected that theory in *United States v. O'Brien,* 391 U.S. 367, 376 (1968):

"We cannot accept the view that an apparently limitless variety of conduct can be labeled 'speech' whenever the person engaging in the conduct intends thereby to express an idea."

Plaintiffs also seem to advance the view that their conduct was protected because it was largely peaceful and nonviolent and involved little if any destruction of college property. But that characteristic alone does not make the conduct protected speech.

There seems to be a tendency in this country—and it is especially prevalent among students—toward the view that if one only believes strongly enough that his cause is right, then one may use in advancing that cause any means that seem effective at the moment, whether they are lawful or unlawful and whether or not they are consistent with the interests of others. The law, of course, cannot and does not take that position, and those who do must not expect to receive substantive protection from the law; to the contrary, they must expect to be punished when they violate laws and college regulations which are part of a system designed to protect the rights and interests of all.

## III. Work and Practice Teaching Programs

Plaintiffs also complain that certain of their campus jobs were terminated and that certain of them were not permitted to begin or to resume their participation in the practice teaching program after the college was reopened because of their participation in the "demonstrations." Plaintiffs contend that this was summary punishment without a hearing that violated their procedural rights and that it was punishment for engaging in constitutionally protected activity in violation of their rights under the First Amendment.

The First Amendment issue has already been decided above adversely to the plaintiffs. The issue of whether due process requires a hearing before participation in work and practice teaching programs may be terminated—a question of first impression—is now moot with respect to those students whose dismissals and suspensions have been upheld and is premature with respect to those students who have been reinstated.

## IV. Defendant's Counterclaim

Defendants have taken the position in this case that the activities for which most of the students were suspended or dismissed were not constitutionally protected and that the plaintiffs were afforded procedural due process. They further allege that although plaintiffs have been dismissed or suspended, many of them have remained on campus and have engaged in activities designed to reverse the administration's decision; that such activities have interfered with the rights of other students and otherwise disrupted the orderly operation of the college as an educational institution. As indicated above, when these allegations were substantiated by affidavits, the Court issued a temporary restraining order against the plaintiffs. That order was based on this Court's consistently held position that when a party brings a dispute with another party into court for a judicial resolution both parties are under an obligation not to resort to other means, including those which in other circumstances would be constitutionally protected, of forcing a settlement of the dispute in their favor. This requirement is grounded in the nature of the judicial process. That process nearly always requires a certain period of time prior to a hearing and to a decision, although in this case and similar cases it may be only a few days. During that time, in order for the court to retain complete jurisdiction over the subject matter, the status quo as of the time of the filing of the suit must be maintained. Moreover, it is imperative for the integrity of an independent judiciary that the court be free from pressures, direct or indirect, tending to preclude thoughtful, deliberate and unemotional consideration of the legal issues.

It is also imperative that those who invoke the judicial process recognize the finality of a judicial resolution of the controversy. A decision of this Court, of course, may be appealed to higher courts; the Alabama Legislature may be prevailed upon to change the rules with respect to student conduct. But those students whose dismissals and suspensions by Alabama State College have been upheld by this Court may not resort to direct action on the campus of Alabama State College for the purpose of exerting pressure on the officials, *i.e.*, the defendants in this suit, to change their decision concerning the dismissals and suspensions. The temporary restraining order will be enlarged into a preliminary injunction.

In accordance with the foregoing, it is the ORDER, JUDGMENT and DECREE of this Court that the plaintiffs' motion for a preliminary injunction, except insofar as that motion relates to plaintiffs Joshua Booker, Murry A. Hardy, and Leroy W. Dunbar, be and the same is hereby denied.

It is further ORDERED that plaintiffs Joshua Booker, Murry A. Hardy, and Leroy W. Dunbar be reinstated as students at Alabama State College with the same right which attached to their status as students prior to their suspension, pending, if defendant officials wish to proceed further against these plaintiffs, a more detailed specification of charges and an additional hearing.

It is further ORDERED that the motion of defendants Alabama State Board of Education and Governor Albert P. Brewer, as ex officio Chairman thereof, to dismiss this action against them as parties defendant, be and the same is hereby granted.

It is further ORDERED that the named plaintiffs Sylvester Scott, Ernestine Wilson, Helen Brown, Timothy Mays, Wheeler M. Washington, and Alexander S. Anderson; all other plaintiffs whose dismissals or suspensions by Alabama State College have been upheld by this Court; and those students or nonstudents acting in concert with them and having actual notice of this order, be and each is hereby enjoined and restrained from:

(1) Failing and refusing to leave the campus of Alabama State College after having been dismissed or indefinitely suspended as a student;

(2) Failing to leave the grounds or any building located on the campus of Alabama State College when requested to do so by officials of said college;

(3) Taking possession or failing and refusing to surrender possession of any of the buildings located on the grounds of Alabama State College;

(4) Harassing, threatening or intimidating any faculty or staff member, employee, student or official of Alabama State College, or any of its several colleges and departments;

(5) Obstructing or preventing the attendance in classes of students and faculty members;

(6) Destroying or attempting to destroy, defacing or

attempting to deface any structures, buildings, materials or equipment used, held for use, maintained, operated or controlled by Alabama State College; and

(7) Committing any other act or acts disrupting the orderly processes or operations of Alabama State College, or any of its several colleges and departments.

It is further ORDERED that the court costs incurred in this cause be and they are hereby taxed two-thirds against the plaintiffs and one-third against the defendant officials of Alabama State College, for which execution may issue.

Done, this the 14th day of May, 1969.

/s/Frank M. Johnson, Jr.
UNITED STATES DISTRICT JUDGE

Attest: A True Copy
Certified to May 14, 1969.
R. C. Dobson
Clerk, U.S. District Court
Middle District of Alabama.

By
Deputy Clerk

# I

## MODEL CODE FOR STUDENT RIGHTS RESPONSIBILITIES AND CONDUCT

The Model Code reproduced below was prepared by the Committee on Student Rights & Responsibilities, Law Student Division, American Bar Association. The text of the Model Code has not been submitted to the House of Delegates of the Law Student Division of the American Bar Association for approval and does not represent the views or actions of the Division or the American Bar Association. Mr. Marvin R. Peebles was Chairman of the Committee which prepared the Code. The Commentary which follows the Code was written by Mr. Peebles to assist in its interpretation. The Code is offered by the Committee as an aid to college and university administrators and students in developing rules and regulations.*

### Short Title

§ 1. These rules shall be known as the _____ [insert name of institution] Code of Conduct.

### Bill of Rights

§ 2. The following enumeration of rights shall not be construed to deny or disparage others retained by students in their capacity as members of the student body or as citizens of the community at large;

    A.    Free inquiry, expression and assembly are guaranteed to all students.

    B.    Students are free to pursue their educational goals; appropriate opportunities for learning in the classroom and

---

*Reprinted by permission of the American Bar Association.

327

on the campus shall be provided by the institution.

C.  The right of students to be secure in their persons, living quarters, papers and effects against unreasonable searches and seizures is guaranteed.

D.  No disciplinary sanctions may be imposed upon any student without notice to the accused of the nature and cause of the charges, and a fair hearing which shall include confrontation of witnesses against him and the assistance of a person of his own choosing.

E.  A student accused of violating institutional regulations is entitled, upon request, to a hearing before a judicial body composed solely of students.


**Definitions**

§  3. When used in this Code-

(1)  The term "institution" means _____ [insert name of college or university] and, collectively, those responsible for its control and operation.

(2)  The term "student" includes all persons taking courses at the institution both full-time and part-time pursuing undergraduate, graduate or extensions studies.

(3)  The term "instructor" means any person hired by the institution to conduct classroom activities. In certain situations a person may be both "student" and "instructor." Determination of his status in a particular situation shall be determined by the surrounding facts.

(4)  The term "legal compulsion" means a judicial or legislative order which requires some action by the person to whom it is directed.

(5)  The term "organization" means a number of persons who have complied with the formal requirements of institution recognition as provided in § 11.

(6)  The term "group" means a number of persons who

have not yet complied with the formal requirements for becoming an organization.

(7) The term "student press" means either an organization whose primary purpose is to publish and distribute any publication on campus or a regular publication of an organization.

(8) The term "shall" is used in the imperative sense.

(9) The term "may" is used in the permissive sense.

(10) All other terms have their natural meaning unless the context dicates otherwise.

## Access to Higher Education

§ 4. Within the limits of its facilities, the institution shall be open to all applicants who are qualified according to its admission requirements.

A. The institution shall make clear the characteristics and expectations of students which it considers relevant to its programs.

B. Under no circumstances may an applicant be denied admission because of race or ethnic background.

C. (Optional) Religious preference for applicants shall be clearly and publicly stated.

## Classroom Expression

§ 5. Discussion and expression of all views relevant to the subject matter is permitted in the classroom subject only to the responsibility of the instructor to maintain order.

A. Students are responsible for learning the content of any course for which they are enrolled.

B. Requirements of participation in classroom discussion and submission of written exercises are not inconsistent with this Section.

§ 6. Academic Evaluation of student performances shall be neither prejudicial nor capricious.

§ 7. Information about student views, beliefs, and political associations acquired by professors in the course of their work as instructors, advisors, and counselors, is confidential and is not to be disclosed to others unless under legal compulsion.

A.     Questions relating to intellectual or skills capacity are not subject to this section except that disclosure must be accompanied by notice to the student.

## Campus Expression

§ 8. Discussion and expression of all views is permitted within the institution subject only to requirements for the maintenance of order.

A.     Support of any cause by orderly means which do not disrupt the operation of the institution is permitted.

§ 9. Students, groups, and campus organizations may invite and hear any persons of their own choosing subject only to the requirements for use of institutional facilities (§ 14, *infra*).

## Campus Organizations

§10. Organizations and groups may be established within the institution for any legal purpose. Affiliation with an extramural organization shall not, in itself, disqualify the institution branch or chapter from institution privileges.

§11.

A.     A group shall become an organization when formally recognized by the institution. All groups that meet the following requirements shall be recognized:

1.     Submission of a list of officers and copies of the

constitution and by-laws to the appropriate institution official or body. All changes and amendments shall be submitted within one week after they become effective.

2.   Where there is affiliation with an extramural organization, that organization's constitution and by-laws shall be filed with the appropriate institution official or body. All amendments shall be submitted within a reasonable time after they become effective.

3.   All sources of outside funds shall be disclosed.

B.   Upon recognition of an organization, the institution shall make clear that said recognition infers neither approval or disapproval of the aims, objectives and policies of the organization.

C.   Groups of a continuing nature must institute proceedings for formal recognition if they are to continue receiving the benefits of § 14, 16, and 17.

D.   Any organization which engages in illegal activities, on or off campus, may have sanctions imposed against it, including withdrawal of institution recognition for a period not exceeding one year.

E.   Any group which engages in illegal activities on campus may have sanctions imposed against it, including withdrawal of institution recognition for a period not exceeding one year.

§ 12. Membership in all institution-related organizations, within the limits of their facilities, shall be open to any member of the institution community who is willing to subscribe to the stated aims and meet the stated obligations of the organization.

§ 13. Membership lists are confidential and solely for the use of the organization except that names and addresses of officers may be required as a condition of access to institution funds.

§14. Institution facilities shall be assigned to organizations, groups, and individuals within the institution community for regular business meetings, for social programs, and for programs open to the public.

    A.    Reasonable conditions may be imposed to regulate the timeliness of requests, to determine the appropriateness of the space assigned, to regulate time and use, and to insure proper maintenance.

    B.    Preference may be given to programs designed for audiences consisting primarily of members of the institutional community.

    C.    Allocation of space shall be made based on priority of requests and the demonstrated needs of the organization, group, or individual.

    D.    The institution may delegate the assignment function to an administrative official.

    D.    (Alternate Provision) The institution may delegate the assignment function to a student committee on organizations.

    E.    Charges may be imposed for any unusual costs for use of facilities.

    F.    Physical abuse of assigned facilities shall result in reasonable limitations on future allocation of space to offending parties and restitution for damages.

    G.    The individual, group, or organization requesting space must inform the institution of the general purpose of any meeting open to persons other than members and the names of outside speakers.

§15. The authority to allocate institutional funds derived from student fees for use by organizations shall be delegated to a body in which student participation in the decisional process is assured.

    A.    Approval of requests for funds is conditioned upon submission of budgets to, and approval by this body.

B.    Financial accountability is required for all allocated funds, including statement of income and expenses on a regular basis. Otherwise, organizations shall have independent control over the expenditure of allocated funds.

C.    (Optional) Any organization seeking access to institutional funds shall choose a faculty member to be a consultant on institution relations. Such a person may not have a veto power.

§16. No individual, group, or organization may use the institution name without the express authorization of the institution except to identify the institutional affiliation. Institution approval or disapproval of any policy may not be stated or implied by any individual, group, or organization.

## Publications

§17. A student, group, or organization may distribute written material on campus without prior approval providing such distribution does not disrupt the operations of the institution.

§18. The student press is to be free of censorship. The editors and managers shall not be arbitrarily suspended because of student, faculty, administration, alumni, or community disapproval of editorial policy or content. Similar freedom is assured oral statements of views on an institution controlled and student operated radio or television station.

A.    This editorial freedom entails a corollary obligation under the canons of responsible journalism and applicable regulations of the Federal Communications Commission.

§19. All student communications shall explicitly state on the editorial page or in broadcast that the opinions expressed are not necessarily those of the institution or its student body.

## Institutional Government

§ 20. All constitutents of the the institutional community are free, individually and collectively, to express their views on issues of institutional policy and on matters of interest to the student body. Clearly defined means shall be provided for student expression on all institutional policies affecting academic and student affairs.

§ 21. The role of student government and its responsibilities shall be made explicit. There should be no review of student government actions except where review procedures are agreed upon in advance.

§ 22. Where the institution owns and operates residence halls, the students shall have final authority to make all decisions affecting their personal lives including the imposition of sanctions for violations of stated norms of conduct, except that the institution may impose minimal standards to insure compliance with all federal, state, and local laws.

§ 23. On questions of educational policy, students are entitled to a participatory function.

    A.    Faculty-student committees shall be created to consider questions of policy affecting student life.

    B.    Students shall be designated as members of standing and special committees concerned with institutional policy affecting academic and student affairs, including those concerned with curriculum, discipline, admissions, and allocation of student funds.

    C.    (Optional) There shall be an ombudsman who shall hear and investigate complaints and recommend appropriate remedial action.

## Protest

§24. The right of peaceful protest is granted within the institutional community. The institution retains the right to assure the safety of individuals, the protection of property, and the continuity of the educational process.

§25. Orderly picketing and other forms of peaceful protest are permitted on institution premises.
    A.    Interference with ingress to and egress from institution facilities, interruption of classes, or damage to property exceeds permissible limits.
    B.    Even though remedies are available through local enforcement bodies, the institution may choose to impose its own disciplinary sanctions.

§26. Orderly picketing and orderly demonstrations are permitted in public areas within institution buildings subject to the requirements of non-interference in §25A.

§27. Every student has the right to be interviewed on campus by any legal organization desiring to recruit at the institution.
    A.    Any student, group, or organization may protest against any such organization provided that protest does not interfere with any other student's right to have such an interview.

## Violation of Law and University Discipline

§28. If a student is charged with, or convicted of, an off-campus violation of law, the matter is of no disciplinary concern to institution unless the student is incarcerated and unable to comply with academic requirements, except,
    A.    The institution may impose sanctions for grave misconduct demonstrating flagrant disregard for the right of

others. In such cases, expulsion is not permitted until the student has been adjudged guilty in a court of law, and;

B.    Once a student is adjudged guilty in a court of law the institution may impose sanctions if it considers the misconduct to be so grave as to demonstrate flagrant disregard for the rights of others.

§29. Under §28A, the institution shall reinstate the student if he is acquitted or the charges are withdrawn.

§30. The institution may institute its own proceedings against a student who violates a law on campus which is also a violation of a published institution regulation.

**Privacy**

§31. Students have the same rights of privacy as any other citizen and surrender none of those rights by becoming members of the academic community. These rights of privacy extend to residence hall living. Nothing in the institutional relationship or residence hall contract may expressly or impliedly give the institution or residence hall officials authority to consent to a search of a student's room by police or other government officials.

§32. The institution is neither arbiter or enforcer of student morals. No inquiry is permitted into the activities of students away from the campus where their behavior is subject to regulation and control by public authorities. Social morality on campus, not in violation of law, is of no disciplinary concern to the institution.

§33. When the institution seeks access to a student room in a residence hall to determine compliance with provisions of applicable multiple dwelling unit laws or for improvement or repairs, the occupant shall be notified of such action not less than twenty-four hours in advance. There may be entry without notice in emergencies where imminent danger to life, safety, health, or property is reasonably feared.

§34. The institution may conduct a search of a student room in a residence hall to determine compliance with federal, state and local criminal law where there is probable cause to believe that a violation has occurred or is taking place. "Probably cause" exists where the facts and circumstances within the knowledge of the institution and of which it has reasonably trustworthy information are sufficient in themselves to warrant a man of reasonable caution in the belief that an offense has been or is being committed.

**Student Records**

§35. The privacy and confidentiality of all student records shall be preserved.   Official student academic records, supporting documents, and other student files shall be maintained only by full-time members of the institution staff employed for that purpose. Separate files shall be maintained of the following; academic records, supporting documents, and general educational records; records of discipline proceedings; medical and psychiatric records; financial aid records.

§36. No entry may be made on a student's academic record and no document may be placed in his file without actual notice to the students. Publication of grades and announcement of honors constitute notice.

§37. Access to his records and files is guaranteed every student subject only to reasonable regulation as to time, place, and supervision.

    A.   A student may challenge the accuracy of any entry or

the presence of any item by bringing the equivalent of an equitable action against the appropriate person before the judicial body to which the student would be responsible under §52.

§38. No record may be made in relation to any of the following matters except upon the express written request of the student;

    A.    Race;

    B.    Religion; (omit if §4C is enacted)

    C.    Political or social views; and

    D.    Membership in any organization other than honorary and professional organizations directly related to the educational process.

§39. No information in any student file may be released to anyone except with the prior written consent of the student concerned or as stated below;

    A.    Members of the faculty with administrative assignments may have access for internal educational purposes as well as routinely necessary administrative and statistical purposes.

    B.    The following data may be given any inquirer; school or division of enrollment, periods of enrollment, and degrees awarded, honors, major field, and date.

    C.    If an inquiry is made in person or by mail, the following information may be given in addition to that in Subsection B; address and telephone number, date of birth, and confirmation of signature.

    D.    Properly identified officials from federal, state and local government agencies may be given the following information upon express request in addition to that in Subsections B and C; name and address of parent or guardian if student is a minor, and any information required under legal compulsion.

E.     Unless under legal compulsion, personal access to a student's file shall be denied to any person making an inquiry.

§40. Upon graduation or withdrawal from the institution, the records and files of former students shall continue to be subject to the provisions of this Code of Conduct.


## Sanctions

§41. The following sanctions may be imposed upon students;

A.     *Admonitions:* An oral statement to a student that he is violating or has violated institution rules.

B.     *Warning:* Notice, orally or in writing, that continuation or repetition of conduct found wrongful, within a period of time stated in the warning, may be cause for more severe disciplinary action.

C.     *Censure:* A written reprimand for violation of specified regulations, including the possibility of more severe disciplinary sanctions in the event of the finding of a violation of any institution regulation within a stated period of time.

D.     *Disciplinary probation:* Exclusion from participation in privileged or extracurricular institution activities as set forth in the notice for a period of time not exceeding one school year.

E.     *Restitution:* Reimbursement for damage to or misappropriation of property. This may take the form of appropriate service or other compensation.

F.     *Suspension:* Exclusion from classes and other privileges or activities as set forth in the notice for a definite period of time not to exceed two years.

G.     *Expulsion:* Termination of student status for an indefinite period. The conditions of readmission, if any, shall be stated in the order of expulsion.

§42. No sanctions may be imposed for violations of rules and regulations for which there is not actual or constructive notice.

## Proscribed Conduct

§43. Generally, institutional discipline shall be limited to conduct which adversely affects the institutional community's pursuit of its educational objectives. The following misconduct is subject to disciplinary action:

A.    All forms of dishonesty including cheating, plagiarism, knowingly furnishing false information to the institution, and forgery, alteration or use of institution documents or instruments of indentification with intent to defraud.

B.    Intentional disruption or obstruction of teaching, research, administration, disciplinary proceedings or other institution activities.

C.    Physical abuse of any person on institution premises or at institution sponsored or supervised functions.

D.    Theft from or damage to institution premises or damage to property of a member of the institutional community on institution premises.

E.    Failure to comply with directions of institution officials acting in performance of their duties.

F.    Violation of published institutional regulations including those relating to entry and use of institutional facilities, the rules in this Code of Conduct, and any other regulations which may be enacted.

G.    Violation of published rules governing residence halls.

H.    Violation of law on institutional premises or residence halls in a way that affects the institutional community's pursuit of its proper educational purposes.

## Procedural Standards in Discipline Proceedings

§44. Any academic or administrative official, faculty member or student may file charges against any student for misconduct. In extraordinary circumstances the student may be suspended pending consideration of the case. Such suspension shall not exceed a reasonable time.

§45. The institution may make a preliminary investigation to determine if the charges can be disposed of informally by mutual consent without the initiation of disciplinary proceedings.

§45. (Alternate) The institution may make a preliminary investigation to determine if the charges can be disposed of informally by mutual consent without the initiation of disciplinary proceedings. Such disposal will be final and there shall be no subsequent proceedings or appeals.

§46. All charges shall be presented to the accused student in written form and he shall respond within seven school days. The time may be extended for such response. A time shall be set for a hearing which shall not be less than seven or more than fifteen school days after the student's response.

§47. A calendar of the hearings in a disciplinary proceeding shall be fixed after consultation with the parties. The institution shall have discretion to alter the calendar for good cause.

§48. Hearings shall be conducted in such manner as to do substantial justice.

    A.    Hearings shall be private if requested by the accused student. In hearings involving more than one student, severance shall be allowed upon request.

    B.    An accused student has the right to be represented by counsel or an adviser who may come from within or without the institution.

C.    Any party to the proceedings may request the privilege of presenting witnesses subject to the right of cross-examination by the other parties.

D.    Production of records and other exhibits may be required.

§49. In the absence of a transcript, there shall be both a digest and a verbatim record, such as a tape recording, of the hearing in cases that may result in the imposition of the sanctions of restitution, as suspension, and expulsion as defined in §41.

§50. No recommendation for the imposition of sanctions may be based solely upon the failure of the accused student to answer the charges or appear at the hearing. In such a case, the evidence in support of the charges shall be presented and considered.

§51. An appeal from a decision by the initial hearing board may be made by any party to the appropriate appeal board within ten days of the decision.

A.    An appeal shall be limited to a review of the full report of the hearing board for the purpose of determining whether it acted fairly in light of the charges and evidence presented.

B.    An appeal may not result in a more severe sanction for the accused student.

C.    An appeal by the institution, in which the decision is reversed, shall be remanded to the initial hearing board for a determination of the appropriate sanction.

### Judicial Authority

§52. Appropriate judicial bodies shall be formed to handle all questions of student discipline. The initial hearing board shall be composed solely of students and any appeal board shall have voting student representation.

§53. The judicial bodies may formulate procedural rules which are not inconsistent with the provision of this Code.

§54. The judicial bodies may give advisory opinions, at their sole discretion, on issues not before any judicial body and where no violation of institutional regulations has taken place. Such opinions shall not be binding on the party making the request nor may it be used as precedent in future proceedings.

§55. A judicial body may be designated as arbiter of disputes within the institutional community. All parties must agree to arbitration and agree to be bound by the decision with no right of appeal.

## COMMENTS TO THE
## MODEL CODE

### Short Title

§ 1. By designating a short title, any statement referring to the "Code of Conduct" will be a reference to the official document.

### Bill of Rights

§ 2. This section is intended to resemble the Federal Bill of Rights and that of many state constitutions. It sets up basic principles upon which more specific rules will be dependent. If specific situations that arise are not covered by the Code of Conduct then it may be necessary to refer back to these *broad* statements of student rights and interpret them.

§ 2A. Debate and freedom of intellectual endeavor is implicit in the definition of a college or university. There should be no fear of adverse consequences as a result of such an exercise of free expression. A fairly recent case held that the granting of a privilege (in this case, attending a state university) cannot be dependent upon 'the renunciation of a constitutional right (freedom of speech). *Dixon v. Alabama Board of Education*, 294 F.2d 150, 156 (5th Cir.), *reversing* 186 F.Supp. 945 (M.D. Ala. 1960), *cert. denied*, 368 U.S. 930 (1961). A 1968 case concerning the free speech of teachers might also be applicable to students;

> (The suggestion) that teachers may consistently be compelled to relinquish the First Amendment rights they would otherwise enjoy as citizens to comment on matters of public interest in connection with the operation of the public schools in which they work (is) a premise that has been unequivocally rejected in numerous prior decision of this court.

*Pickering v. Board of Education*, 391 U.S. 563, 568 (1968).

§ 2B. No comment

§ 2C. This section, like the Fourth Amendment, is designed to guarantee minimal rights of privacy. Students, by virtue of their membership in the academic community, should not be required to surrender any of their constitutionally guaranteed rights of privacy.

§ 2D,E. These are "due process of law" provisions which insure that disciplinary proceedings will be fair and impartial.

## Definitions

§ 3. A definite failing of most college codes and rules is the failure to adequately define the important terms used within. Individual institutions may find it necessary to add definitions to this section to fit their particular situations.

§ 3(1) No comment

§ 3(2) No comment

§ 3(3) Many larger institutions hire graduate students to conduct basic undergraduate courses. If, for example, such a person while attending a class as a student, suddenly disrupts classroom activities, he is subject to the provisions of this Code. He may also be subject to the rules and regulations covering faculty members. If, however, he engages in a demonstration by faculty members which disrupt the operations of the institution, he is not subject to the provisions of this Code.

§ 3(4) The usual form of legal compulsion is the subpoena which is available to legislative bodies and courts.

§ 3(5) *cross reference:* §11.

§ 3(6) No comment

§ 3(7) All printed materials or those who print them cannot constitute the "student press". As defined, it must be an organization and not a "group" as defined in subsection (6) *supra.*

§ 3(8)(9) Drafting tip; When a negative designation is used, "may" is the proper term. It negates both permission and the mandate. For example, "A person *shall* not engage in certain activities."—This merely means that he is not mandated to do it. He still may do it. For example, "A person *may* not engage in certain activities." This is an absolute prohibition.

§ 3(10) Regular rules of English construction should apply.

### Access to Higher Education

§ 4. It is inconsistent with the role of an institution of higher learning for it to be discriminatory or prejudicial in selecting applicants for enrollment except under clearly specified and relevant criteria. Race or ethnic background is not relevant because it has no effect on the ability of the institution to achieve its function—education. Prior grades, extracurricular activities, college board scores are relevant criteria because they determine an applicant's capability to meet educational requirements of the institution.

§ 4(A) This would be embodied in the statement of admission requirements of the institution.

§ 4(B) No comment

§ 4(C) Some institutions are incorporated as institutions related to particular religious bodies primarily for the purpose of educating persons of that religion. Such institutions may desire to indicate a preference for members of the related denomination. All institutions, however, should make provisions so that there will be non-members in attendance. Absolute conformity of views, in any respect, should not be encouraged at any college or university.

### Classroom Expression

§ 5. This section is designed to encourage freedom of discussion and the expression of views in the classroom. "Relevant to the subject matter" may be a phrase of some difficulty—its determination is a matter of the instructor's discretion, this being the only practical way to handle the matter. Students will always have the opportunity to discuss those ideas which they deem relevant to a context outside the classroom. The instructor is the ultimate authority in the classroom, but it is expected that he will exercise that authority with reason, restraint, and within the confines of academic freedom for faculty and students alike.

*cross reference:* § §2A, 8.

§ 5(A) Determination of content is, primarily, a matter for the institution and the instructor. However, in some instances, students should be involved in the determination.

*cross reference:* § §20, 23.

§ 5(B) Such requirements merely assist the instructor in determining progress and in determining course content for the remainder of the course.

§ 6. Academic evaluation should be based on the performance of the student and not on extraneous matters. For example, there was a situation where marginal students were allegedly told that unless they took tutoring lessons from an individual who was a close friend of the instructor, they would fail the course. If true, this would be violative of this section.

Similarly, a set percentage for failures would fit into this category. Either a student meets the minimal standards set up by the instructor or he does not. His successful completion of a course should not depend on his ranking among his classmates.

§ 7. This section refers to faculty members giving information to outsiders. It is normal and expected for the faculty to discuss among themselves the progress and views of their students. All such information should remain within the walls of the institution. The only exception is "legal compulsion." There are constitutional standards as to what type of information a person is required to divulge and the mere service of a subpoena, for example, should not cause a person to become an "open book." Rather, he should seek the advice of a competent attorney as to what must, may and should not be answered.

*definitions:* § 3(4).


## Campus Expression

§ 8. This section refers to all views which are constitutionally permitted. In times of national emergency, a 1919 case (*Schenck v. United States*, 249 U.S. 47) is still applicable law. In the words of Justice Holmes:

> We admit that in many places and in ordinary times the defendants in saying all that was said in the circular, would have been within their constitutional rights. But, the character of every act depends upon the circumstances in which it is done. . . The question in every case is whether the words used are used in such circumstances and are of such a nature as to create a *clear and present danger* that they will bring about the substantive evils that Congress has a right to prevent. It is a question of proximity and degree. When a nation is at war many things that might be said in time of peace are such a hindrance to its effort that their utterance will not be endured so long as men fight, and that no Court could regard them as protected by any constitutional right. (emphasis added).

The requirement of lawfulness of views is not present in this section but other sections do require organizations and groups to be legal and to engage only in legal activities.

*cross reference:* § § 10, 11.


§ 9. Speakers' bans for state institutions have been declared unconstitutional in at least two cases. Any institution, private or public, must permit all views if it is to act consistently with the principles of academic freedom. Although there is no specific section on this point, it is expected that students, groups, and organizations will adhere to the concept of all views being expressed and will permit all persons to be heard. Speakers' ban laws have been overturned in Illinois and California; In Illinois the District Court held that the "Clabaugh Act" which prohibited the use of campus facilities for certain specified types of activities as unconstitutional because (1) it lacked the necessary precise language for a statute as closely intertwined with First Amendment rights and, (2) the prior restraint of speech was unjustified, and, (3) procedural safeguards were lacking. *Snyder v. Board of Trustees*, 236 F. Supp. 927 (N.D. Ill. 1968).

In North Carolina, the District Court overturned a rule by the Board of Trustees banning speakers who hold certain beliefs. *Dickson v. Sitterson*, 280 F. Supp. 484 (M.D. N.C. 1968). For additional background see Comment, "The North Carolina Speaker Ban Law: A Study in Context," 55 KY. L.J. 255 (1967), and Van Alstyne, "Political Speakers at State Universities: Some Constitutional Considerations," 11 U. PA.L.REV. 328 (1963).
*cross reference:* § § 8A, 24, 25, 26, 43B.


## Campus Organizations

§ 10. "Legal purpose" is the only qualification for forming organizations or groups. An organization that *advocates* the violent overthrow of the United States Government would not be for a legal purpose. Similarly, an organization or group that has as its policy destruction of property and other such unlawful activity could not be established within the institution. If an extramural organization does not exist for a legal purpose or has illegal policies, *but* the campus branch disavows such purposes or policies, then the branch is not disqualified. If the extramural organization insists that branches adhere to policies which violate either institution regulations or law, then this would be ample cause to disqualify the institution branch.
*cross reference:* § 11D, E.
*definitions:* § 3(5), (6).

§11. The first draft of the Code did not include the provisions of this section. Upon deliberation, the drafting committee felt that it was absolutely essential to distinguish between groups and organizations and what privileges are permitted each. Basically, groups are entitled to the same privileges as organizations unless they are of a "continuing nature," with the exceptions of publications (see commentary on §3(7) *supra.*) and the right to use funds derived from student fees.

*cross reference:* § §3(7), 15.

§11(A) No comment

§11(B) Since the institution should be an open market place for ideas, it follows that the institution, as an entity, should divorce itself from the aims, objectives and policies of all organizations that it recognizes.

§11(C) Whether or not a group is of a "continuing nature" is a subjective determination depending on the facts of each particular situation. Once it is determined that it is such a group, then it becomes incumbent upon the group to initiate formal recognition proceedings if they are not to be denied certain benefits. It would seem advantageous for most groups to seek organization status since they could then share in student activities fees upon a showing of need.

*cross reference:* § §14, 15, 16, 17.

§11(D) *Cross reference:* §10.

§11(E) Since a group is not formally recognized by the institution, it is unreasonable to permit sanctions where it engages in wrongful activities off campus. This would be inconsistent with § 28. In appropriate serious cases the institution may be able to take action against individuals within the group.

*cross reference:* §28.


§12. Where facilities are limited, then relevant selection criteria would be operable. Where selection criteria are irrelevant to the stated aims and obligations of the organization then this section is violated. For example, a campus chapter of the Republican or Democratic Parties may not discriminate against Negroes. This is irrelevant (as well as possibly illegal) to organization membership and the section is violated. Most state universities have regulations requiring fraternities and sororities to expunge discrimination clauses in their charters. In such cases, those clauses would violate this section as well as § 11D.

*cross reference:* § 11D.

§ 13. For an excellent rationale of such a provision, see the "Statement on Confidentiality of Student Records," of the American Council on Education (Washington, D.C., July 7, 1967). Basically it asserted that the disadvantages of the maintenance of such membership lists outweighs the advantages and that the institution only needs the names of officers to adequately deal with the organization.

There was dissent within the Code drafting committee based on the concept that a person should be willing to stand up for what he believes in and take whatever consequences follow. The majority of the committee, considering that the college experience is often experimental and developmental, felt that possible present or future condemnation for views held during this period would inhibit such experiment and development.

*cross reference:* § 38.

§ 14. As members of the academic community, students, their groups and organizations should have access to the facilities of the institution for their activities.

*cross reference:* § 11C.

§ 14(A) "Reasonable conditions" is the key phrase.

§ 14(B) No comment

§ 14(C) No comment

§ 14(D) Alternate provisions. The Committee expressed no preference for either method.

§14(E) No comment

§14(F) *cross reference:* §4IE.

§14(G) This section gives the institution notice so that, if necessary, it may take or insist upon certain precautionary measures.

*cross reference:* §9.

§15. Only organizations are entitled to funds derived from student fees. This is an additional incentive for groups to seek institution recognition. Participation in the "decisional process" refers to voting participation.

*cross reference:* §11C.

§15(A) No comment

§15(B) It would be expected that where there is no proper financial accountability, this would be a part of the considerations of the allocating body in the future. It is the duty of the members of an organization to see that their officers are responsible. In the event of misappropriation of funds there may be sanctions against the individuals involved.

*cross reference:* §43A.

§15(C) Some institutions are insistent upon faculty advisors. They should consult but should not have veto powers. If an organization is unable to find an advisor after making a reasonable effort, this provision should be waived.

§16. For example, a group would be permitted to identify itself as "The Political Society of John Doe College," but can go no further. Any public statements to the effect that John Doe College approves or disapproves of aims, objectives, or policies would violate this section.

*cross reference:* §11B.

## Publications

§17. This section refers to distribution only. With one exception, no student, group, or organization has the "right" to use institution facilities to publish. The majority of the committee felt that the institution should not be required to provide the use of its printing facilities for publications whose policies and views the institution disagrees with. The dissent argued that, if the institution is an open market place for ideas, it should allow full use of its facilities for the printing of such ideas.

This section does not apply to the "student press," because denial of facilities would be a form of censorship.

*cross reference:* §18.

§18. The prohibitions implied in §17 as not applicable since denial of facilities would be a form of censorship.

*cross reference:* §17.

*definition:* §3(7).

§18(A) Special note should be made of the corresponding responsibility.

§19. No comment.

## Institutional Government

§20. One of the loudest and most legitimate gripes of students is that they do not have a voice in shaping institutional policy. This section calls for effective means to be provided. It merely grants the right of students to be *heard* on matters of institutional policy.

§21. It is expected that student governments will be given a responsible role in shaping institution policy. Many of the guarantees (for example, §20) can be assured by making student government the vehicle of student expression and decision making.

§22. The drafting committee discussed, with more than the usual depth, the role of the institution when owning and operating residence halls. The conclusions are embodied in this section; The institution is more than a landlord, it is a landlord *plus* and can thus not only impose minimal sanctions but also take appropriate action (see §34). Dissent was for the position that the institution has no greater status than a landlord and no additional regulations beyond those of the civil and criminal law are required. The majority rejected this concept as it considered the total relationship of the student and the institution and regarded this relationship as adding something "extra." However, the Committee unanimously rejected any implication that this is a return to the doctrine of *in loco parentis* and strongly warns against considering it as such.

§23. At minimum, "participatory function" means a non-voting seat on the bodies that form educational policy. It can be extended to a voting position on various bodies.
§23(A) No comment
§23(B) No comment
§23(C) The ombudsman concept is relatively new and is presently being attempted at the University of Chicago (a student) and New York University (a faculty member) and at other colleges. An ombudsman is somewhat of a "super-administrator" but who has no powers beyond those of reason and persuasion. He hears complaints and makes investigations followed by a report or recommendation to the appropriate individual or body. There are numerous articles on the concept and those considering creating such a post are advised to read them.

**Protest**

§24. The institution must be allowed to function and protect the members of the academic community, property and perform its

function of education.
*cross reference:* § §25, 26, 27A, 43B, C, D, E.

§25. No comment
§25(A) Two recent cases involving state institutions are the basis for this provision. In the first, students carrying placards entered the stands after a peaceful demonstration during half-time of a football game. They became "abusive" and "disorderly" and subsequently prevented the college president and others from viewing the game. The court held that they had exceeded their right to bring grievances to the attention of college officials, had violated college rules and regulations, and it was the duty of college officials to invoke disciplinary procedures (including suspension) against the responsible parties. *Barker v. Hardway* (President of Bluefield College), 283 F. Supp. 228 (S.D. W. Va. 1968).
See also, *Zanders v. Louisiana State Board of Education,* 281 F. Supp. 228 (W.D., La. 1968).
*cross reference:* § §24, 43B, E, F.
§25(B) This is a situation where the institution regulations which are similar to law are proper because of their direct relevance to maintaining the continuity of the educational process.
*cross reference:* §43H.

§26. *cross reference:* § §24, 43B, E, F, H.

§27. No comment
§27(A) In *Buttny v. Smiley,* 281 F. Supp. 280 (D.C.D., 1968), students at a state university physically blocked the entrances to the university placement service and, in effect, denied an interview to those who wished to be interviewed. The court held that the First Amendment does not give state university students participating in a protest demonstration the right to prevent lawful access to campus facilities. Furthermore, "plaintiffs in the present

case had a right to be where they were at the time in question, but they did not have the right to exclude others from free movement in the area."
*cross reference:* § §24, 26, 43B, E, F.


### Violation of Law and University Discipline

§28. Multiplication of penalties should be avoided whenever the additional penalty has no relationship to the interest to be protected. Most violations of law in no way affect a person's ability to pursue his education or hinder others from pursuing their educational objectives.

§28(A)(B) There are crimes (for example, homicide, rape and attempted rape, sale of highly dangerous drugs) which *may* be considered as grave enough for the instituion to add its own sanctions. For off campus activity, this section supersedes §43, generally, by the use of §43F.
*cross reference:* §43F.


§29. In the eyes of the law, the student would be considered absolved of the charges and any institution imposition of sanctions would be an imposition of its own standards as to what amounts to guilt. This is a task for the courts.


§30. Institution regulations should not be a duplication of existing law. The regulations that could be instituted would be limited by § §28 and 43. Thus, a blanket prohibition such as "all laws of the state must be obeyed on campus and the institution can punish for any violation of this provision," would be improper. Internal discipline must be related to the functions of the institution.
*cross reference:* § §28, 43F, H.

## Privacy

§31. A private landlord has no general authority to consent to a police search without a warrant. *Chapman v. United States*, 365 U.S. 610 (1960). The "landlord plus" concept created by the majority of the drafting committee was not extended to avoid this rule (see commentary to §22). Even where a key is retained with an implied authority for maids, janitors, and repairmen to enter, the rule is not altered. *Stoner v. California*, 376 U.S. 473 (1963). This section prohibits the institution from cooperating with police where they are either too lax to get a search warrant or are unable to get one because of the absence of "probable cause."
In this section, any analogy of the institution acting in the role of a parent was totally rejected by the Committee.
*cross reference:* §22.

§32. A total freedom from interference is given where activity occurs off campus. On campus, the institution may be concerned and may engage in counseling and advice, but no disciplinary action can result. For example, if the use of certain words and phrases are not legally obscene, then their use on the campus is not a disciplinary matter.
*cross reference:* §28.

§33. The only reasons for spot inspections are (1) a deterrent effect and, (2) the finding of violators for exemplary punishment. Too often, the motive is the latter and can be abused. Students are entitled to privacy just as other adults. That which is not permitted police or landlords should not be permitted of the institution. An exception does exist—emergencies (for example, the smell of smoke indicating a fire).
*cross reference:* §22.

§34. The majority of the drafting committee believed this section necessary to aid in keeping police off the campus. The institution *is* under a legal obligation to report to police any finding of illegal activity, otherwise institution officials could be an accessory after the fact (particularly where felonies are involved and, in a few jurisdictions, even for misdemeanors). A very strong dissent was expressed. It was contended that the matter of law enforcement is primarily up to the police and where the institution has "probable cause" it should immediately go to the police where there can then be a judicial determination as to the legal existence of "probable cause." The committee took no position as to what sanctions, if any, should be imposed upon an institution official who violates this provision. However, some action by the institution would be appropriate if this rule is to have any effect. Also, the idea of the institution securing some type of "search warrant" was rejected as unwieldy and not feasible.

### Student Records

§35. Colleges and universities, "have an obligation to protect their students from unwarranted intrusion into their lives and from hurtful or threatening interference in the exploration of ideas and their consequences that education entails. . . Finally, requests for information about a student's beliefs and associations inevitably imply the spectre of reprisals. To the extent that they do, they put at hazard the intellectual freedom of the college and the university." "Statement on Confidentiality of Records," by the American Council on Education (7 July 1967, Washington, D.C.).

§36. No comment

§37. No comment
§37(A) This is the only action against an institution official provided in this Model Code. An "equitable action" is one in which the tribunal is asked, in the interest of justice and fair play,

to remedy a wrong for which there is no other adequate remedy. In this situation, the decision would be an order directing the expunging, amending, or other alteration of the student record. A strong dissent was registered as to the right of students to see such items as subjective faculty recommendations and evaluations (which may not be particularly praiseworthy of the student). The section, as it reads, was termed a "whitewash" which will inhibit and perhaps prevent internal evaluations of students by faculty.

§38. No comment
§38(A) No comment
§38(B) *cross reference:* §4C.
§38(C)(D) If institution records are not available on these matters, then they cannot be obtained through legal compulsion of the institution or its officials and it becomes necessary, and preferable, to go to the individual being investigated. Committee dissent took the position that a student should be willing to go on record where his views and the organizations he belongs to are concerned.

§39. See comment to §13.
§39(A) No comment
§39(B) No comment
§39(C) No comment
§39(D)(E) *definitions:* §3(4)

§40. The original draft of the Code provided for the destruction of various types of records. It was decided that the institution may still have a legitimate interest in such records (for example, in seeking future employment). Since the records that are permitted can have little adverse effect (with the exception of grades), and a highly beneficial effect, it was deemed preferable to permit their retention subject to the provisions of the Code.
*cross reference:* § §35, 36, 39.

## Sanctions

§41. These are the traditional penalties invoked at most colleges and universities.

§42. In conjunction with the requirement of specificity of rules, there must be publication, availability of publication, and notice that the publicized rules are available and that the students are subject to them. If an accused student can prove that he was unaware of the rule in question and that a copy was unavailable or, after reasonable diligence on his part (e.g., reading the university catalog), there was no general notice of the availability of the published rules, then sanctions may not be imposed against him. The best procedure would be for the institution to hand copies of regulations to all students upon registration and to have some accessible place within the institution where copies are always available (if only for reading on the premises).
*cross reference:* §43F.

## Proscribed Conduct

§43. This section should not be considered as covering every possibility.·
§43(A) No comment
§43(B) *cross reference:* § §5, 8, 24, 25, 26, 27.
§43(C) *cross reference:* §24.
§43(D) No comment
§43(E) No comment
§43(F) *cross reference:* § §25A, 42.
§43(G) *cross reference:* § §22, 42.
§43(H) The key question is what is a "proper educational purpose?" This will vary from academic community to academic community and must be determined by them. Avoided, however, should be ridiculous attempts to define certain violations (e.g. parking laws) as affecting educational purpose. Relevance is the

test. A recent case involving high school students demonstrates this point. Their expulsions, for distributing freedom buttons on school premises, was overturned, the court holding that rules must be reasonable as well as materially and substantially related to appropriate discipline requirements. *Burnside v. Byars*, 363 F. 2d. 744 (5th Cir. 1966).

## Procedural Standards

§44. "Extraordinary circumstances" are basically the more serious crimes for which there is good reason to fear for the safety of the academic community (e.g., an indictment for murder).
*cross reference:* § §28, 29.

§45. (Alternatives) This avoids overburdening the student judicial system and leaves it those cases in which there may be serious questions of fact which must be ascertained. The Committee was split as to whether or not there could be a continuation of proceedings on the part of the student or the institution.

§46. No comment

§47. No comment

§48. This is basically a due process provision with certain specified requirements. Those who hear cases, initially and on appeal, will be unbiased and disinterested parties to the proceedings.

§49. This avoids overburdening the institution and the judicial system. Only the potentially most serious cases are subject to this provision. In other cases it would seem that a digest by the chairman of the judicial body would be sufficient. If it appears that a case is more serious than originally contemplated, then it would be wise to start the proceedings from the beginning.
*cross reference:* § §41E, F, G.

§50. No comment.

§51. No comment

§51(A) This is the type of procedure which appellate courts utilize in reviewing the decisions of lower courts and, particularly, administrative boards. Appeals bodies should not conduct a new hearing ("de novo" review).

§51(B) This provision applies to appeals by both institution and student.

§51(C) For example, although an appeals body may find a student guilty, it is not permitted to establish the penalty. It is the initial hearing Board which is fully aware of all the facts and extenuating circumstances and is better able to set the penalty.

## Judicial Authority

§52. Some question was raised as to the desirability of having joint faculty-student judiciaries for violations such as plagiarism or cheating on examinations. It was felt that the initial hearing board should consist solely of students and any appeal body could have joint representation.

§53. No comment

§54. No comment

§55. There is a need for some arbitration procedure within the modern institution and it is hoped that students, groups, organizations and other members of the academic community will take advantage of such a service.

# Bibliography

## Books

*Academic Freedom and Civil Liberties of Students in Colleges and Universities.* New York: American Civil Liberties Union, 1965.

American Association for Higher Education. Smith, G. Kerry, Ed. *Stress and Campus Response.* San Francisco: Jossey-Bass, Inc., Publishers. 1968.

Barzun, Jacques. *The American University: How it Runs, Where it Is Going.* New York, Evanston, and London: Harper and Row, 1968.

Birenbaum, William M. *Overlive: Power, Poverty, and the University.* New York: Delacorte, 1969.

Blackwell, Thomas E. *College Law/A Guide for Administrators.* Washington, D.C.: American Council on Education, 1961.

Chomsky, Noam. *American Power and the New Mandarins.* New York: Pantheon Books, 1969.

Feuer, Lewis S. *The Conflict of Generations: The Character and Significance of Student Movements.* New York: Basic Books, 1969.

Fortas, Abe. *Concerning Dissent and Civil Disobedience.* New York: New American Library, 1968.

Jencks, C.; Riesman, D. *The Academic Revolution.* New York: Doubleday and Co., 1968.

Kennan, George. *Democracy and the Student Left.* Boston: Atlantic Monthly Press, 1968.

Kerr, Clark. *The Uses of a University.* Boston: Harvard University Press, 1963.

Kunen, J. S. *Strawberry Statement: Notes of a College Revolutionist.* New York: Random House, 1969.

Miller, M. V. *Revolution at Berkeley.* New York: The Dial Press, Inc., 1965.

Perkins, James A. *The University in Transition.* Princeton, N.J.: Princeton University Press, 1967.

Ridgeway, James. *The Closed Corporation.* New York: Random House, 1968.

Schlesinger, Arthur M., Jr. *The Crisis of Confidence.* Boston: Houghton Mifflin Co., 1969.

Wallerstein, Immanuel. *University in Turmoil: The Politics of Change.* New York: Atheneum, 1969.

## Periodicals

Alexander, L. I. *Campus Peace Restored Through Student Bargaining,* L.A.B. Bull. 44:253 (1969).

Andrews, J. R. *Confrontation at Columbia: A Case Study in Coercive Rhetoric,* Q.J. of Speech 55:9 (1969).

Anon. *Faculty Participation in Strikes,* A.A.U.P. Bull. 54:155 (1968).

Ashbaugh, C. R. *High School Student Activism: Nine Tested Approaches for Coping With Conflict Situations,* Nation's Schools 83:94 (1969).

Baker. *Students, Parents and the College,* Amer. Alumni Council Bull. 53:325 (1967).

Beaney, William M. *Students, Higher Education, and the Law,* Denver L.J. 45:511 (1968).

Bowen, H. R. *Student Unrest in the United States,* International Bureau of Education Bull. 42:236 (1968).

Byse, Clark. *The University and Due Process: A Somewhat Different View* in *Proceedings of the 54th Annual Meeting of the American Association of University Professors,* (1968).

Cohen, William. *The Private-Public Legal Aspects of Institutions of Higher Education,* Denver L.J. 45:643 (1968).

Commager, Henry Steele. *The University and Freedom: 'Lehrfreiheit' and 'Lehrnfreiheit',* 34 J. Higher Ed. 34:361 (1963).

Comment. *Academic Freedom—Its Constitutional Context,* U. Colo. L. Rev. 40:600 (1968).

Comment. Johnson, Michael T. *The Constitutional Rights of College Students,* Texas L. Rev. 42:344 (1964).

Comment. *Procedural Limitations on the Expulsion of College and University Students,* St. Louis U.L.J. 10:542 (1966).

Comment. *School Expulsions and Due Process,* Kansas L. Rev. 14:108 (1965).

Developments in the Law. *Academic Freedom,* Harv. L. Rev. 81:1045 (1968).

Dorsen, Norman. *Racial Discrimination in "Private" Schools,* Wm. & Mary L. Rev. 9:39 (1967).

Gillespie, J. R. *Introduction to Urban Affairs: The University,* Ad. Law Rev. 21:41 (1968).

Goldman, Alvin L. *The University and the Liberty of Its Students—A Fiduciary Theory,* Ky. L.J. 54:643 (1966).

Henderson, A. D. *The Administrator/Student Conflict,* Ad. Law Rev. 21:    (1968).

Hook, S. *Trojan Horse in American Higher Education,* Ed. Rec. 50:21 (1969).

Jacobson, Sol. *Student and Faculty Due Process,* A.A.U.P. Bull. 196 (1966).

———.*The Expulsion of Students and Due Process of Law,* J. Higher Ed. 34:250 (1963).

Kadish, S. H. *Strike and the Professoriate,* A.A.U.P. Bull. 54:160 (1968).

Kurland, P. B. *Revolting Student,* U. Chi. L.S. Rec. 16:10 (1968).

Kutner, L. Habeas Scholastica: *An Ombudsman for Academic Due Process—A Proposal,* Miami L. Rev. 23:107 (1968).

Legislation. *College Discipline Proceedings*, Vand. L. Rev. 18:819 (1965).

Lunsford, Terry. *Who Are Members of the University Community?* Denver L.J. 45:545 (1968).

Majault, J. *Crisis in the University*, International Bureau of Education Bull. 42:235 (1968).

Malone, D. H. *Testimony on Student Unrest Before California Legislative Committee*, A.A.U.P. Bull. 55:91 (1969).

Means, R. L. *Who Is Responsible for Student Violence?* America 120:352 (1969).

Monypenny, Phillip. *The Student as a Student*, Denver L.J. 45:649 (1968).

———.*Toward a Standard for Academic Freedom*, Law and Contemp. Prob. 28:625 (1963).

———.*University Purpose, Discipline and Due Process*, N.D.L. Rev. 43:739 (1967).

Murphy, William P. *Educational Freedom in the Courts*, A.A.U.P. Bull. 49:309 (1963).

Note. *The College Student and Due Process in Discipline Proceedings*, U. Ill. L.F. 1962:438 (1962).

———. *Degree of Discretionary Authority Possessed by University Officials in Student Discipline Matters—The Availability of Mandamus*, Sw. L.J. 21:664 (1967).

———. *Due Process in Public Colleges and Universities—Need for Trial-Type Hearings*, How. L.J. 13:414 (1967).

———. *Expulsion of College and Professional Students—Rights and Remedies*, Notre Dame Law. 38:174 (1963).

———. *Private Government on the Campus—Judicial Review of University Expulsions*, Yale L.J. 72:1362 (1963).

———. *Reasonable Rules, Reasonably Enforced—Guidelines for University Disciplinary Proceedings*, Minn. L. Rev. 53:301 (1968).

———. *Uncertainty in College Disciplinary Regulations*, Ohio St. L.J. 29:1023 (1968).

Perkins, James A. *University and Due Process,* Am. Library Assoc. Bull. 62:977 (1968).

Ryman, C. R. *Student Revolt Against Society or Against Institutions?,* International Bureau of Education Bull. 42:247 (1968).

Seavey, Warren A. *Dismissal of Students: "Due Process",* Harv. L. Rev. 70:1406 (1957).

Stanmeyer, W. A. *New Left and the Old Law,* A.B.A.J. (1969).

Student Comment. *Mississippi's Campus Speaker Ban: Constitutional Considerations and the Academic Freedom of Students,* Miss. L.J. 38:488 (1967).

*Symposium-Student Rights and Campus Rules,* (five articles), Calif. L. Rev. 54:1 (1966).

Torres, Ruben D. *The Constitutional Rights of Students,* Philippine L.J. 40:587 (1965).

Van Alstyne, William W. *Procedural Due Process and State University Students,* U.C.L.A. L. Rev. 10:368 (1963).

———.*Student Academic Freedom and the Rule-Making Powers of Public Universities: Some Constitutional Considerations,* Law in Transition Q. 2:1 (1965).

———.*The Student as University Resident,* Denver L.J. 45:582 (1968).

Van Patten, J. *Rights vs. Responsibilities,* School and Community 55:7 (1969).

Van Waes, Robert. *Student Freedoms and Educational Reform* in *Stress and Campus Response,* a Publication of the American Association for Higher Education. San Francisco: Jossey-Bass, Inc., 1968.

Vogel, C. S. *Student Demonstrations, Trespass Laws, Private Colleges,* L.A.B. Bull. 43:457 (1968).

Williamson, E. G. *Do Students Have Academic Freedom?,* College and University 39:466 (1964).

———.*Students' Academic Freedom,* Ed. Rec. 44:214 (1963).

Wilson, Logan. *Campus Freedom and Order,* Denver L.J. 45:502 (1968).

———.*Protest Politics and Campus Reform,* Ad. Law Rev. 21: (1968).

Yegge, Robert B. *Emerging Legal Rights for Students* in *Stress and Campus Response,* a Publication of the American Association for Higher Education. San Francisco: Jossey-Bass, Inc., Publishers, 1968.

# Table of Cases

369

# Index

**NOTE:**

This index does not cover the appendixes section, as the materials included therein are reproduced from other sources. Names of cases are not included in the index. All references to cases may be found in the Table of Cases.